MARVEL RISING

HEROES OF THE ROUND TABLE

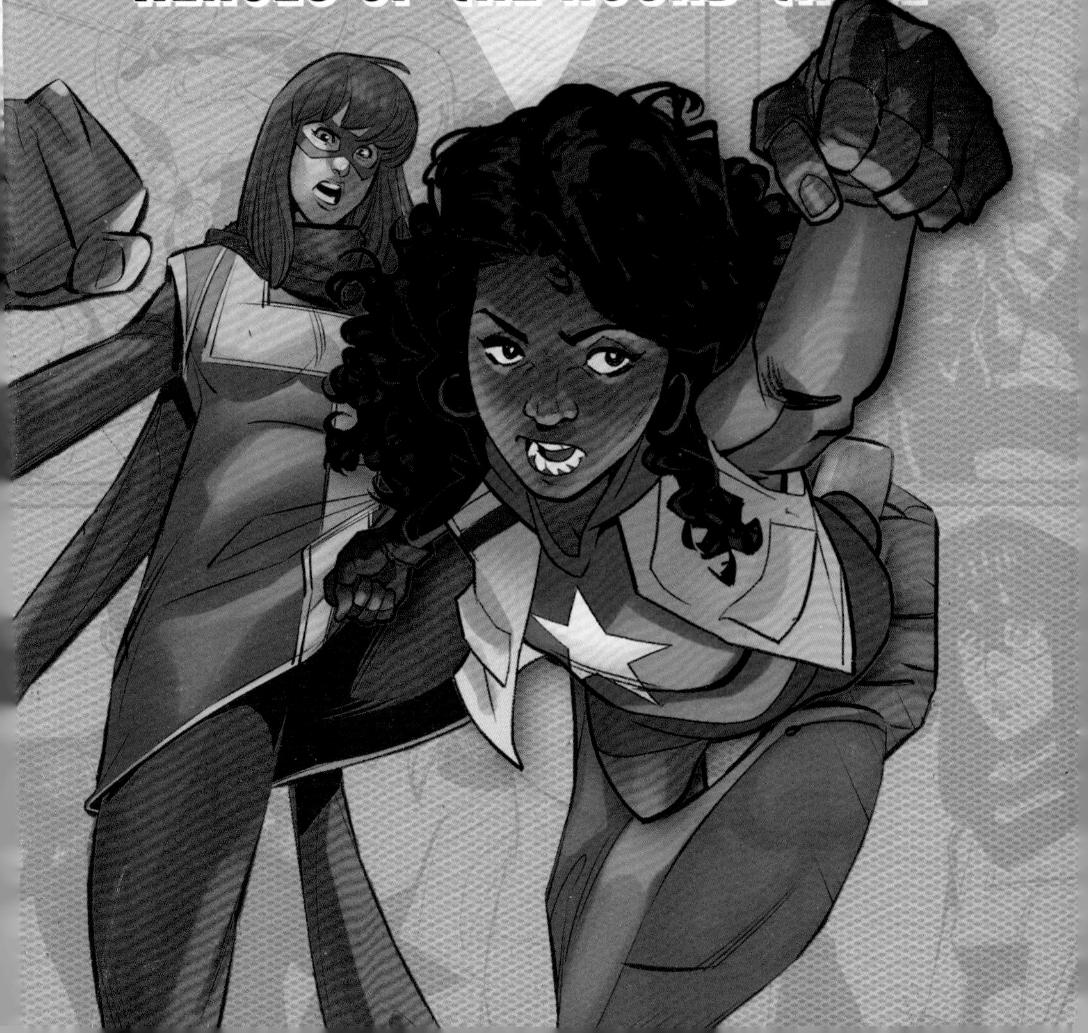

DOREEN GREEN,
A.K.A. THE
UNBEATABLE
SQUIRREL GIRL!

TIPPY-TOE,
THE SQUIRREL WHO
NEEDS NO OTHER
NAME!

KAMALA KHAN,
A.K.A. THE
MAGNIFICENT
MS. MARVEL!

MILES MORALES,
A.K.A. THE
SPECTACULAR
SPIDER-MAN!

AMERICA CHAVEZ,
A.K.A. THE BADDEST
CHICK YOU KNOW!

DAISY JOHNSON,
A.K.A. THE EARTH-
SHATTERING QUAKE!

DANTE PERTUZ,
A.K.A. THE
INCREDIBLE INFERNO!

COLLECTION EDITOR Jennifer Grünwald
ASSISTANT EDITOR Caitlin O'Connell
ASSOCIATE MANAGING EDITOR Kateri Woody
EDITOR, SPECIAL PROJECTS Mark D. Beazley
VP PRODUCTION & SPECIAL PROJECTS Jeff Youngquist
BOOK DESIGNERS Stacie Zucker with
Adam Del Re & Jay Bowen

SVP PRINT, SALES & MARKETING David Gabriel
DIRECTOR, LICENSED PUBLISHING Sven Larsen
EDITOR IN CHIEF C.B. Cebulski
CHIEF CREATIVE OFFICER Joe Quesada
PRESIDENT Dan Buckley
EXECUTIVE PRODUCER Alan Fine

MARVEL RISING: HEROES OF THE ROUND TABLE. Contains material originally published in magazine form as MARVEL RISING #1-5. First printing 2019. ISBN 978-1-302-91826-2. Published by MARVEL WORLDWIDE, INC., a subsidiary of MARVEL ENTERTAINMENT, LLC. OFFICE OF PUBLICATION: 135 West 50th Street, New York, NY 10020. © 2019 MARVEL No similarity between any of the names, characters, persons, and/or institutions in this magazine with those of any living or dead person or institution is intended, and any such similarity which may exist is purely coincidental. **Printed in Canada.** DAN BUCKLEY, President, Marvel Entertainment; JOHN NEE, Publisher; JOE QUESADA, Chief Creative Officer; TOM BREVOORT, SVP of Publishing; DAVID BOGART, Associate Publisher & SVP of Talent Affairs; DAVID GABRIEL, SVP of Sales & Marketing, Publishing; JEFF YOUNGQUIST, VP of Production & Special Projects; DAN CARR, Executive Director of Publishing Technology; ALEX MORALES, Director of Publishing Operations; DAN EDINGTON, Managing Editor; SUSAN CRESPI, Production Manager; STAN LEE, Chairman Emeritus. For information regarding advertising in Marvel Comics or on Marvel.com, please contact Vit DeBellis, Custom Solutions & Integrated Advertising Manager, at vdebellis@marvel.com. For Marvel subscription inquiries, please call 888-511-5480. **Manufactured between 8/2/2019 and 9/3/2019 by SOLISCO PRINTERS, SCOTT, QC, CANADA.**

10 9 8 7 6 5 4 3 2 1

MARVEL RISING

HEROES OF THE ROUND TABLE

WRITER Nilah Magruder

ARTISTS Roberto Di Salvo (#1-5) & Georges Duarte (#3-5)

COLOR ARTIST Rachelle Rosenberg

LETTERER VC's Clayton Cowles

COVER ART Audrey Mok

EDITOR Sarah Brunstad

SPECIAL THANKS TO SANA AMANAT

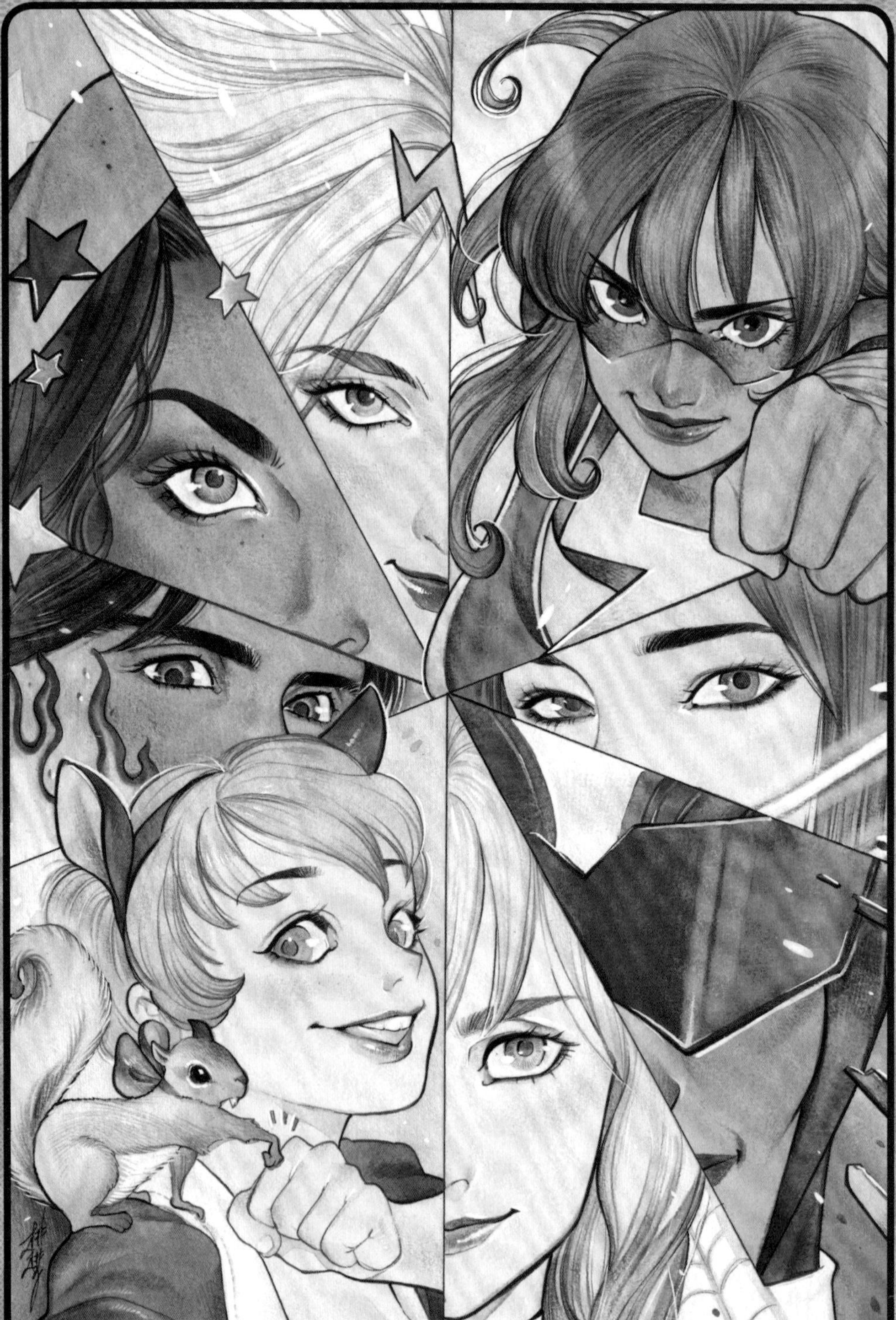

1 VARIANT BY
PEACH MOMOKO

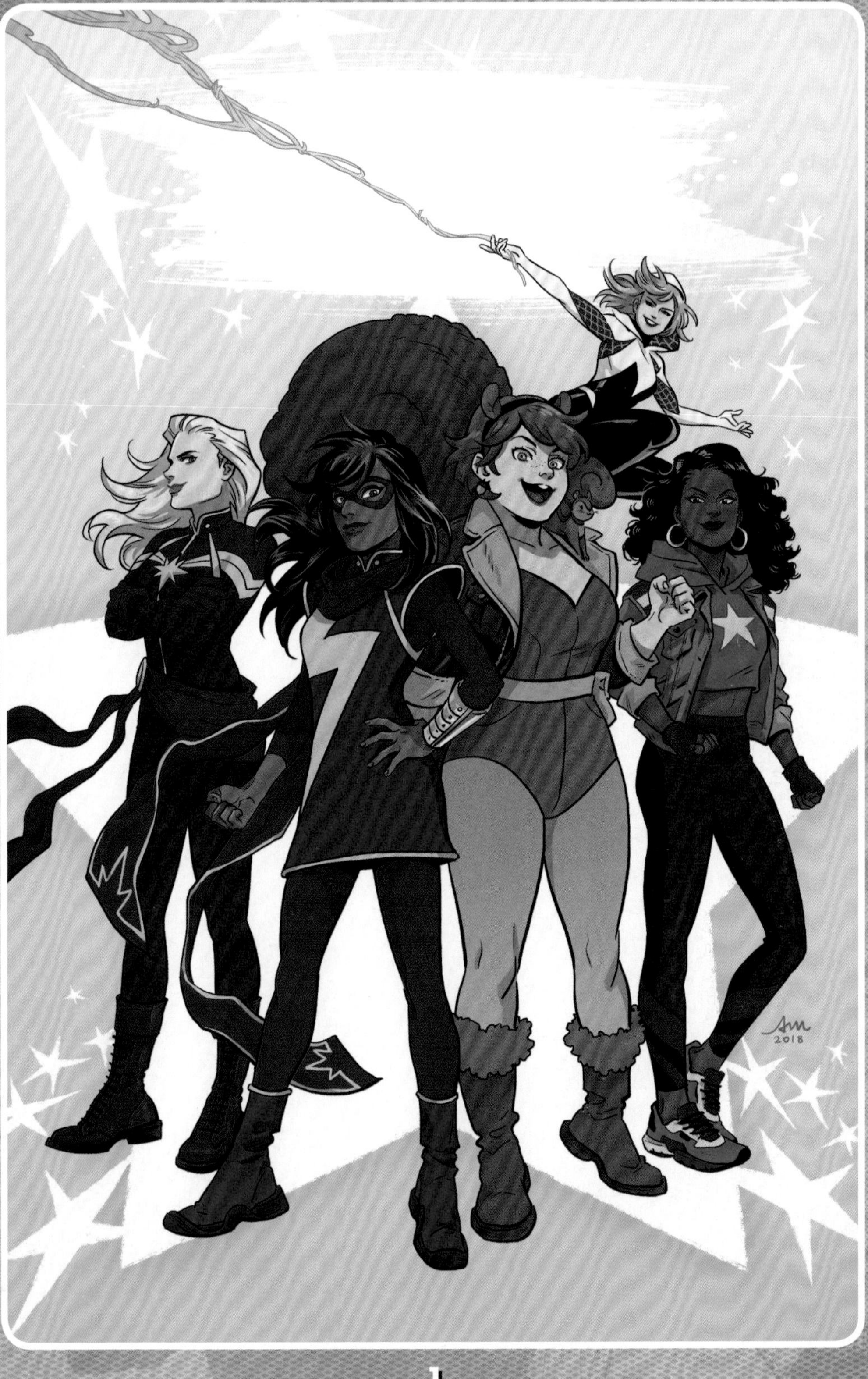
2018

1

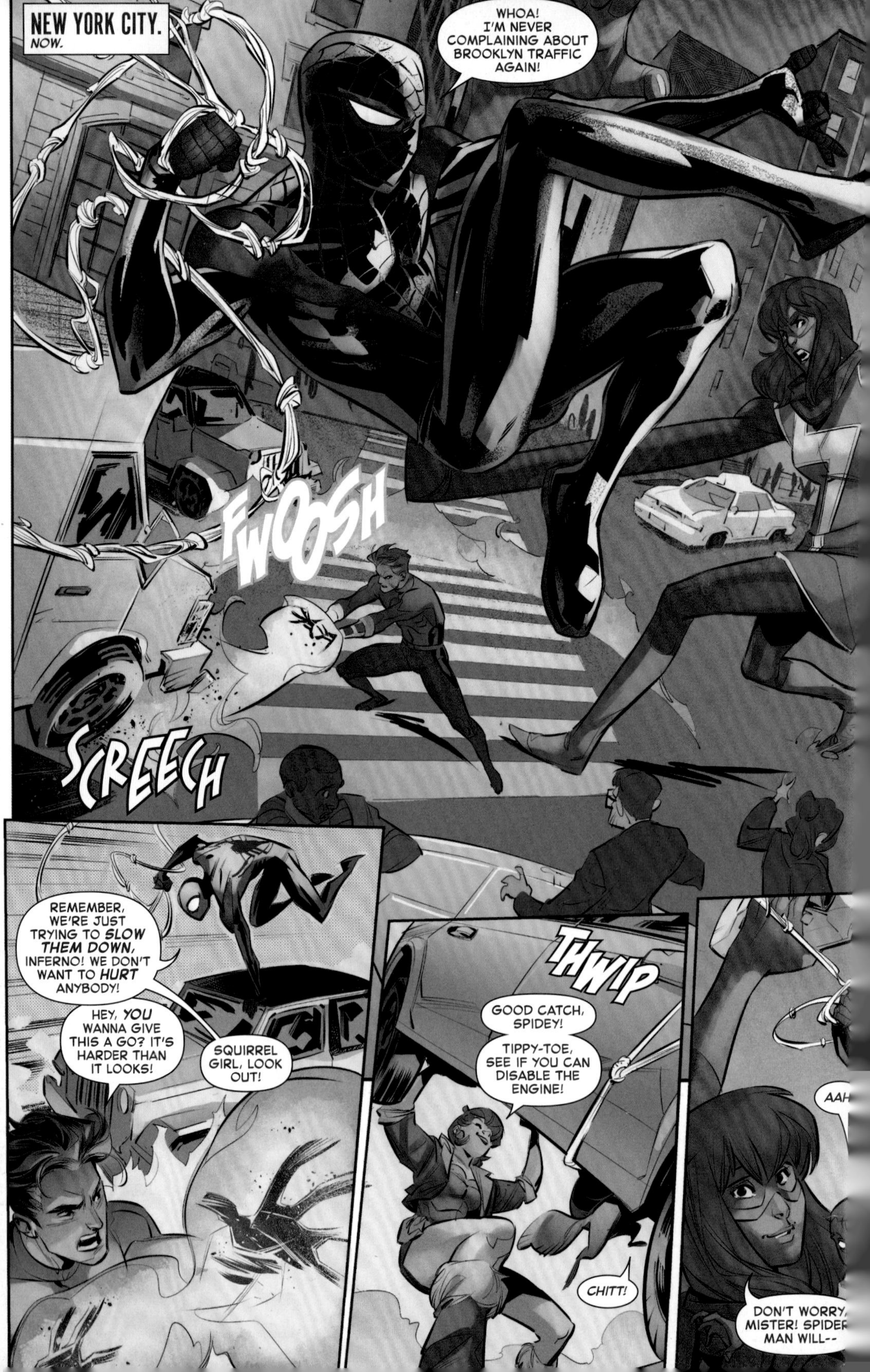
NEW YORK CITY.
NOW.
WHOA! I'M NEVER COMPLAINING ABOUT BROOKLYN TRAFFIC AGAIN!
FWOOSH
SCREECH
REMEMBER, WE'RE JUST TRYING TO SLOW THEM DOWN, INFERNO! WE DON'T WANT TO HURT ANYBODY!
HEY, YOU WANNA GIVE THIS A GO? IT'S HARDER THAN IT LOOKS!
SQUIRREL GIRL, LOOK OUT!
THWIP
GOOD CATCH, SPIDEY!
TIPPY-TOE, SEE IF YOU CAN DISABLE THE ENGINE!
CHITT!
AAH
DON'T WORRY, MISTER! SPIDER MAN WILL--

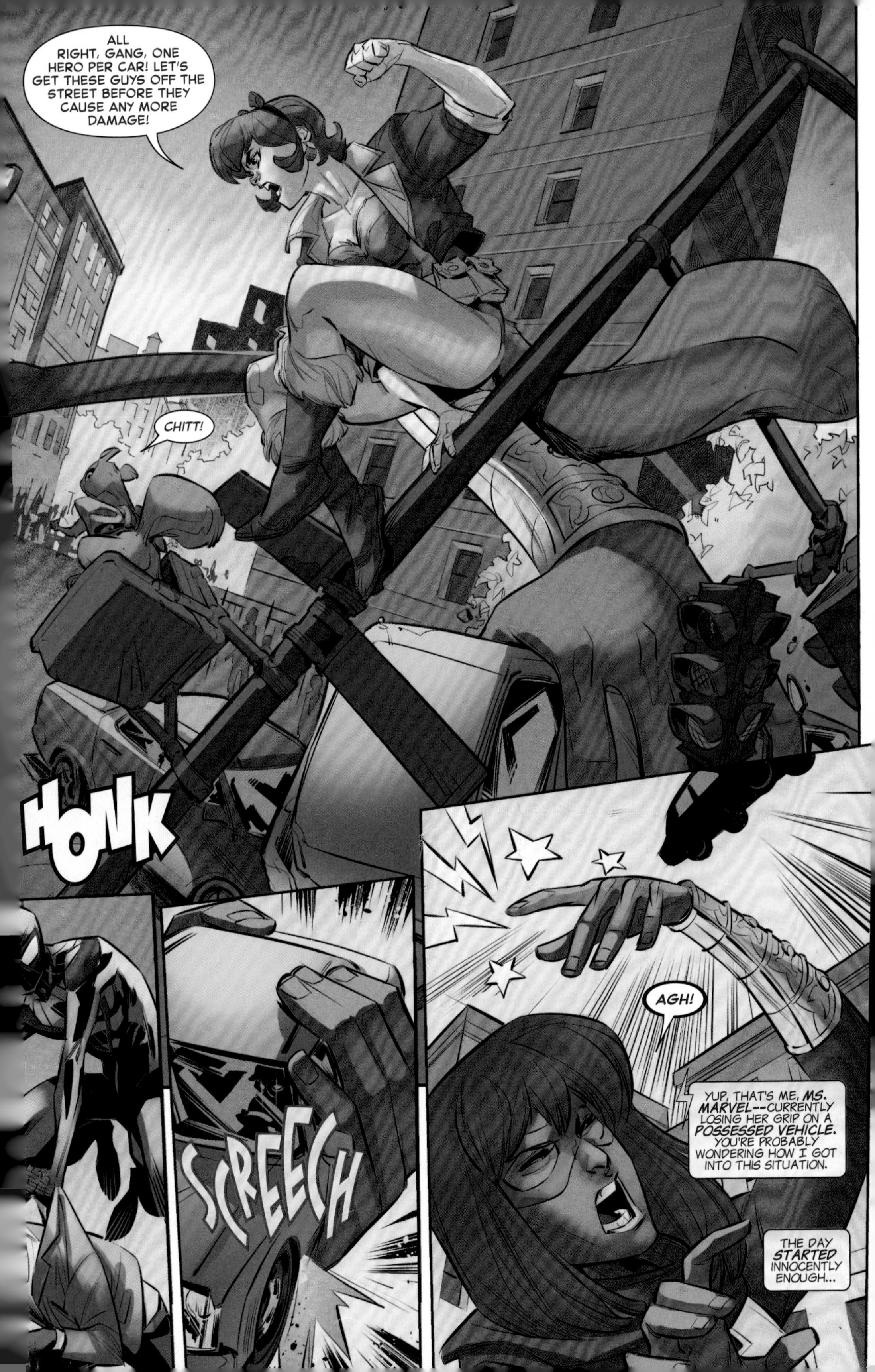

ALL RIGHT, GANG, ONE HERO PER CAR! LET'S GET THESE GUYS OFF THE STREET BEFORE THEY CAUSE ANY MORE DAMAGE!
CHITT!
HONK
AGH!
SCREECH
YUP, THAT'S ME, MS. MARVEL--CURRENTLY LOSING HER GRIP ON A POSSESSED VEHICLE. YOU'RE PROBABLY WONDERING HOW I GOT INTO THIS SITUATION.
THE DAY STARTED INNOCENTLY ENOUGH...

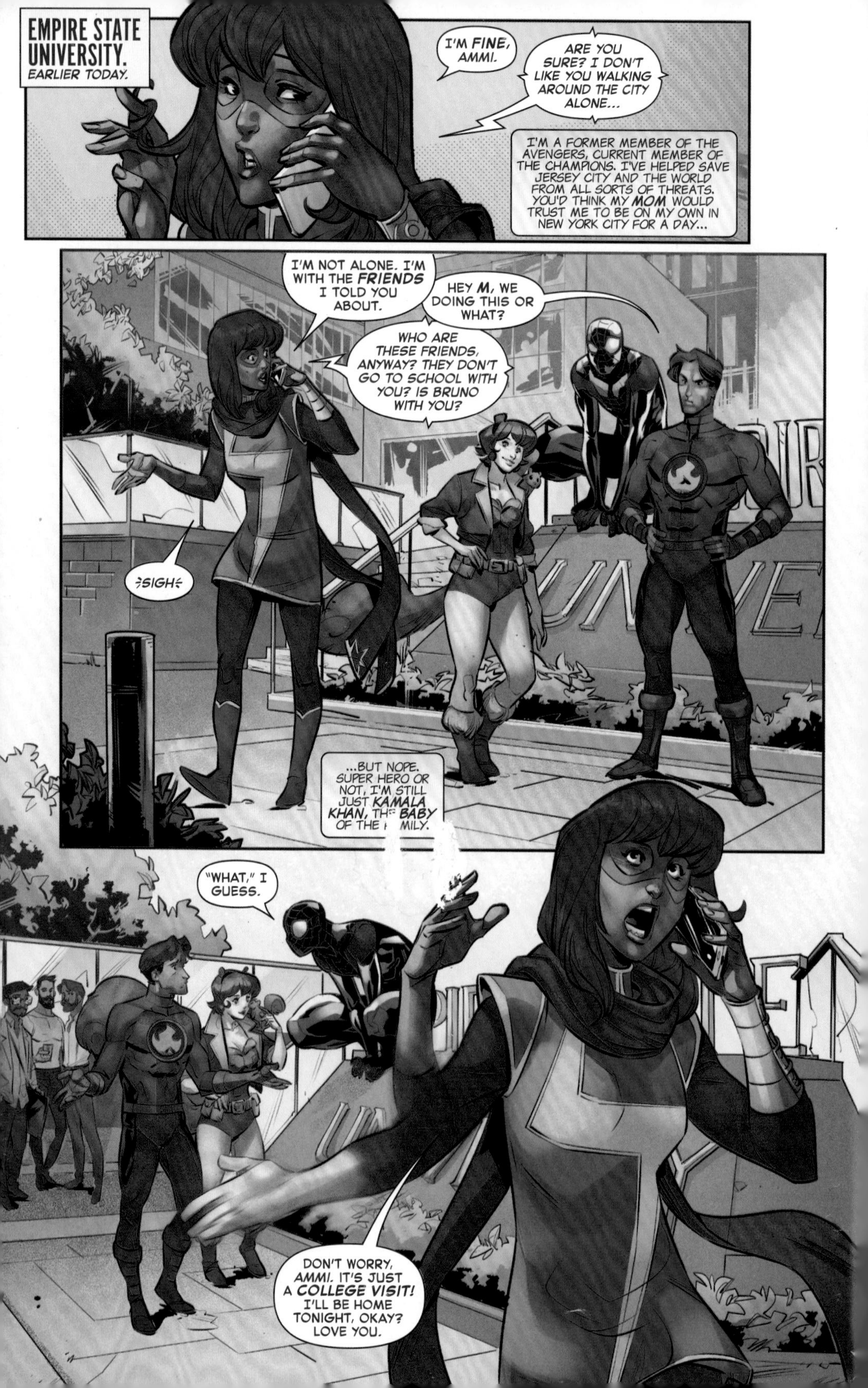
EMPIRE STATE UNIVERSITY.
EARLIER TODAY.
I'M FINE, AMMI.
ARE YOU SURE? I DON'T LIKE YOU WALKING AROUND THE CITY ALONE...
I'M A FORMER MEMBER OF THE AVENGERS, CURRENT MEMBER OF THE CHAMPIONS. I'VE HELPED SAVE JERSEY CITY AND THE WORLD FROM ALL SORTS OF THREATS. YOU'D THINK MY MOM WOULD TRUST ME TO BE ON MY OWN IN NEW YORK CITY FOR A DAY...
I'M NOT ALONE. I'M WITH THE FRIENDS I TOLD YOU ABOUT.
HEY M, WE DOING THIS OR WHAT?
WHO ARE THESE FRIENDS, ANYWAY? THEY DON'T GO TO SCHOOL WITH YOU? IS BRUNO WITH YOU?
SIGH
...BUT NOPE. SUPER HERO OR NOT, I'M STILL JUST KAMALA KHAN, TH BABY OF THE MILY.
"WHAT," I GUESS.
DON'T WORRY, AMMI. IT'S JUST A COLLEGE VISIT! I'LL BE HOME TONIGHT, OKAY? LOVE YOU.

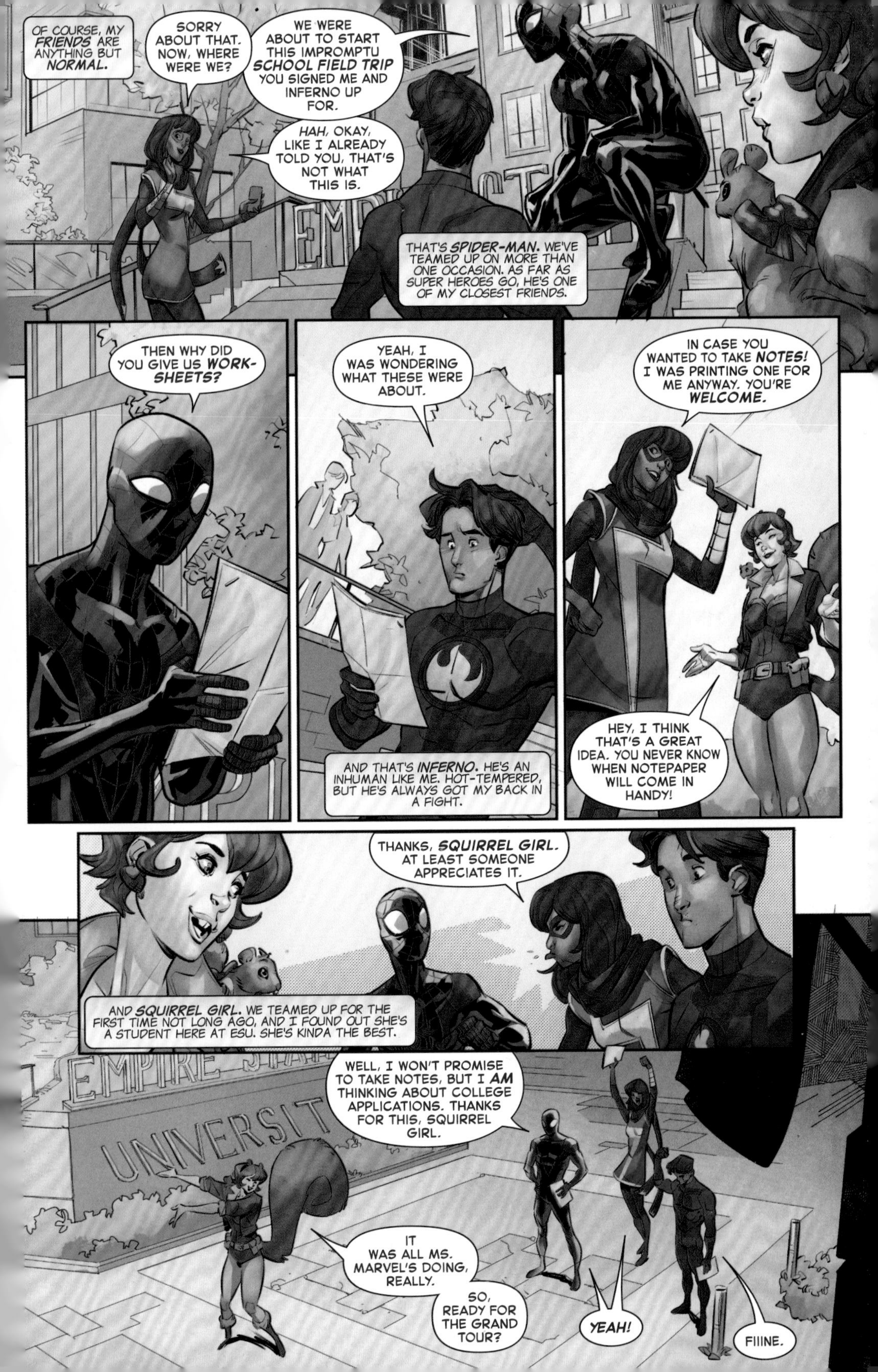
OF COURSE, MY FRIENDS ARE ANYTHING BUT NORMAL.
SORRY ABOUT THAT. NOW, WHERE WERE WE?
WE WERE ABOUT TO START THIS IMPROMPTU SCHOOL FIELD TRIP YOU SIGNED ME AND INFERNO UP FOR.
HAH, OKAY, LIKE I ALREADY TOLD YOU, THAT'S NOT WHAT THIS IS.
THAT'S SPIDER-MAN. WE'VE TEAMED UP ON MORE THAN ONE OCCASION. AS FAR AS SUPER HEROES GO, HE'S ONE OF MY CLOSEST FRIENDS.
THEN WHY DID YOU GIVE US WORK-SHEETS?
YEAH, I WAS WONDERING WHAT THESE WERE ABOUT.
AND THAT'S INFERNO. HE'S AN INHUMAN LIKE ME. HOT-TEMPERED, BUT HE'S ALWAYS GOT MY BACK IN A FIGHT.
IN CASE YOU WANTED TO TAKE NOTES! I WAS PRINTING ONE FOR ME ANYWAY. YOU'RE WELCOME.
HEY, I THINK THAT'S A GREAT IDEA. YOU NEVER KNOW WHEN NOTEPAPER WILL COME IN HANDY!
THANKS, SQUIRREL GIRL. AT LEAST SOMEONE APPRECIATES IT.
AND SQUIRREL GIRL. WE TEAMED UP FOR THE FIRST TIME NOT LONG AGO, AND I FOUND OUT SHE'S A STUDENT HERE AT ESU. SHE'S KINDA THE BEST.
WELL, I WON'T PROMISE TO TAKE NOTES, BUT I AM THINKING ABOUT COLLEGE APPLICATIONS. THANKS FOR THIS, SQUIRREL GIRL.
IT WAS ALL MS. MARVEL'S DOING, REALLY.
SO, READY FOR THE GRAND TOUR?
YEAH!
FIIINE.

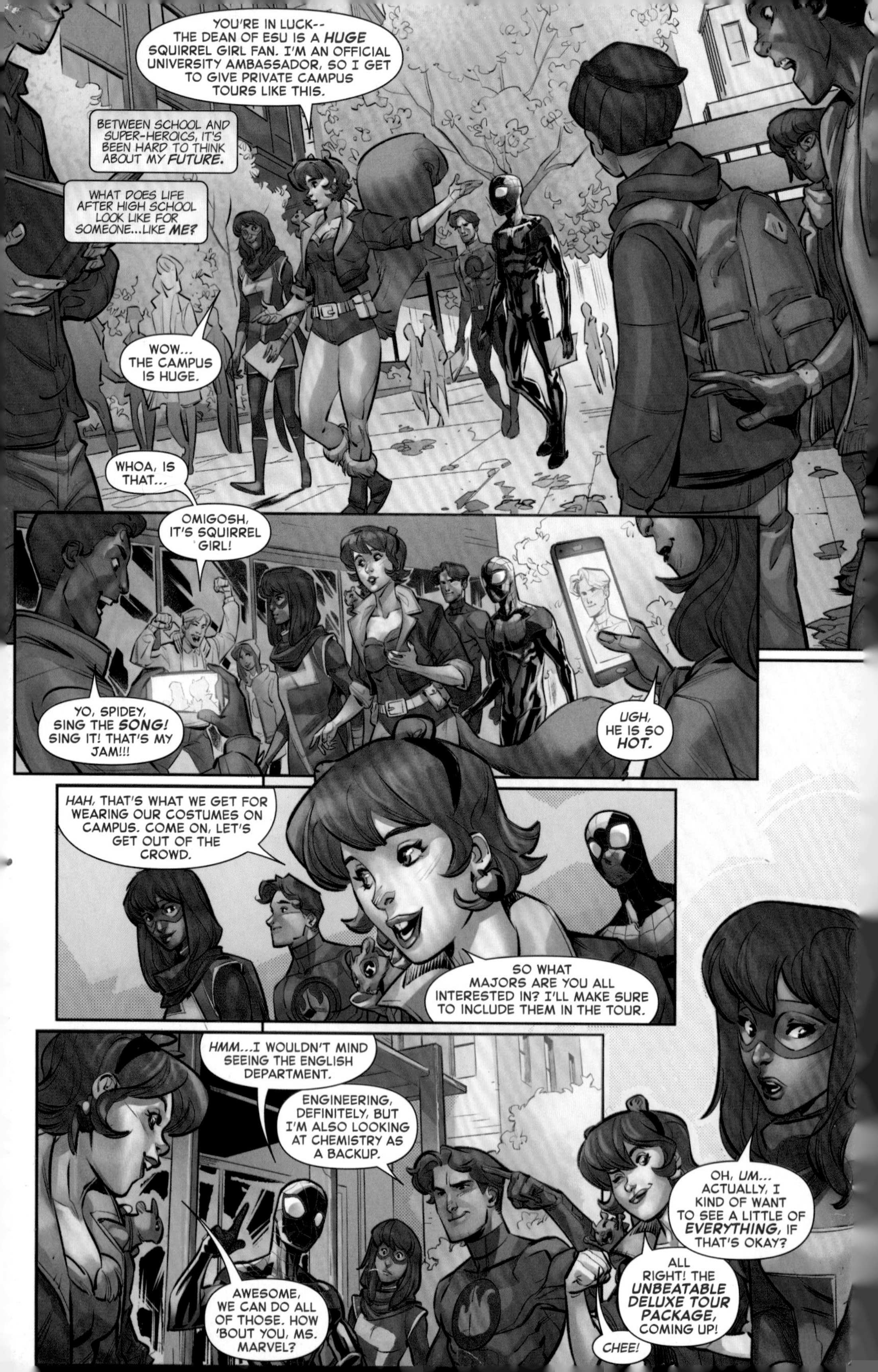
YOU'RE IN LUCK-- THE DEAN OF ESU IS A HUGE SQUIRREL GIRL FAN. I'M AN OFFICIAL UNIVERSITY AMBASSADOR, SO I GET TO GIVE PRIVATE CAMPUS TOURS LIKE THIS.
BETWEEN SCHOOL AND SUPER-HEROICS, IT'S BEEN HARD TO THINK ABOUT MY FUTURE.
WHAT DOES LIFE AFTER HIGH SCHOOL LOOK LIKE FOR SOMEONE...LIKE ME?
WOW... THE CAMPUS IS HUGE.
WHOA, IS THAT...
OMIGOSH, IT'S SQUIRREL GIRL!
YO, SPIDEY, SING THE SONG! SING IT! THAT'S MY JAM!!!
UGH, HE IS SO HOT.
HAH, THAT'S WHAT WE GET FOR WEARING OUR COSTUMES ON CAMPUS. COME ON, LET'S GET OUT OF THE CROWD.
SO WHAT MAJORS ARE YOU ALL INTERESTED IN? I'LL MAKE SURE TO INCLUDE THEM IN THE TOUR.
HMM...I WOULDN'T MIND SEEING THE ENGLISH DEPARTMENT.
ENGINEERING, DEFINITELY, BUT I'M ALSO LOOKING AT CHEMISTRY AS A BACKUP.
AWESOME, WE CAN DO ALL OF THOSE. HOW 'BOUT YOU, MS. MARVEL?
OH, UM... ACTUALLY, I KIND OF WANT TO SEE A LITTLE OF EVERYTHING, IF THAT'S OKAY?
ALL RIGHT! THE UNBEATABLE DELUXE TOUR PACKAGE, COMING UP!
CHEE!

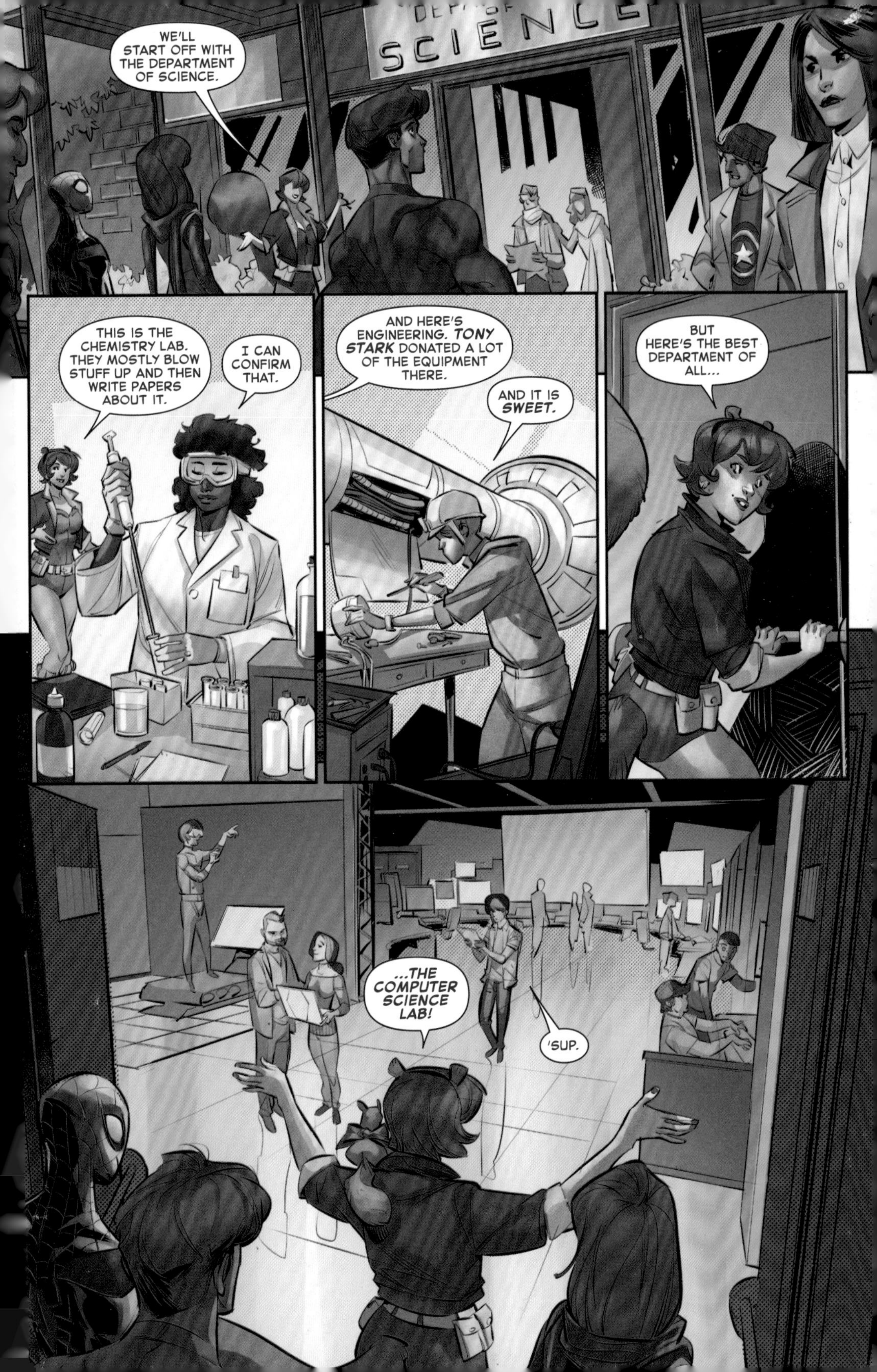

SCIENCE
WE'LL START OFF WITH THE DEPARTMENT OF SCIENCE.
THIS IS THE CHEMISTRY LAB. THEY MOSTLY BLOW STUFF UP AND THEN WRITE PAPERS ABOUT IT.
I CAN CONFIRM THAT.
AND HERE'S ENGINEERING. *TONY STARK* DONATED A LOT OF THE EQUIPMENT THERE.
AND IT IS *SWEET.*
BUT HERE'S THE BEST DEPARTMENT OF ALL...
...THE COMPUTER SCIENCE LAB!
'SUP.

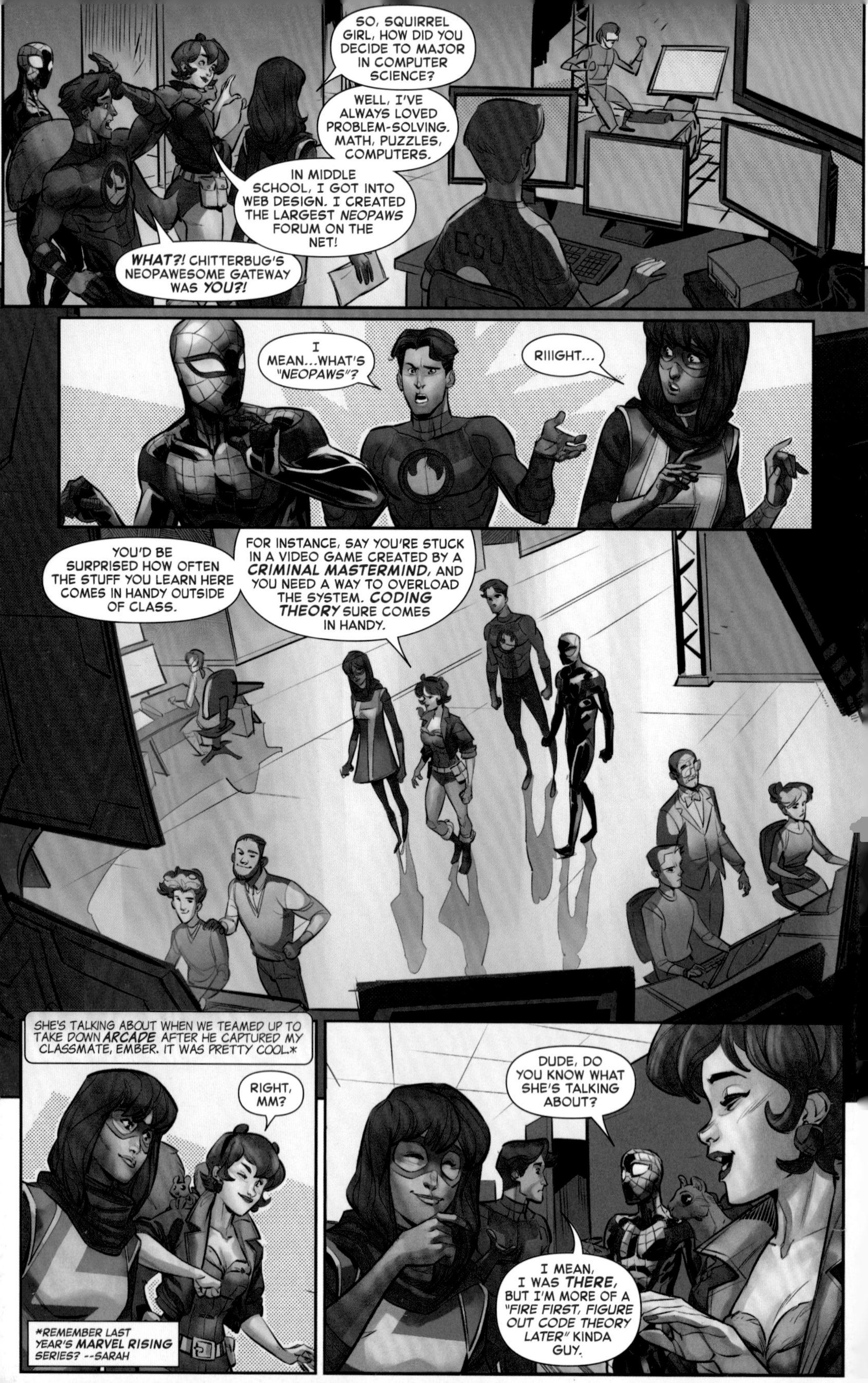
SO, SQUIRREL GIRL, HOW DID YOU DECIDE TO MAJOR IN COMPUTER SCIENCE?
WELL, I'VE ALWAYS LOVED PROBLEM-SOLVING. MATH, PUZZLES, COMPUTERS.
IN MIDDLE SCHOOL, I GOT INTO WEB DESIGN. I CREATED THE LARGEST NEOPAWS FORUM ON THE NET!
WHAT?! CHITTERBUG'S NEOPAWESOME GATEWAY WAS YOU?!
ESU
I MEAN...WHAT'S "NEOPAWS"?
RIIIGHT...
YOU'D BE SURPRISED HOW OFTEN THE STUFF YOU LEARN HERE COMES IN HANDY OUTSIDE OF CLASS.
FOR INSTANCE, SAY YOU'RE STUCK IN A VIDEO GAME CREATED BY A CRIMINAL MASTERMIND, AND YOU NEED A WAY TO OVERLOAD THE SYSTEM. CODING THEORY SURE COMES IN HANDY.
SHE'S TALKING ABOUT WHEN WE TEAMED UP TO TAKE DOWN ARCADE AFTER HE CAPTURED MY CLASSMATE, EMBER. IT WAS PRETTY COOL.*
RIGHT, MM?
*REMEMBER LAST YEAR'S MARVEL RISING SERIES? --SARAH
DUDE, DO YOU KNOW WHAT SHE'S TALKING ABOUT?
I MEAN, I WAS THERE, BUT I'M MORE OF A "FIRE FIRST, FIGURE OUT CODE THEORY LATER" KINDA GUY.

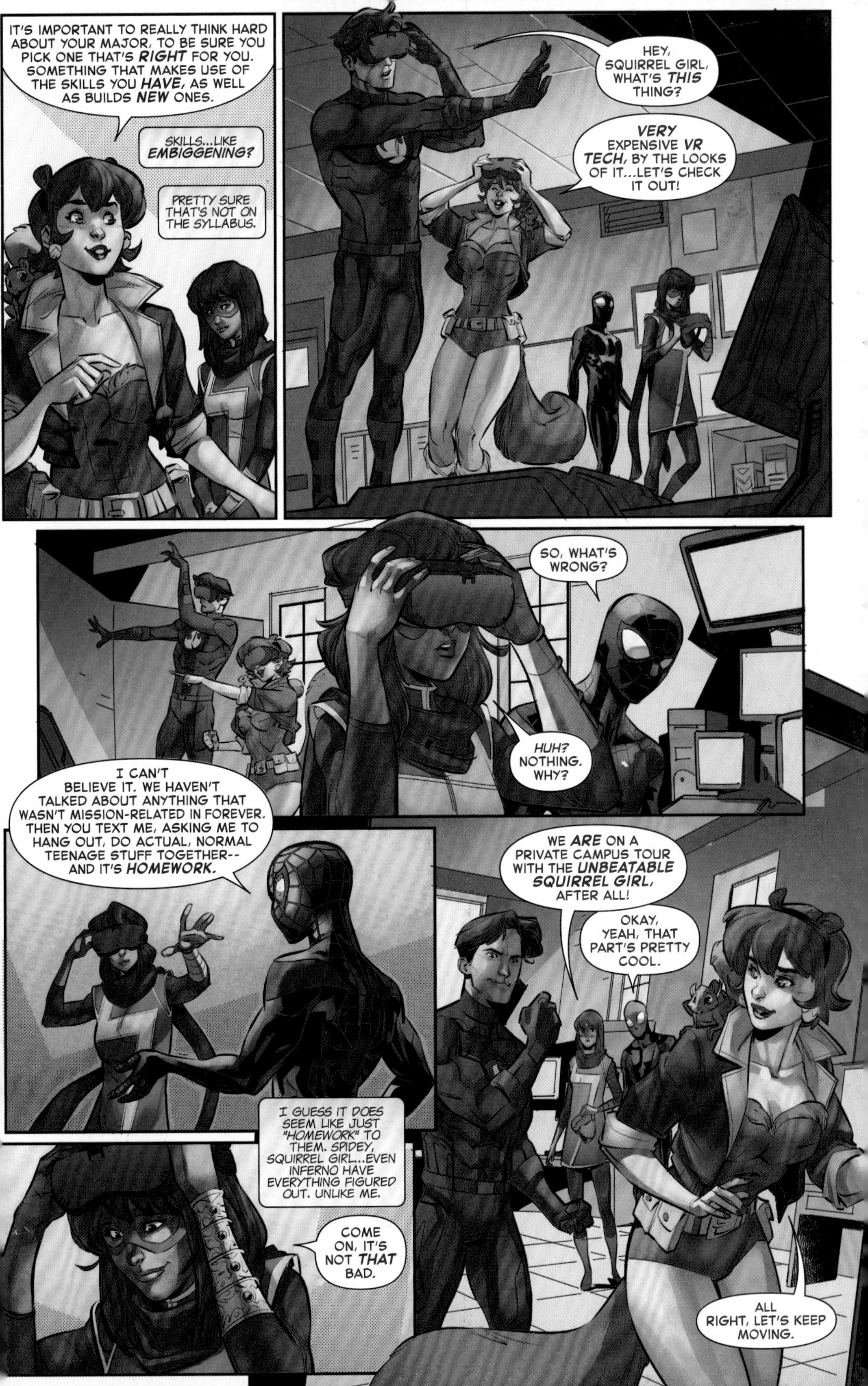
IT'S IMPORTANT TO REALLY THINK HARD ABOUT YOUR MAJOR, TO BE SURE YOU PICK ONE THAT'S **RIGHT** FOR YOU. SOMETHING THAT MAKES USE OF THE SKILLS YOU **HAVE,** AS WELL AS BUILDS **NEW** ONES.
SKILLS...LIKE **EMBIGGENING?**
PRETTY SURE THAT'S NOT ON THE SYLLABUS.
HEY, SQUIRREL GIRL, WHAT'S **THIS** THING?
VERY EXPENSIVE **VR TECH,** BY THE LOOKS OF IT...LET'S CHECK IT OUT!
SO, WHAT'S WRONG?
HUH? NOTHING. WHY?
I CAN'T BELIEVE IT. WE HAVEN'T TALKED ABOUT ANYTHING THAT WASN'T MISSION-RELATED IN FOREVER. THEN YOU TEXT ME, ASKING ME TO HANG OUT, DO ACTUAL, NORMAL TEENAGE STUFF TOGETHER-- AND IT'S **HOMEWORK.**
WE **ARE** ON A PRIVATE CAMPUS TOUR WITH THE **UNBEATABLE SQUIRREL GIRL,** AFTER ALL!
OKAY, YEAH, THAT PART'S PRETTY COOL.
I GUESS IT DOES SEEM LIKE JUST "HOMEWORK" TO THEM. SPIDEY, SQUIRREL GIRL...EVEN INFERNO HAVE EVERYTHING FIGURED OUT. UNLIKE ME.
COME ON, IT'S NOT **THAT** BAD.
ALL RIGHT, LET'S KEEP MOVING.

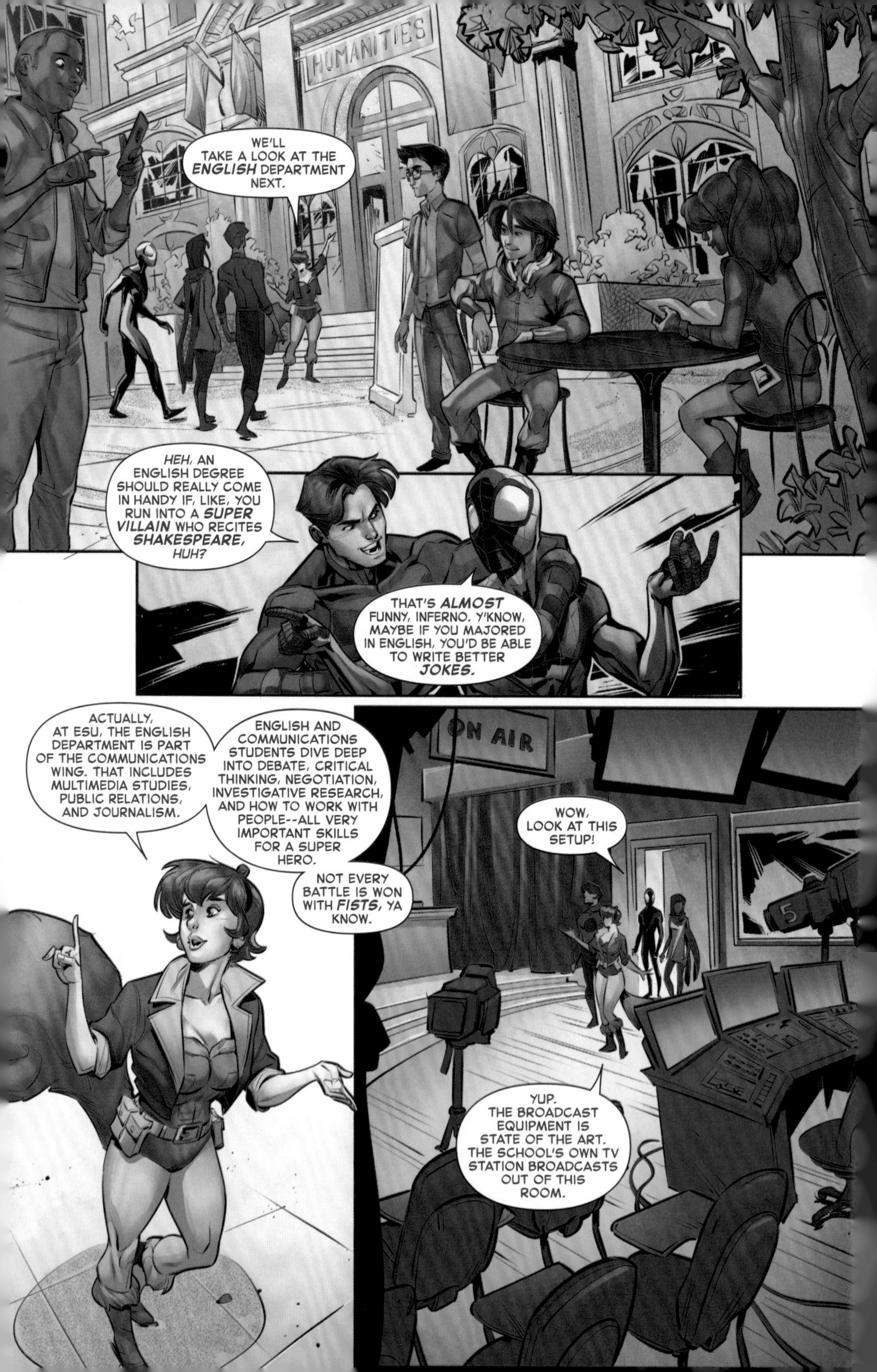
WE'LL TAKE A LOOK AT THE ENGLISH DEPARTMENT NEXT.
HUMANITIES
HEH, AN ENGLISH DEGREE SHOULD REALLY COME IN HANDY IF, LIKE, YOU RUN INTO A SUPER VILLAIN WHO RECITES SHAKESPEARE, HUH?
THAT'S ALMOST FUNNY, INFERNO. Y'KNOW, MAYBE IF YOU MAJORED IN ENGLISH, YOU'D BE ABLE TO WRITE BETTER JOKES.
ACTUALLY, AT ESU, THE ENGLISH DEPARTMENT IS PART OF THE COMMUNICATIONS WING. THAT INCLUDES MULTIMEDIA STUDIES, PUBLIC RELATIONS, AND JOURNALISM.
ENGLISH AND COMMUNICATIONS STUDENTS DIVE DEEP INTO DEBATE, CRITICAL THINKING, NEGOTIATION, INVESTIGATIVE RESEARCH, AND HOW TO WORK WITH PEOPLE--ALL VERY IMPORTANT SKILLS FOR A SUPER HERO.
NOT EVERY BATTLE IS WON WITH FISTS, YA KNOW.
ON AIR
WOW, LOOK AT THIS SETUP!
YUP. THE BROADCAST EQUIPMENT IS STATE OF THE ART. THE SCHOOL'S OWN TV STATION BROADCASTS OUT OF THIS ROOM.

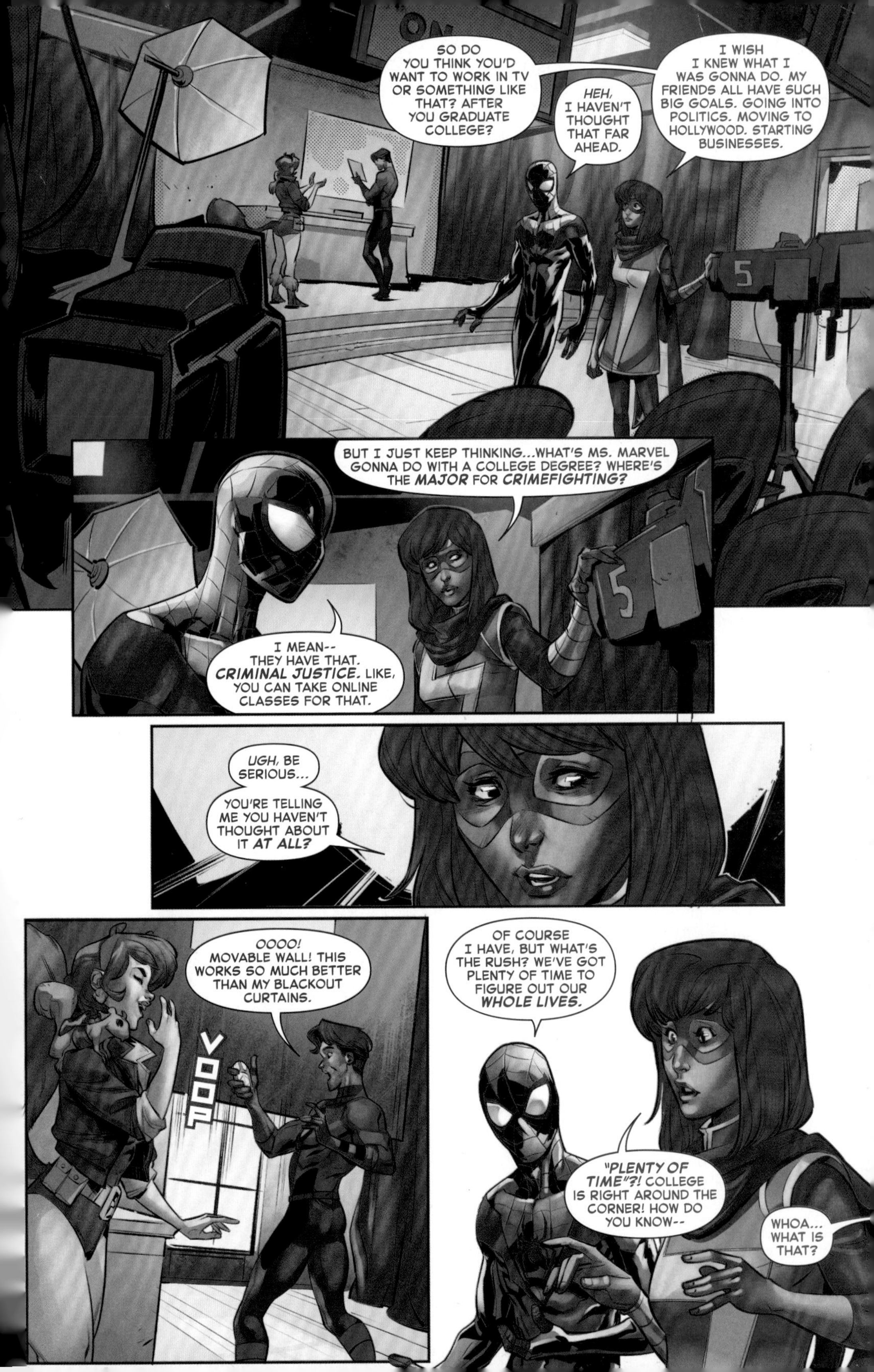
SO DO YOU THINK YOU'D WANT TO WORK IN TV OR SOMETHING LIKE THAT? AFTER YOU GRADUATE COLLEGE?
HEH, I HAVEN'T THOUGHT THAT FAR AHEAD.
I WISH I KNEW WHAT I WAS GONNA DO. MY FRIENDS ALL HAVE SUCH BIG GOALS. GOING INTO POLITICS. MOVING TO HOLLYWOOD. STARTING BUSINESSES.
BUT I JUST KEEP THINKING...WHAT'S MS. MARVEL GONNA DO WITH A COLLEGE DEGREE? WHERE'S THE MAJOR FOR CRIMEFIGHTING?
I MEAN-- THEY HAVE THAT. CRIMINAL JUSTICE. LIKE, YOU CAN TAKE ONLINE CLASSES FOR THAT.
UGH, BE SERIOUS...
YOU'RE TELLING ME YOU HAVEN'T THOUGHT ABOUT IT AT ALL?
OOOO! MOVABLE WALL! THIS WORKS SO MUCH BETTER THAN MY BLACKOUT CURTAINS.
VOOP
OF COURSE I HAVE, BUT WHAT'S THE RUSH? WE'VE GOT PLENTY OF TIME TO FIGURE OUT OUR WHOLE LIVES.
"PLENTY OF TIME"?! COLLEGE IS RIGHT AROUND THE CORNER! HOW DO YOU KNOW--
WHOA... WHAT IS THAT?

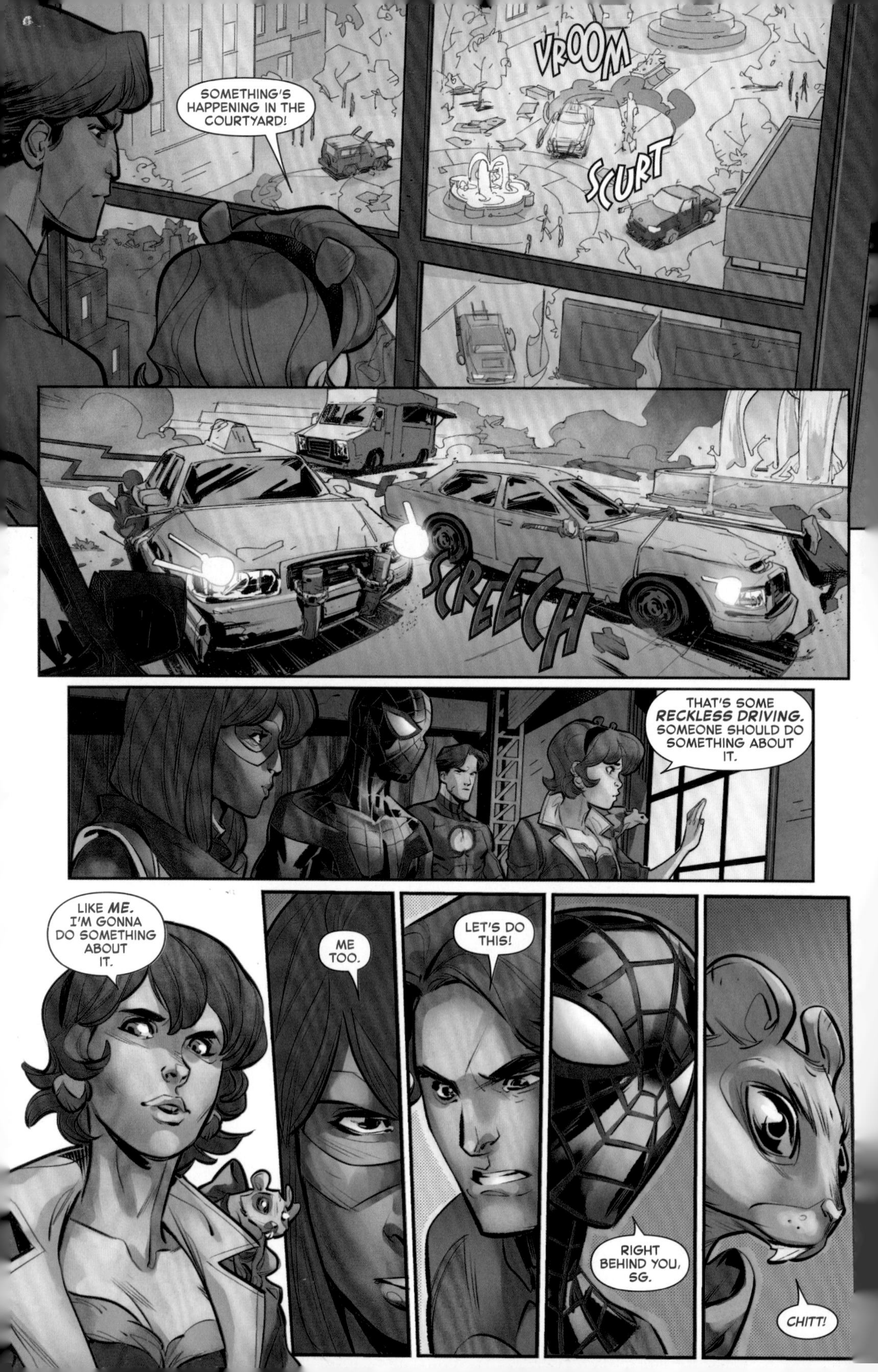
SOMETHING'S HAPPENING IN THE COURTYARD!
VROOM
SCURT
SCREECH
THAT'S SOME RECKLESS DRIVING. SOMEONE SHOULD DO SOMETHING ABOUT IT.
LIKE ME. I'M GONNA DO SOMETHING ABOUT IT.
ME TOO.
LET'S DO THIS!
RIGHT BEHIND YOU, SG.
CHITT!

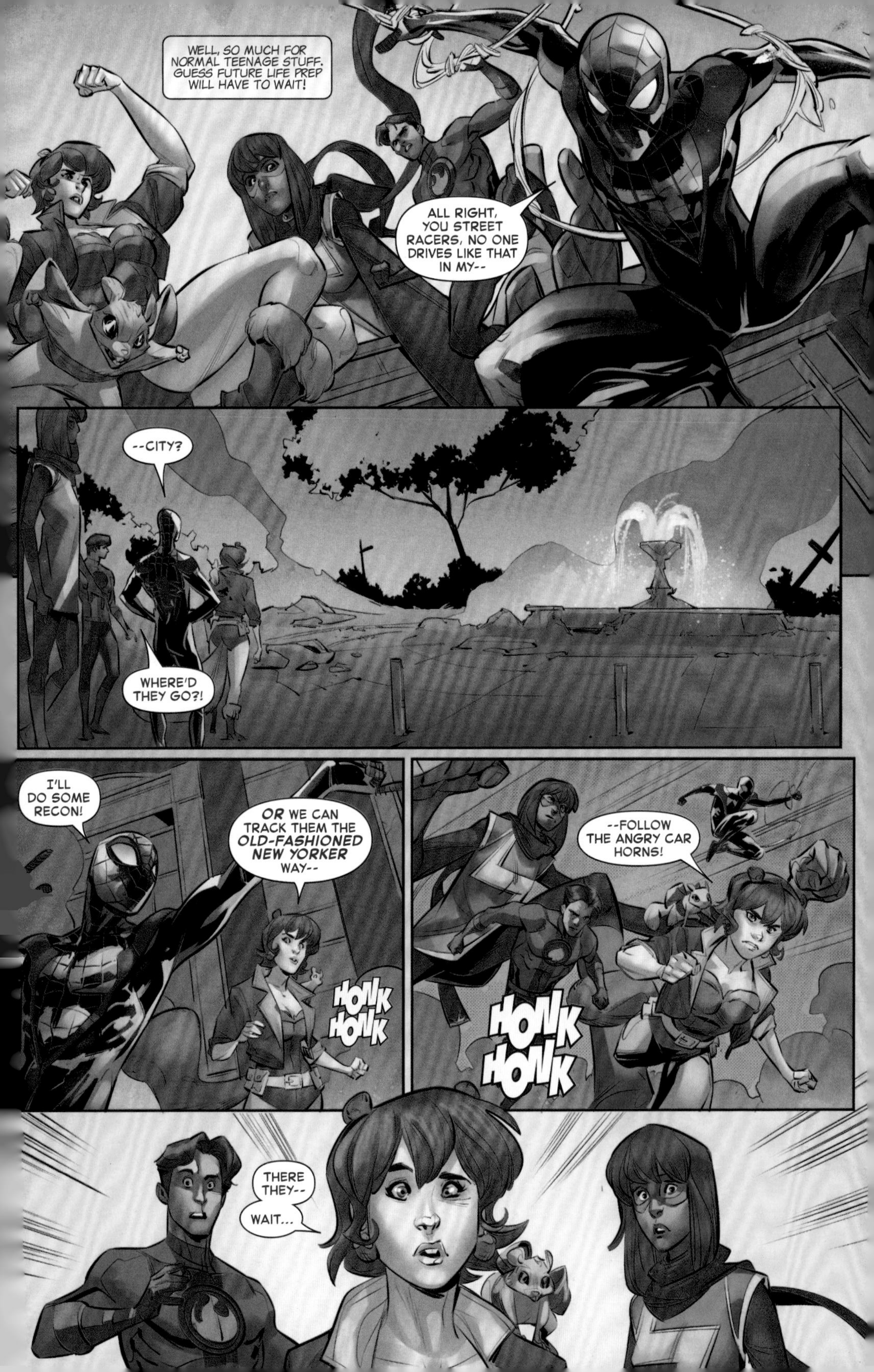
WELL, SO MUCH FOR NORMAL TEENAGE STUFF. GUESS FUTURE LIFE PREP WILL HAVE TO WAIT!
ALL RIGHT, YOU STREET RACERS, NO ONE DRIVES LIKE THAT IN MY--
--CITY?
WHERE'D THEY GO?!
I'LL DO SOME RECON!
OR WE CAN TRACK THEM THE *OLD-FASHIONED NEW YORKER* WAY--
HONK HONK
--FOLLOW THE ANGRY CAR HORNS!
HONK HONK
THERE THEY--
WAIT...

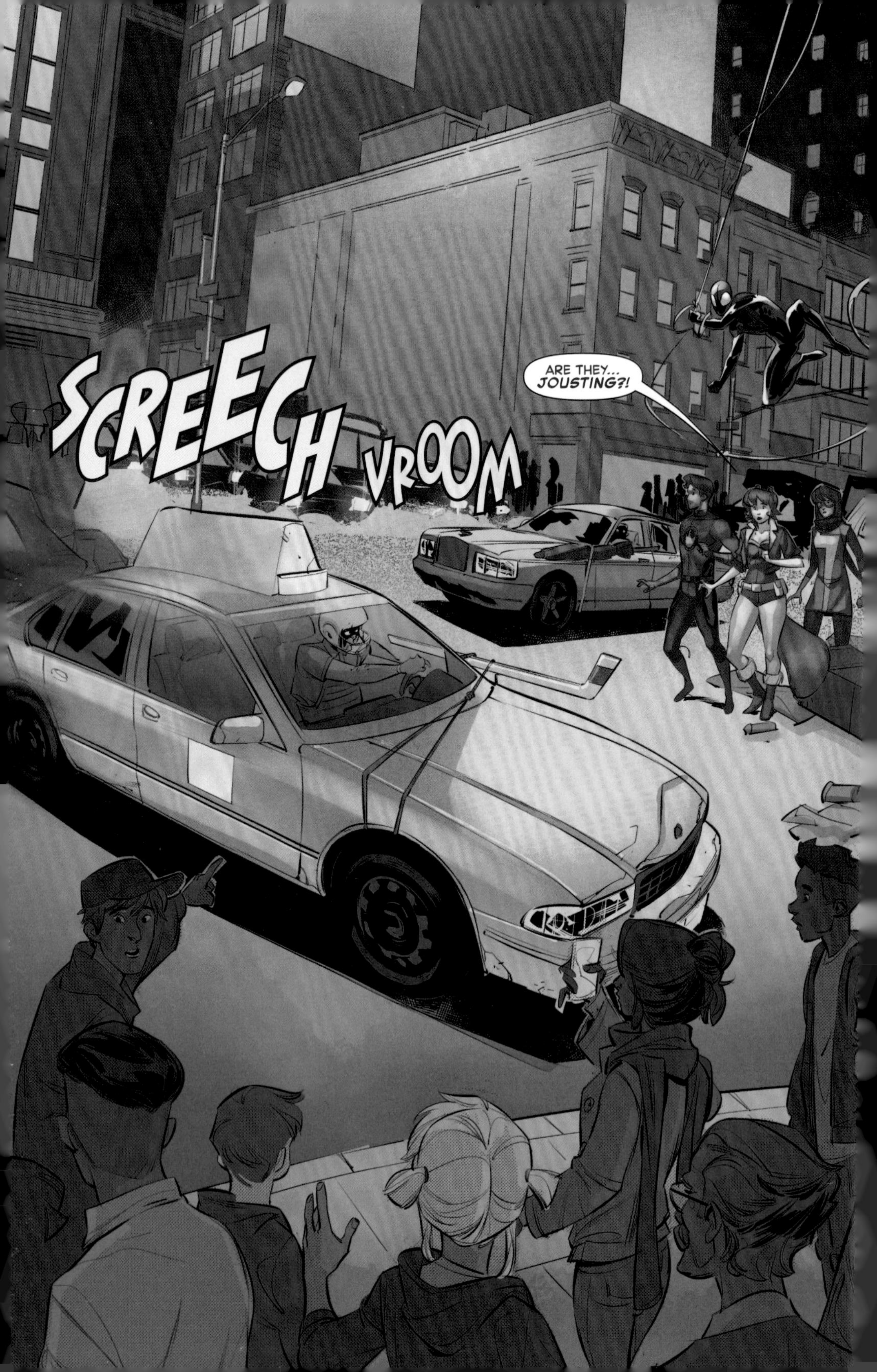
SCREECH
VROOM
ARE THEY... JOUSTING?!

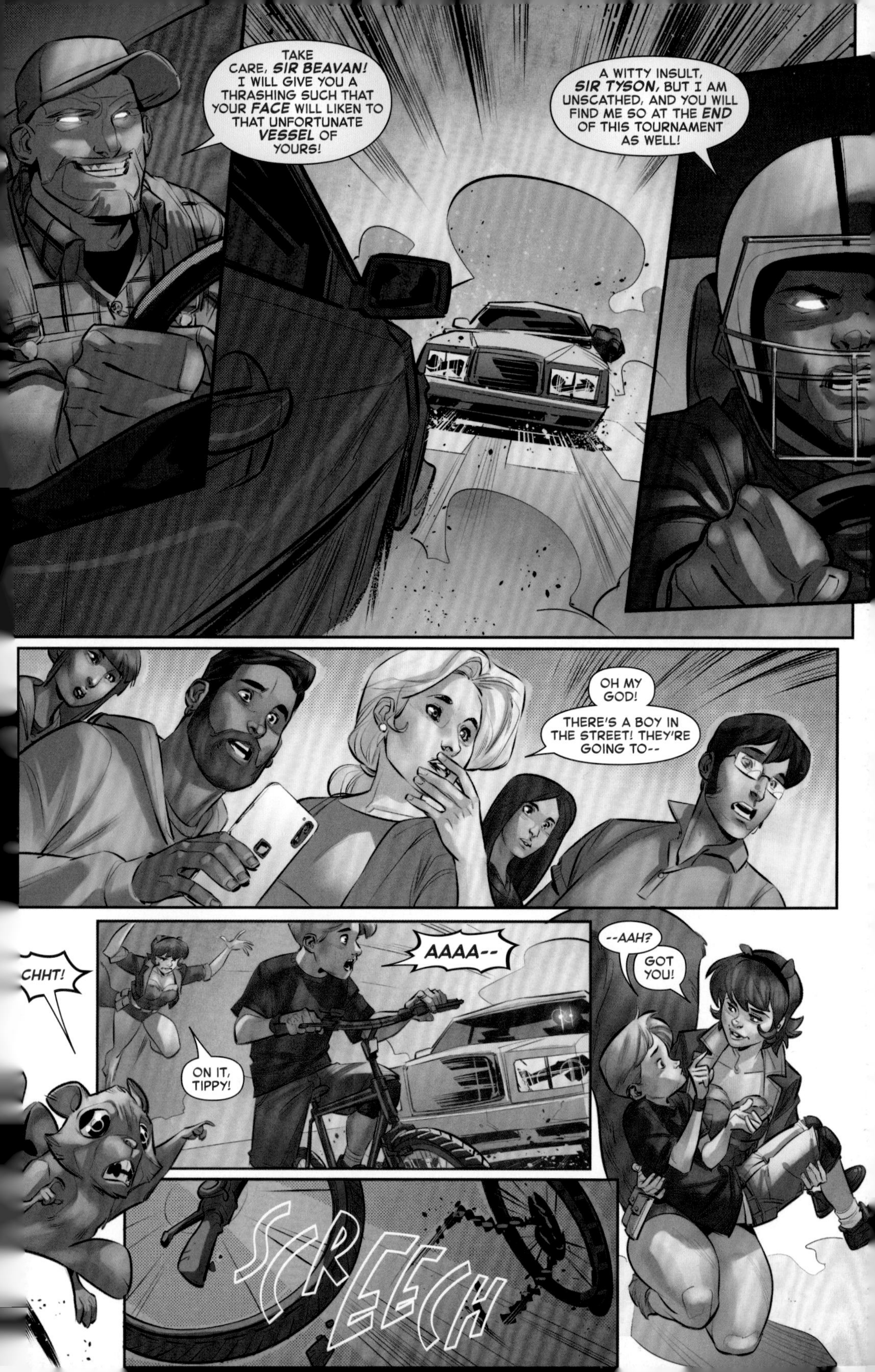
TAKE CARE, SIR BEAVAN! I WILL GIVE YOU A THRASHING SUCH THAT YOUR FACE WILL LIKEN TO THAT UNFORTUNATE VESSEL OF YOURS!
A WITTY INSULT, SIR TYSON, BUT I AM UNSCATHED, AND YOU WILL FIND ME SO AT THE END OF THIS TOURNAMENT AS WELL!
OH MY GOD!
THERE'S A BOY IN THE STREET! THEY'RE GOING TO--
CHHT!
AAAA--
ON IT, TIPPY!
--AAH?
GOT YOU!
SCREECH

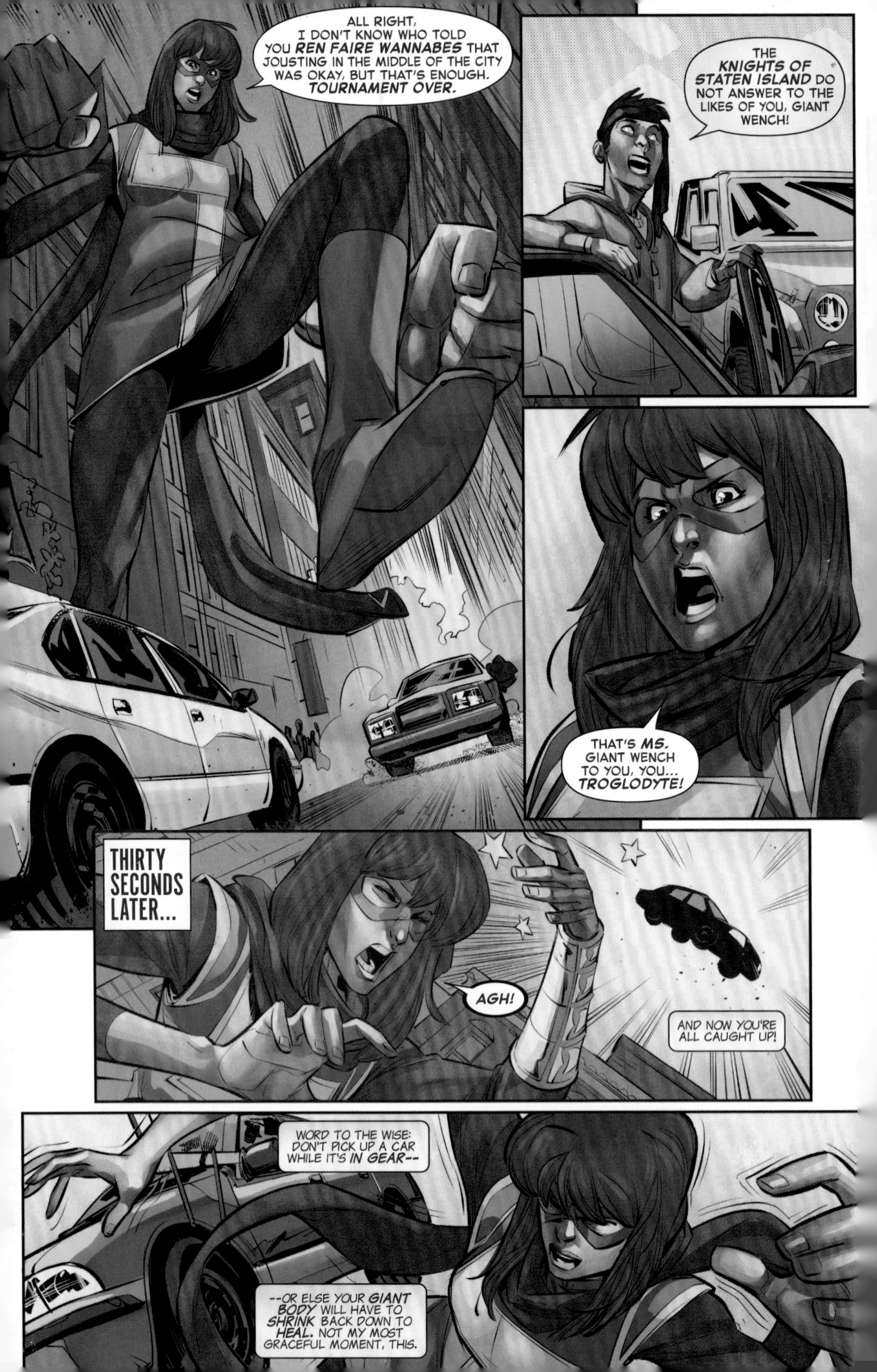
ALL RIGHT, I DON'T KNOW WHO TOLD YOU REN FAIRE WANNABES THAT JOUSTING IN THE MIDDLE OF THE CITY WAS OKAY, BUT THAT'S ENOUGH. TOURNAMENT OVER.
THE KNIGHTS OF STATEN ISLAND DO NOT ANSWER TO THE LIKES OF YOU, GIANT WENCH!
THAT'S MS. GIANT WENCH TO YOU, YOU... TROGLODYTE!
THIRTY SECONDS LATER...
AGH!
AND NOW YOU'RE ALL CAUGHT UP!
WORD TO THE WISE: DON'T PICK UP A CAR WHILE IT'S IN GEAR--
--OR ELSE YOUR GIANT BODY WILL HAVE TO SHRINK BACK DOWN TO HEAL. NOT MY MOST GRACEFUL MOMENT, THIS.

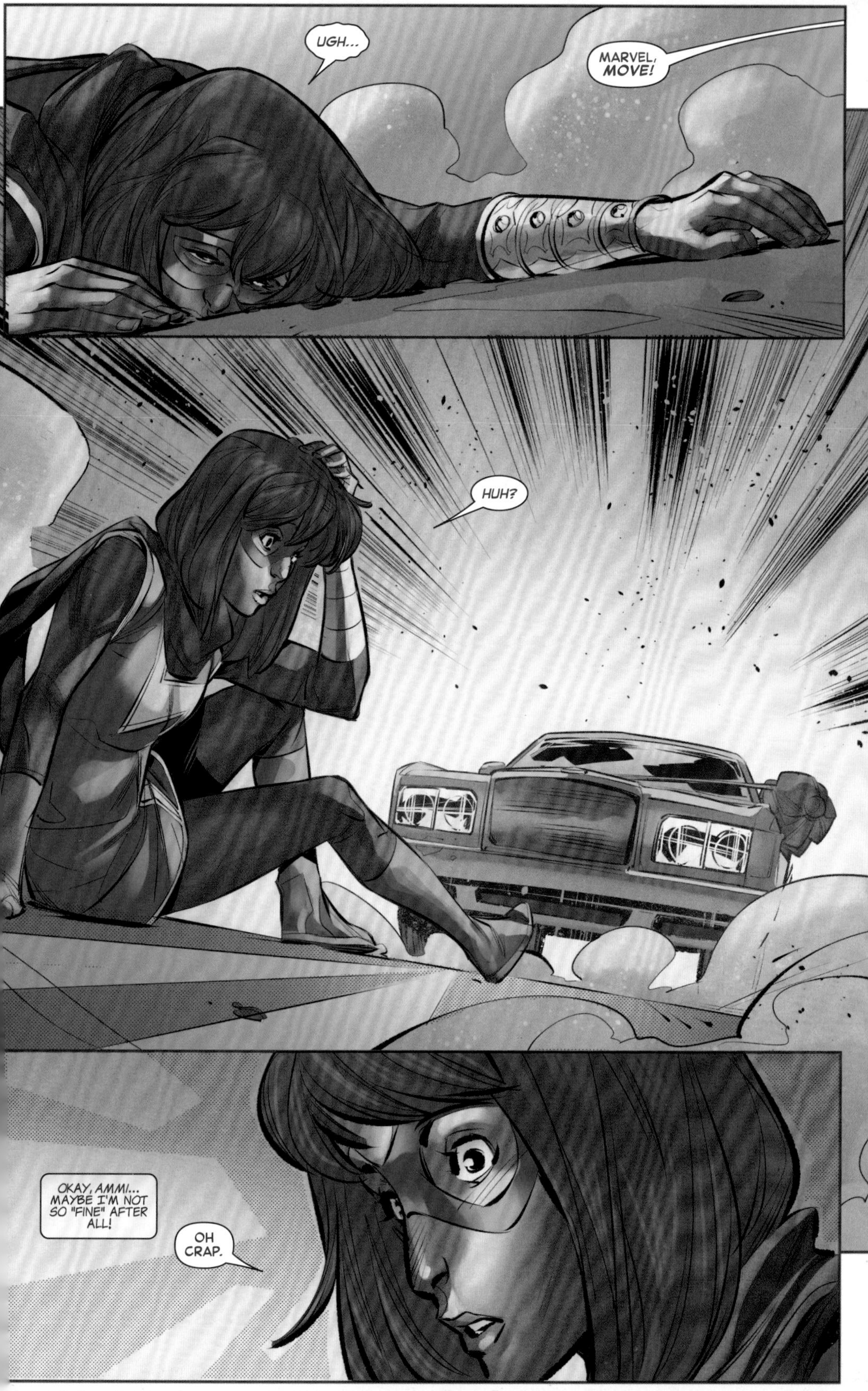

UGH...
MARVEL, MOVE!
HUH?
OKAY, AMMI... MAYBE I'M NOT SO "FINE" AFTER ALL!
OH CRAP.

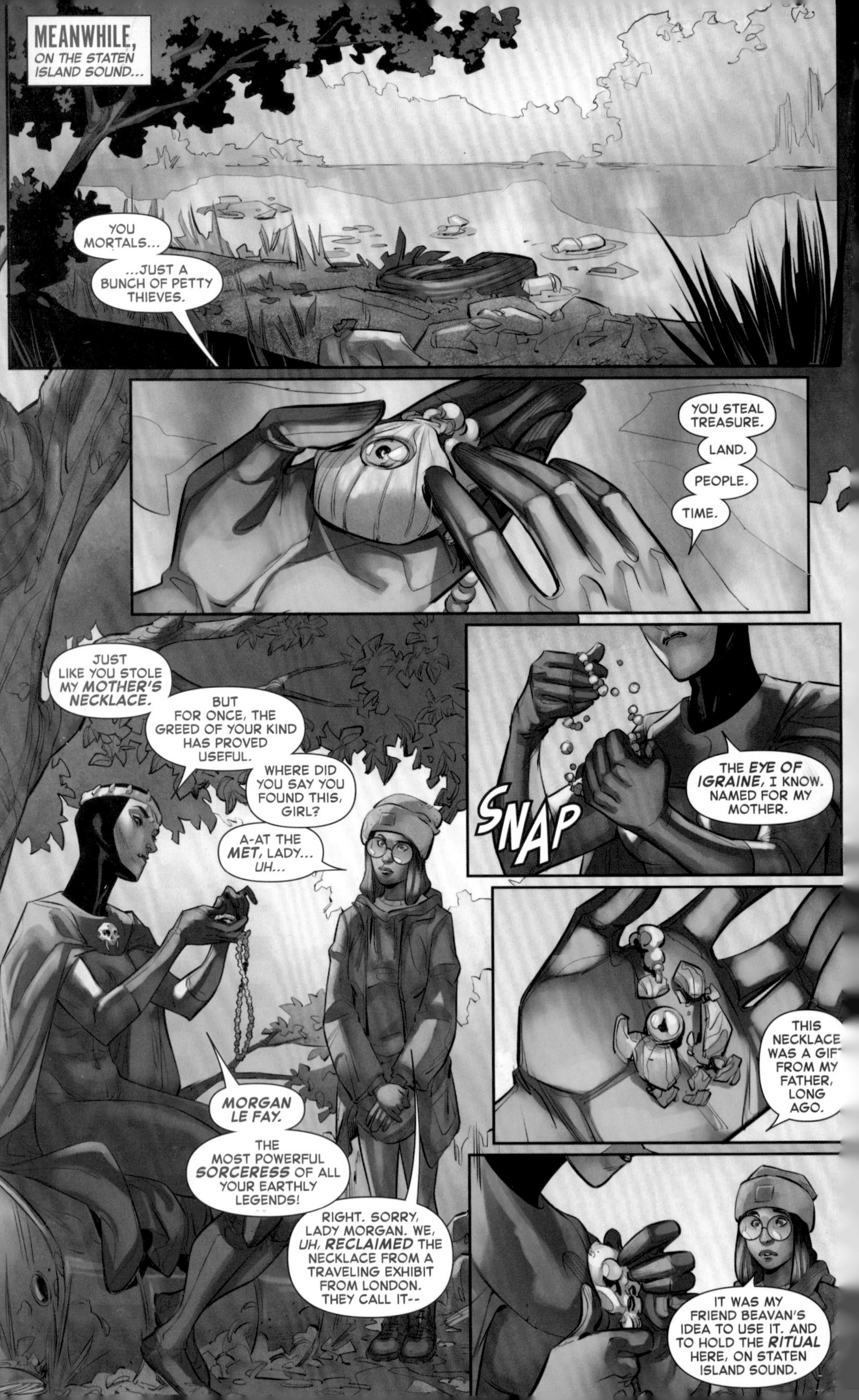
MEANWHILE, ON THE STATEN ISLAND SOUND...
YOU MORTALS...
...JUST A BUNCH OF PETTY THIEVES.
YOU STEAL TREASURE.
LAND.
PEOPLE.
TIME.
JUST LIKE YOU STOLE MY MOTHER'S NECKLACE.
BUT FOR ONCE, THE GREED OF YOUR KIND HAS PROVED USEFUL.
WHERE DID YOU SAY YOU FOUND THIS, GIRL?
A-AT THE MET, LADY... UH...
MORGAN LE FAY.
THE MOST POWERFUL SORCERESS OF ALL YOUR EARTHLY LEGENDS!
RIGHT. SORRY, LADY MORGAN. WE, UH, RECLAIMED THE NECKLACE FROM A TRAVELING EXHIBIT FROM LONDON. THEY CALL IT--
SNAP
THE EYE OF IGRAINE, I KNOW. NAMED FOR MY MOTHER.
THIS NECKLACE WAS A GIFT FROM MY FATHER, LONG AGO.
IT WAS MY FRIEND BEAVAN'S IDEA TO USE IT. AND TO HOLD THE RITUAL HERE, ON STATEN ISLAND SOUND.

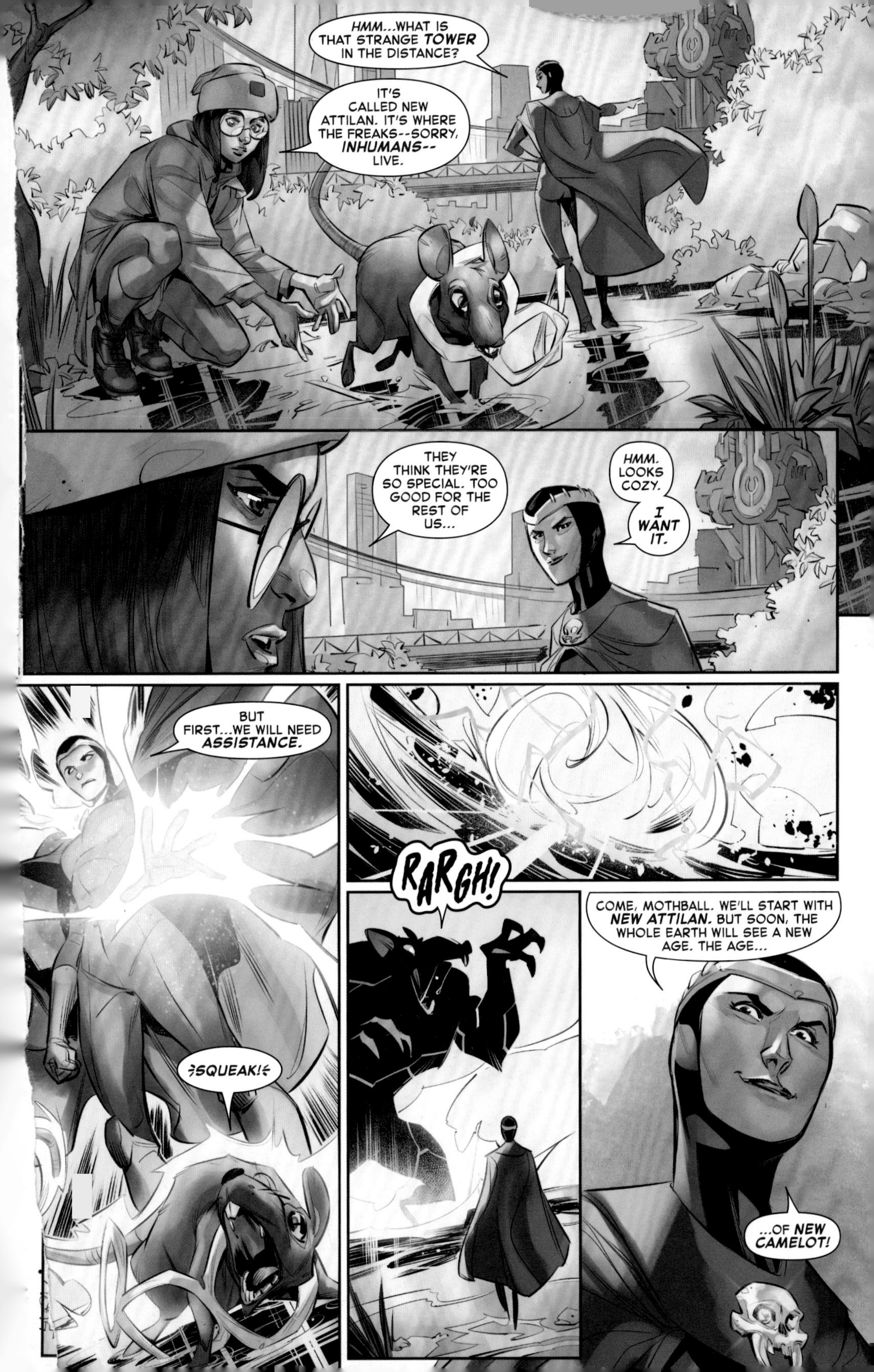
HMM...WHAT IS THAT STRANGE TOWER IN THE DISTANCE?
IT'S CALLED NEW ATTILAN. IT'S WHERE THE FREAKS--SORRY, INHUMANS-- LIVE.
THEY THINK THEY'RE SO SPECIAL. TOO GOOD FOR THE REST OF US...
HMM. LOOKS COZY.
I WANT IT.
BUT FIRST...WE WILL NEED ASSISTANCE.
SQUEAK!
RARGH!
COME, MOTHBALL. WE'LL START WITH NEW ATTILAN. BUT SOON, THE WHOLE EARTH WILL SEE A NEW AGE. THE AGE...
...OF NEW CAMELOT!

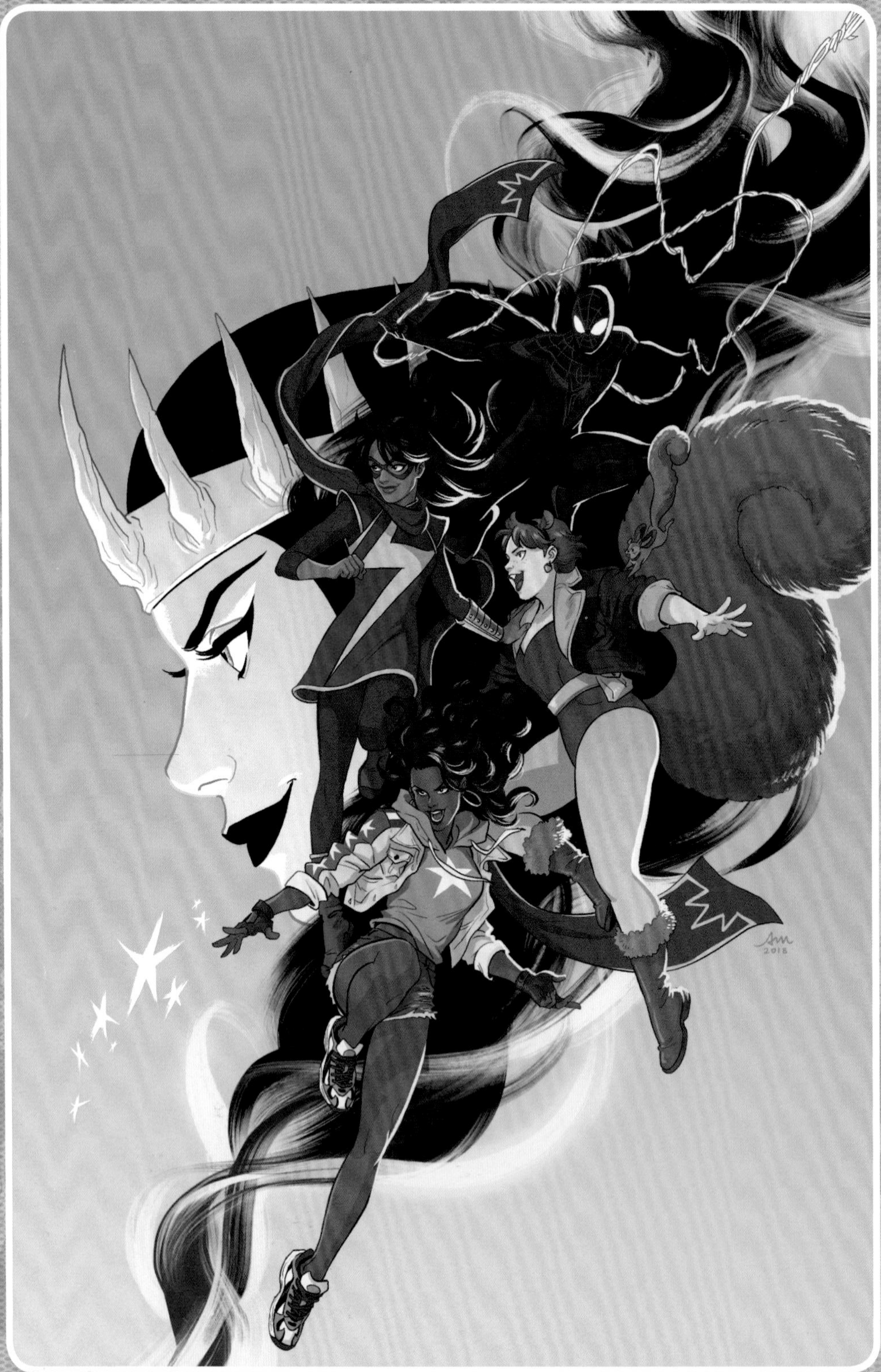

AM
2018

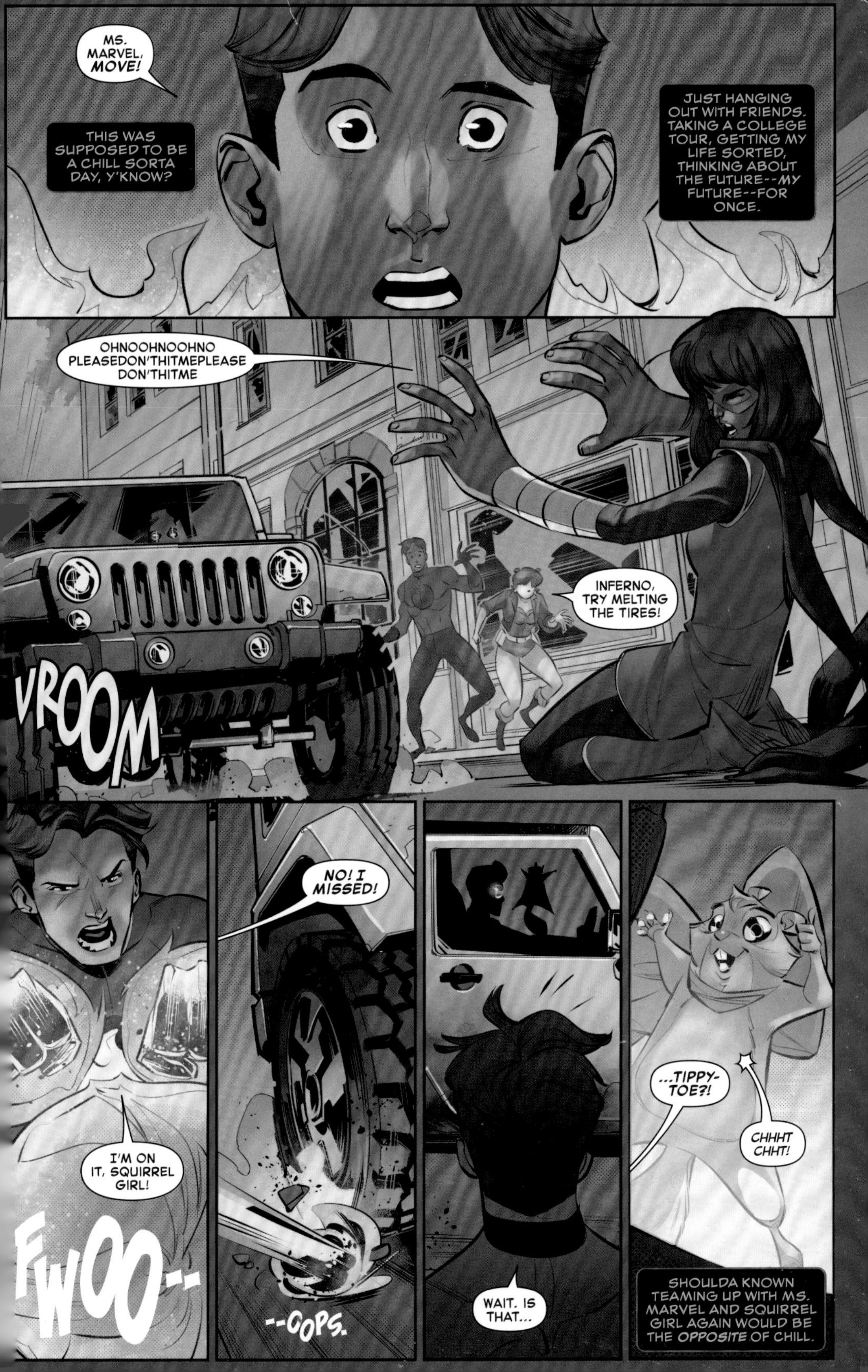
MS. MARVEL, MOVE!
THIS WAS SUPPOSED TO BE A CHILL SORTA DAY, Y'KNOW?
JUST HANGING OUT WITH FRIENDS. TAKING A COLLEGE TOUR, GETTING MY LIFE SORTED, THINKING ABOUT THE FUTURE--MY FUTURE--FOR ONCE.
OHNOOHNOOHNO PLEASEDON'THITMEPLEASE DON'THITME
INFERNO, TRY MELTING THE TIRES!
VROOM
I'M ON IT, SQUIRREL GIRL!
FWOO--
NO! I MISSED!
--OOPS.
WAIT. IS THAT...
...TIPPY-TOE?!
CHHHT CHHT!
SHOULDA KNOWN TEAMING UP WITH MS. MARVEL AND SQUIRREL GIRL AGAIN WOULD BE THE OPPOSITE OF CHILL.

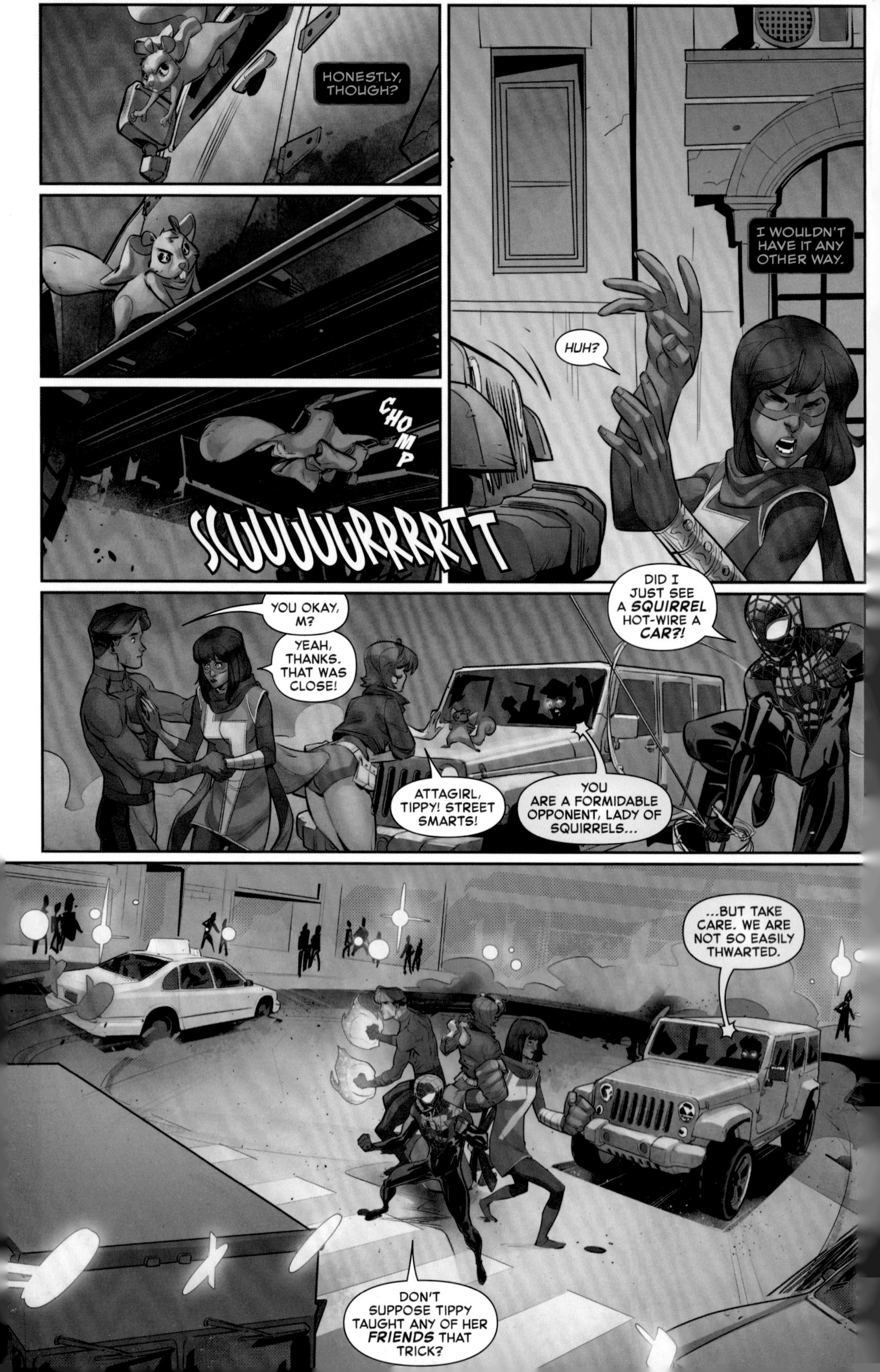
HONESTLY, THOUGH?
I WOULDN'T HAVE IT ANY OTHER WAY.
CHOMP
SCUUUUUURRRRTT
HUH?
YOU OKAY, M?
YEAH, THANKS. THAT WAS CLOSE!
DID I JUST SEE A SQUIRREL HOT-WIRE A CAR?!
ATTAGIRL, TIPPY! STREET SMARTS!
YOU ARE A FORMIDABLE OPPONENT, LADY OF SQUIRRELS...
...BUT TAKE CARE. WE ARE NOT SO EASILY THWARTED.
DON'T SUPPOSE TIPPY TAUGHT ANY OF HER FRIENDS THAT TRICK?

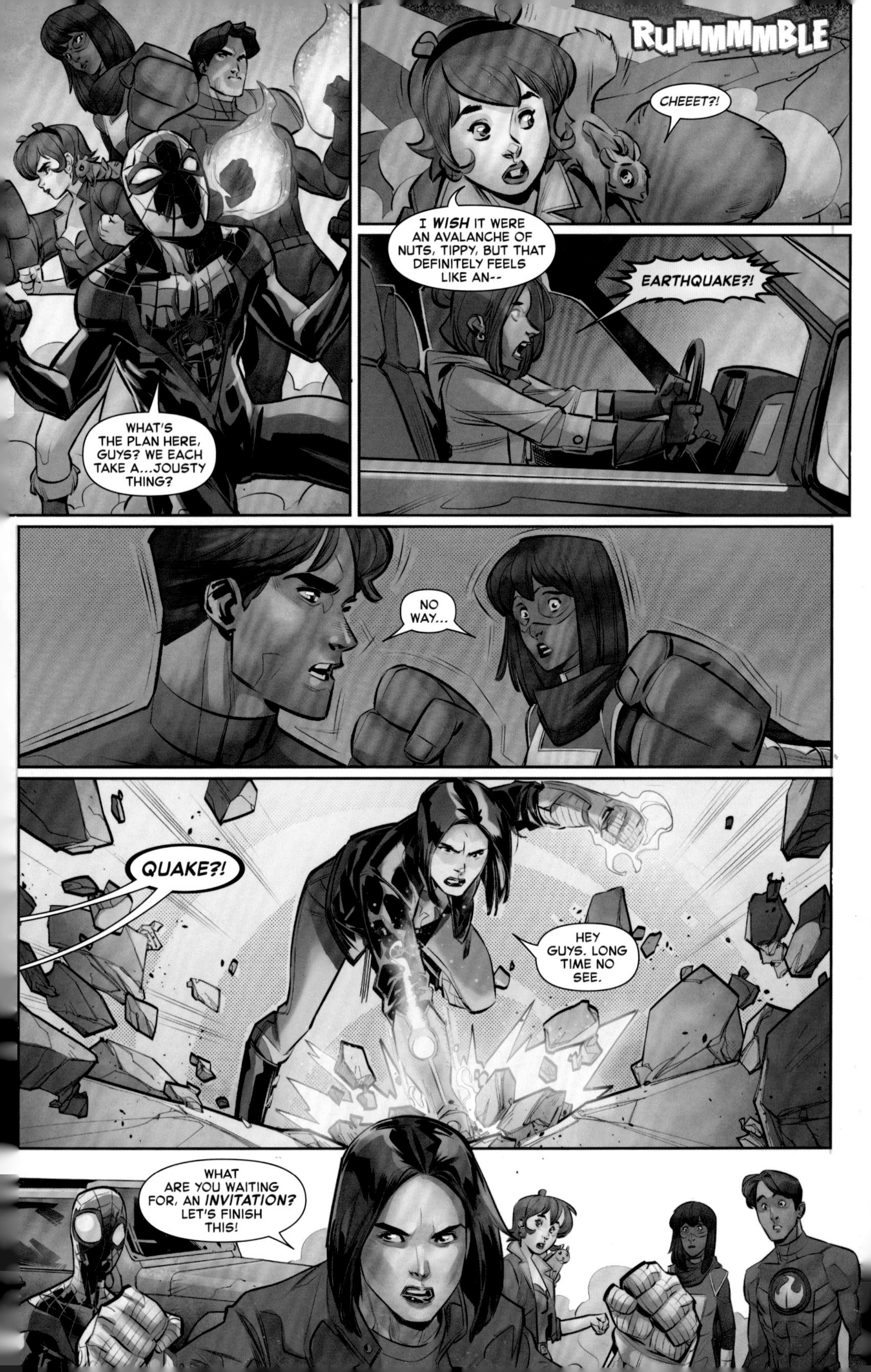
WHAT'S THE PLAN HERE, GUYS? WE EACH TAKE A...JOUSTY THING?
RUMMMMBLE
CHEEET?!
I WISH IT WERE AN AVALANCHE OF NUTS, TIPPY, BUT THAT DEFINITELY FEELS LIKE AN--
EARTHQUAKE?!
NO WAY...
QUAKE?!
HEY GUYS. LONG TIME NO SEE.
WHAT ARE YOU WAITING FOR, AN INVITATION? LET'S FINISH THIS!

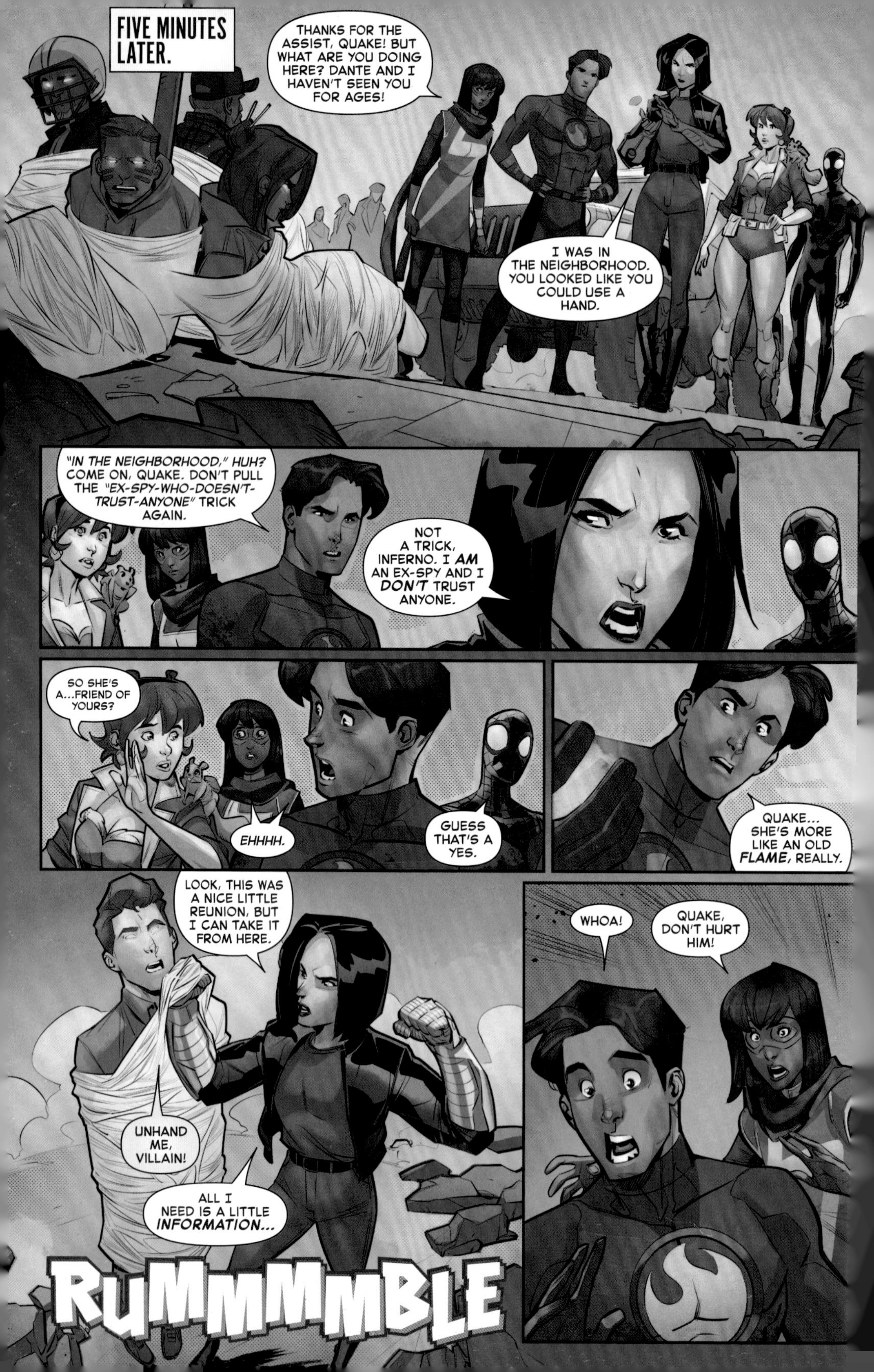
FIVE MINUTES LATER.
THANKS FOR THE ASSIST, QUAKE! BUT WHAT ARE YOU DOING HERE? DANTE AND I HAVEN'T SEEN YOU FOR AGES!
I WAS IN THE NEIGHBORHOOD. YOU LOOKED LIKE YOU COULD USE A HAND.
"IN THE NEIGHBORHOOD," HUH? COME ON, QUAKE. DON'T PULL THE "EX-SPY-WHO-DOESN'T-TRUST-ANYONE" TRICK AGAIN.
NOT A TRICK, INFERNO. I AM AN EX-SPY AND I DON'T TRUST ANYONE.
SO SHE'S A...FRIEND OF YOURS?
EHHHH.
GUESS THAT'S A YES.
QUAKE... SHE'S MORE LIKE AN OLD FLAME, REALLY.
LOOK, THIS WAS A NICE LITTLE REUNION, BUT I CAN TAKE IT FROM HERE.
UNHAND ME, VILLAIN!
ALL I NEED IS A LITTLE INFORMATION...
RUMMMMBLE
WHOA!
QUAKE, DON'T HURT HIM!

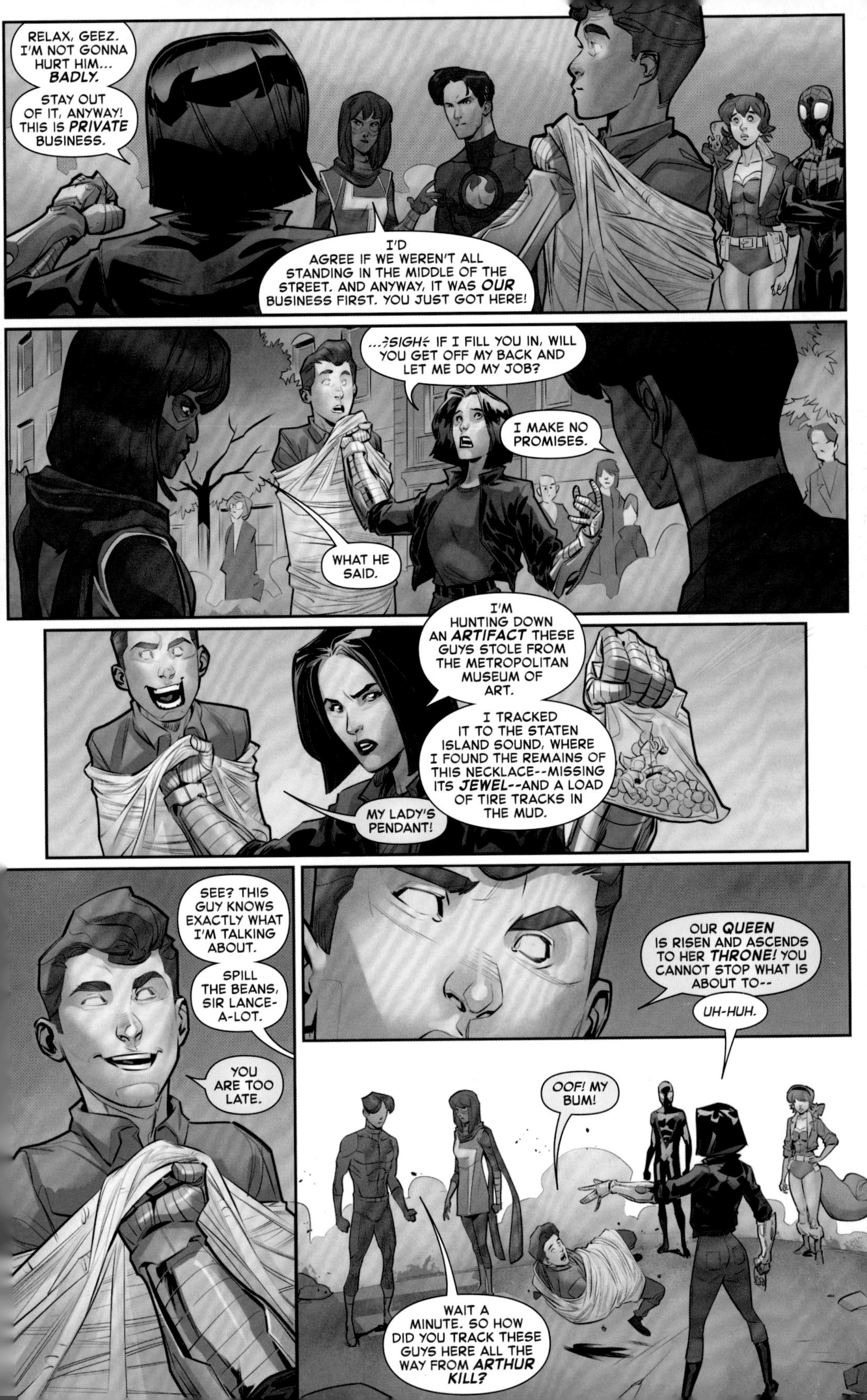
RELAX, GEEZ. I'M NOT GONNA HURT HIM... BADLY.
STAY OUT OF IT, ANYWAY! THIS IS PRIVATE BUSINESS.
I'D AGREE IF WE WEREN'T ALL STANDING IN THE MIDDLE OF THE STREET. AND ANYWAY, IT WAS OUR BUSINESS FIRST. YOU JUST GOT HERE!
...SIGH IF I FILL YOU IN, WILL YOU GET OFF MY BACK AND LET ME DO MY JOB?
I MAKE NO PROMISES.
WHAT HE SAID.
I'M HUNTING DOWN AN ARTIFACT THESE GUYS STOLE FROM THE METROPOLITAN MUSEUM OF ART.
I TRACKED IT TO THE STATEN ISLAND SOUND, WHERE I FOUND THE REMAINS OF THIS NECKLACE--MISSING ITS JEWEL--AND A LOAD OF TIRE TRACKS IN THE MUD.
MY LADY'S PENDANT!
SEE? THIS GUY KNOWS EXACTLY WHAT I'M TALKING ABOUT.
SPILL THE BEANS, SIR LANCE-A-LOT.
YOU ARE TOO LATE.
OUR QUEEN IS RISEN AND ASCENDS TO HER THRONE! YOU CANNOT STOP WHAT IS ABOUT TO--
UH-HUH.
OOF! MY BUM!
WAIT A MINUTE. SO HOW DID YOU TRACK THESE GUYS HERE ALL THE WAY FROM ARTHUR KILL?

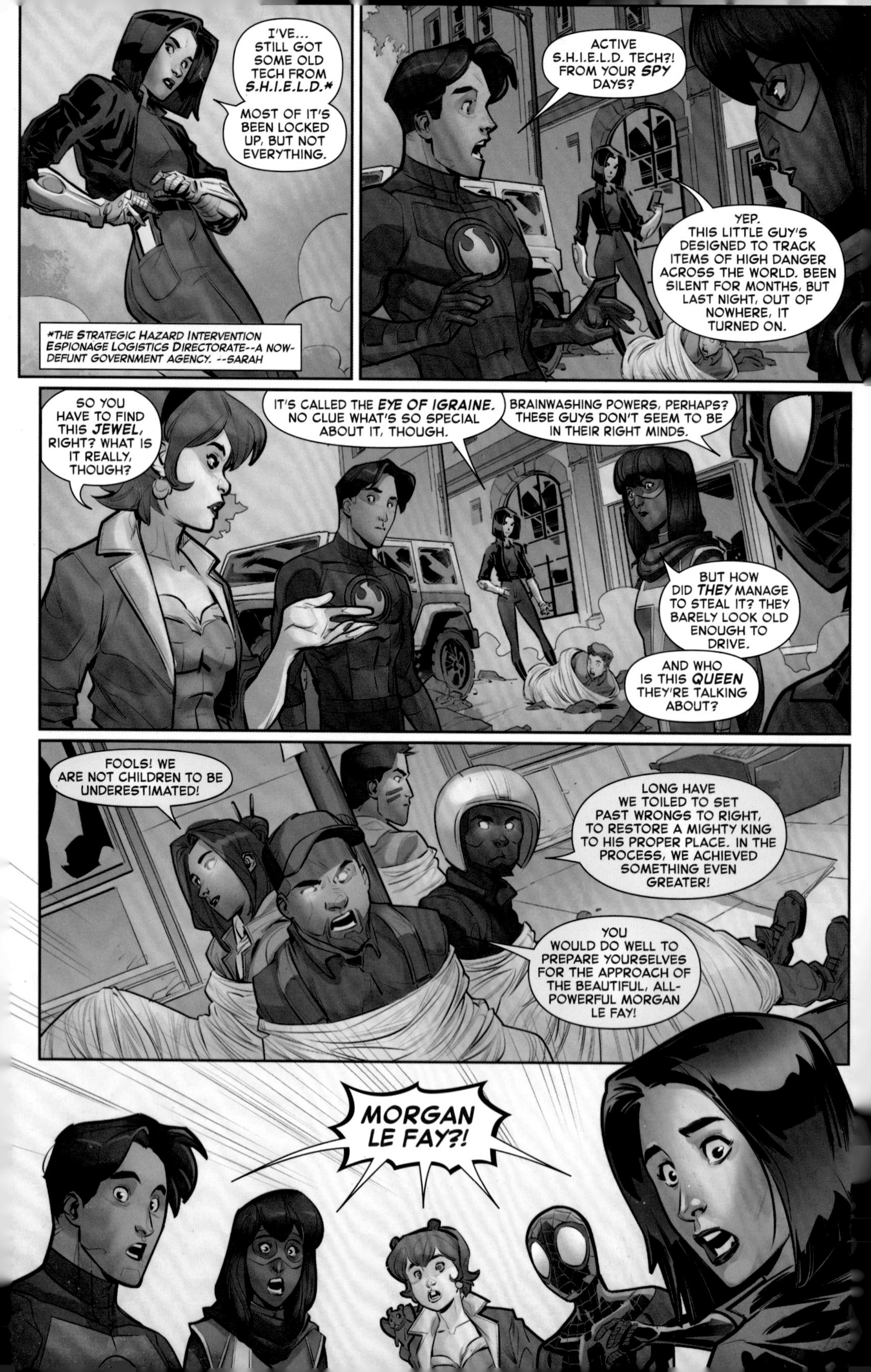
I'VE... STILL GOT SOME OLD TECH FROM S.H.I.E.L.D.*
MOST OF IT'S BEEN LOCKED UP, BUT NOT EVERYTHING.
*THE STRATEGIC HAZARD INTERVENTION ESPIONAGE LOGISTICS DIRECTORATE--A NOW-DEFUNT GOVERNMENT AGENCY. --SARAH
ACTIVE S.H.I.E.L.D. TECH?! FROM YOUR SPY DAYS?
YEP. THIS LITTLE GUY'S DESIGNED TO TRACK ITEMS OF HIGH DANGER ACROSS THE WORLD. BEEN SILENT FOR MONTHS, BUT LAST NIGHT, OUT OF NOWHERE, IT TURNED ON.
SO YOU HAVE TO FIND THIS JEWEL, RIGHT? WHAT IS IT REALLY, THOUGH?
IT'S CALLED THE EYE OF IGRAINE. NO CLUE WHAT'S SO SPECIAL ABOUT IT, THOUGH.
BRAINWASHING POWERS, PERHAPS? THESE GUYS DON'T SEEM TO BE IN THEIR RIGHT MINDS.
BUT HOW DID THEY MANAGE TO STEAL IT? THEY BARELY LOOK OLD ENOUGH TO DRIVE.
AND WHO IS THIS QUEEN THEY'RE TALKING ABOUT?
FOOLS! WE ARE NOT CHILDREN TO BE UNDERESTIMATED!
LONG HAVE WE TOILED TO SET PAST WRONGS TO RIGHT, TO RESTORE A MIGHTY KING TO HIS PROPER PLACE. IN THE PROCESS, WE ACHIEVED SOMETHING EVEN GREATER!
YOU WOULD DO WELL TO PREPARE YOURSELVES FOR THE APPROACH OF THE BEAUTIFUL, ALL-POWERFUL MORGAN LE FAY!
MORGAN LE FAY?!

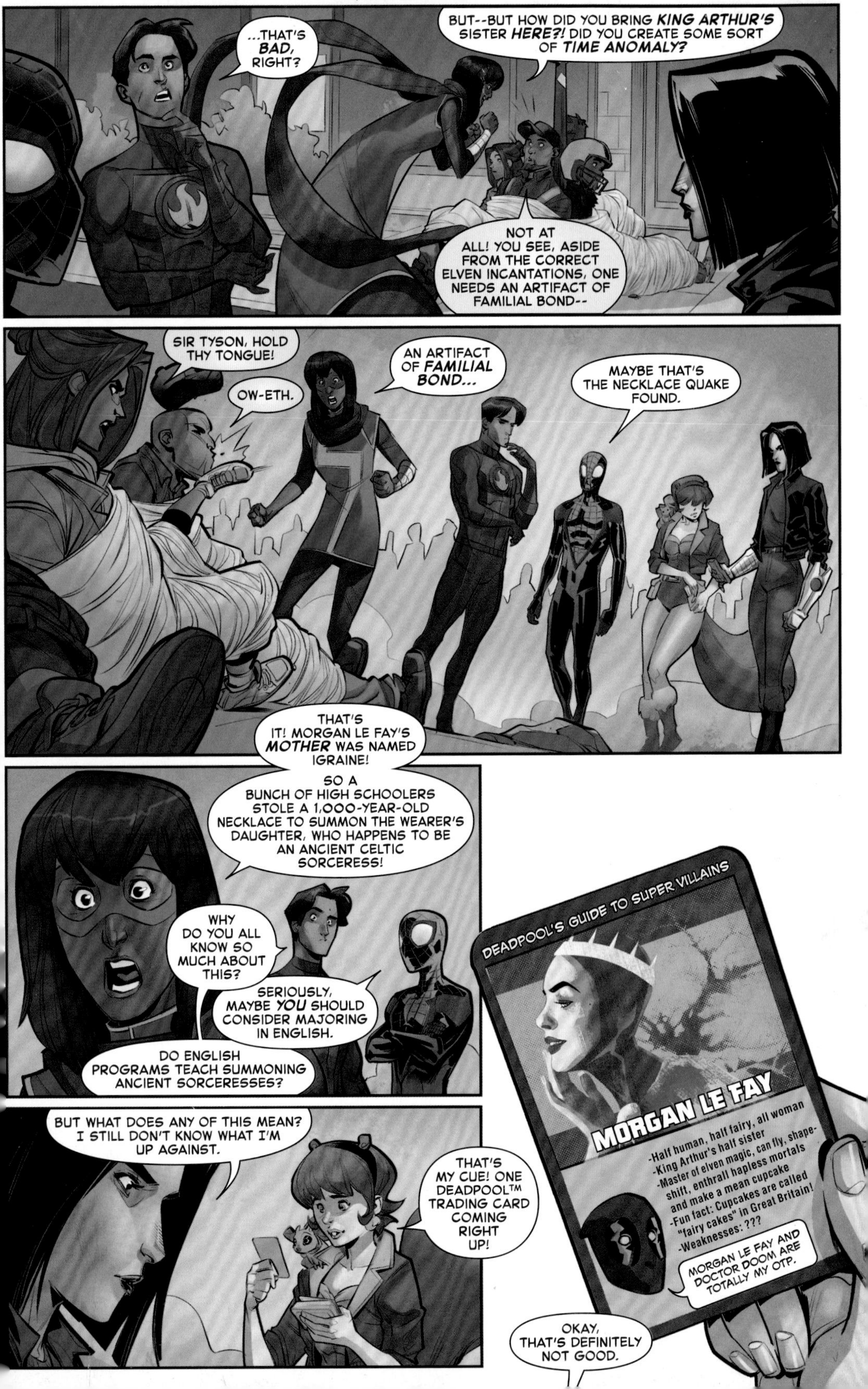
...THAT'S BAD, RIGHT?
BUT--BUT HOW DID YOU BRING KING ARTHUR'S SISTER HERE?! DID YOU CREATE SOME SORT OF TIME ANOMALY?
NOT AT ALL! YOU SEE, ASIDE FROM THE CORRECT ELVEN INCANTATIONS, ONE NEEDS AN ARTIFACT OF FAMILIAL BOND--
SIR TYSON, HOLD THY TONGUE!
OW-ETH.
AN ARTIFACT OF FAMILIAL BOND...
MAYBE THAT'S THE NECKLACE QUAKE FOUND.
THAT'S IT! MORGAN LE FAY'S MOTHER WAS NAMED IGRAINE!
SO A BUNCH OF HIGH SCHOOLERS STOLE A 1,000-YEAR-OLD NECKLACE TO SUMMON THE WEARER'S DAUGHTER, WHO HAPPENS TO BE AN ANCIENT CELTIC SORCERESS!
WHY DO YOU ALL KNOW SO MUCH ABOUT THIS?
SERIOUSLY, MAYBE YOU SHOULD CONSIDER MAJORING IN ENGLISH.
DO ENGLISH PROGRAMS TEACH SUMMONING ANCIENT SORCERESSES?
BUT WHAT DOES ANY OF THIS MEAN? I STILL DON'T KNOW WHAT I'M UP AGAINST.
THAT'S MY CUE! ONE DEADPOOL™ TRADING CARD COMING RIGHT UP!
DEADPOOL'S GUIDE TO SUPER VILLAINS
MORGAN LE FAY
-Half human, half fairy, all woman
-King Arthur's half sister
-Master of elven magic, can fly, shape-shift, enthrall hapless mortals and make a mean cupcake
-Fun fact: Cupcakes are called "fairy cakes" in Great Britain!
-Weaknesses: ???
MORGAN LE FAY AND DOCTOR DOOM ARE TOTALLY MY OTP.
OKAY, THAT'S DEFINITELY NOT GOOD.

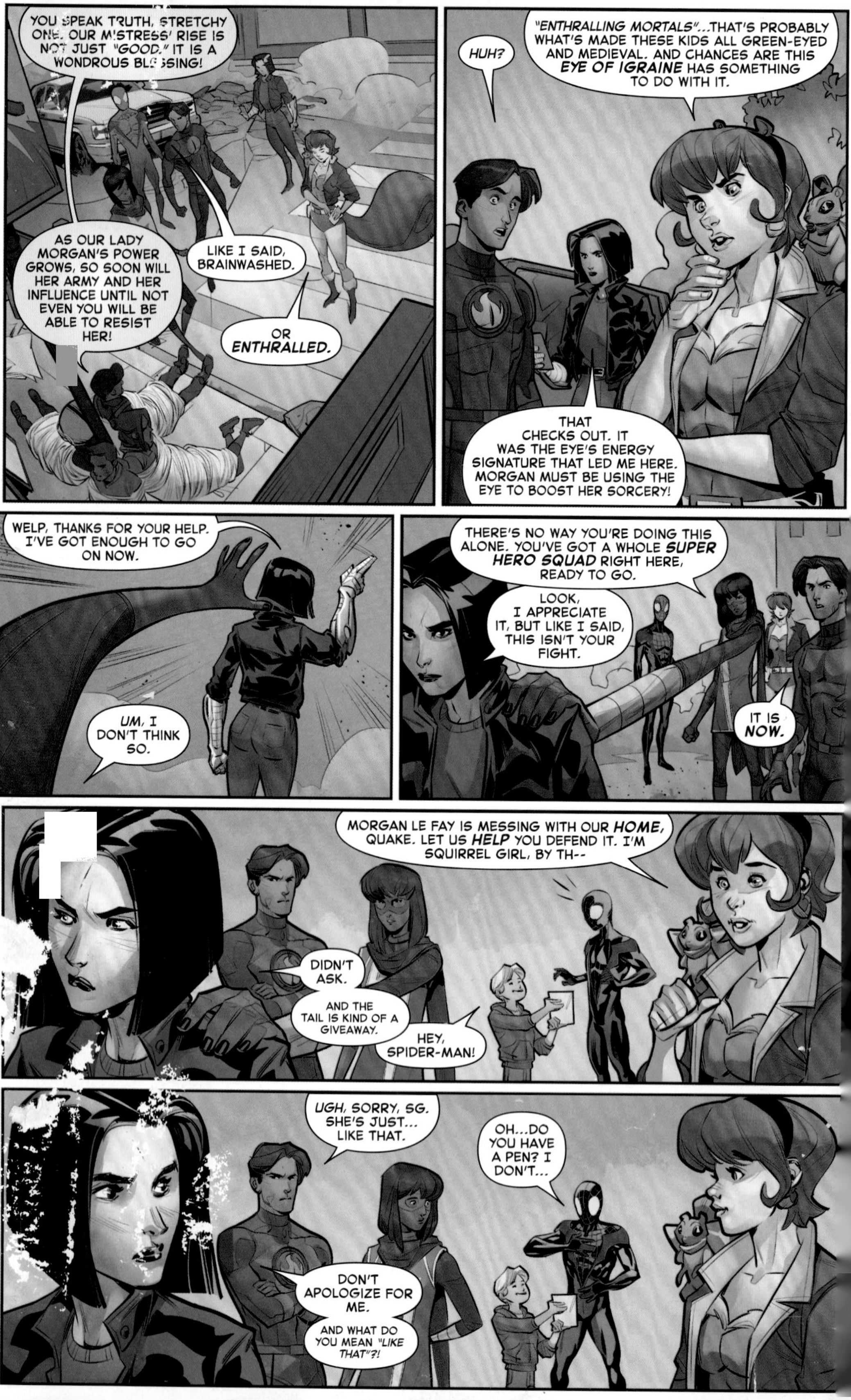
YOU SPEAK TRUTH, STRETCHY ONE. OUR MISTRESS' RISE IS NOT JUST "GOOD." IT IS A WONDROUS BLESSING!
AS OUR LADY MORGAN'S POWER GROWS, SO SOON WILL HER ARMY AND HER INFLUENCE UNTIL NOT EVEN YOU WILL BE ABLE TO RESIST HER!
LIKE I SAID, BRAINWASHED.
OR *ENTHRALLED.*
HUH?
"ENTHRALLING MORTALS"...THAT'S PROBABLY WHAT'S MADE THESE KIDS ALL GREEN-EYED AND MEDIEVAL. AND CHANCES ARE THIS *EYE OF IGRAINE* HAS SOMETHING TO DO WITH IT.
THAT CHECKS OUT. IT WAS THE EYE'S ENERGY SIGNATURE THAT LED ME HERE. MORGAN MUST BE USING THE EYE TO BOOST HER SORCERY!
WELP, THANKS FOR YOUR HELP. I'VE GOT ENOUGH TO GO ON NOW.
UM, I DON'T THINK SO.
THERE'S NO WAY YOU'RE DOING THIS ALONE. YOU'VE GOT A WHOLE *SUPER HERO SQUAD* RIGHT HERE, READY TO GO.
LOOK, I APPRECIATE IT, BUT LIKE I SAID, THIS ISN'T YOUR FIGHT.
IT IS *NOW.*
MORGAN LE FAY IS MESSING WITH OUR *HOME,* QUAKE. LET US *HELP* YOU DEFEND IT. I'M SQUIRREL GIRL, BY TH--
DIDN'T ASK.
AND THE TAIL IS KIND OF A GIVEAWAY.
HEY, SPIDER-MAN!
UGH, SORRY, SG. SHE'S JUST... LIKE THAT.
OH...DO YOU HAVE A PEN? I DON'T...
DON'T APOLOGIZE FOR ME.
AND WHAT DO YOU MEAN *"LIKE THAT"*?!

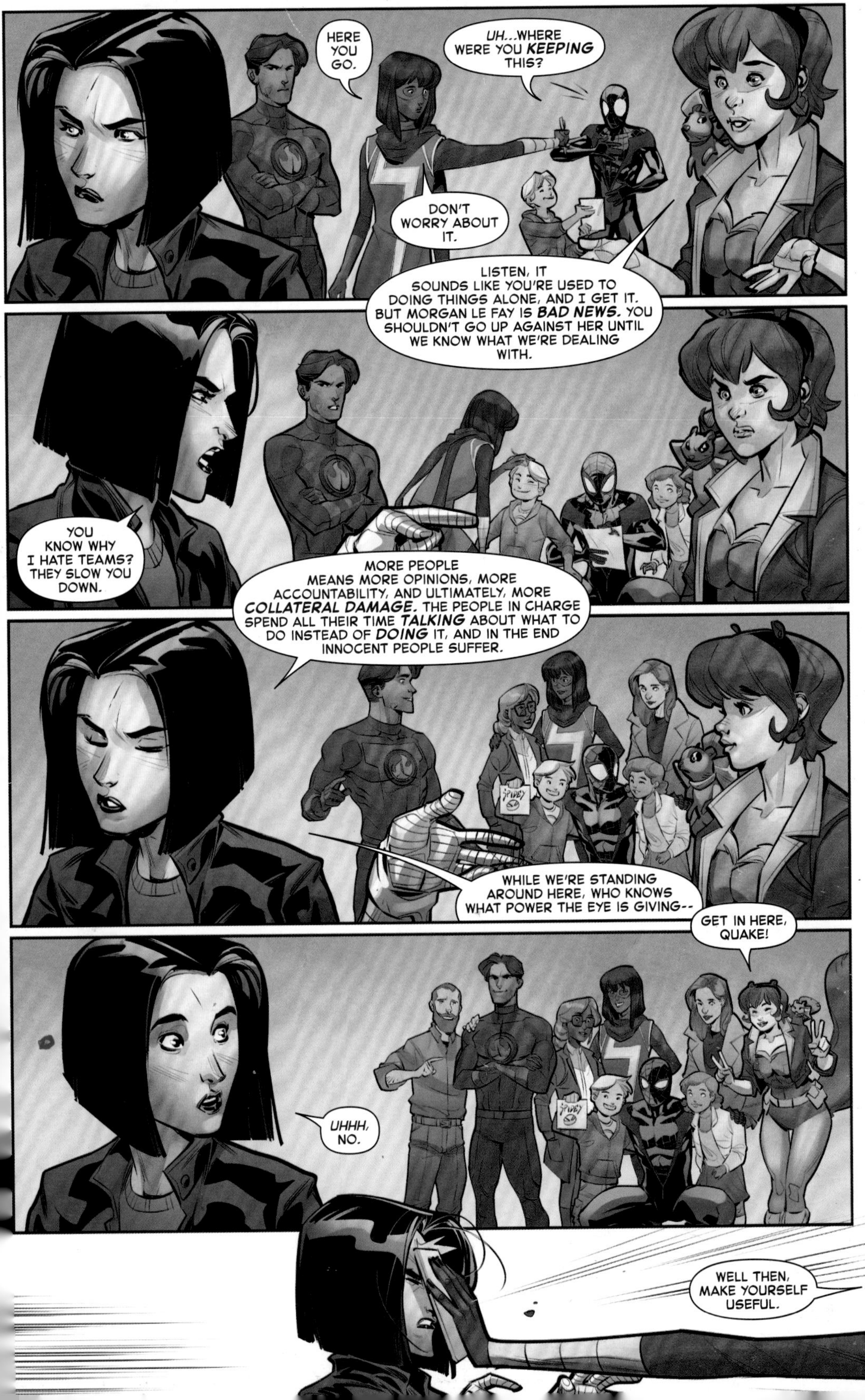
HERE YOU GO.
UH...WHERE WERE YOU KEEPING THIS?
DON'T WORRY ABOUT IT.
LISTEN, IT SOUNDS LIKE YOU'RE USED TO DOING THINGS ALONE, AND I GET IT. BUT MORGAN LE FAY IS BAD NEWS. YOU SHOULDN'T GO UP AGAINST HER UNTIL WE KNOW WHAT WE'RE DEALING WITH.
YOU KNOW WHY I HATE TEAMS? THEY SLOW YOU DOWN.
MORE PEOPLE MEANS MORE OPINIONS, MORE ACCOUNTABILITY, AND ULTIMATELY, MORE COLLATERAL DAMAGE. THE PEOPLE IN CHARGE SPEND ALL THEIR TIME TALKING ABOUT WHAT TO DO INSTEAD OF DOING IT, AND IN THE END INNOCENT PEOPLE SUFFER.
SPIDEY
WHILE WE'RE STANDING AROUND HERE, WHO KNOWS WHAT POWER THE EYE IS GIVING--
GET IN HERE, QUAKE!
SPIDEY
UHHH, NO.
WELL THEN, MAKE YOURSELF USEFUL.

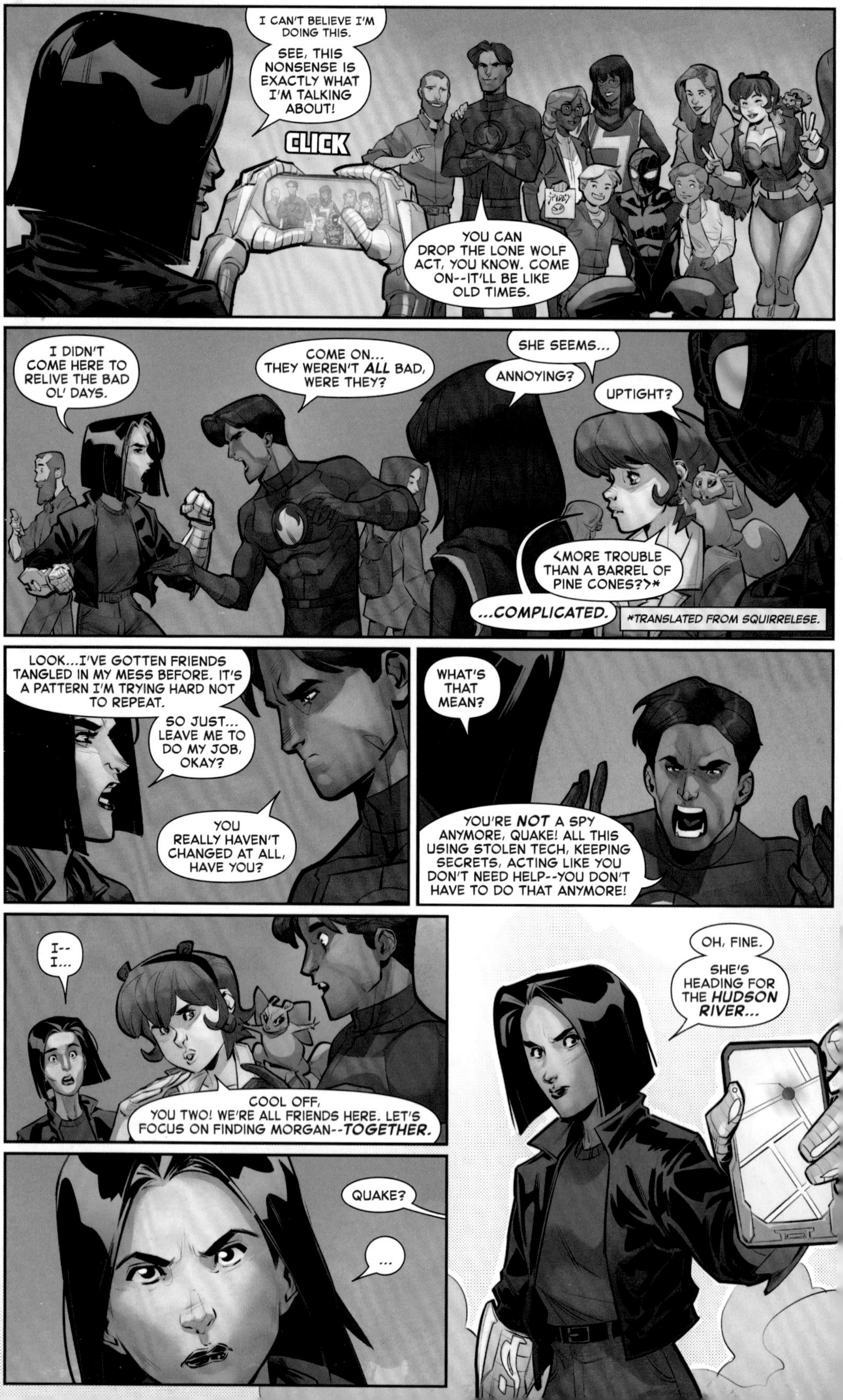

I CAN'T BELIEVE I'M DOING THIS.
SEE, THIS NONSENSE IS EXACTLY WHAT I'M TALKING ABOUT!
CLICK
YOU CAN DROP THE LONE WOLF ACT, YOU KNOW. COME ON--IT'LL BE LIKE OLD TIMES.
I DIDN'T COME HERE TO RELIVE THE BAD OL' DAYS.
COME ON... THEY WEREN'T ALL BAD, WERE THEY?
SHE SEEMS...
ANNOYING?
UPTIGHT?
<MORE TROUBLE THAN A BARREL OF PINE CONES?>*
...COMPLICATED.
*TRANSLATED FROM SQUIRRELESE.
LOOK...I'VE GOTTEN FRIENDS TANGLED IN MY MESS BEFORE. IT'S A PATTERN I'M TRYING HARD NOT TO REPEAT.
SO JUST... LEAVE ME TO DO MY JOB, OKAY?
YOU REALLY HAVEN'T CHANGED AT ALL, HAVE YOU?
WHAT'S THAT MEAN?
YOU'RE NOT A SPY ANYMORE, QUAKE! ALL THIS USING STOLEN TECH, KEEPING SECRETS, ACTING LIKE YOU DON'T NEED HELP--YOU DON'T HAVE TO DO THAT ANYMORE!
I-- I...
COOL OFF, YOU TWO! WE'RE ALL FRIENDS HERE. LET'S FOCUS ON FINDING MORGAN--TOGETHER.
QUAKE?
...
OH, FINE.
SHE'S HEADING FOR THE HUDSON RIVER...

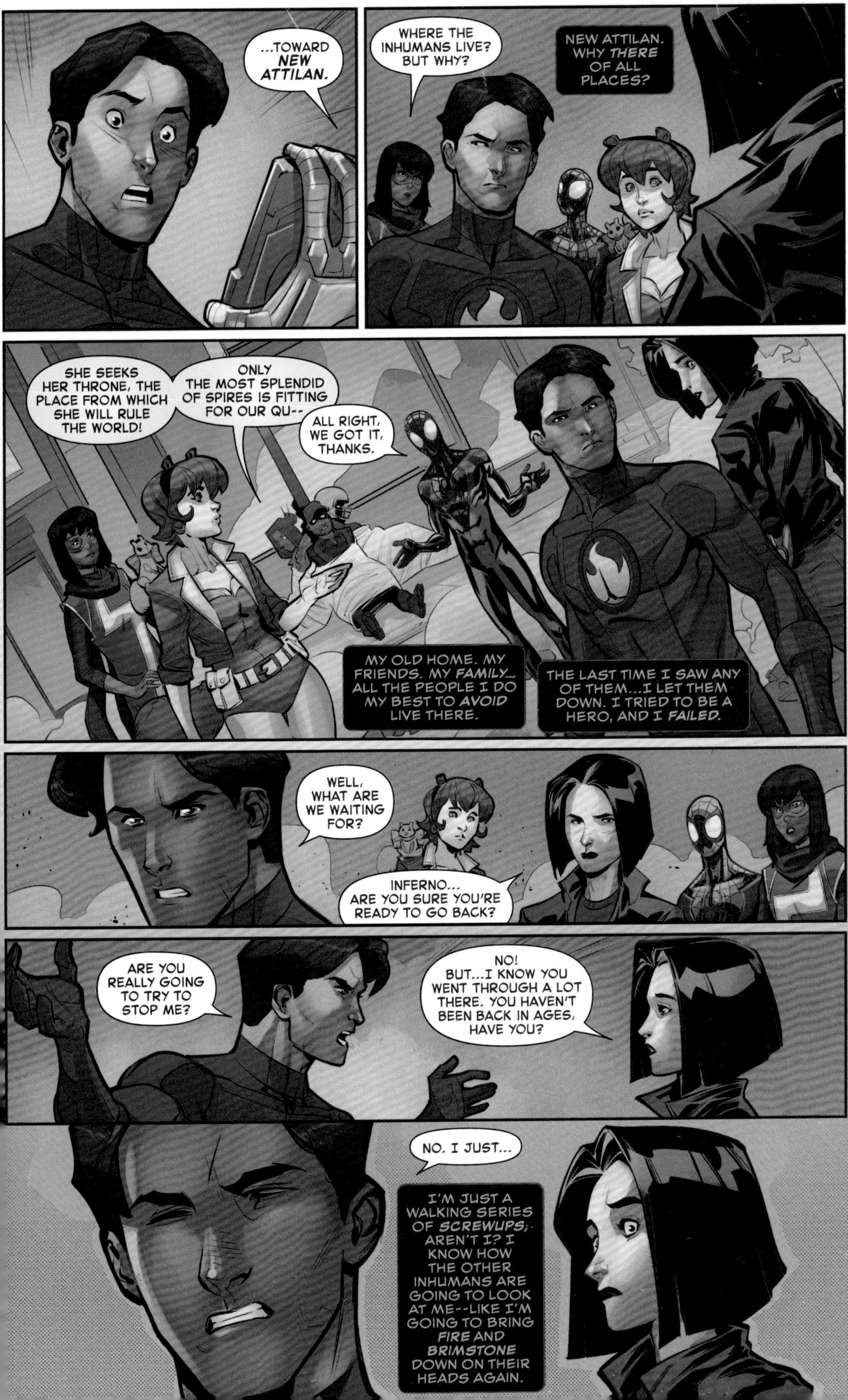
...TOWARD NEW ATTILAN.
WHERE THE INHUMANS LIVE? BUT WHY?
NEW ATTILAN. WHY THERE OF ALL PLACES?
SHE SEEKS HER THRONE, THE PLACE FROM WHICH SHE WILL RULE THE WORLD!
ONLY THE MOST SPLENDID OF SPIRES IS FITTING FOR OUR QU--
ALL RIGHT, WE GOT IT, THANKS.
MY OLD HOME. MY FRIENDS. MY FAMILY... ALL THE PEOPLE I DO MY BEST TO AVOID LIVE THERE.
THE LAST TIME I SAW ANY OF THEM...I LET THEM DOWN. I TRIED TO BE A HERO, AND I FAILED.
WELL, WHAT ARE WE WAITING FOR?
INFERNO... ARE YOU SURE YOU'RE READY TO GO BACK?
ARE YOU REALLY GOING TO TRY TO STOP ME?
NO! BUT...I KNOW YOU WENT THROUGH A LOT THERE. YOU HAVEN'T BEEN BACK IN AGES, HAVE YOU?
NO. I JUST...
I'M JUST A WALKING SERIES OF SCREWUPS, AREN'T I? I KNOW HOW THE OTHER INHUMANS ARE GOING TO LOOK AT ME--LIKE I'M GOING TO BRING FIRE AND BRIMSTONE DOWN ON THEIR HEADS AGAIN.

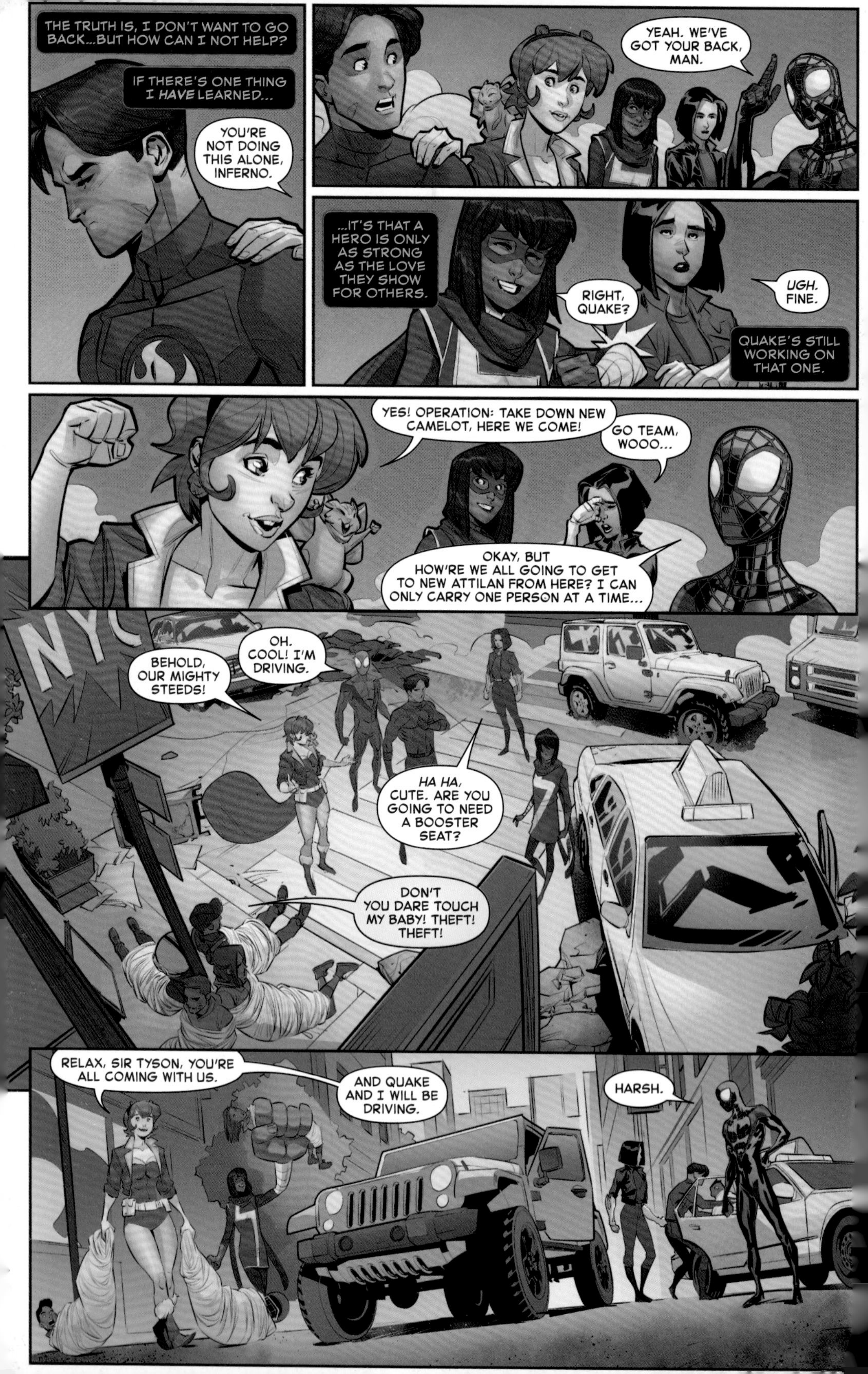
THE TRUTH IS, I DON'T WANT TO GO BACK...BUT HOW CAN I NOT HELP?
IF THERE'S ONE THING I *HAVE* LEARNED...
YOU'RE NOT DOING THIS ALONE, INFERNO.
YEAH. WE'VE GOT YOUR BACK, MAN.
...IT'S THAT A HERO IS ONLY AS STRONG AS THE LOVE THEY SHOW FOR OTHERS.
RIGHT, QUAKE?
UGH. FINE.
QUAKE'S STILL WORKING ON THAT ONE.
YES! OPERATION: TAKE DOWN NEW CAMELOT, HERE WE COME!
GO TEAM, WOOO...
OKAY, BUT HOW'RE WE ALL GOING TO GET TO NEW ATTILAN FROM HERE? I CAN ONLY CARRY ONE PERSON AT A TIME...
NYC
BEHOLD, OUR MIGHTY STEEDS!
OH. COOL! I'M DRIVING.
HA HA, CUTE. ARE YOU GOING TO NEED A BOOSTER SEAT?
DON'T YOU DARE TOUCH MY BABY! THEFT! THEFT!
RELAX, SIR TYSON, YOU'RE ALL COMING WITH US.
AND QUAKE AND I WILL BE DRIVING.
HARSH.

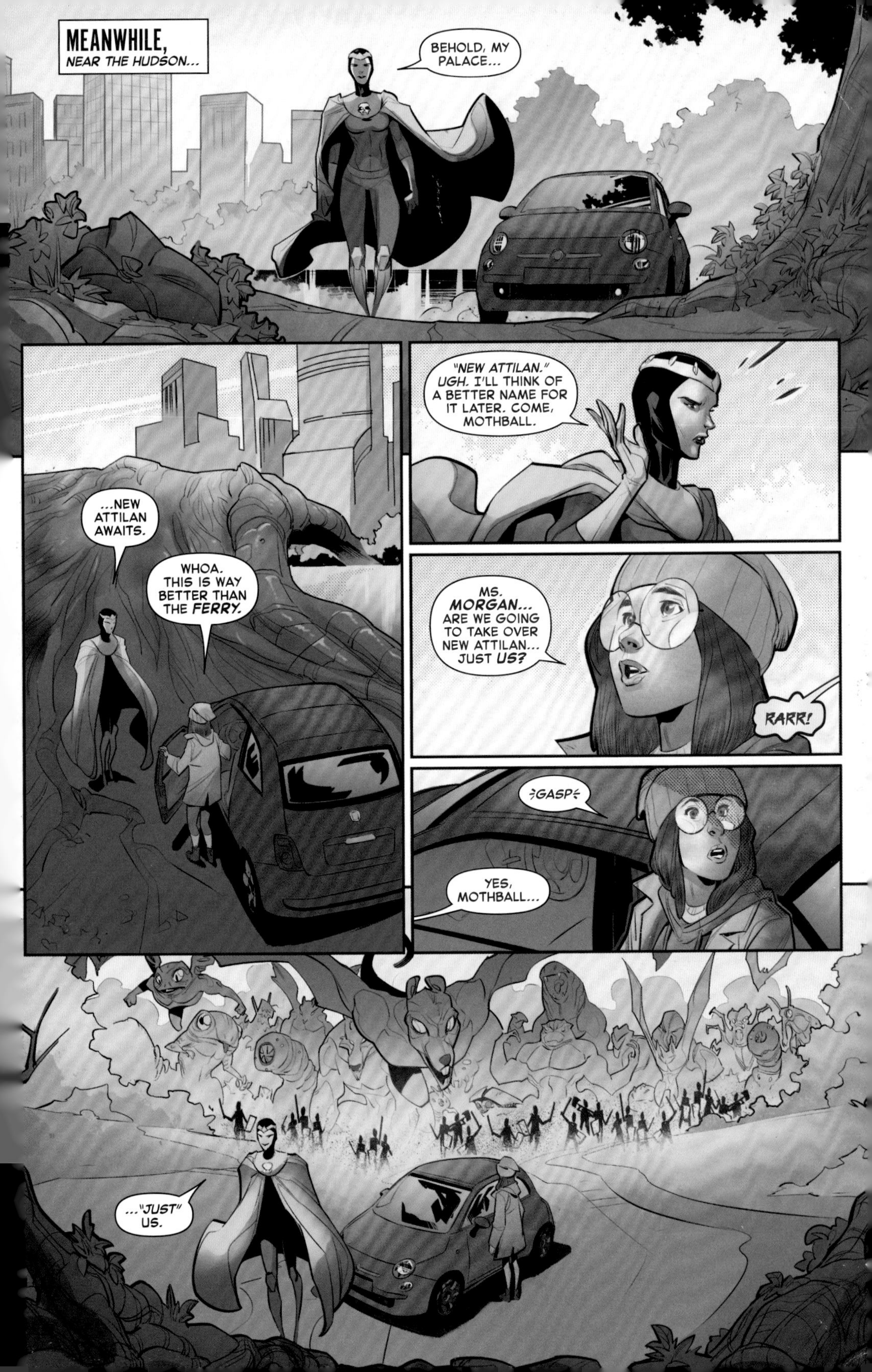
MEANWHILE,
NEAR THE HUDSON...
BEHOLD, MY PALACE...
...NEW ATTILAN AWAITS.
WHOA. THIS IS WAY BETTER THAN THE FERRY.
"NEW ATTILAN." UGH. I'LL THINK OF A BETTER NAME FOR IT LATER. COME, MOTHBALL.
MS. MORGAN... ARE WE GOING TO TAKE OVER NEW ATTILAN... JUST US?
RARR!
GASP
YES, MOTHBALL...
..."JUST" US.

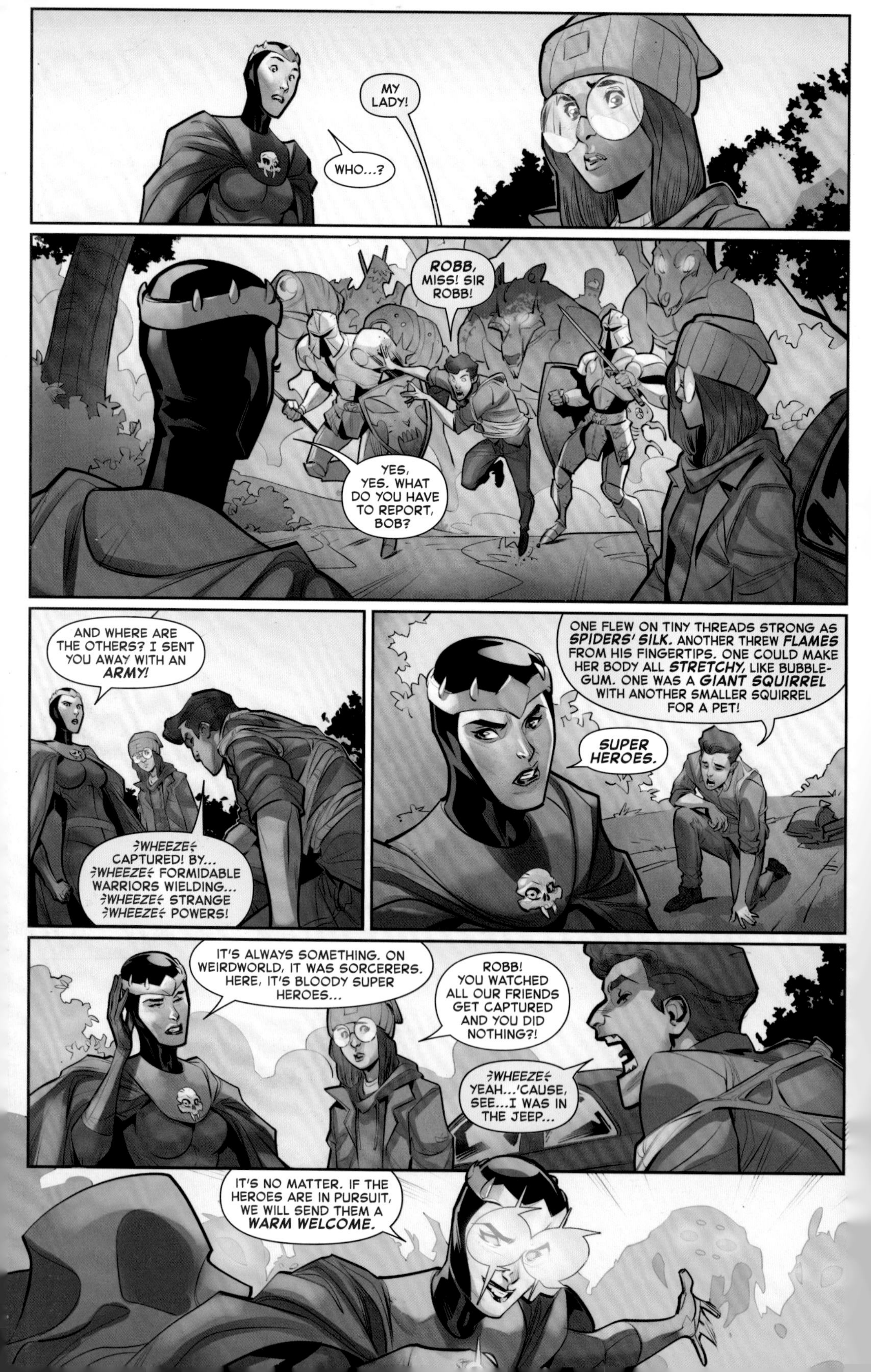
MY LADY!
WHO...?
ROBB, MISS! SIR ROBB!
YES, YES. WHAT DO YOU HAVE TO REPORT, BOB?
AND WHERE ARE THE OTHERS? I SENT YOU AWAY WITH AN ARMY!
≶WHEEZE≷ CAPTURED! BY... ≶WHEEZE≷ FORMIDABLE WARRIORS WIELDING... ≶WHEEZE≷ STRANGE ≶WHEEZE≷ POWERS!
ONE FLEW ON TINY THREADS STRONG AS SPIDERS' SILK. ANOTHER THREW FLAMES FROM HIS FINGERTIPS. ONE COULD MAKE HER BODY ALL STRETCHY, LIKE BUBBLE-GUM. ONE WAS A GIANT SQUIRREL WITH ANOTHER SMALLER SQUIRREL FOR A PET!
SUPER HEROES.
IT'S ALWAYS SOMETHING. ON WEIRDWORLD, IT WAS SORCERERS. HERE, IT'S BLOODY SUPER HEROES...
ROBB! YOU WATCHED ALL OUR FRIENDS GET CAPTURED AND YOU DID NOTHING?!
≶WHEEZE≷ YEAH...'CAUSE, SEE...I WAS IN THE JEEP...
IT'S NO MATTER. IF THE HEROES ARE IN PURSUIT, WE WILL SEND THEM A WARM WELCOME.

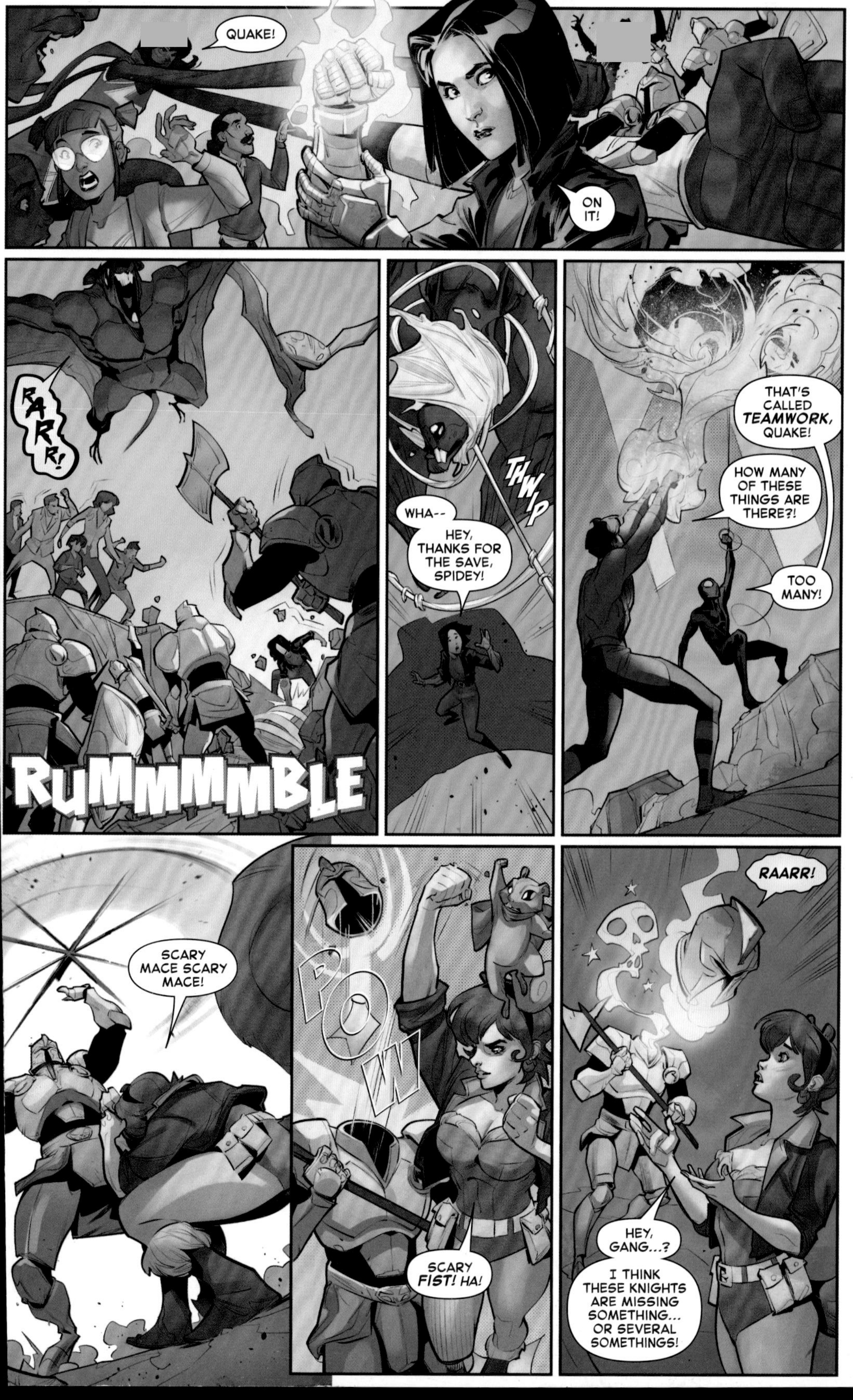
QUAKE!
ON IT!
RARR!
RUMMMMBLE
THWIP
WHA--
HEY, THANKS FOR THE SAVE, SPIDEY!
THAT'S CALLED *TEAMWORK,* QUAKE!
HOW MANY OF THESE THINGS ARE THERE?!
TOO MANY!
SCARY MACE SCARY MACE!
POW
SCARY *FIST!* HA!
RAARR!
HEY, GANG...?
I THINK THESE KNIGHTS ARE MISSING SOMETHING... OR SEVERAL SOMETHINGS!

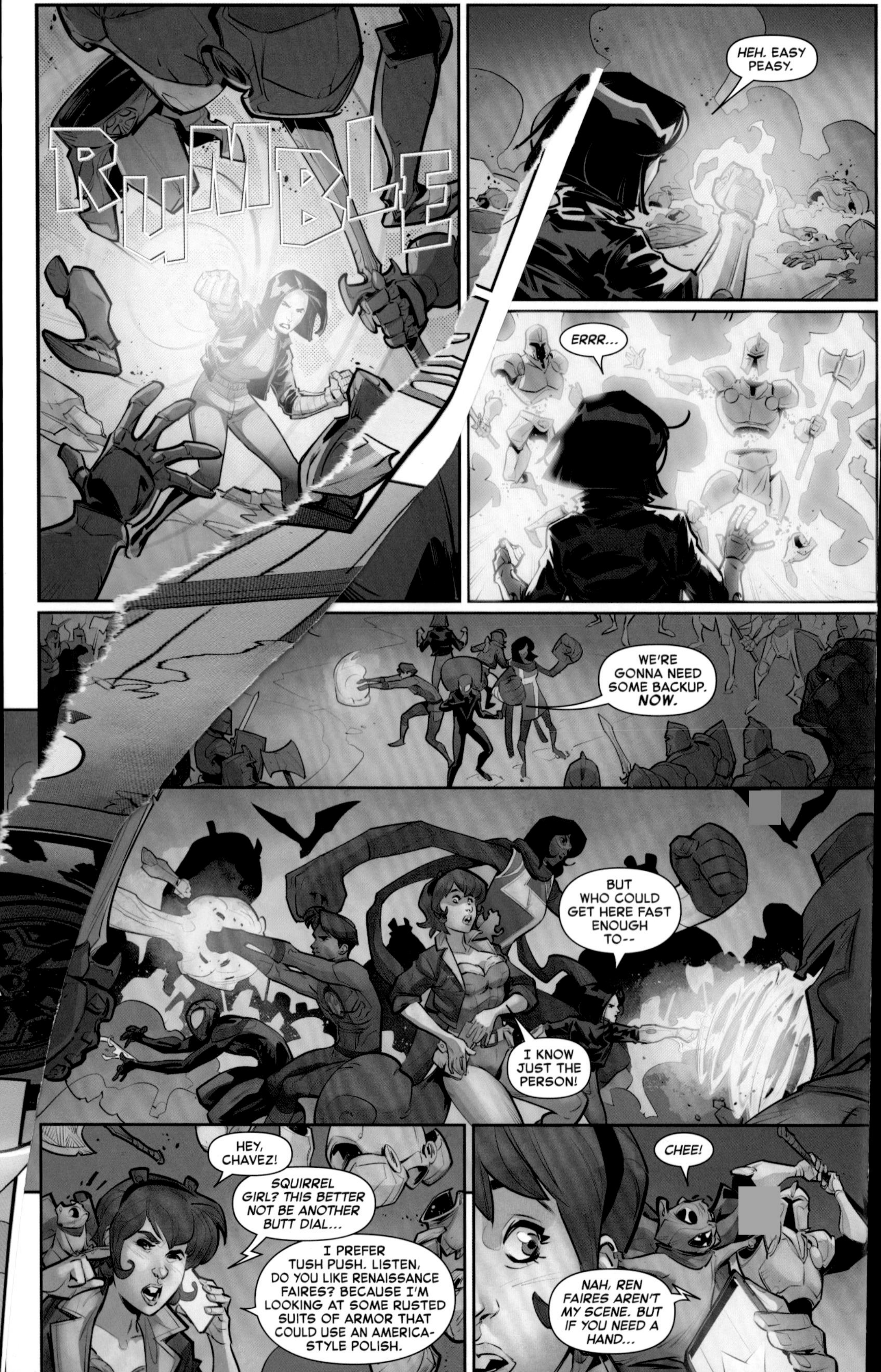
RUMBLE
HEH. EASY PEASY.
ERRR...
WE'RE GONNA NEED SOME BACKUP. NOW.
BUT WHO COULD GET HERE FAST ENOUGH TO--
I KNOW JUST THE PERSON!
HEY, CHAVEZ!
SQUIRREL GIRL? THIS BETTER NOT BE ANOTHER BUTT DIAL...
I PREFER TUSH PUSH. LISTEN, DO YOU LIKE RENAISSANCE FAIRES? BECAUSE I'M LOOKING AT SOME RUSTED SUITS OF ARMOR THAT COULD USE AN AMERICA-STYLE POLISH.
CHEE!
NAH, REN FAIRES AREN'T MY SCENE. BUT IF YOU NEED A HAND...

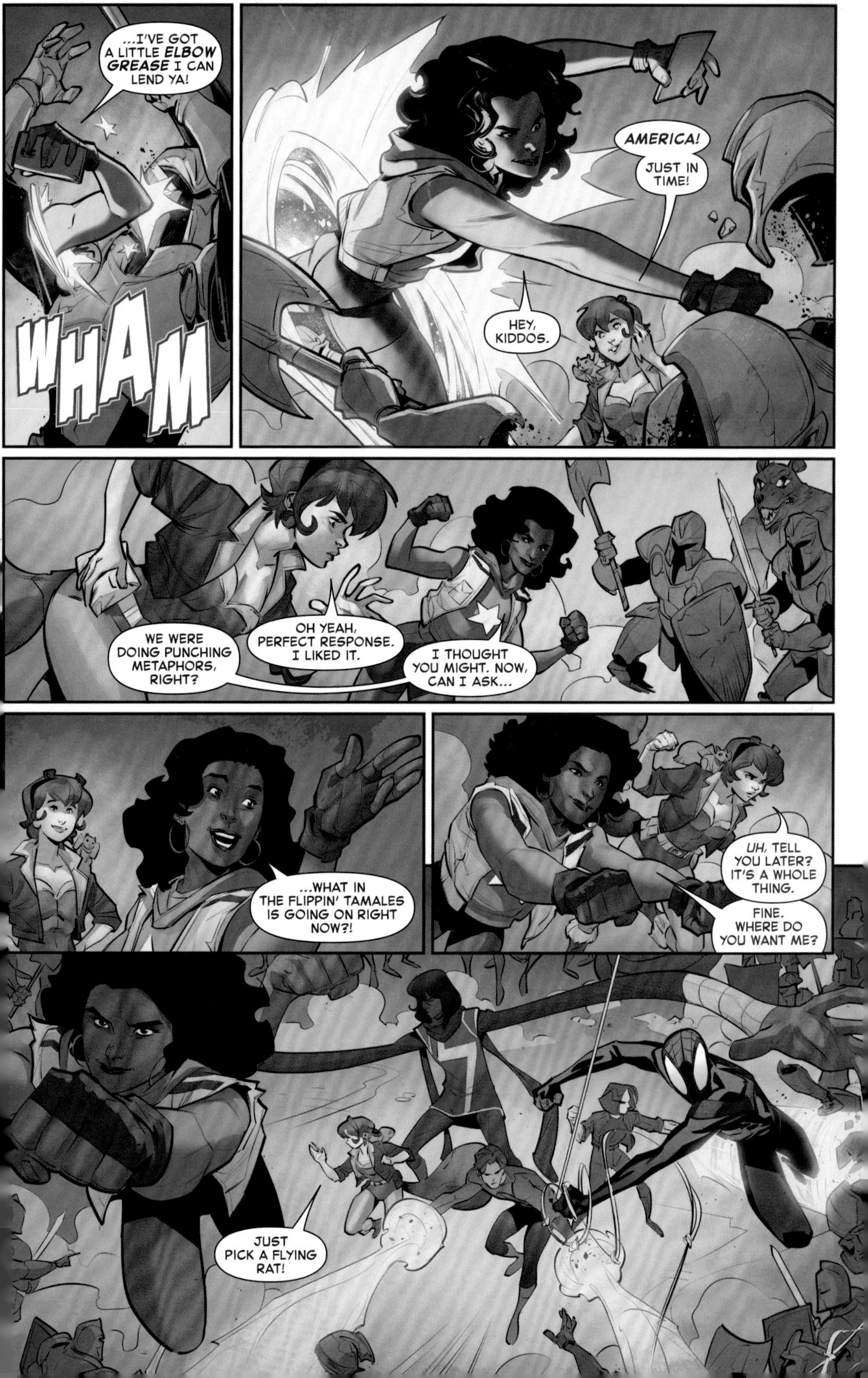
...I'VE GOT A LITTLE ELBOW GREASE I CAN LEND YA!
WHAM
AMERICA!
JUST IN TIME!
HEY, KIDDOS.
WE WERE DOING PUNCHING METAPHORS, RIGHT?
OH YEAH, PERFECT RESPONSE. I LIKED IT.
I THOUGHT YOU MIGHT. NOW, CAN I ASK...
...WHAT IN THE FLIPPIN' TAMALES IS GOING ON RIGHT NOW?!
UH, TELL YOU LATER? IT'S A WHOLE THING.
FINE. WHERE DO YOU WANT ME?
JUST PICK A FLYING RAT!

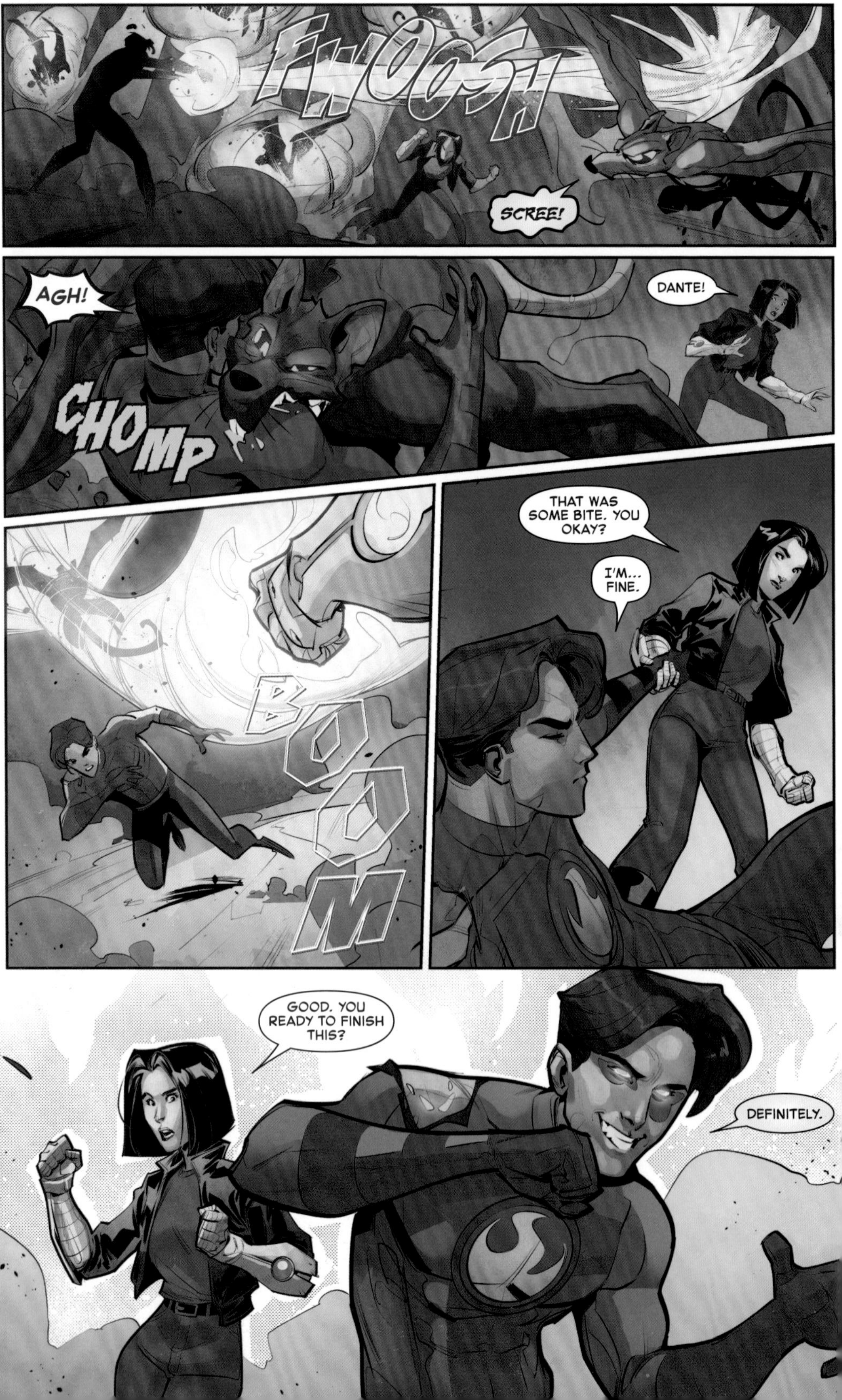
FWOOSH
SCREE!
AGH!
CHOMP
DANTE!
BOOOOM
THAT WAS SOME BITE. YOU OKAY?
I'M... FINE.
GOOD. YOU READY TO FINISH THIS?
DEFINITELY.

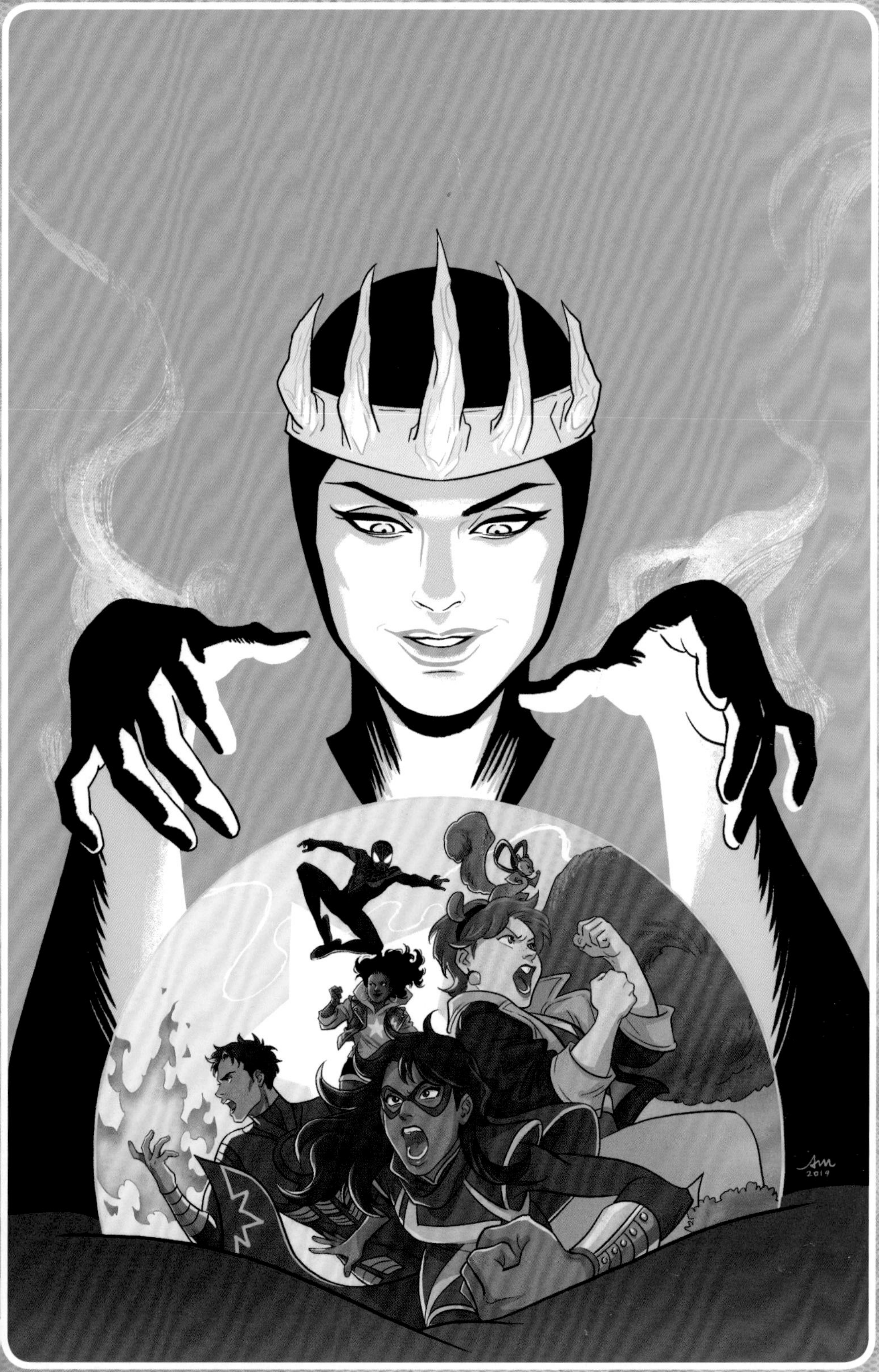
AM
2019

3

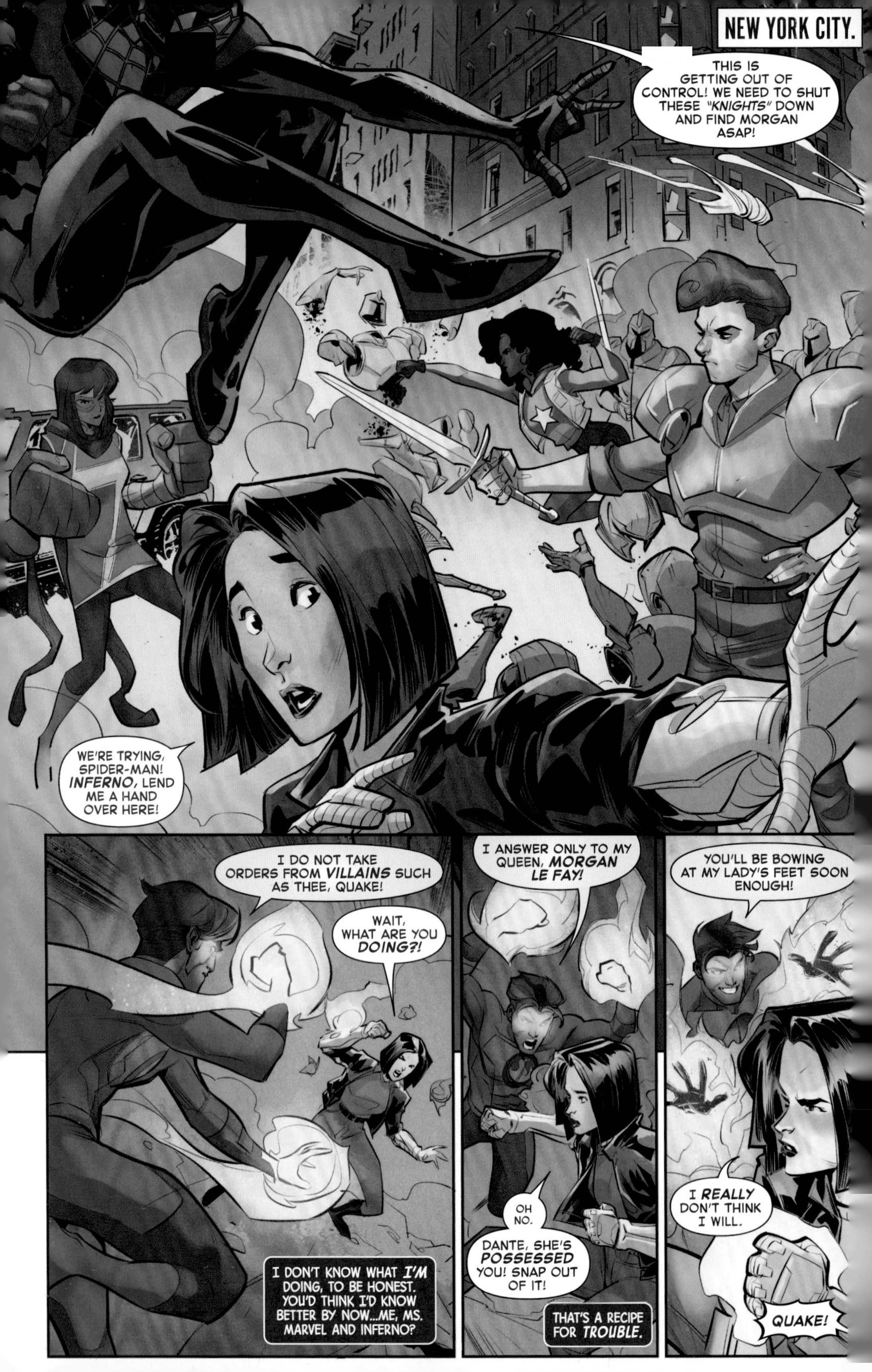
NEW YORK CITY.
THIS IS GETTING OUT OF CONTROL! WE NEED TO SHUT THESE "KNIGHTS" DOWN AND FIND MORGAN ASAP!
WE'RE TRYING, SPIDER-MAN! INFERNO, LEND ME A HAND OVER HERE!
I DO NOT TAKE ORDERS FROM VILLAINS SUCH AS THEE, QUAKE!
WAIT, WHAT ARE YOU DOING?!
I DON'T KNOW WHAT I'M DOING, TO BE HONEST. YOU'D THINK I'D KNOW BETTER BY NOW...ME, MS. MARVEL AND INFERNO?
I ANSWER ONLY TO MY QUEEN, MORGAN LE FAY!
OH NO.
DANTE, SHE'S POSSESSED YOU! SNAP OUT OF IT!
THAT'S A RECIPE FOR TROUBLE.
YOU'LL BE BOWING AT MY LADY'S FEET SOON ENOUGH!
I REALLY DON'T THINK I WILL.
QUAKE!

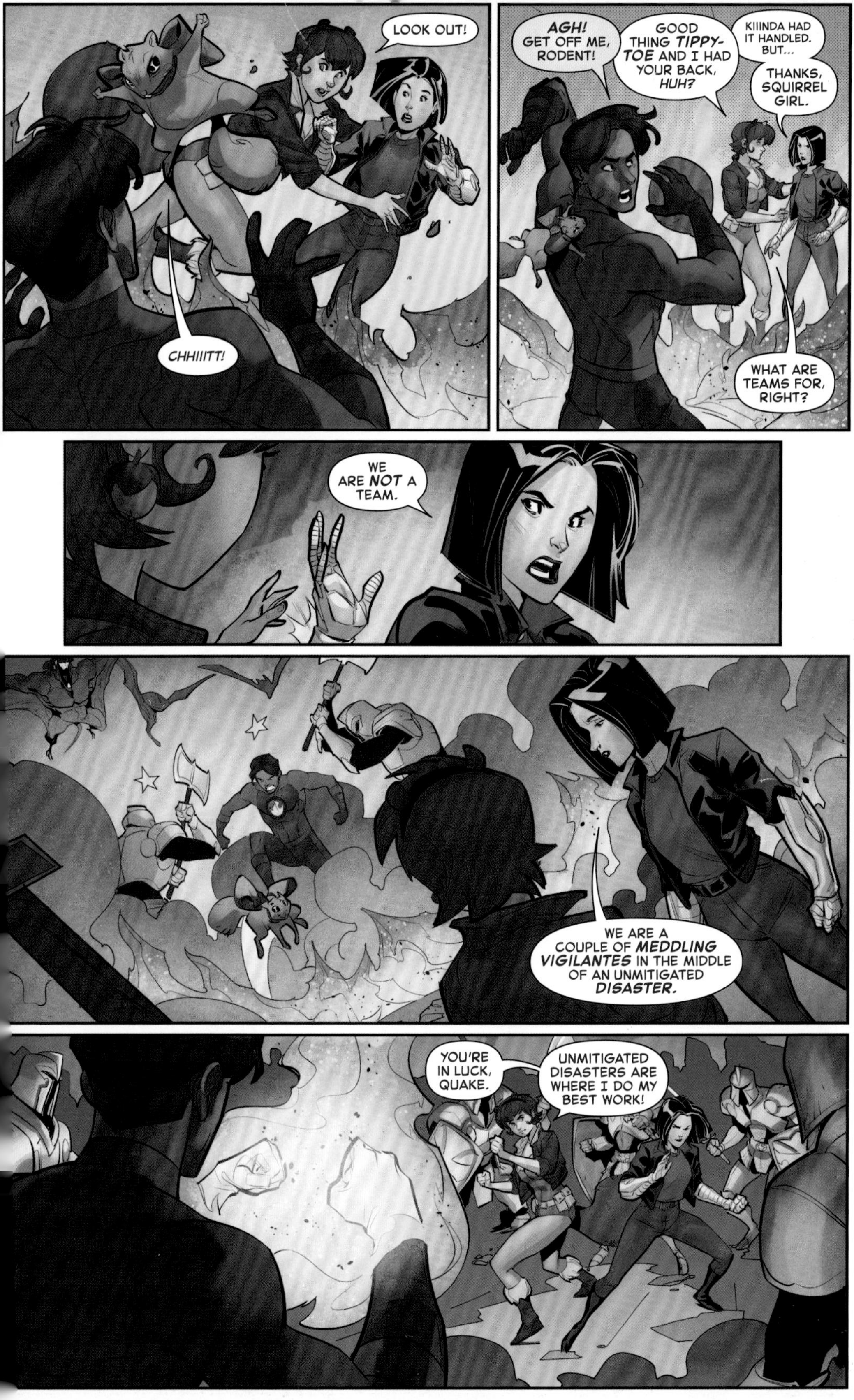
LOOK OUT!
CHHIIITT!
AGH! GET OFF ME, RODENT!
GOOD THING TIPPY-TOE AND I HAD YOUR BACK, HUH?
KIIINDA HAD IT HANDLED. BUT...
THANKS, SQUIRREL GIRL.
WHAT ARE TEAMS FOR, RIGHT?
WE ARE NOT A TEAM.
WE ARE A COUPLE OF MEDDLING VIGILANTES IN THE MIDDLE OF AN UNMITIGATED DISASTER.
YOU'RE IN LUCK, QUAKE.
UNMITIGATED DISASTERS ARE WHERE I DO MY BEST WORK!

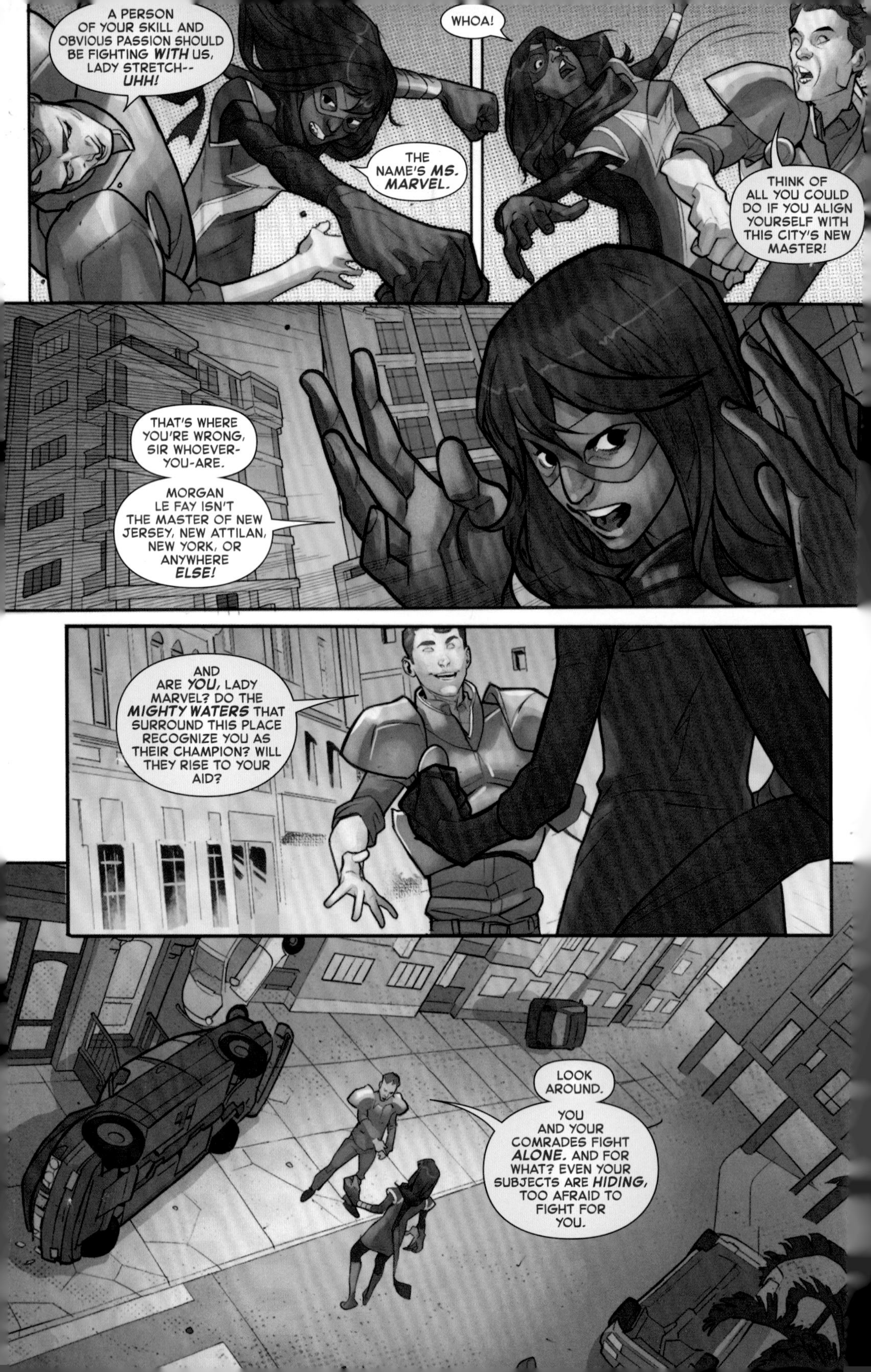
A PERSON OF YOUR SKILL AND OBVIOUS PASSION SHOULD BE FIGHTING WITH US, LADY STRETCH-- UHH!
THE NAME'S MS. MARVEL.
WHOA!
THINK OF ALL YOU COULD DO IF YOU ALIGN YOURSELF WITH THIS CITY'S NEW MASTER!
THAT'S WHERE YOU'RE WRONG, SIR WHOEVER-YOU-ARE.
MORGAN LE FAY ISN'T THE MASTER OF NEW JERSEY, NEW ATTILAN, NEW YORK, OR ANYWHERE ELSE!
AND ARE YOU, LADY MARVEL? DO THE MIGHTY WATERS THAT SURROUND THIS PLACE RECOGNIZE YOU AS THEIR CHAMPION? WILL THEY RISE TO YOUR AID?
LOOK AROUND.
YOU AND YOUR COMRADES FIGHT ALONE. AND FOR WHAT? EVEN YOUR SUBJECTS ARE HIDING, TOO AFRAID TO FIGHT FOR YOU.

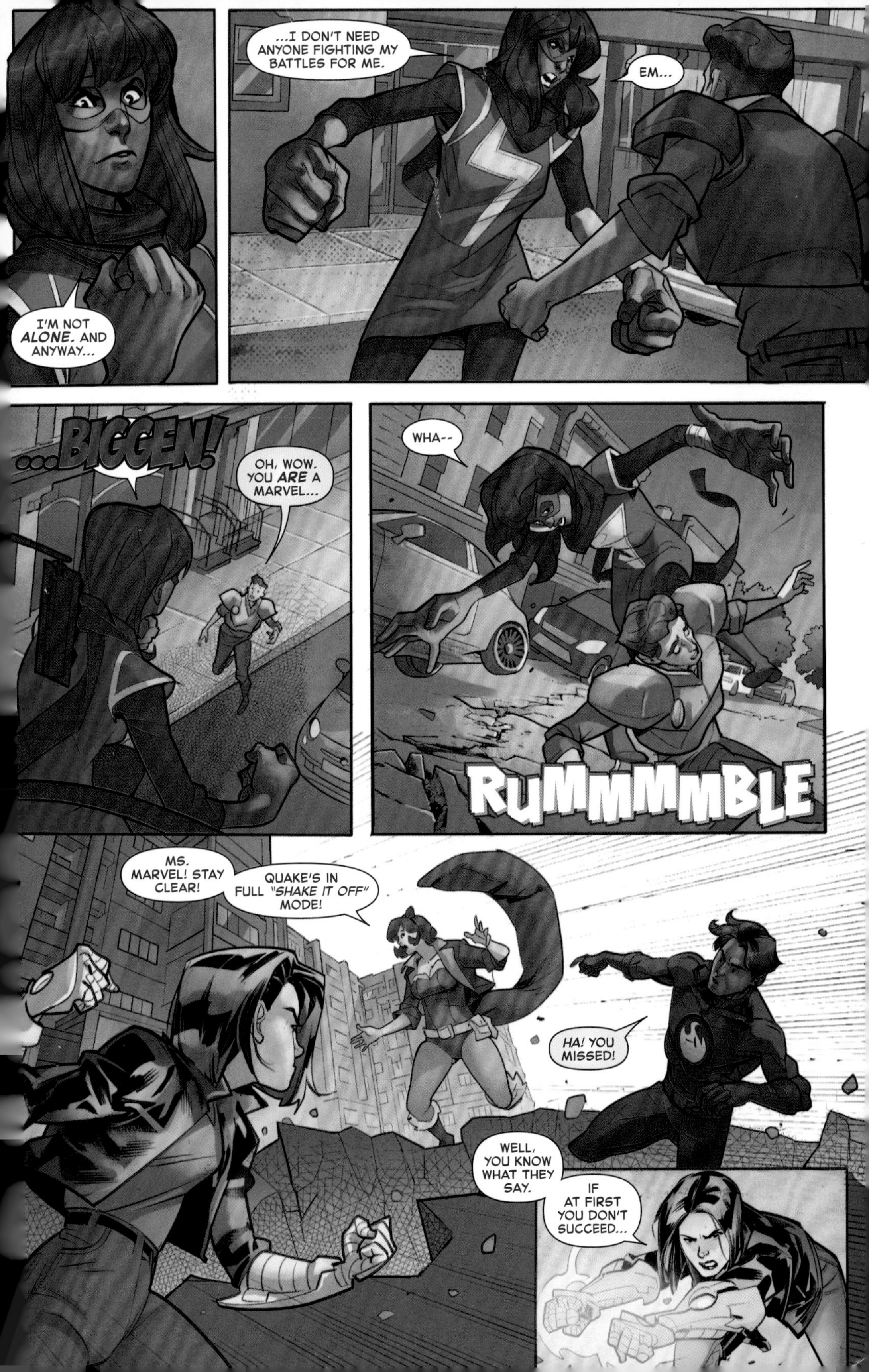

I'M NOT ALONE. AND ANYWAY...
...I DON'T NEED ANYONE FIGHTING MY BATTLES FOR ME.
EM...
...BIGGEN!
OH, WOW. YOU ARE A MARVEL...
WHA--
RUMMMMMBLE
MS. MARVEL! STAY CLEAR!
QUAKE'S IN FULL "SHAKE IT OFF" MODE!
HA! YOU MISSED!
WELL, YOU KNOW WHAT THEY SAY.
IF AT FIRST YOU DON'T SUCCEED...

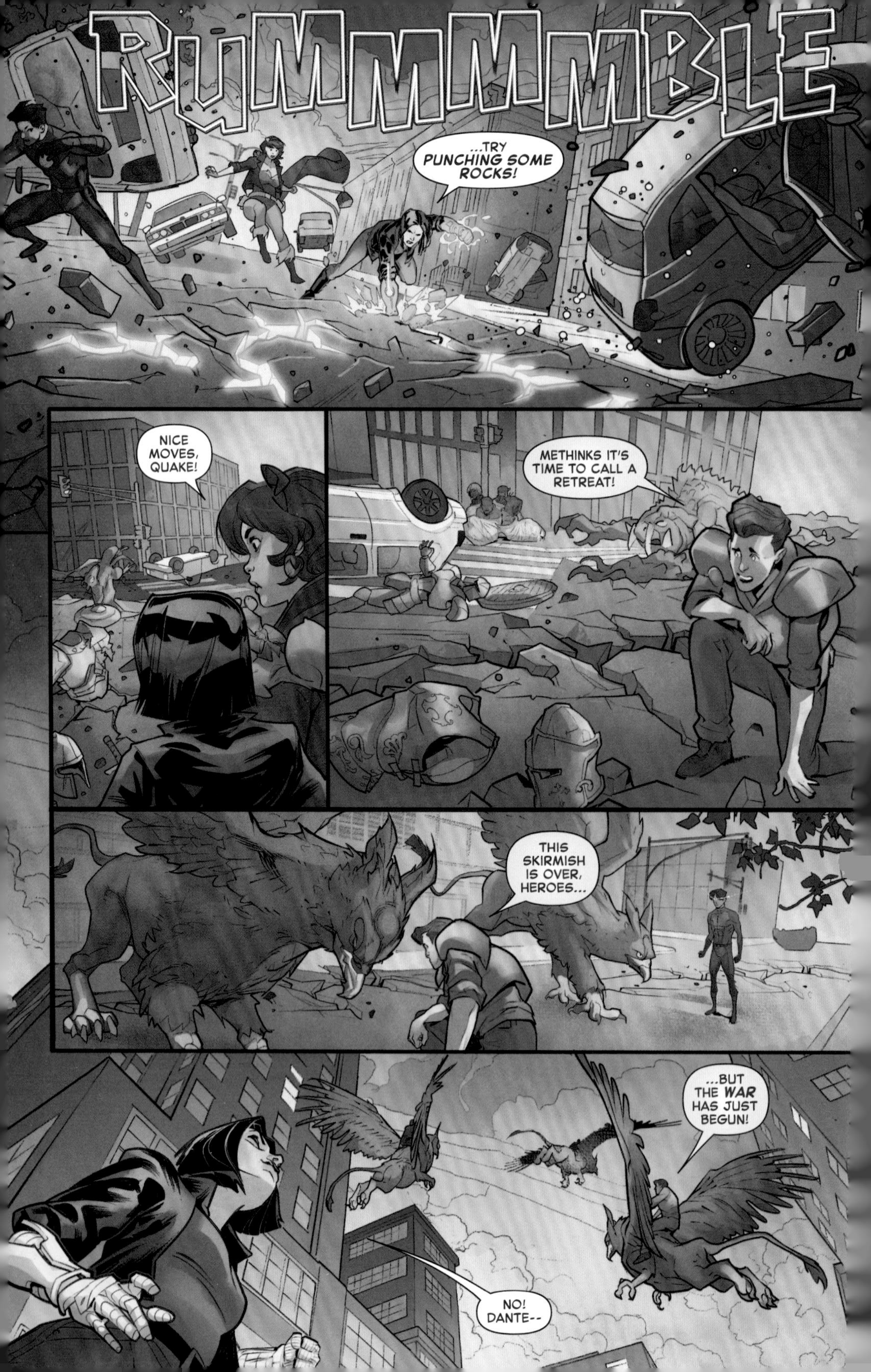
RUMMMMBLE
...TRY PUNCHING SOME ROCKS!
NICE MOVES, QUAKE!
METHINKS IT'S TIME TO CALL A RETREAT!
THIS SKIRMISH IS OVER, HEROES...
...BUT THE WAR HAS JUST BEGUN!
NO! DANTE--

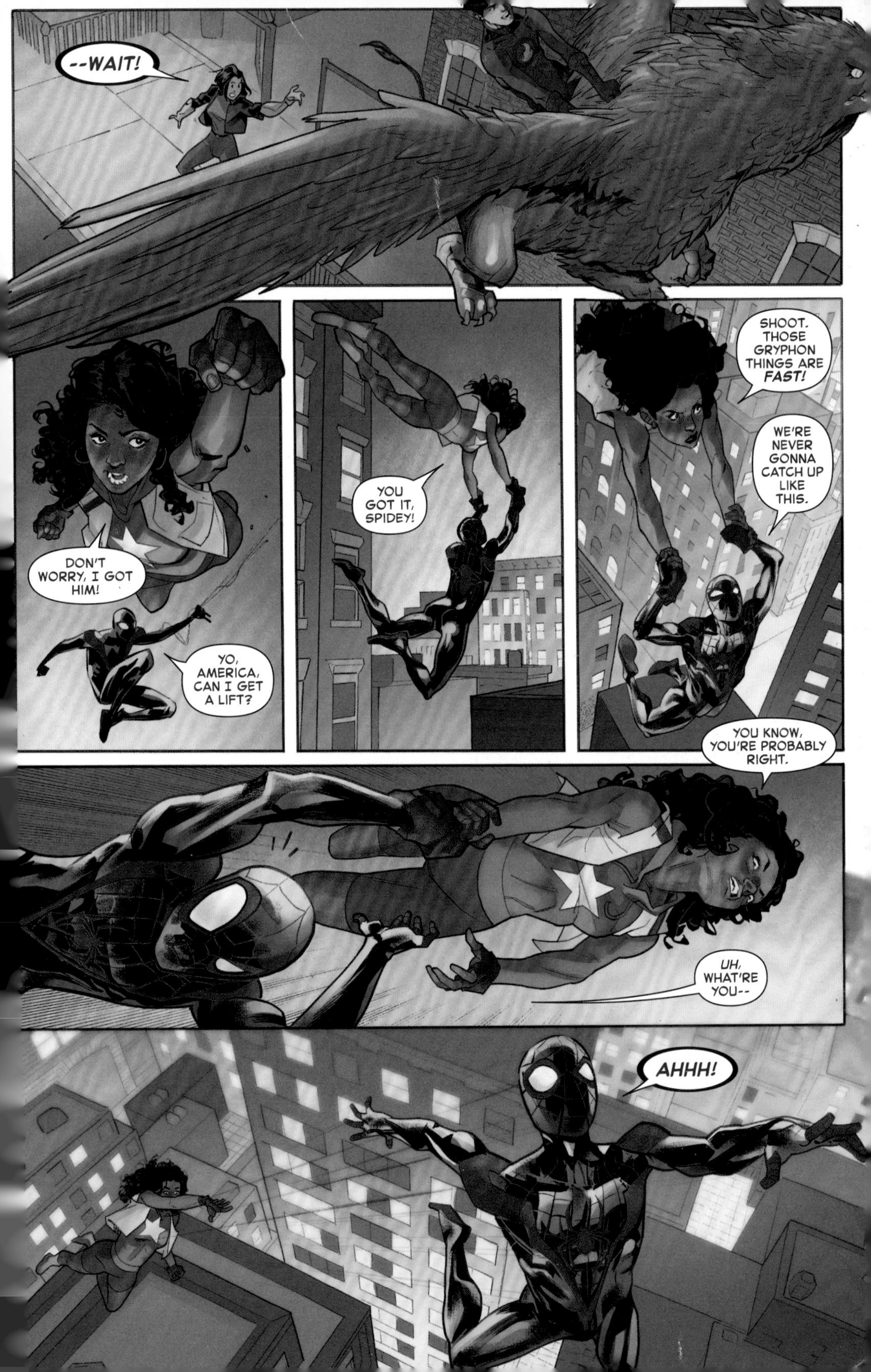
--WAIT!
DON'T WORRY, I GOT HIM!
YO, AMERICA, CAN I GET A LIFT?
YOU GOT IT, SPIDEY!
SHOOT. THOSE GRYPHON THINGS ARE FAST!
WE'RE NEVER GONNA CATCH UP LIKE THIS.
YOU KNOW, YOU'RE PROBABLY RIGHT.
UH, WHAT'RE YOU--
AHHH!

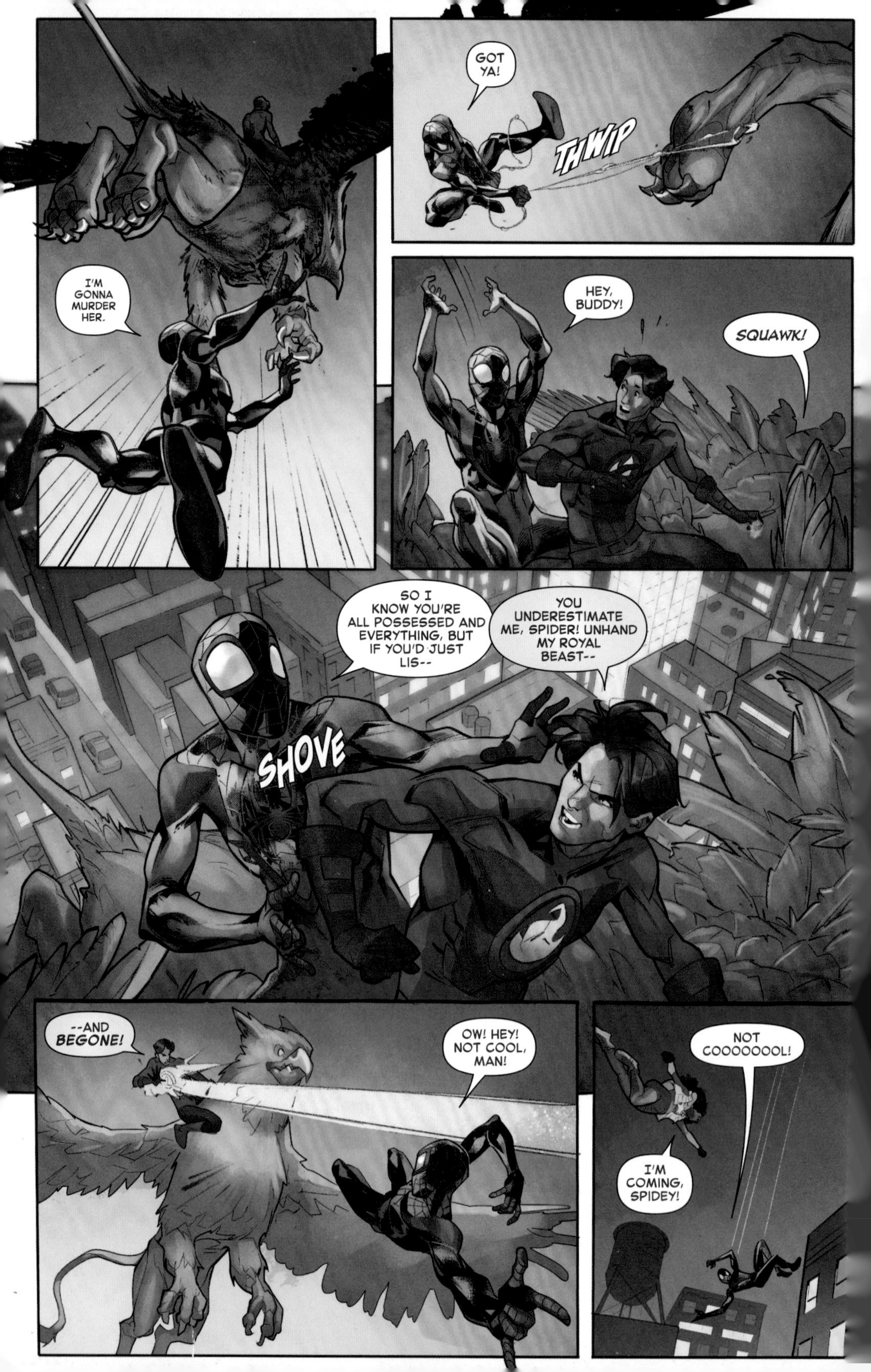

I'M GONNA MURDER HER.
GOT YA!
THWIP
HEY, BUDDY!
SQUAWK!
SO I KNOW YOU'RE ALL POSSESSED AND EVERYTHING, BUT IF YOU'D JUST LIS--
YOU UNDERESTIMATE ME, SPIDER! UNHAND MY ROYAL BEAST--
SHOVE
--AND BEGONE!
OW! HEY! NOT COOL, MAN!
NOT COOOOOOOL!
I'M COMING, SPIDEY!

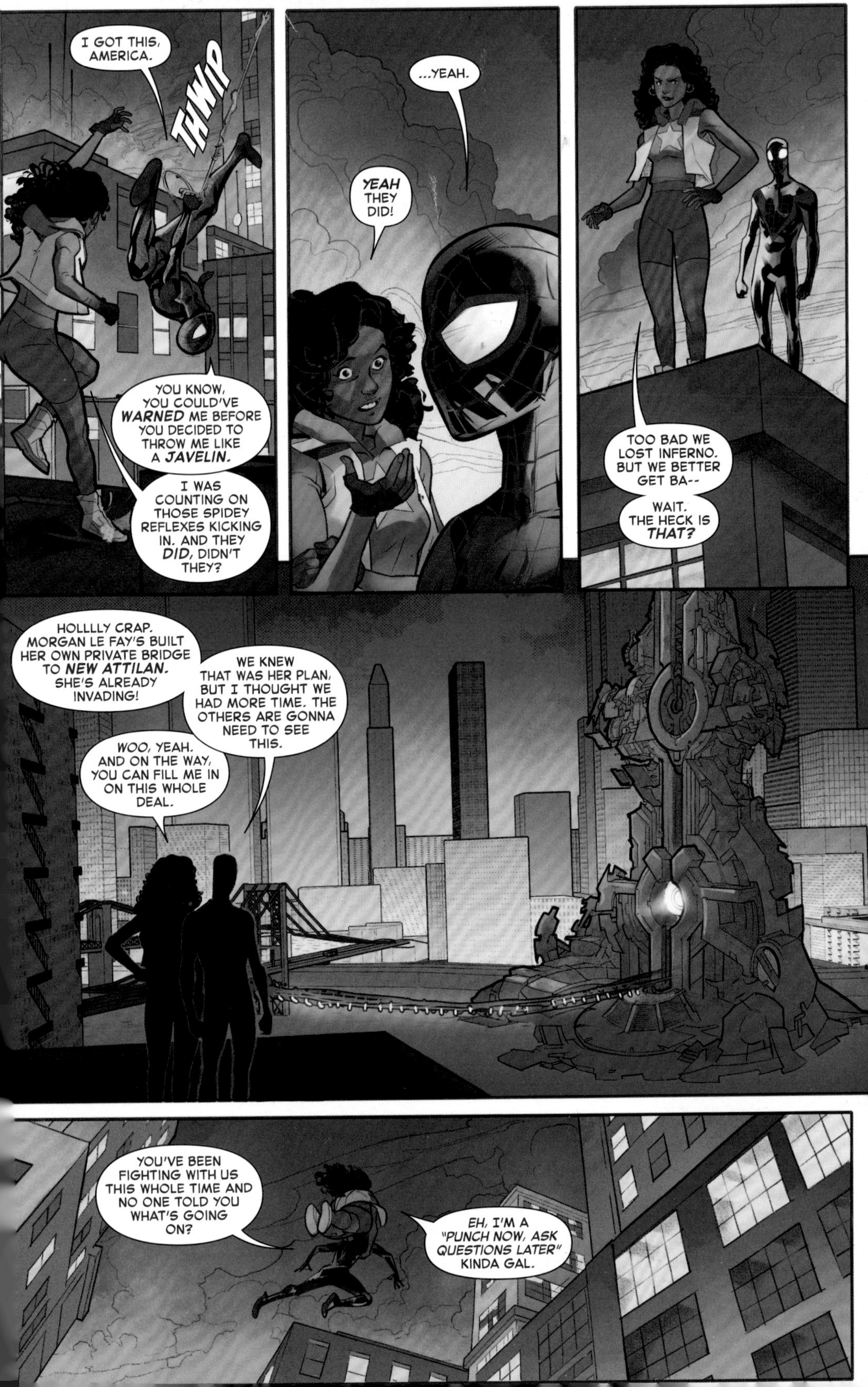
I GOT THIS, AMERICA.
THWIP
YOU KNOW, YOU COULD'VE WARNED ME BEFORE YOU DECIDED TO THROW ME LIKE A JAVELIN.
I WAS COUNTING ON THOSE SPIDEY REFLEXES KICKING IN. AND THEY DID, DIDN'T THEY?
...YEAH.
YEAH THEY DID!
TOO BAD WE LOST INFERNO. BUT WE BETTER GET BA--
WAIT. THE HECK IS THAT?
HOLLLLY CRAP. MORGAN LE FAY'S BUILT HER OWN PRIVATE BRIDGE TO NEW ATTILAN. SHE'S ALREADY INVADING!
WE KNEW THAT WAS HER PLAN, BUT I THOUGHT WE HAD MORE TIME. THE OTHERS ARE GONNA NEED TO SEE THIS.
WOO, YEAH. AND ON THE WAY, YOU CAN FILL ME IN ON THIS WHOLE DEAL.
YOU'VE BEEN FIGHTING WITH US THIS WHOLE TIME AND NO ONE TOLD YOU WHAT'S GOING ON?
EH, I'M A "PUNCH NOW, ASK QUESTIONS LATER" KINDA GAL.

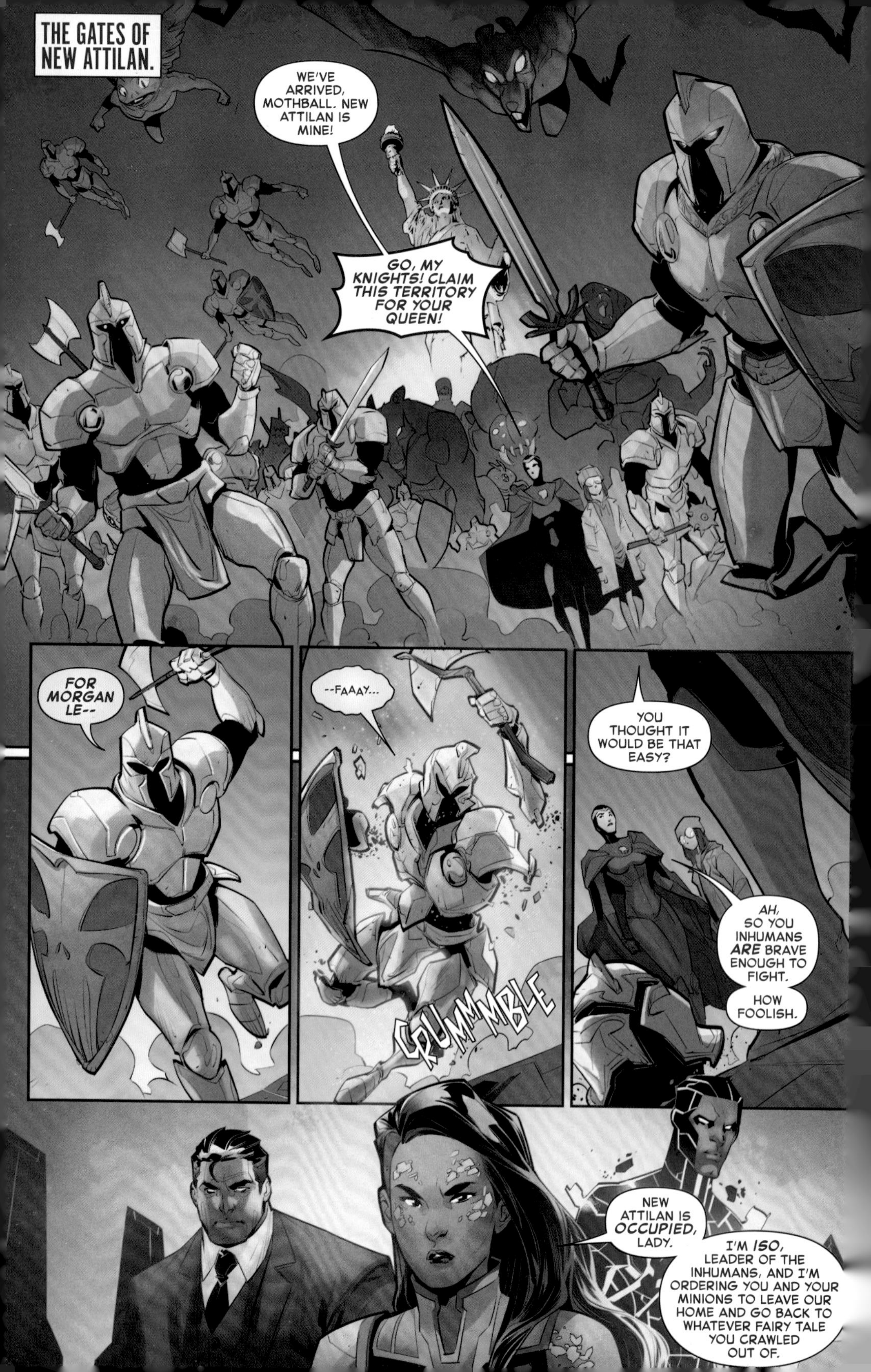
THE GATES OF NEW ATTILAN.
WE'VE ARRIVED, MOTHBALL. NEW ATTILAN IS MINE!
GO, MY KNIGHTS! CLAIM THIS TERRITORY FOR YOUR QUEEN!
FOR MORGAN LE--
--FAAAY...
CRUMMMBLE
YOU THOUGHT IT WOULD BE THAT EASY?
AH, SO YOU INHUMANS ARE BRAVE ENOUGH TO FIGHT.
HOW FOOLISH.
NEW ATTILAN IS OCCUPIED, LADY.
I'M ISO, LEADER OF THE INHUMANS, AND I'M ORDERING YOU AND YOUR MINIONS TO LEAVE OUR HOME AND GO BACK TO WHATEVER FAIRY TALE YOU CRAWLED OUT OF.

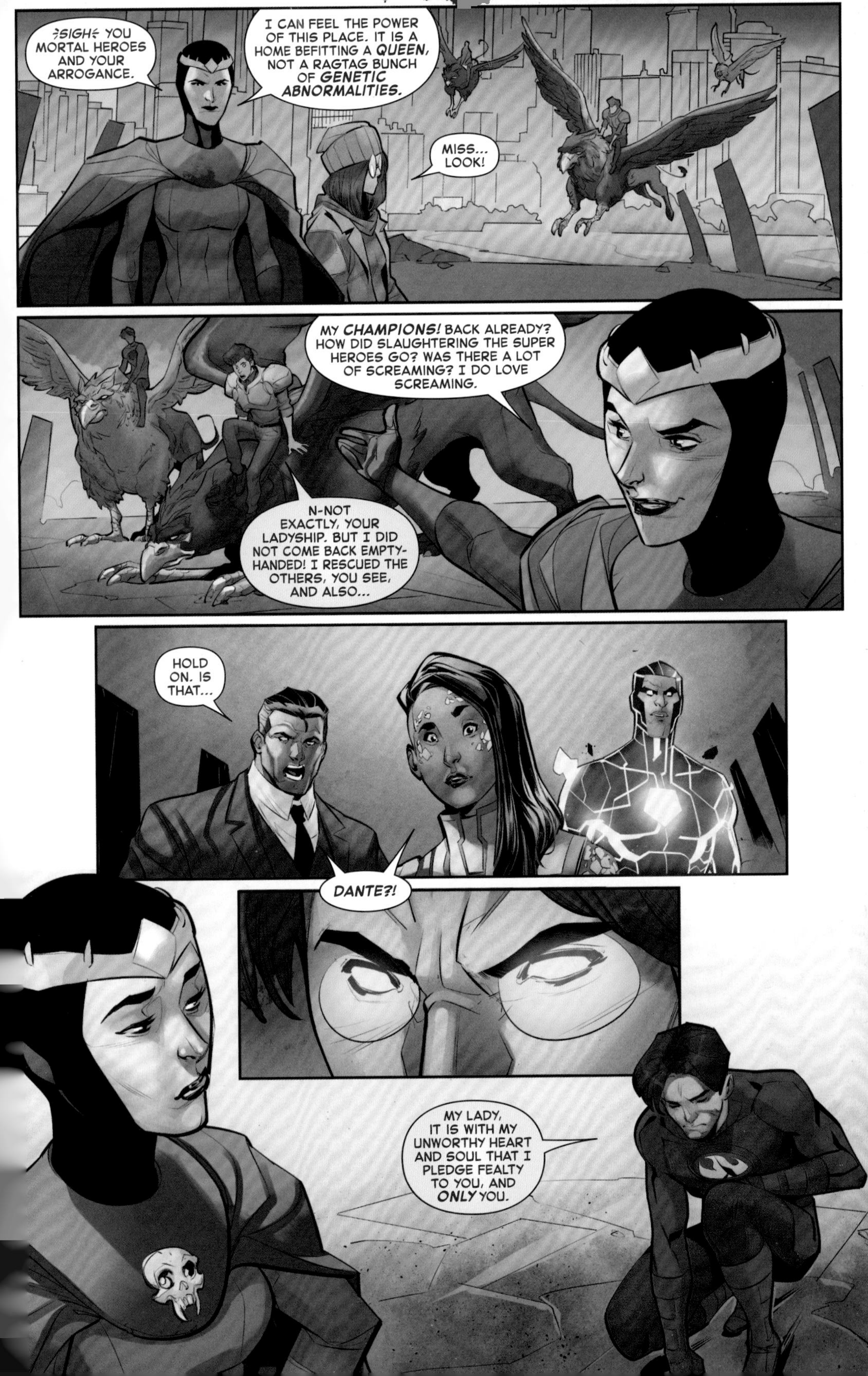

SIGH YOU MORTAL HEROES AND YOUR ARROGANCE.
I CAN FEEL THE POWER OF THIS PLACE. IT IS A HOME BEFITTING A QUEEN, NOT A RAGTAG BUNCH OF GENETIC ABNORMALITIES.
MISS... LOOK!
MY CHAMPIONS! BACK ALREADY? HOW DID SLAUGHTERING THE SUPER HEROES GO? WAS THERE A LOT OF SCREAMING? I DO LOVE SCREAMING.
N-NOT EXACTLY, YOUR LADYSHIP. BUT I DID NOT COME BACK EMPTY-HANDED! I RESCUED THE OTHERS, YOU SEE, AND ALSO...
HOLD ON. IS THAT...
DANTE?!
MY LADY, IT IS WITH MY UNWORTHY HEART AND SOUL THAT I PLEDGE FEALTY TO YOU, AND ONLY YOU.

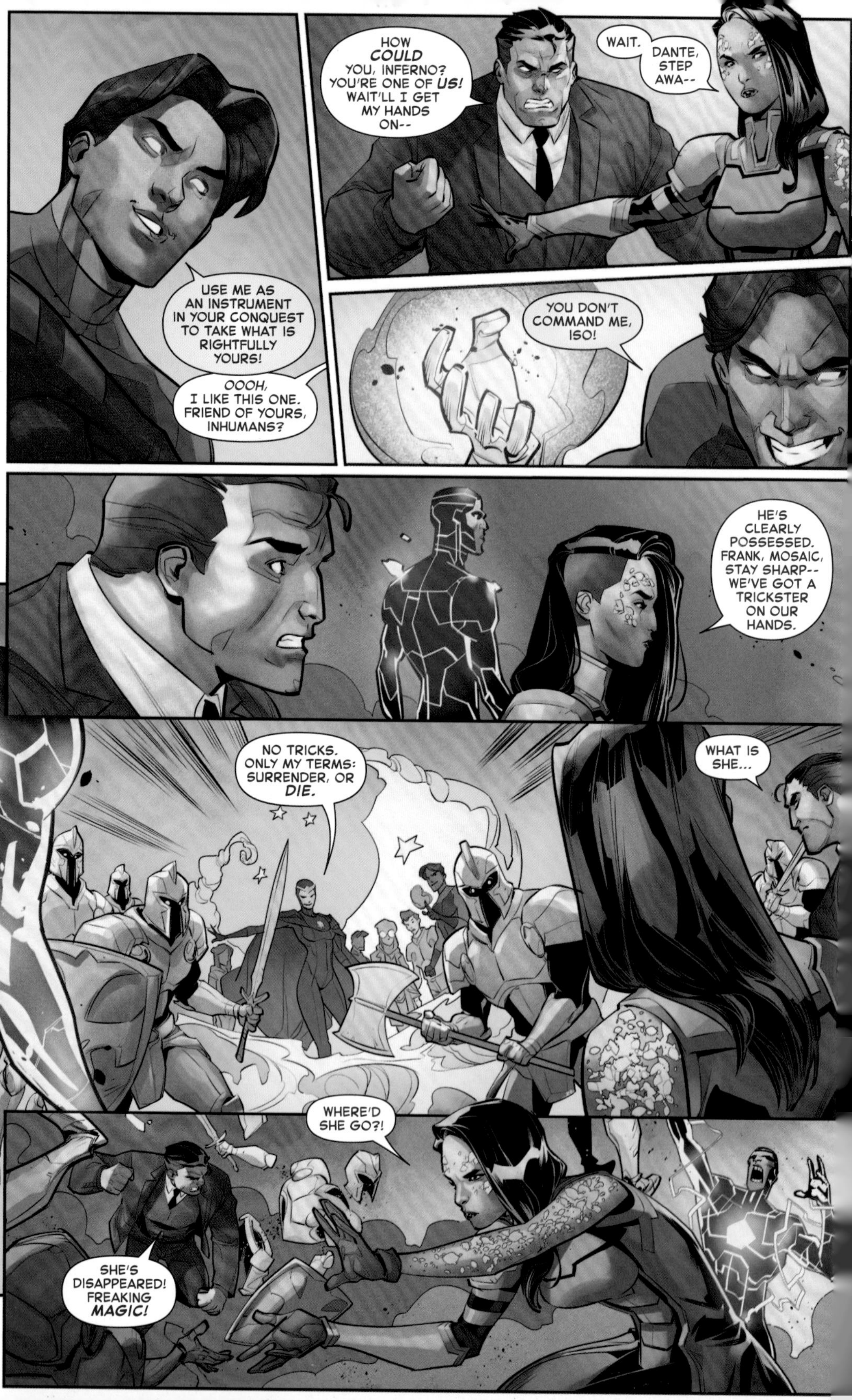
HOW COULD YOU, INFERNO? YOU'RE ONE OF US! WAIT'LL I GET MY HANDS ON--
WAIT.
DANTE, STEP AWA--
USE ME AS AN INSTRUMENT IN YOUR CONQUEST TO TAKE WHAT IS RIGHTFULLY YOURS!
OOOH, I LIKE THIS ONE. FRIEND OF YOURS, INHUMANS?
YOU DON'T COMMAND ME, ISO!
HE'S CLEARLY POSSESSED. FRANK, MOSAIC, STAY SHARP-- WE'VE GOT A TRICKSTER ON OUR HANDS.
NO TRICKS. ONLY MY TERMS: SURRENDER, OR DIE.
WHAT IS SHE...
WHERE'D SHE GO?!
SHE'S DISAPPEARED! FREAKING MAGIC!

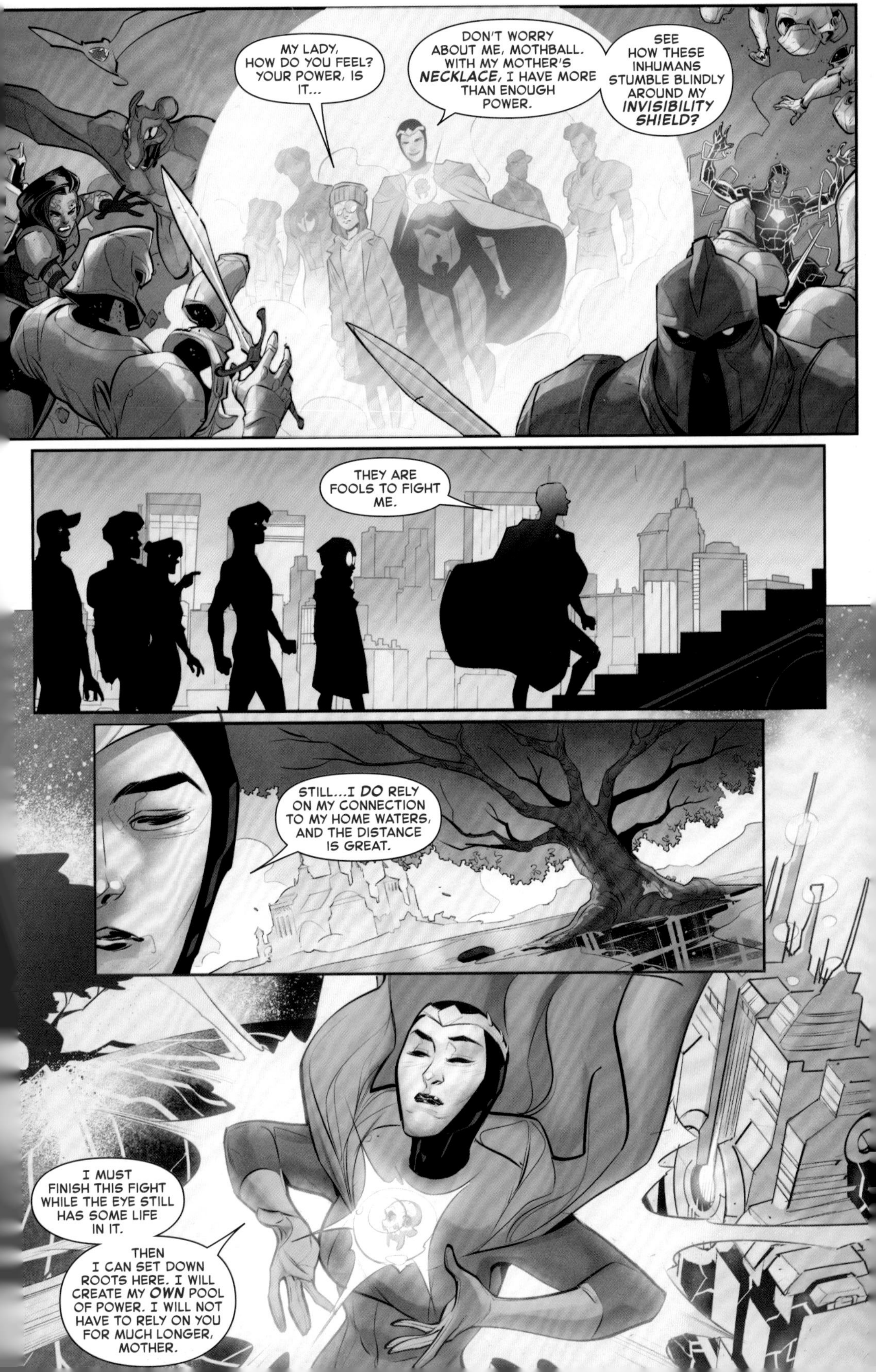
MY LADY, HOW DO YOU FEEL? YOUR POWER, IS IT...
DON'T WORRY ABOUT ME, MOTHBALL. WITH MY MOTHER'S NECKLACE, I HAVE MORE THAN ENOUGH POWER.
SEE HOW THESE INHUMANS STUMBLE BLINDLY AROUND MY INVISIBILITY SHIELD?
THEY ARE FOOLS TO FIGHT ME.
STILL...I DO RELY ON MY CONNECTION TO MY HOME WATERS, AND THE DISTANCE IS GREAT.
I MUST FINISH THIS FIGHT WHILE THE EYE STILL HAS SOME LIFE IN IT.
THEN I CAN SET DOWN ROOTS HERE. I WILL CREATE MY OWN POOL OF POWER. I WILL NOT HAVE TO RELY ON YOU FOR MUCH LONGER, MOTHER.

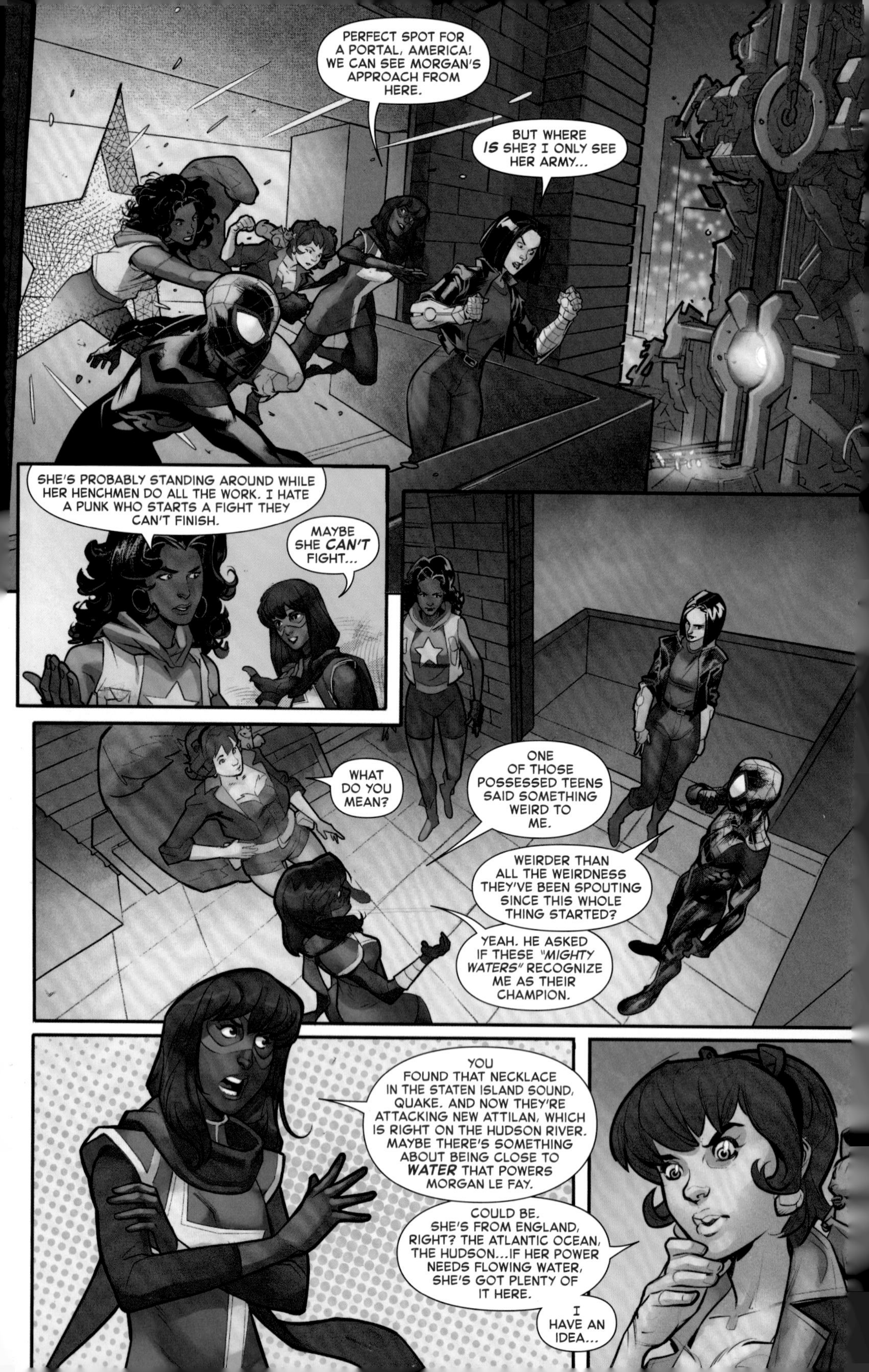
PERFECT SPOT FOR A PORTAL, AMERICA! WE CAN SEE MORGAN'S APPROACH FROM HERE.
BUT WHERE *IS* SHE? I ONLY SEE HER ARMY...
SHE'S PROBABLY STANDING AROUND WHILE HER HENCHMEN DO ALL THE WORK. I HATE A PUNK WHO STARTS A FIGHT THEY CAN'T FINISH.
MAYBE SHE ***CAN'T*** FIGHT...
WHAT DO YOU MEAN?
ONE OF THOSE POSSESSED TEENS SAID SOMETHING WEIRD TO ME.
WEIRDER THAN ALL THE WEIRDNESS THEY'VE BEEN SPOUTING SINCE THIS WHOLE THING STARTED?
YEAH. HE ASKED IF THESE *"MIGHTY WATERS"* RECOGNIZE ME AS THEIR CHAMPION.
YOU FOUND THAT NECKLACE IN THE STATEN ISLAND SOUND, QUAKE. AND NOW THEY'RE ATTACKING NEW ATTILAN, WHICH IS RIGHT ON THE HUDSON RIVER. MAYBE THERE'S SOMETHING ABOUT BEING CLOSE TO ***WATER*** THAT POWERS MORGAN LE FAY.
COULD BE. SHE'S FROM ENGLAND, RIGHT? THE ATLANTIC OCEAN, THE HUDSON...IF HER POWER NEEDS FLOWING WATER, SHE'S GOT PLENTY OF IT HERE.
I HAVE AN IDEA...

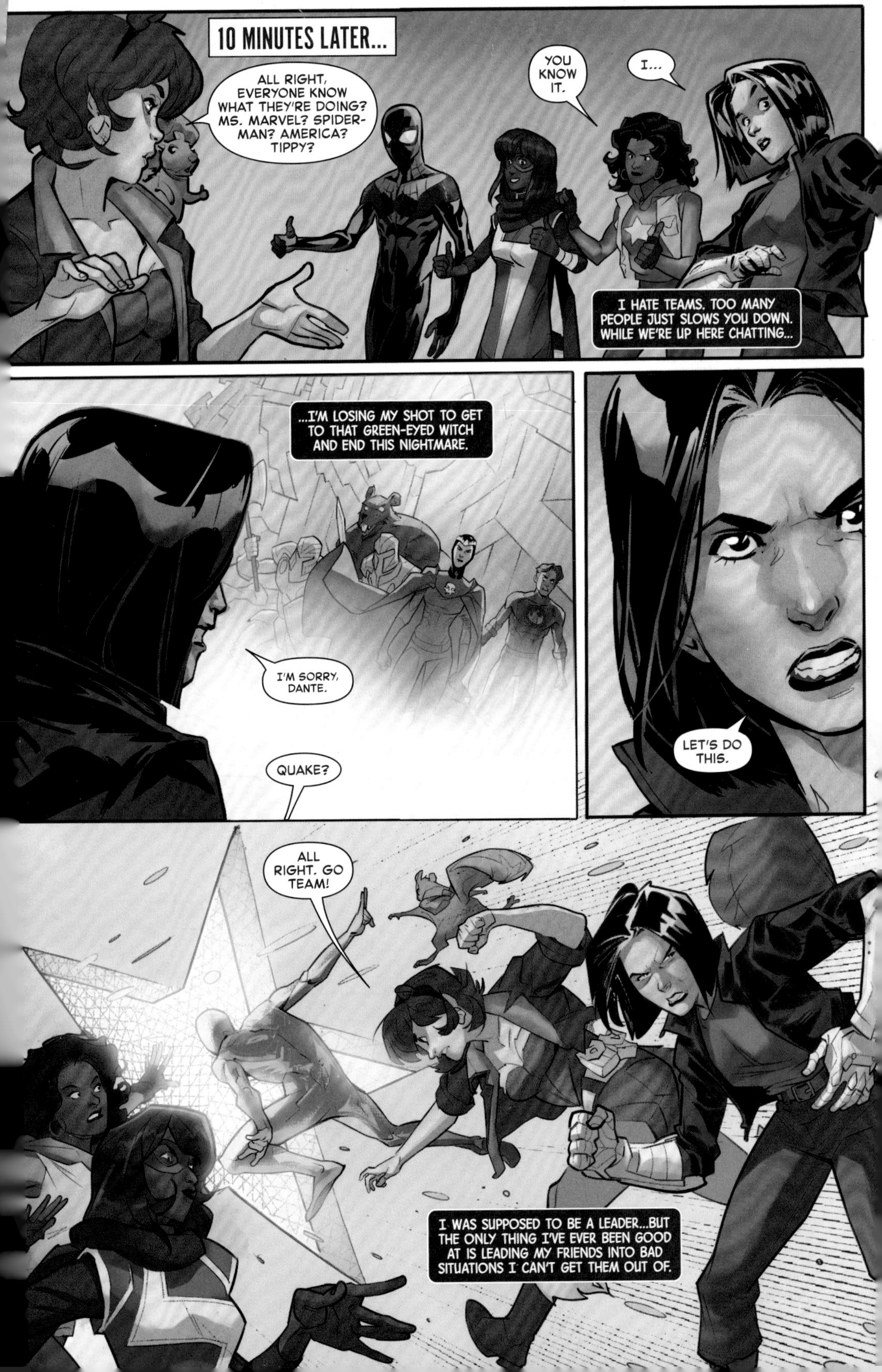
10 MINUTES LATER...
ALL RIGHT, EVERYONE KNOW WHAT THEY'RE DOING? MS. MARVEL? SPIDER-MAN? AMERICA? TIPPY?
YOU KNOW IT.
I...
I HATE TEAMS. TOO MANY PEOPLE JUST SLOWS YOU DOWN. WHILE WE'RE UP HERE CHATTING...
...I'M LOSING MY SHOT TO GET TO THAT GREEN-EYED WITCH AND END THIS NIGHTMARE.
I'M SORRY, DANTE.
QUAKE?
LET'S DO THIS.
ALL RIGHT. GO TEAM!
I WAS SUPPOSED TO BE A LEADER...BUT THE ONLY THING I'VE EVER BEEN GOOD AT IS LEADING MY FRIENDS INTO BAD SITUATIONS I CAN'T GET THEM OUT OF.

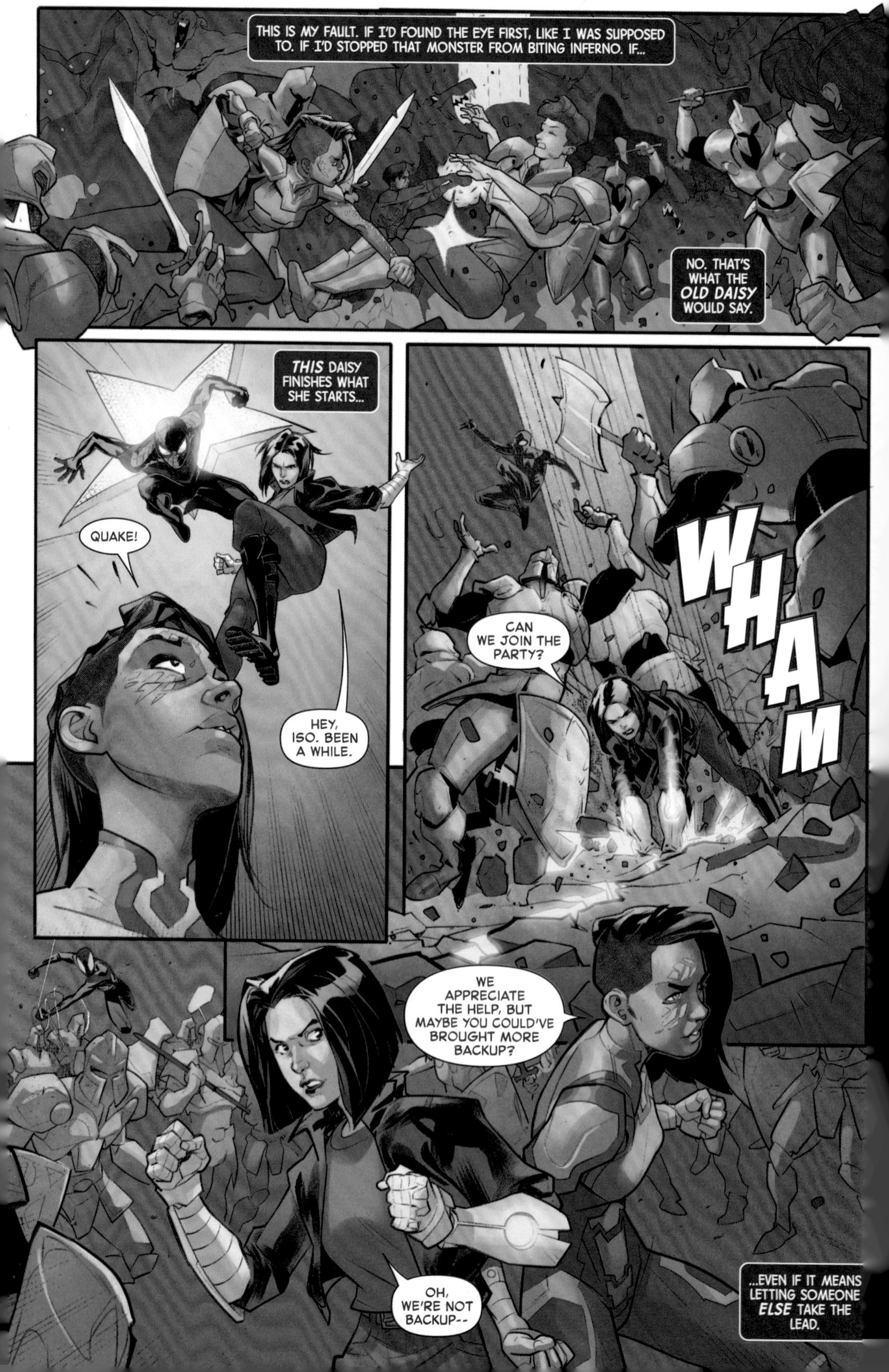

THIS IS MY FAULT. IF I'D FOUND THE EYE FIRST, LIKE I WAS SUPPOSED TO. IF I'D STOPPED THAT MONSTER FROM BITING INFERNO. IF...
NO. THAT'S WHAT THE *OLD DAISY* WOULD SAY.
THIS DAISY FINISHES WHAT SHE STARTS...
QUAKE!
HEY, ISO. BEEN A WHILE.
CAN WE JOIN THE PARTY?
WHAM
WE APPRECIATE THE HELP, BUT MAYBE YOU COULD'VE BROUGHT MORE BACKUP?
OH, WE'RE NOT BACKUP--
...EVEN IF IT MEANS LETTING SOMEONE *ELSE* TAKE THE LEAD.

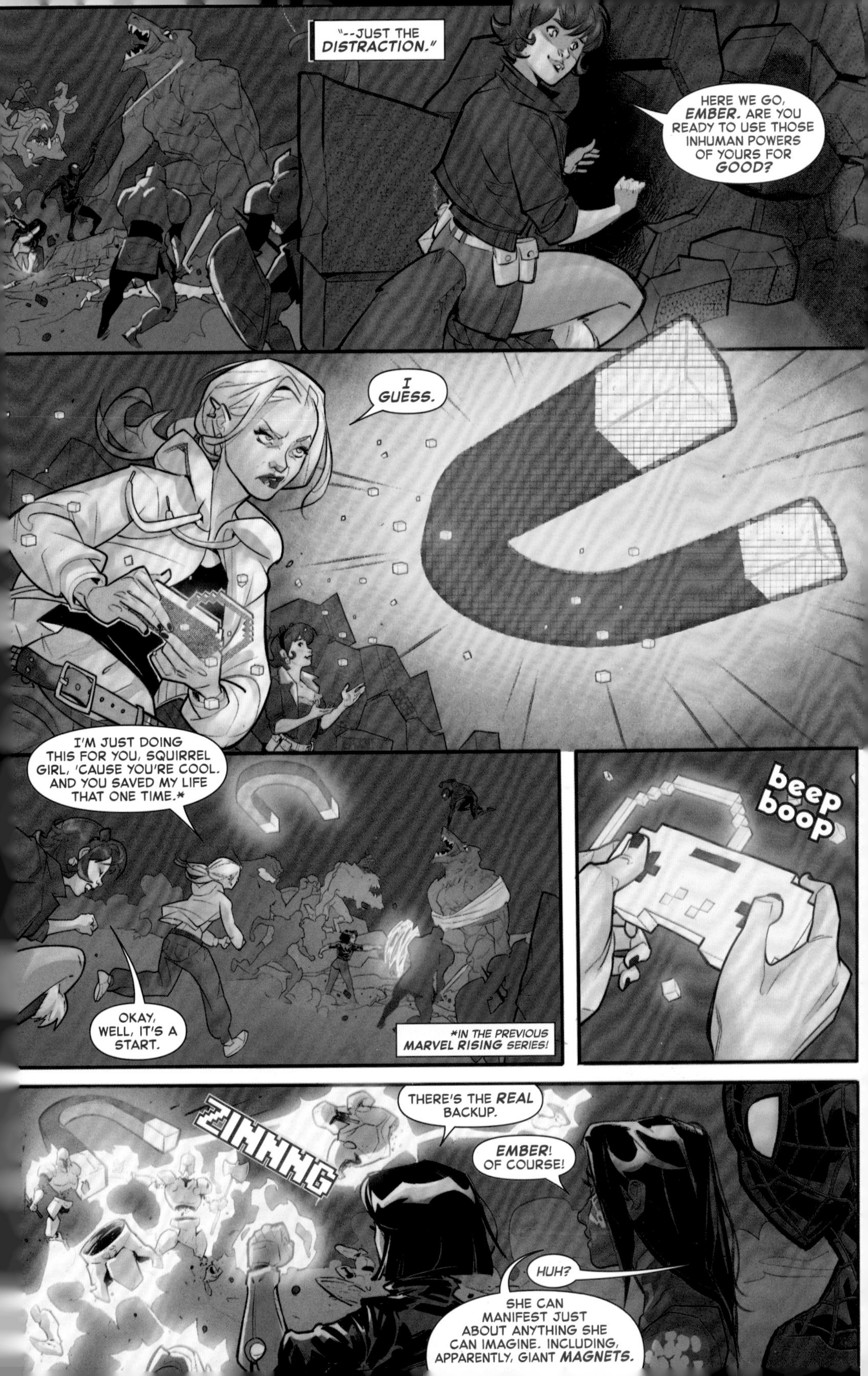
"--JUST THE DISTRACTION."
HERE WE GO, EMBER. ARE YOU READY TO USE THOSE INHUMAN POWERS OF YOURS FOR GOOD?
I GUESS.
I'M JUST DOING THIS FOR YOU, SQUIRREL GIRL, 'CAUSE YOU'RE COOL. AND YOU SAVED MY LIFE THAT ONE TIME.*
OKAY, WELL, IT'S A START.
*IN THE PREVIOUS MARVEL RISING SERIES!
beep boop
ZINNNG
THERE'S THE REAL BACKUP.
EMBER! OF COURSE!
HUH?
SHE CAN MANIFEST JUST ABOUT ANYTHING SHE CAN IMAGINE. INCLUDING, APPARENTLY, GIANT MAGNETS.

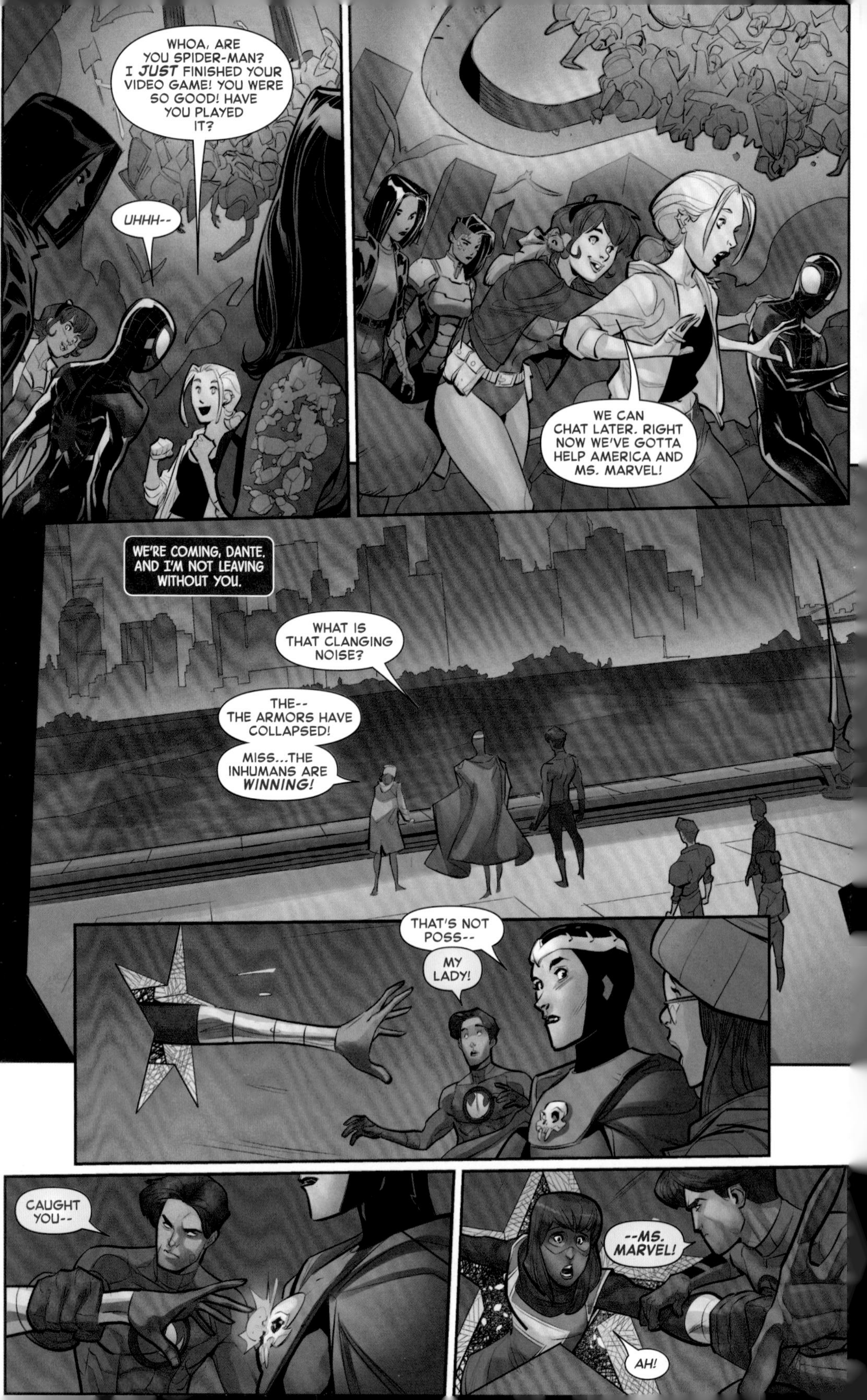

WHOA, ARE YOU SPIDER-MAN? I JUST FINISHED YOUR VIDEO GAME! YOU WERE SO GOOD! HAVE YOU PLAYED IT?
UHHH--
WE CAN CHAT LATER. RIGHT NOW WE'VE GOTTA HELP AMERICA AND MS. MARVEL!
WE'RE COMING, DANTE. AND I'M NOT LEAVING WITHOUT YOU.
WHAT IS THAT CLANGING NOISE?
THE-- THE ARMORS HAVE COLLAPSED!
MISS...THE INHUMANS ARE WINNING!
THAT'S NOT POSS--
MY LADY!
CAUGHT YOU--
--MS. MARVEL!
AH!

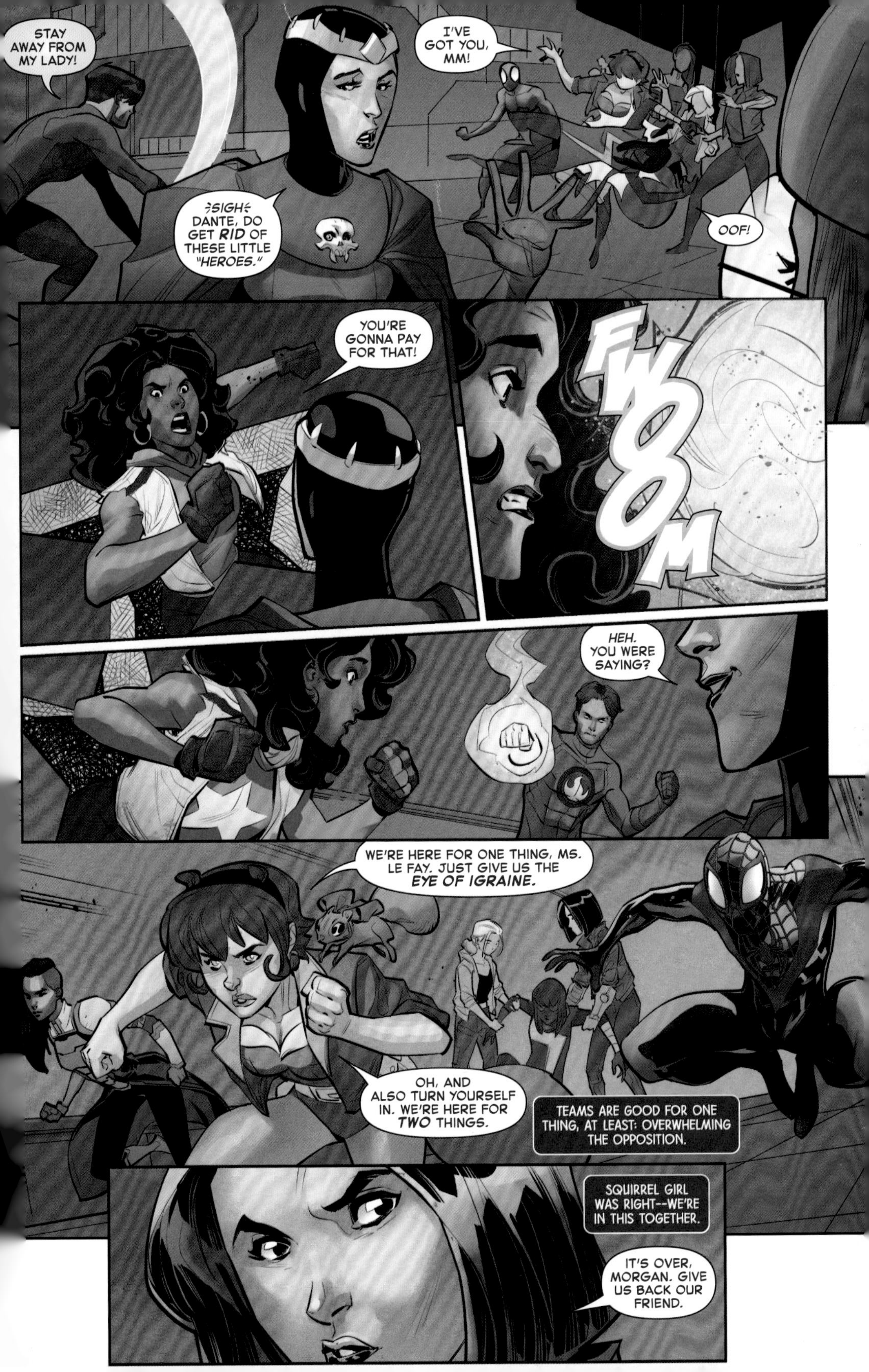
STAY AWAY FROM MY LADY!
I'VE GOT YOU, MM!
⋟SIGH⋞ DANTE, DO GET RID OF THESE LITTLE "HEROES."
OOF!
YOU'RE GONNA PAY FOR THAT!
FWOOM
HEH. YOU WERE SAYING?
WE'RE HERE FOR ONE THING, MS. LE FAY. JUST GIVE US THE EYE OF IGRAINE.
OH, AND ALSO TURN YOURSELF IN. WE'RE HERE FOR TWO THINGS.
TEAMS ARE GOOD FOR ONE THING, AT LEAST: OVERWHELMING THE OPPOSITION.
SQUIRREL GIRL WAS RIGHT--WE'RE IN THIS TOGETHER.
IT'S OVER, MORGAN. GIVE US BACK OUR FRIEND.

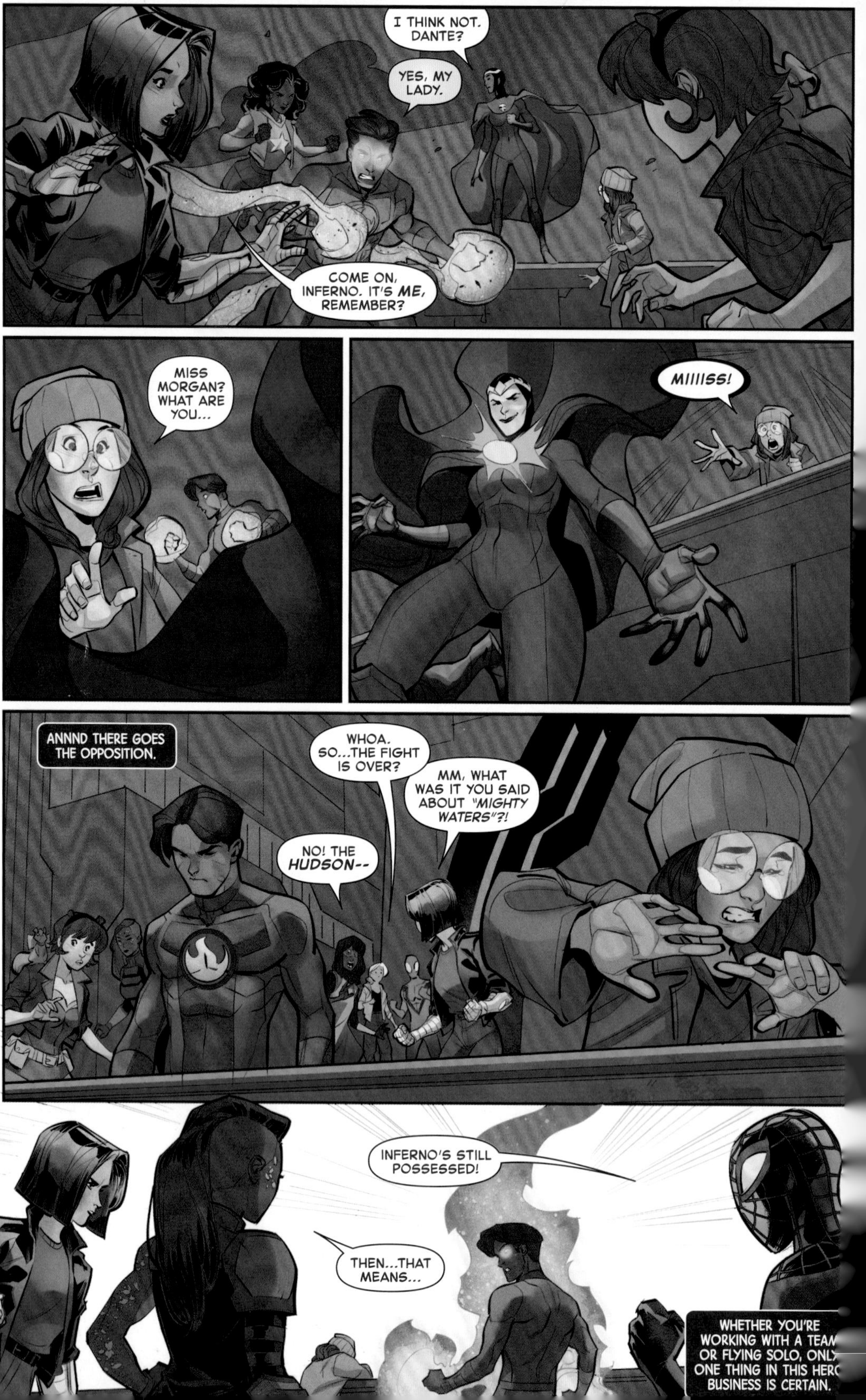
I THINK NOT. DANTE?
YES, MY LADY.
COME ON, INFERNO. IT'S ME, REMEMBER?
MISS MORGAN? WHAT ARE YOU...
MIIIISS!
ANNND THERE GOES THE OPPOSITION.
WHOA. SO...THE FIGHT IS OVER?
MM, WHAT WAS IT YOU SAID ABOUT "MIGHTY WATERS"?!
NO! THE HUDSON--
INFERNO'S STILL POSSESSED!
THEN...THAT MEANS...
WHETHER YOU'RE WORKING WITH A TEAM OR FLYING SOLO, ONLY ONE THING IN THIS HERO BUSINESS IS CERTAIN.

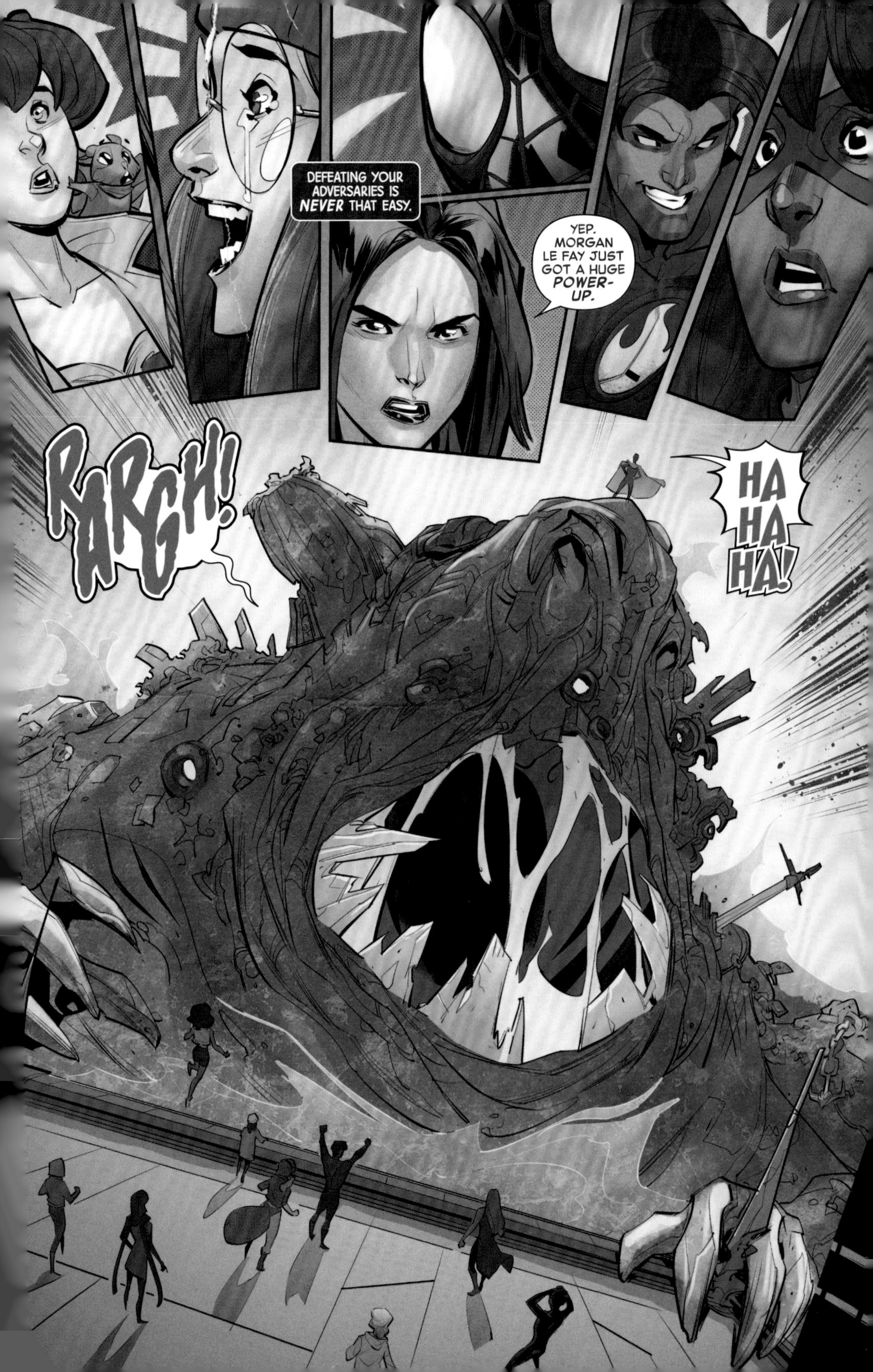

DEFEATING YOUR ADVERSARIES IS NEVER THAT EASY.
YEP. MORGAN LE FAY JUST GOT A HUGE POWER-UP.
RARGH!
HA HA HA HA!

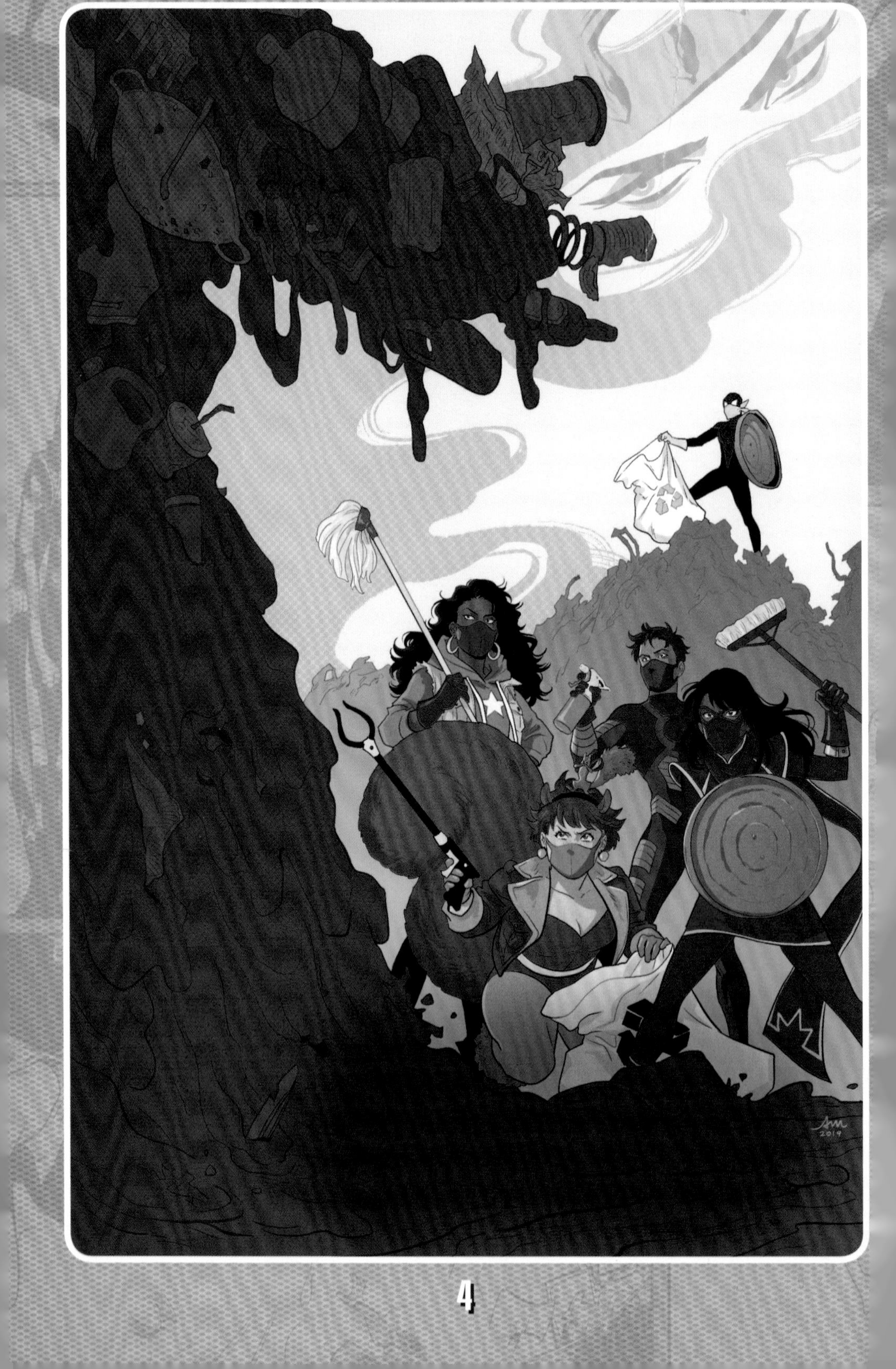

4

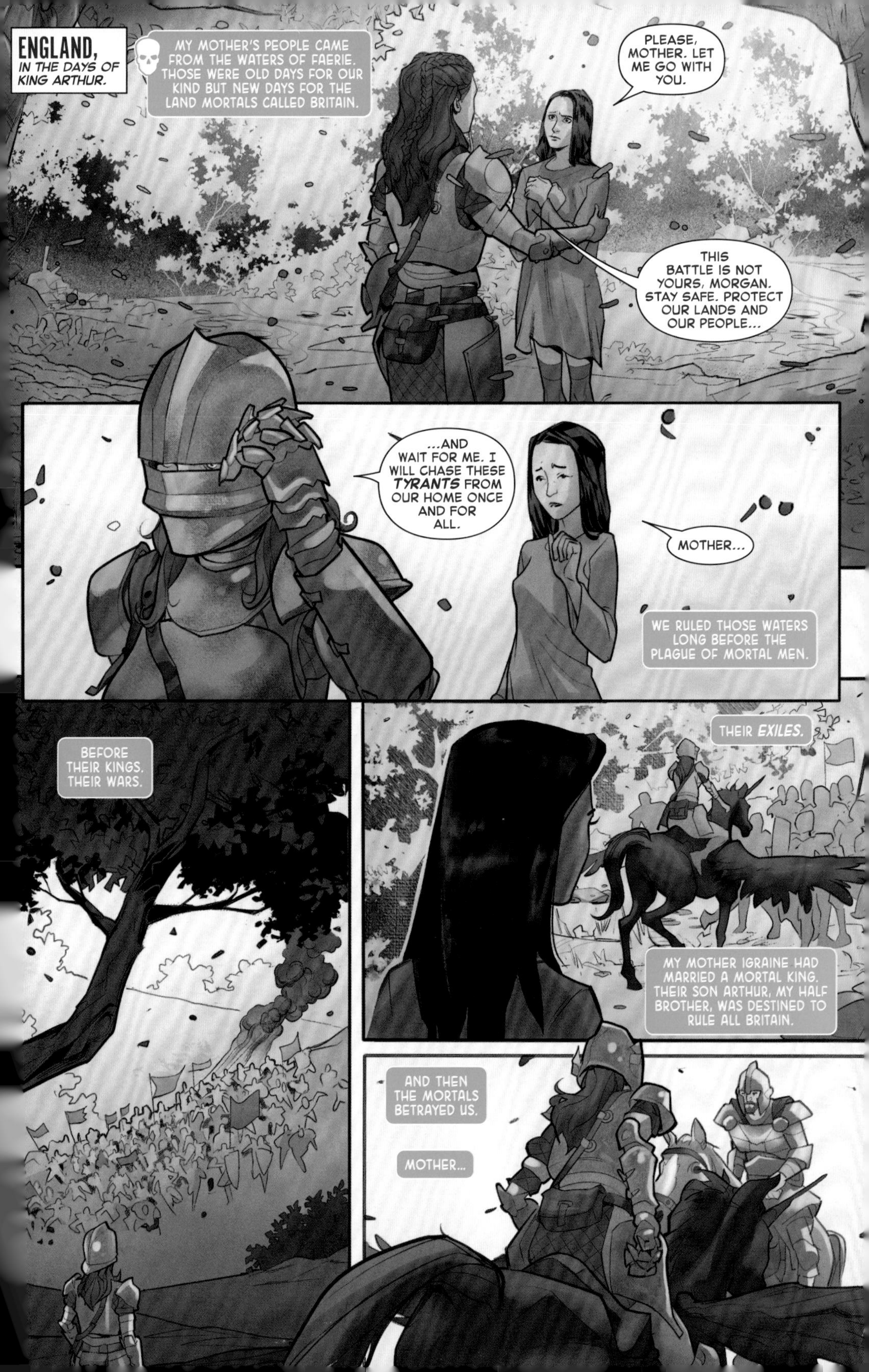
ENGLAND, IN THE DAYS OF KING ARTHUR.
MY MOTHER'S PEOPLE CAME FROM THE WATERS OF FAERIE. THOSE WERE OLD DAYS FOR OUR KIND BUT NEW DAYS FOR THE LAND MORTALS CALLED BRITAIN.
PLEASE, MOTHER. LET ME GO WITH YOU.
THIS BATTLE IS NOT YOURS, MORGAN. STAY SAFE. PROTECT OUR LANDS AND OUR PEOPLE...
...AND WAIT FOR ME. I WILL CHASE THESE TYRANTS FROM OUR HOME ONCE AND FOR ALL.
MOTHER...
WE RULED THOSE WATERS LONG BEFORE THE PLAGUE OF MORTAL MEN.
BEFORE THEIR KINGS. THEIR WARS.
THEIR EXILES.
MY MOTHER IGRAINE HAD MARRIED A MORTAL KING. THEIR SON ARTHUR, MY HALF BROTHER, WAS DESTINED TO RULE ALL BRITAIN.
AND THEN THE MORTALS BETRAYED US.
MOTHER...

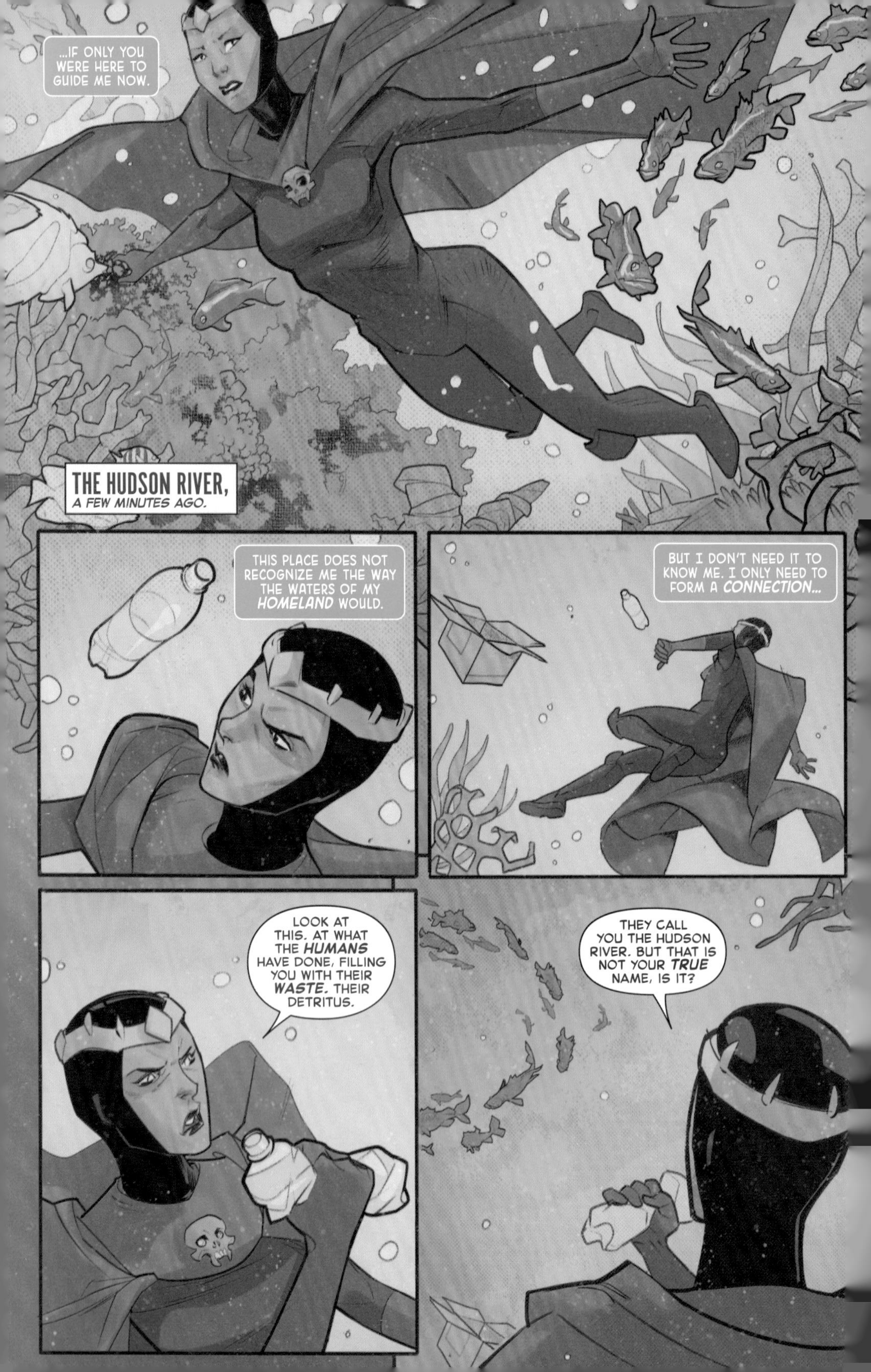
...IF ONLY YOU WERE HERE TO GUIDE ME NOW.
THE HUDSON RIVER, A FEW MINUTES AGO.
THIS PLACE DOES NOT RECOGNIZE ME THE WAY THE WATERS OF MY HOMELAND WOULD.
BUT I DON'T NEED IT TO KNOW ME. I ONLY NEED TO FORM A CONNECTION...
LOOK AT THIS. AT WHAT THE HUMANS HAVE DONE, FILLING YOU WITH THEIR WASTE. THEIR DETRITUS.
THEY CALL YOU THE HUDSON RIVER. BUT THAT IS NOT YOUR TRUE NAME, IS IT?

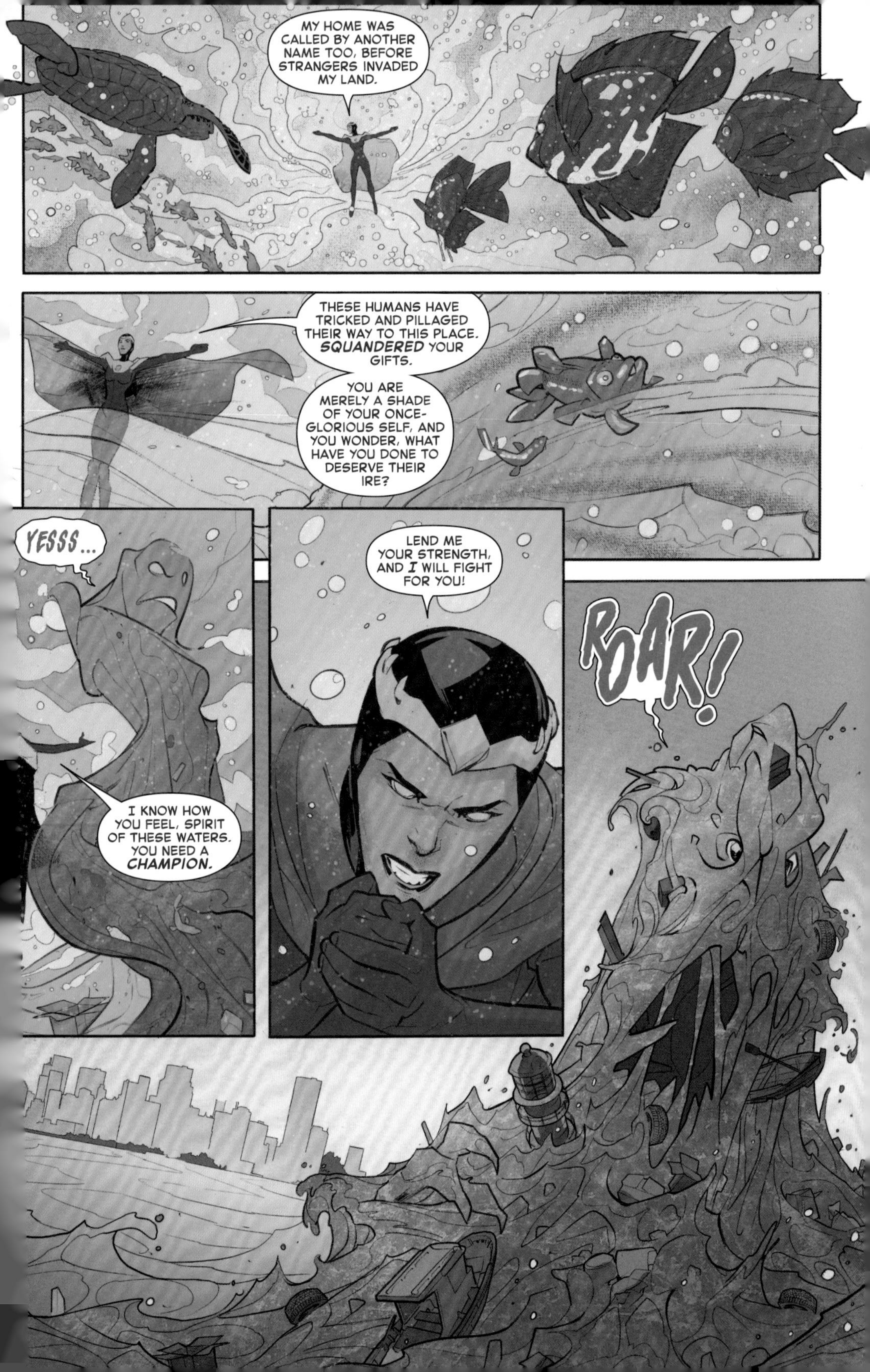

MY HOME WAS CALLED BY ANOTHER NAME TOO, BEFORE STRANGERS INVADED MY LAND.
THESE HUMANS HAVE TRICKED AND PILLAGED THEIR WAY TO THIS PLACE. SQUANDERED YOUR GIFTS.
YOU ARE MERELY A SHADE OF YOUR ONCE-GLORIOUS SELF, AND YOU WONDER, WHAT HAVE YOU DONE TO DESERVE THEIR IRE?
YESSS...
I KNOW HOW YOU FEEL, SPIRIT OF THESE WATERS. YOU NEED A CHAMPION.
LEND ME YOUR STRENGTH, AND I WILL FIGHT FOR YOU!
ROAR!

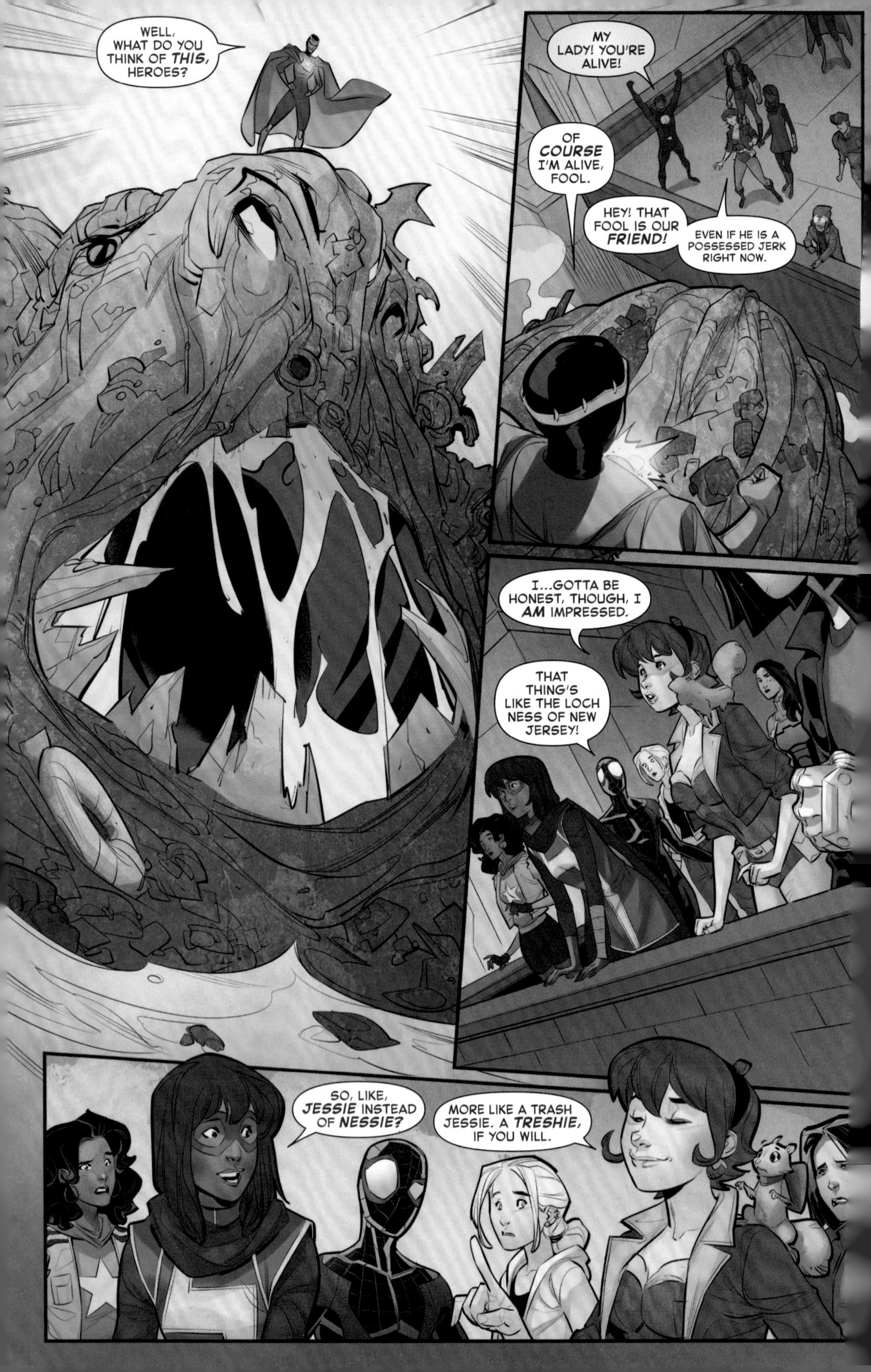
WELL, WHAT DO YOU THINK OF THIS, HEROES?
MY LADY! YOU'RE ALIVE!
OF COURSE I'M ALIVE, FOOL.
HEY! THAT FOOL IS OUR FRIEND!
EVEN IF HE IS A POSSESSED JERK RIGHT NOW.
I...GOTTA BE HONEST, THOUGH, I AM IMPRESSED.
THAT THING'S LIKE THE LOCH NESS OF NEW JERSEY!
SO, LIKE, JESSIE INSTEAD OF NESSIE?
MORE LIKE A TRASH JESSIE. A TRESHIE, IF YOU WILL.

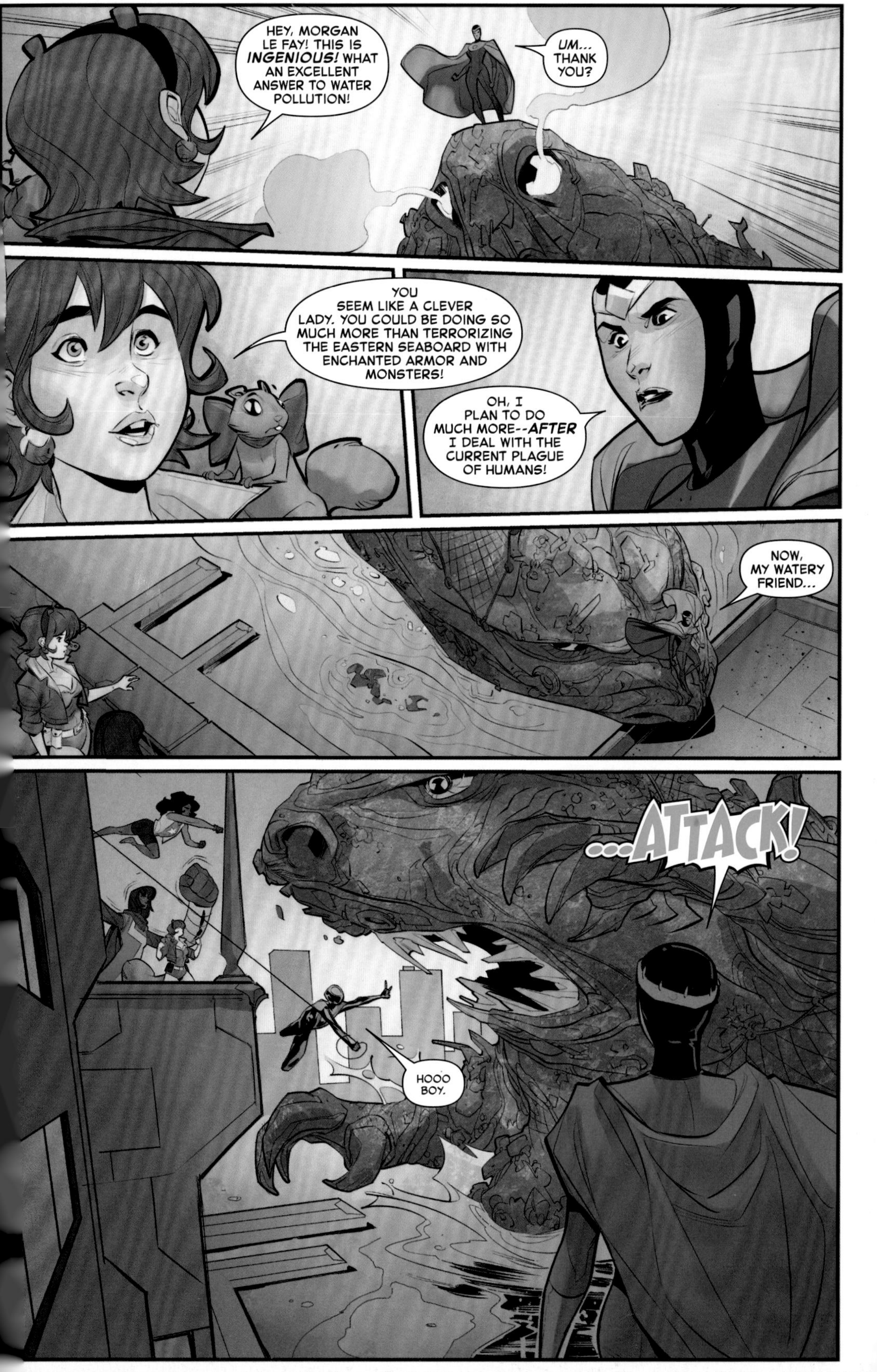
HEY, MORGAN LE FAY! THIS IS INGENIOUS! WHAT AN EXCELLENT ANSWER TO WATER POLLUTION!
UM... THANK YOU?
YOU SEEM LIKE A CLEVER LADY. YOU COULD BE DOING SO MUCH MORE THAN TERRORIZING THE EASTERN SEABOARD WITH ENCHANTED ARMOR AND MONSTERS!
OH, I PLAN TO DO MUCH MORE--AFTER I DEAL WITH THE CURRENT PLAGUE OF HUMANS!
NOW, MY WATERY FRIEND...
...ATTACK!
HOOO BOY.

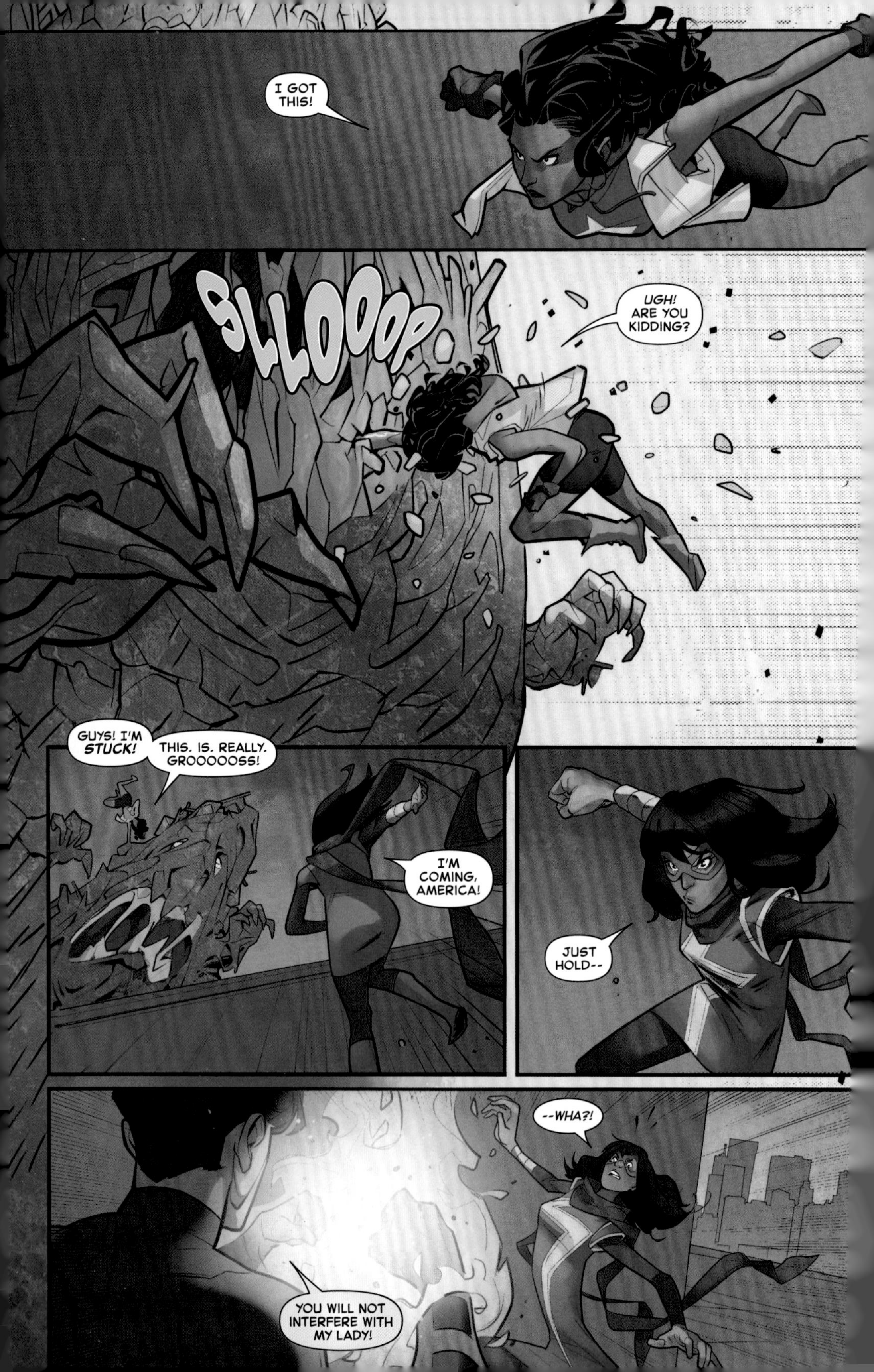
I GOT THIS!
SLLOOOP
UGH! ARE YOU KIDDING?
GUYS! I'M STUCK!
THIS. IS. REALLY. GROOOOOSS!
I'M COMING, AMERICA!
JUST HOLD--
--WHA?!
YOU WILL NOT INTERFERE WITH MY LADY!

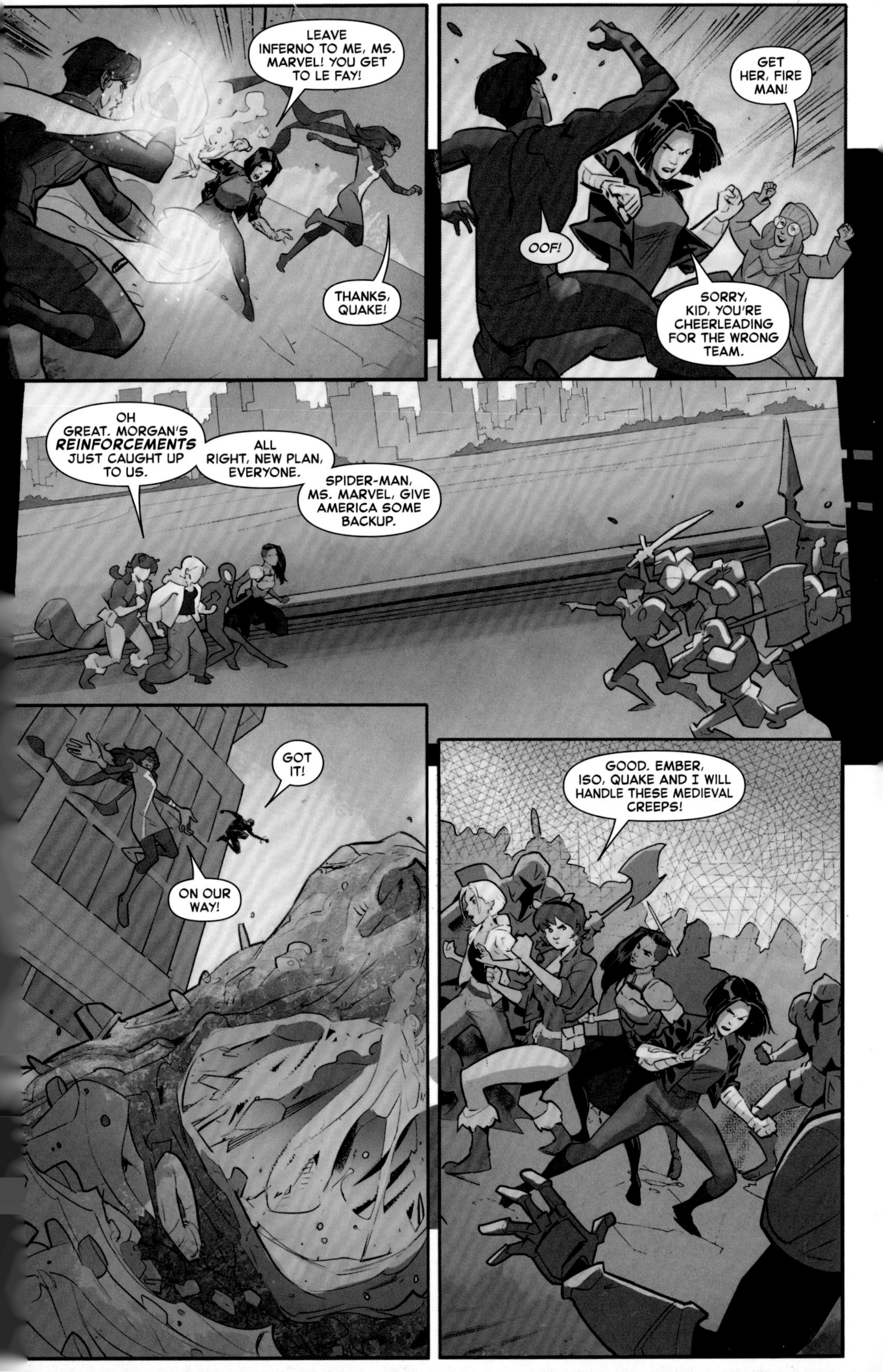
LEAVE INFERNO TO ME, MS. MARVEL! YOU GET TO LE FAY!
THANKS, QUAKE!
GET HER, FIRE MAN!
OOF!
SORRY, KID, YOU'RE CHEERLEADING FOR THE WRONG TEAM.
OH GREAT. MORGAN'S **REINFORCEMENTS** JUST CAUGHT UP TO US.
ALL RIGHT, NEW PLAN, EVERYONE.
SPIDER-MAN, MS. MARVEL, GIVE AMERICA SOME BACKUP.
GOT IT!
ON OUR WAY!
GOOD. EMBER, ISO, QUAKE AND I WILL HANDLE THESE MEDIEVAL CREEPS!

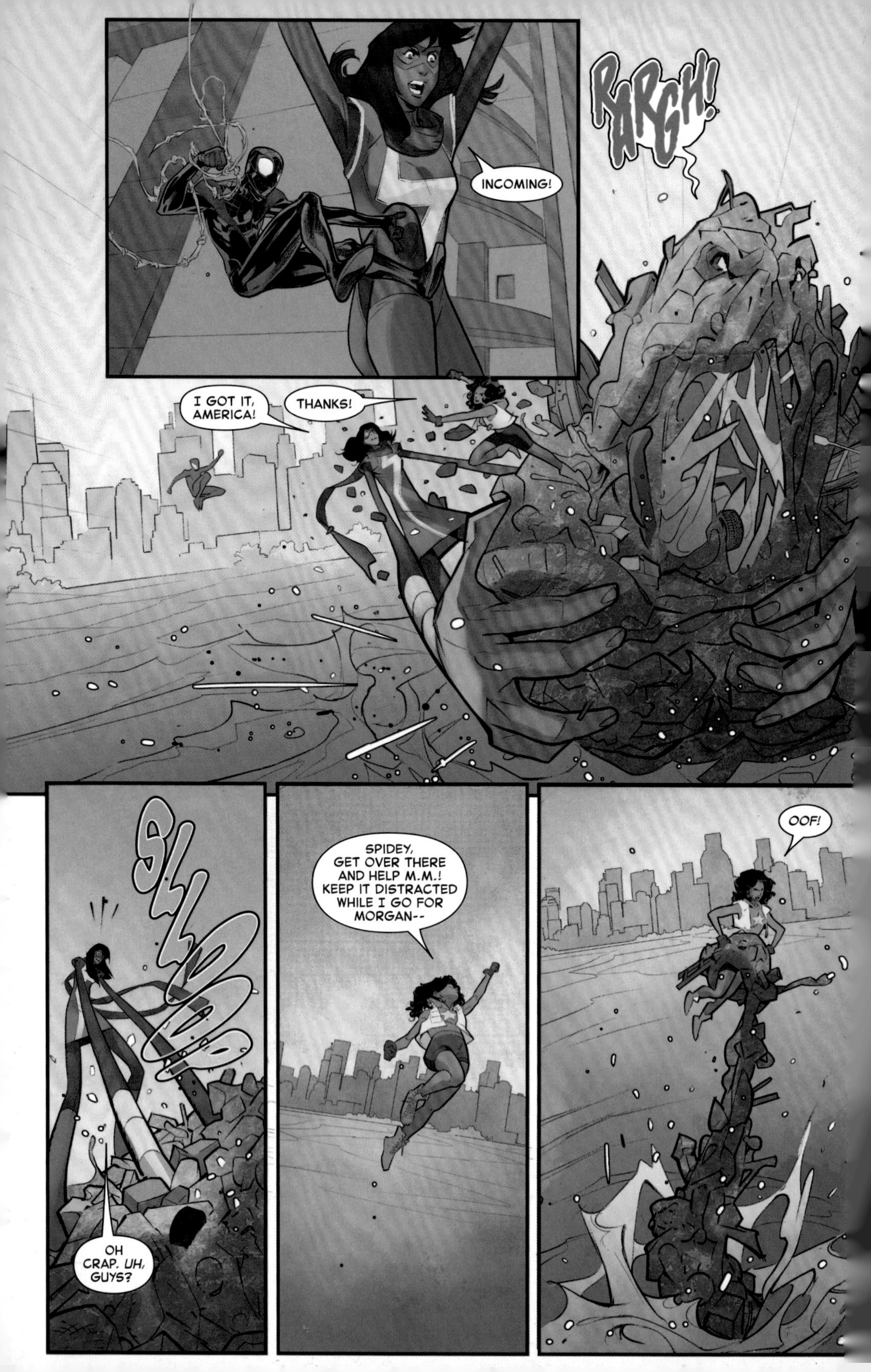
INCOMING!
RARGH!
I GOT IT, AMERICA!
THANKS!
OH CRAP. UH, GUYS?
SPIDEY, GET OVER THERE AND HELP M.M.! KEEP IT DISTRACTED WHILE I GO FOR MORGAN--
OOF!

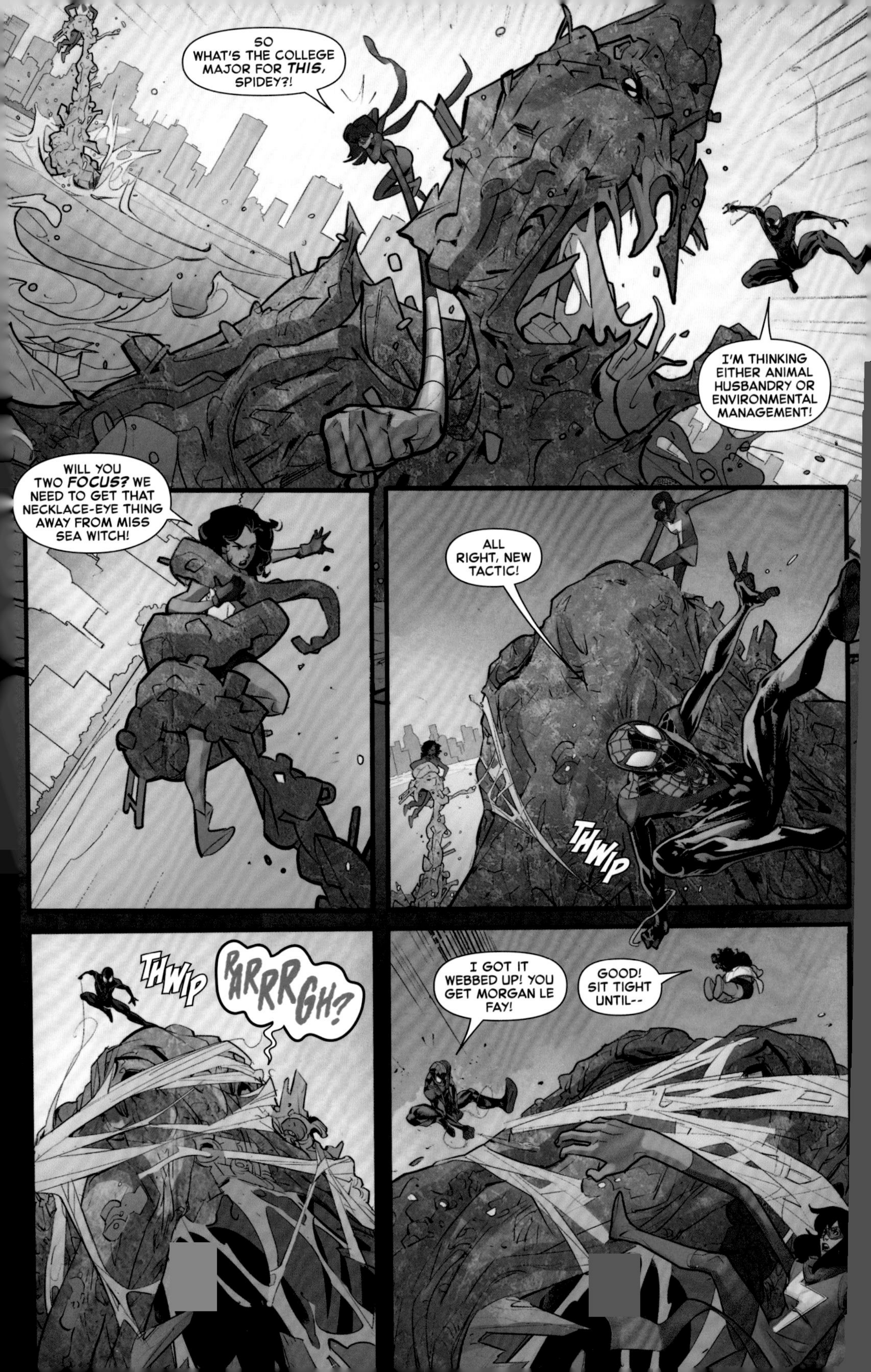
SO WHAT'S THE COLLEGE MAJOR FOR THIS, SPIDEY?!
I'M THINKING EITHER ANIMAL HUSBANDRY OR ENVIRONMENTAL MANAGEMENT!
WILL YOU TWO FOCUS? WE NEED TO GET THAT NECKLACE-EYE THING AWAY FROM MISS SEA WITCH!
ALL RIGHT, NEW TACTIC!
THWIP
THWIP
RARRRGH?
I GOT IT WEBBED UP! YOU GET MORGAN LE FAY!
GOOD! SIT TIGHT UNTIL--

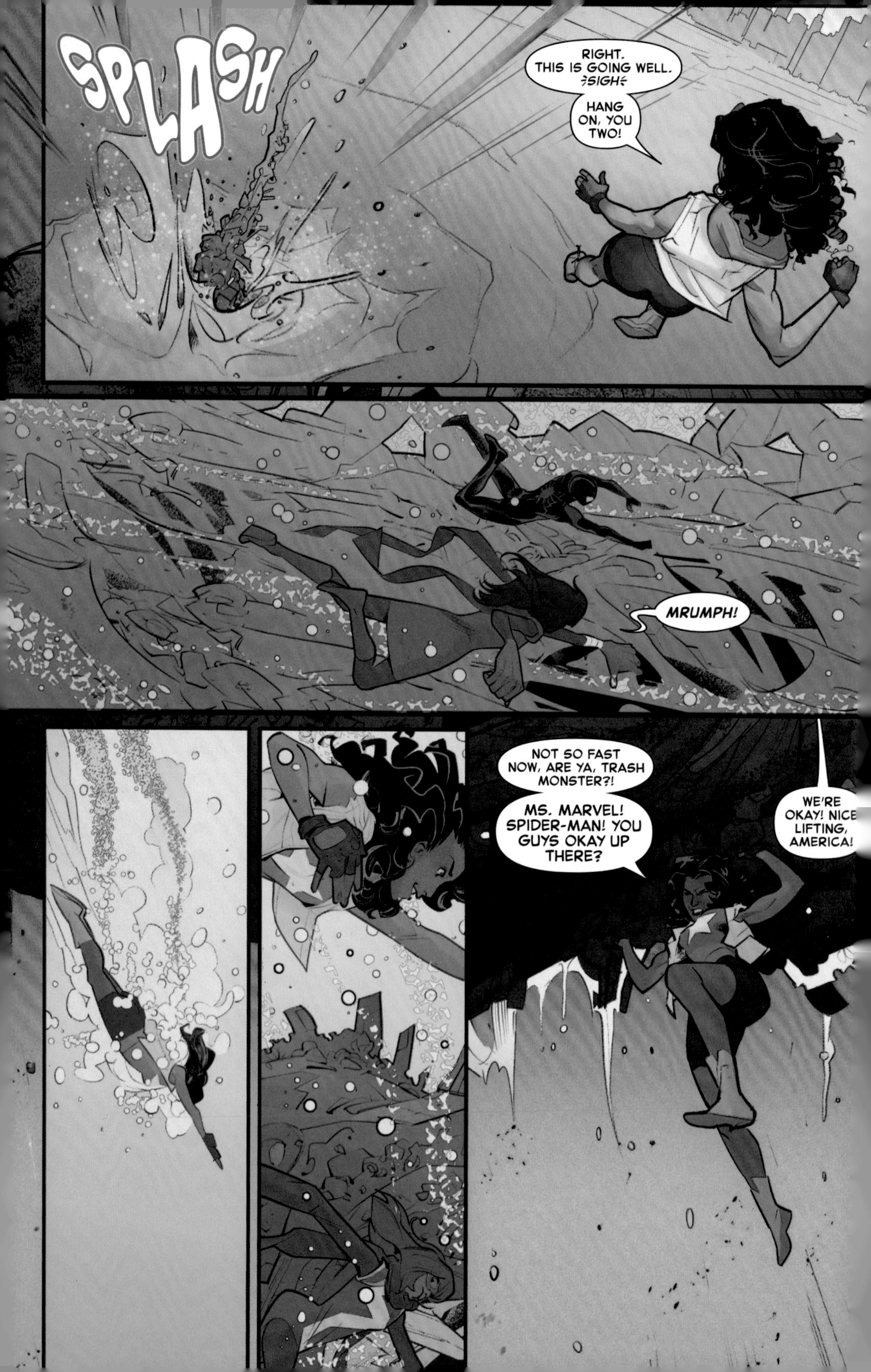
SPLASH
RIGHT. THIS IS GOING WELL. *SIGH*
HANG ON, YOU TWO!
MRUMPH!
NOT SO FAST NOW, ARE YA, TRASH MONSTER?!
MS. MARVEL! SPIDER-MAN! YOU GUYS OKAY UP THERE?
WE'RE OKAY! NICE LIFTING, AMERICA!

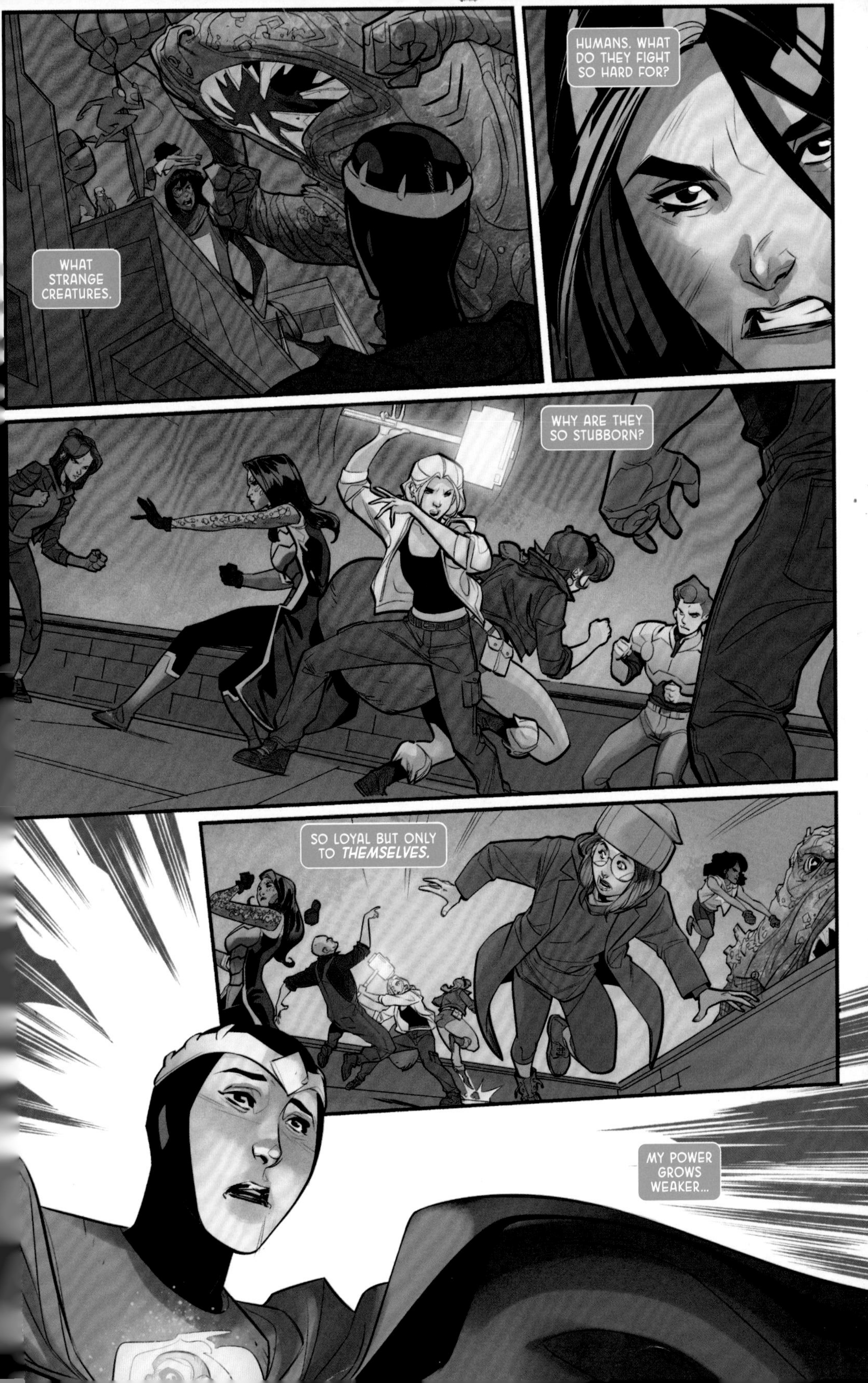
WHAT STRANGE CREATURES.
HUMANS. WHAT DO THEY FIGHT SO HARD FOR?
WHY ARE THEY SO STUBBORN?
SO LOYAL BUT ONLY TO *THEMSELVES.*
MY POWER GROWS WEAKER...

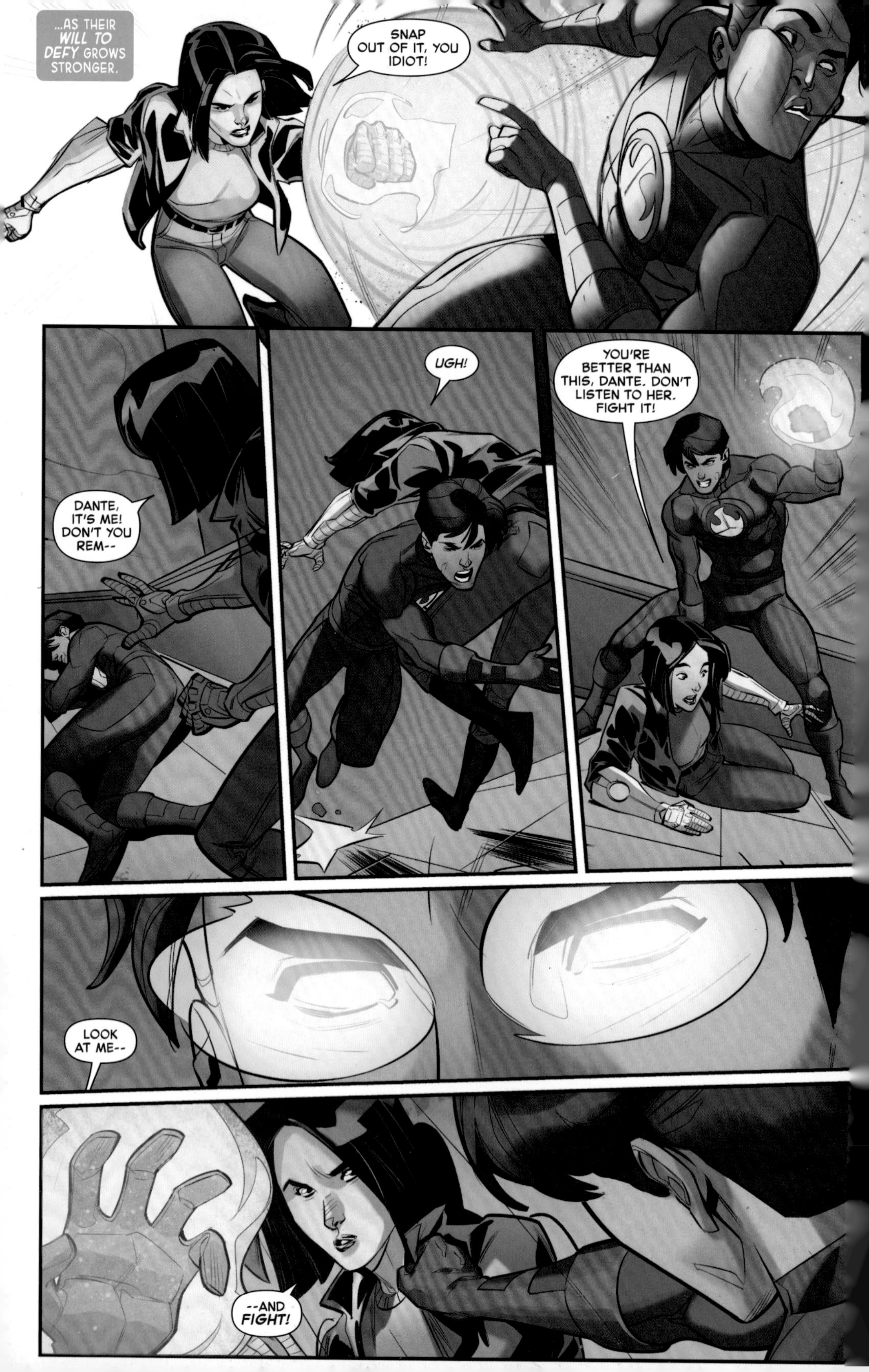
...AS THEIR WILL TO DEFY GROWS STRONGER.
SNAP OUT OF IT, YOU IDIOT!
DANTE, IT'S ME! DON'T YOU REM--
UGH!
YOU'RE BETTER THAN THIS, DANTE. DON'T LISTEN TO HER. FIGHT IT!
LOOK AT ME--
--AND FIGHT!

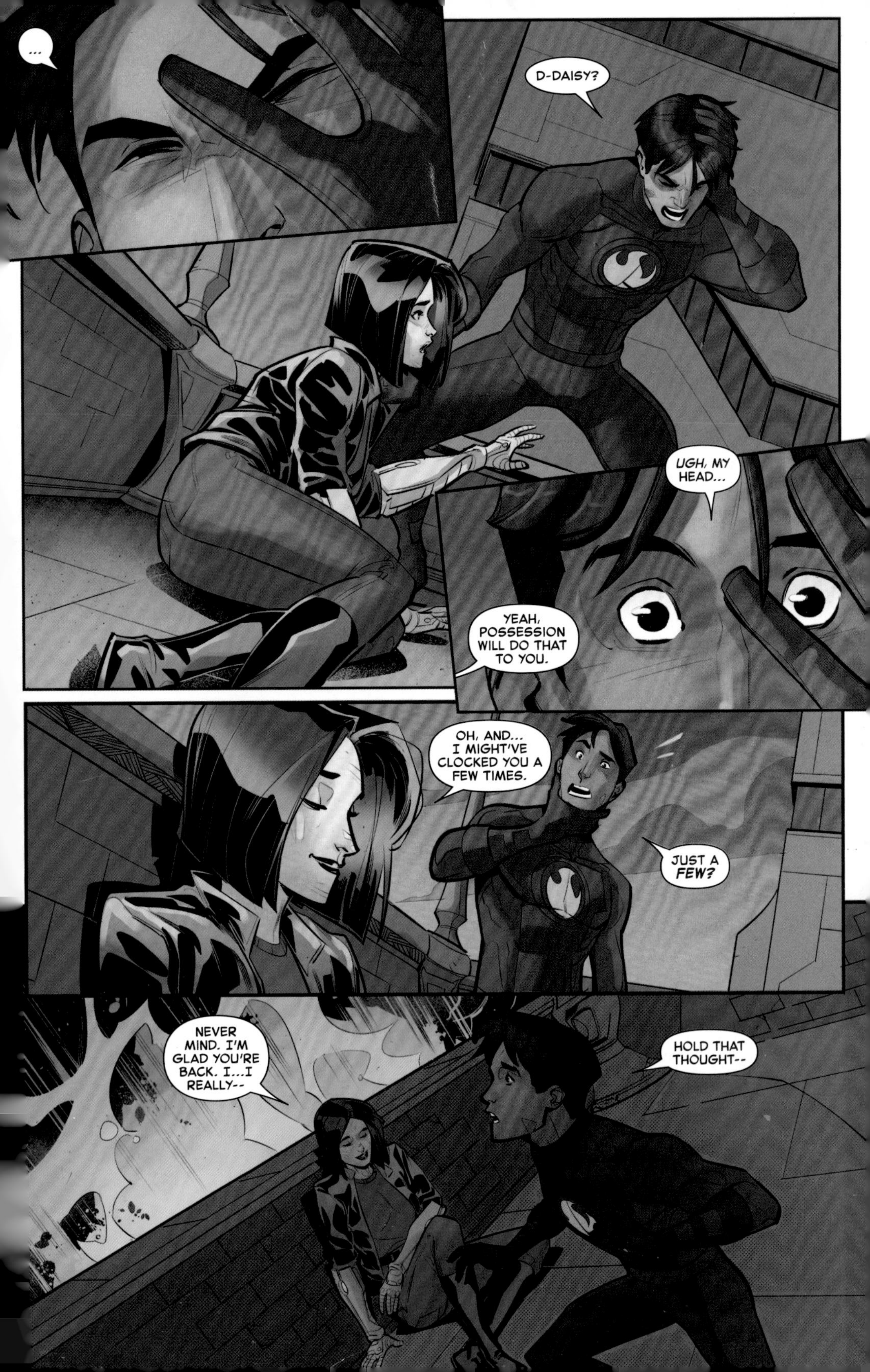
...
D-DAISY?
UGH, MY HEAD...
YEAH, POSSESSION WILL DO THAT TO YOU.
OH, AND... I MIGHT'VE CLOCKED YOU A FEW TIMES.
JUST A *FEW?*
NEVER MIND. I'M GLAD YOU'RE BACK. I...I REALLY--
HOLD THAT THOUGHT--

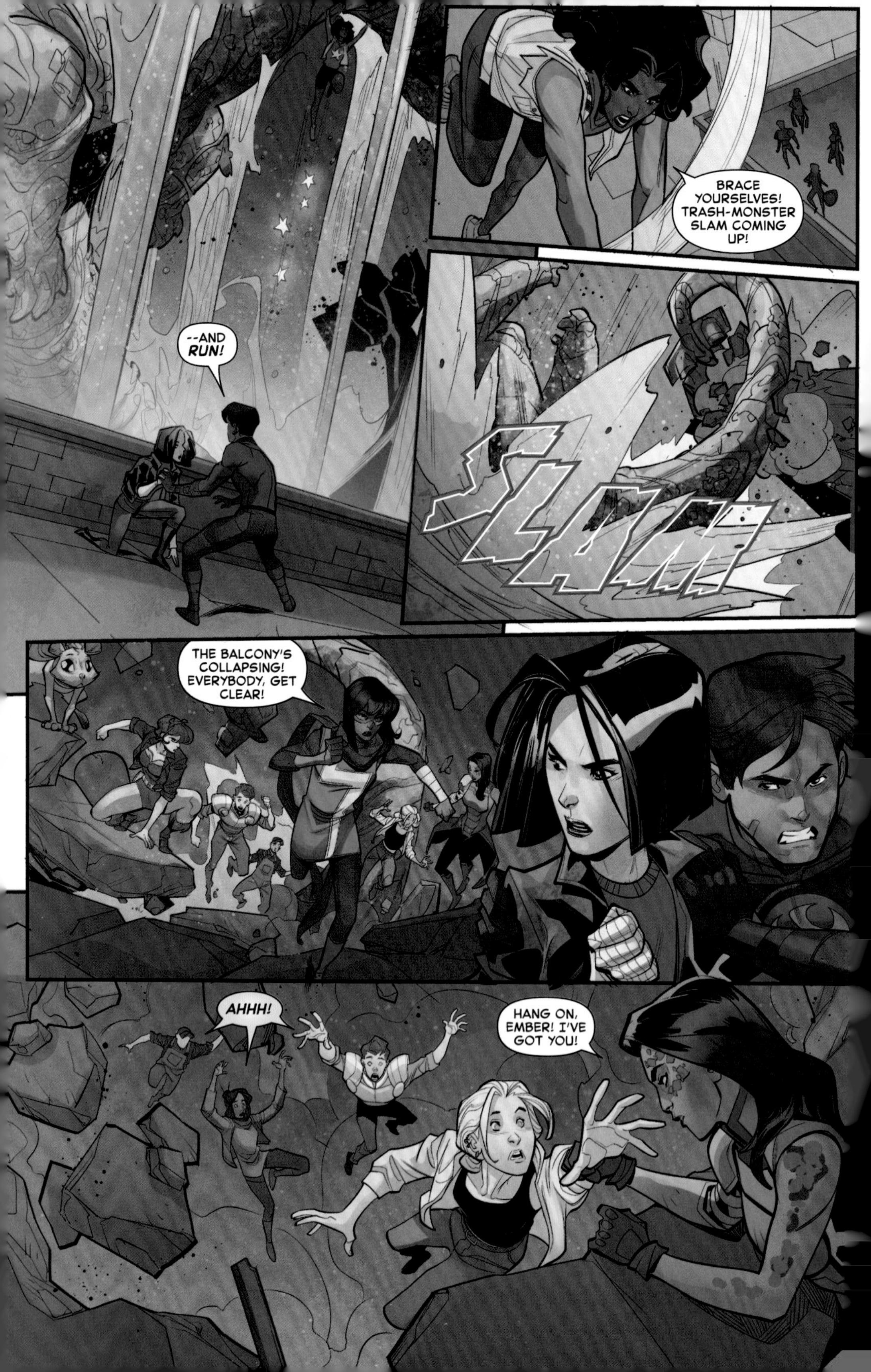
BRACE YOURSELVES! TRASH-MONSTER SLAM COMING UP!
--AND RUN!
SLAM
THE BALCONY'S COLLAPSING! EVERYBODY, GET CLEAR!
AHHH!
HANG ON, EMBER! I'VE GOT YOU!

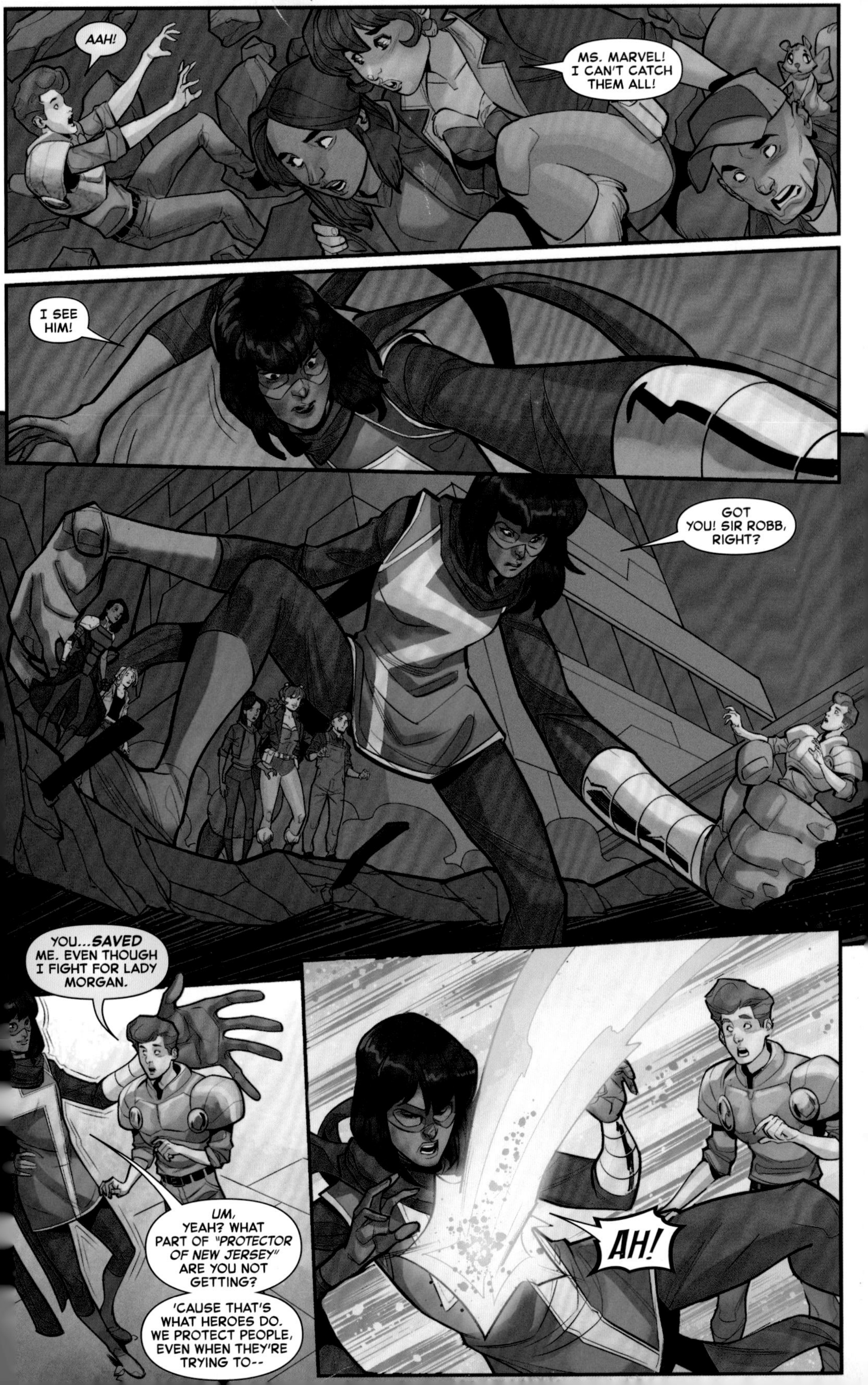
AAH!
MS. MARVEL! I CAN'T CATCH THEM ALL!
I SEE HIM!
GOT YOU! SIR ROBB, RIGHT?
YOU...*SAVED* ME. EVEN THOUGH I FIGHT FOR LADY MORGAN.
UM, YEAH? WHAT PART OF *"PROTECTOR OF NEW JERSEY"* ARE YOU NOT GETTING?
'CAUSE THAT'S WHAT HEROES DO. WE PROTECT PEOPLE, EVEN WHEN THEY'RE TRYING TO--
AH!

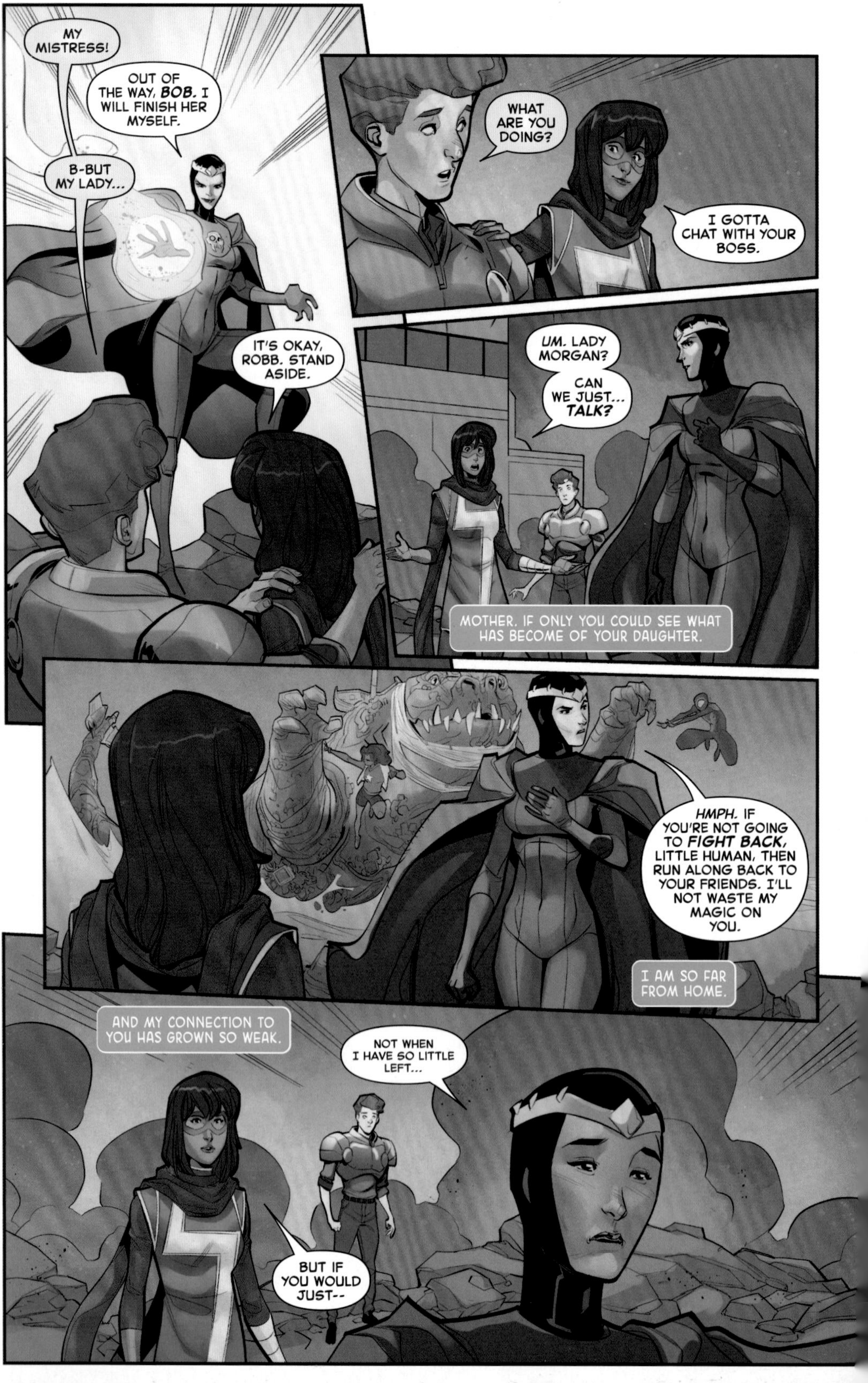
MY MISTRESS!
OUT OF THE WAY, BOB. I WILL FINISH HER MYSELF.
B-BUT MY LADY...
IT'S OKAY, ROBB. STAND ASIDE.
WHAT ARE YOU DOING?
I GOTTA CHAT WITH YOUR BOSS.
UM. LADY MORGAN?
CAN WE JUST... TALK?
MOTHER. IF ONLY YOU COULD SEE WHAT HAS BECOME OF YOUR DAUGHTER.
HMPH. IF YOU'RE NOT GOING TO FIGHT BACK, LITTLE HUMAN, THEN RUN ALONG BACK TO YOUR FRIENDS. I'LL NOT WASTE MY MAGIC ON YOU.
I AM SO FAR FROM HOME.
AND MY CONNECTION TO YOU HAS GROWN SO WEAK.
NOT WHEN I HAVE SO LITTLE LEFT...
BUT IF YOU WOULD JUST--

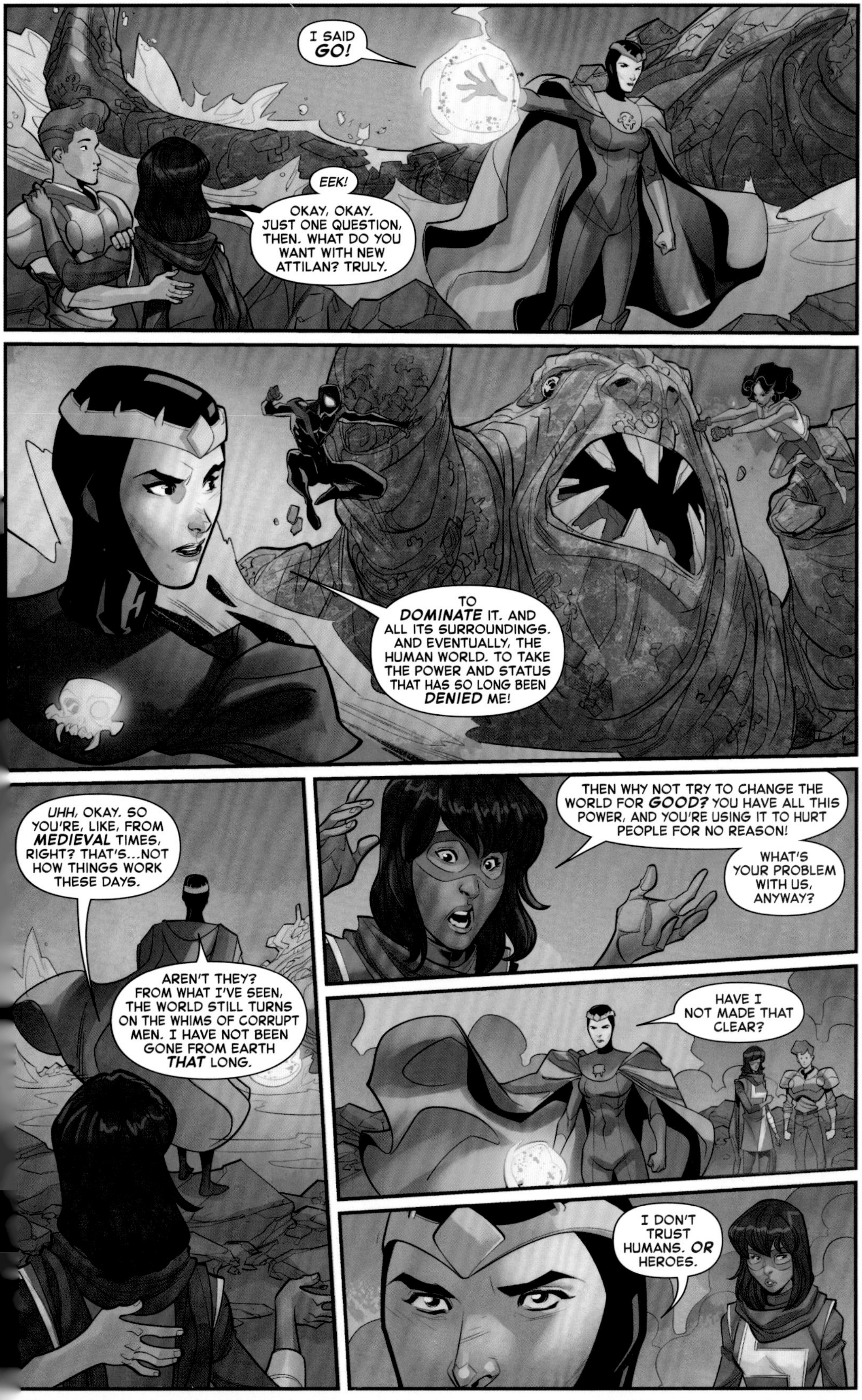
I SAID *GO!*
EEK!
OKAY, OKAY. JUST ONE QUESTION, THEN. WHAT DO YOU WANT WITH NEW ATTILAN? TRULY.
TO *DOMINATE* IT. AND ALL ITS SURROUNDINGS. AND EVENTUALLY, THE HUMAN WORLD. TO TAKE THE POWER AND STATUS THAT HAS SO LONG BEEN *DENIED* ME!
UHH, OKAY. SO YOU'RE, LIKE, FROM *MEDIEVAL* TIMES, RIGHT? THAT'S...NOT HOW THINGS WORK THESE DAYS.
AREN'T THEY? FROM WHAT I'VE SEEN, THE WORLD STILL TURNS ON THE WHIMS OF CORRUPT MEN. I HAVE NOT BEEN GONE FROM EARTH *THAT* LONG.
THEN WHY NOT TRY TO CHANGE THE WORLD FOR *GOOD?* YOU HAVE ALL THIS POWER, AND YOU'RE USING IT TO HURT PEOPLE FOR NO REASON!
WHAT'S YOUR PROBLEM WITH US, ANYWAY?
HAVE I NOT MADE THAT CLEAR?
I DON'T TRUST HUMANS. *OR* HEROES.

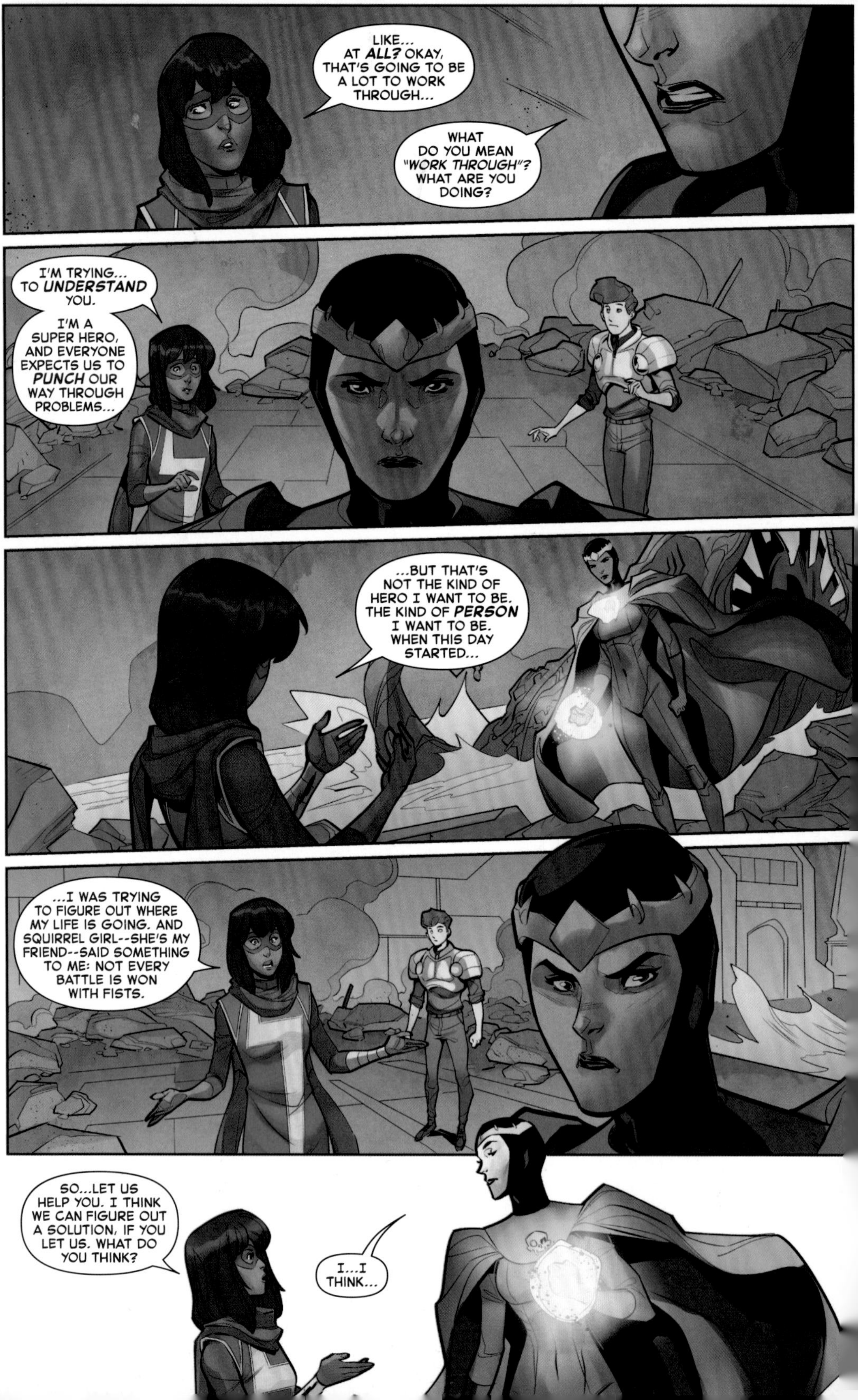
LIKE... AT ALL? OKAY, THAT'S GOING TO BE A LOT TO WORK THROUGH...
WHAT DO YOU MEAN "WORK THROUGH"? WHAT ARE YOU DOING?
I'M TRYING... TO UNDERSTAND YOU.
I'M A SUPER HERO, AND EVERYONE EXPECTS US TO PUNCH OUR WAY THROUGH PROBLEMS...
...BUT THAT'S NOT THE KIND OF HERO I WANT TO BE. THE KIND OF PERSON I WANT TO BE. WHEN THIS DAY STARTED...
...I WAS TRYING TO FIGURE OUT WHERE MY LIFE IS GOING. AND SQUIRREL GIRL--SHE'S MY FRIEND--SAID SOMETHING TO ME: NOT EVERY BATTLE IS WON WITH FISTS.
SO...LET US HELP YOU. I THINK WE CAN FIGURE OUT A SOLUTION, IF YOU LET US. WHAT DO YOU THINK?
I...I THINK...

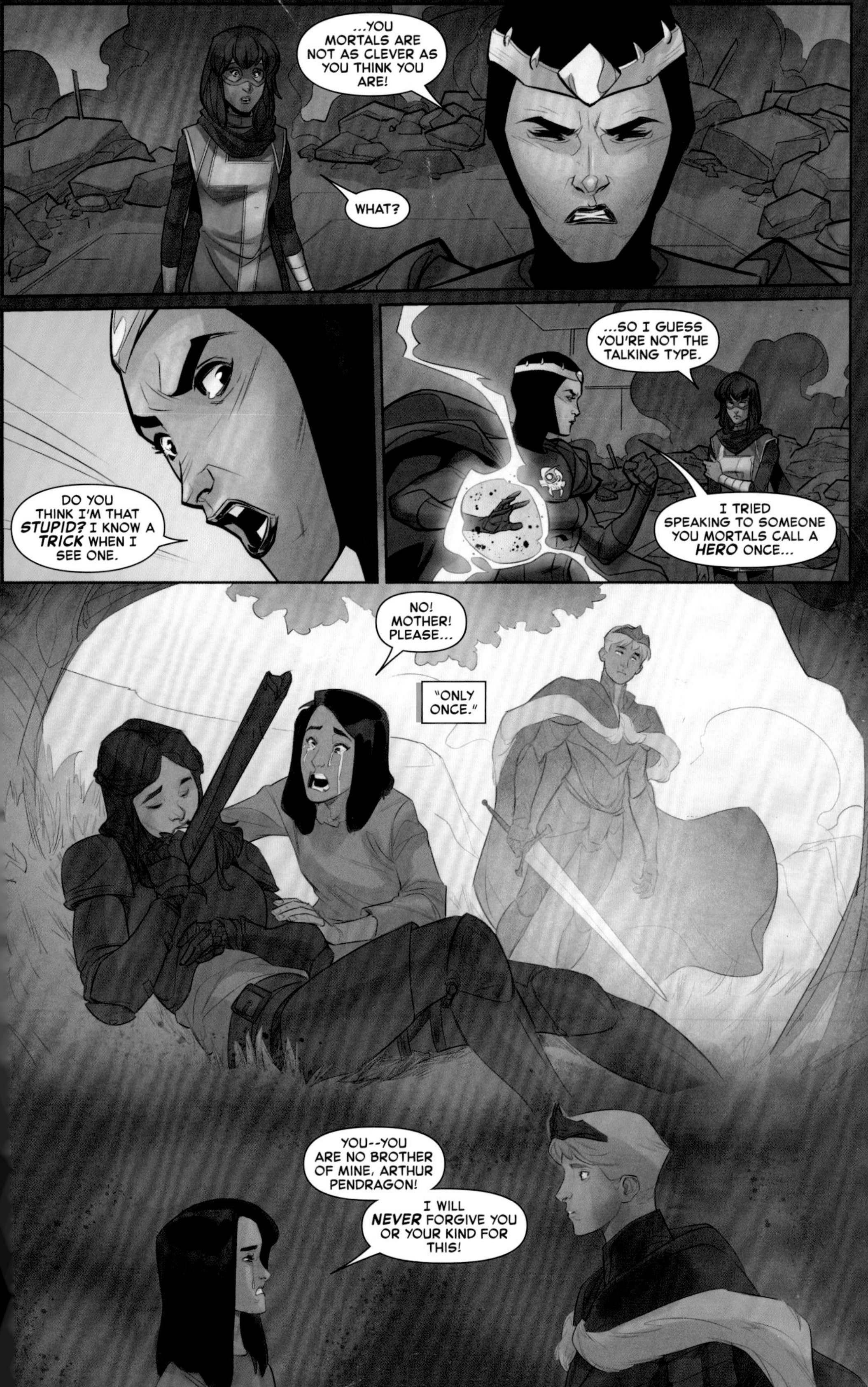
...YOU MORTALS ARE NOT AS CLEVER AS YOU THINK YOU ARE!
WHAT?
DO YOU THINK I'M THAT STUPID? I KNOW A TRICK WHEN I SEE ONE.
...SO I GUESS YOU'RE NOT THE TALKING TYPE.
I TRIED SPEAKING TO SOMEONE YOU MORTALS CALL A HERO ONCE...
NO! MOTHER! PLEASE...
"ONLY ONCE."
YOU--YOU ARE NO BROTHER OF MINE, ARTHUR PENDRAGON!
I WILL NEVER FORGIVE YOU OR YOUR KIND FOR THIS!

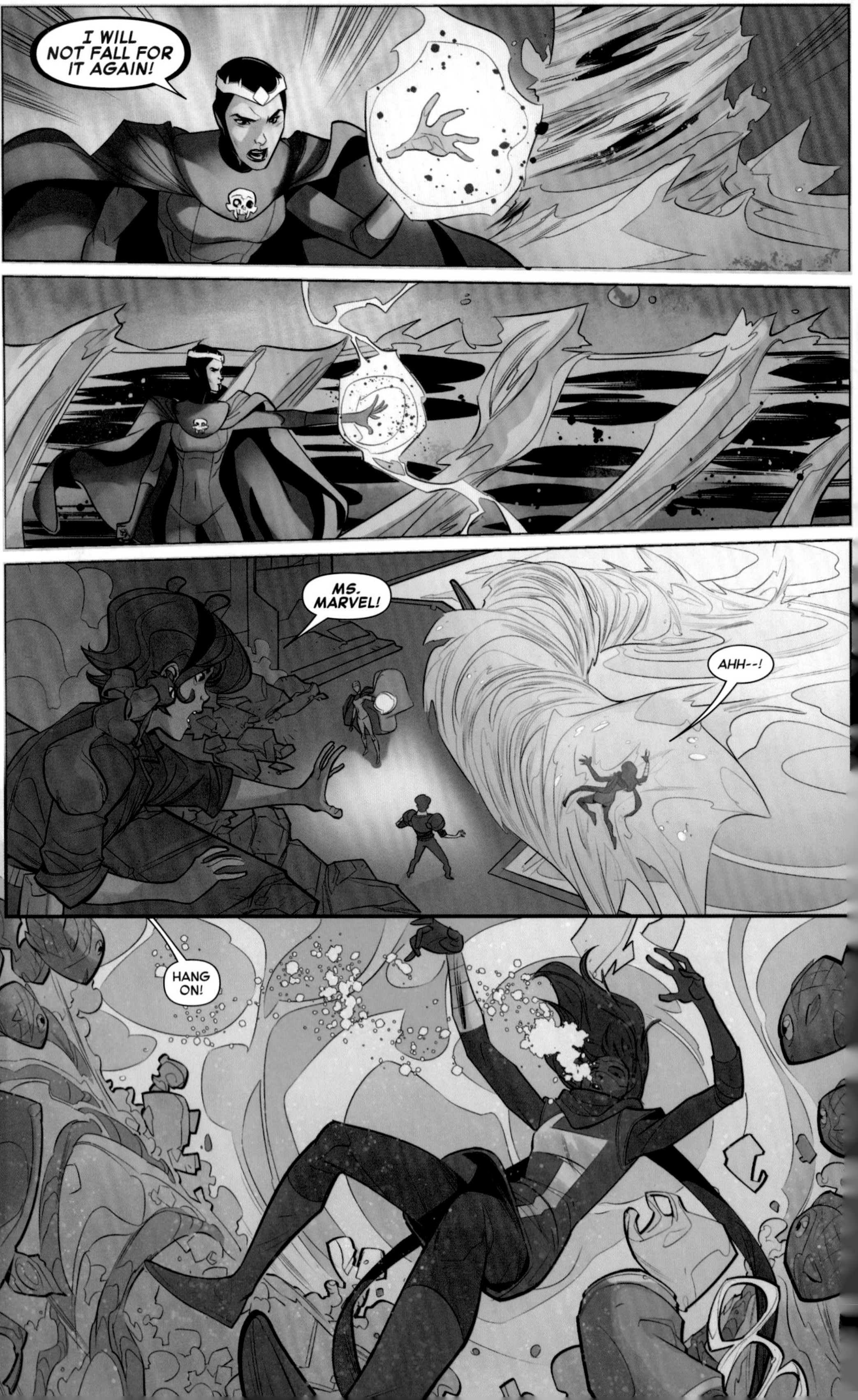
I WILL NOT FALL FOR IT AGAIN!
MS. MARVEL!
AHH--!
HANG ON!

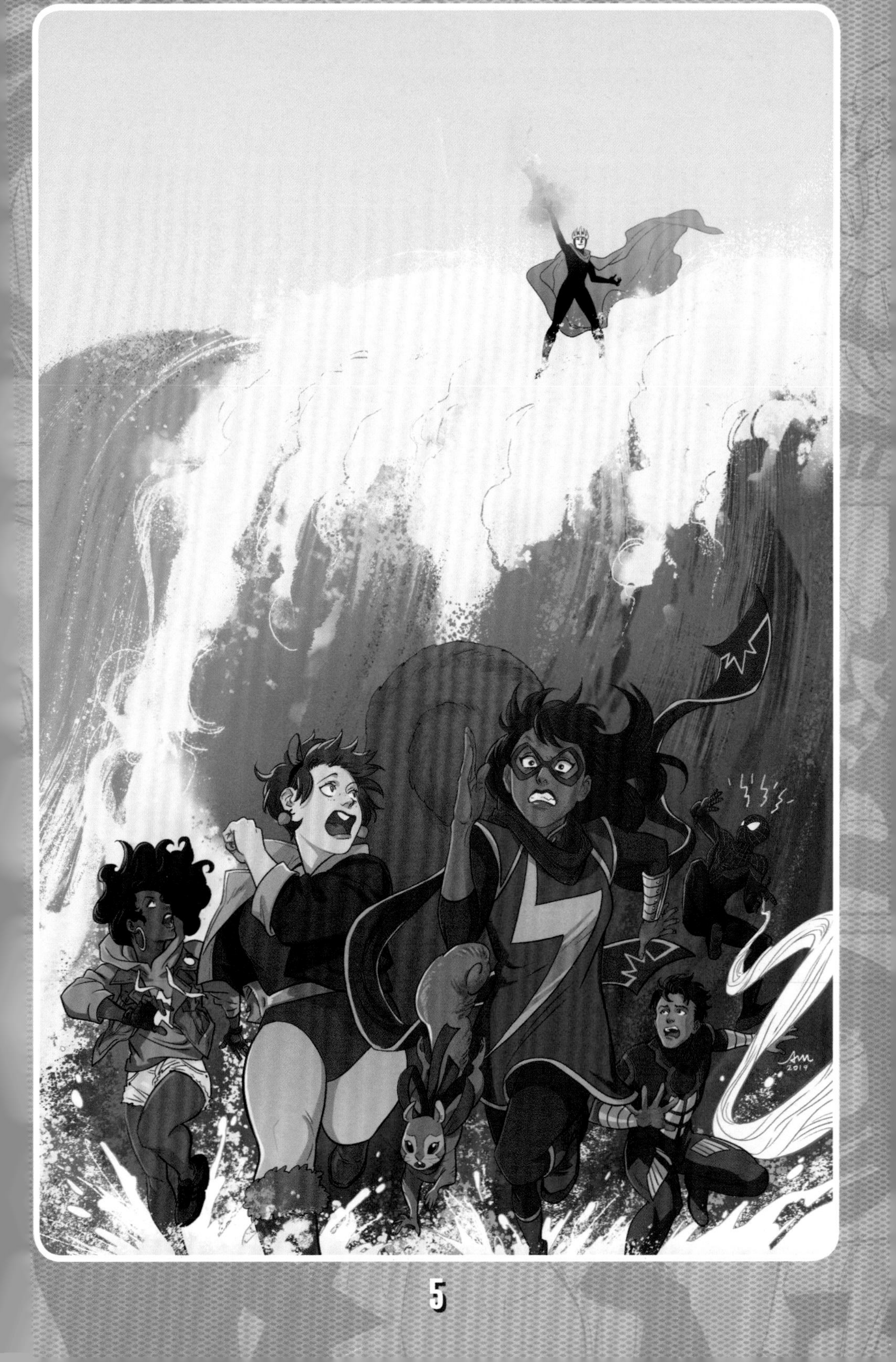

5

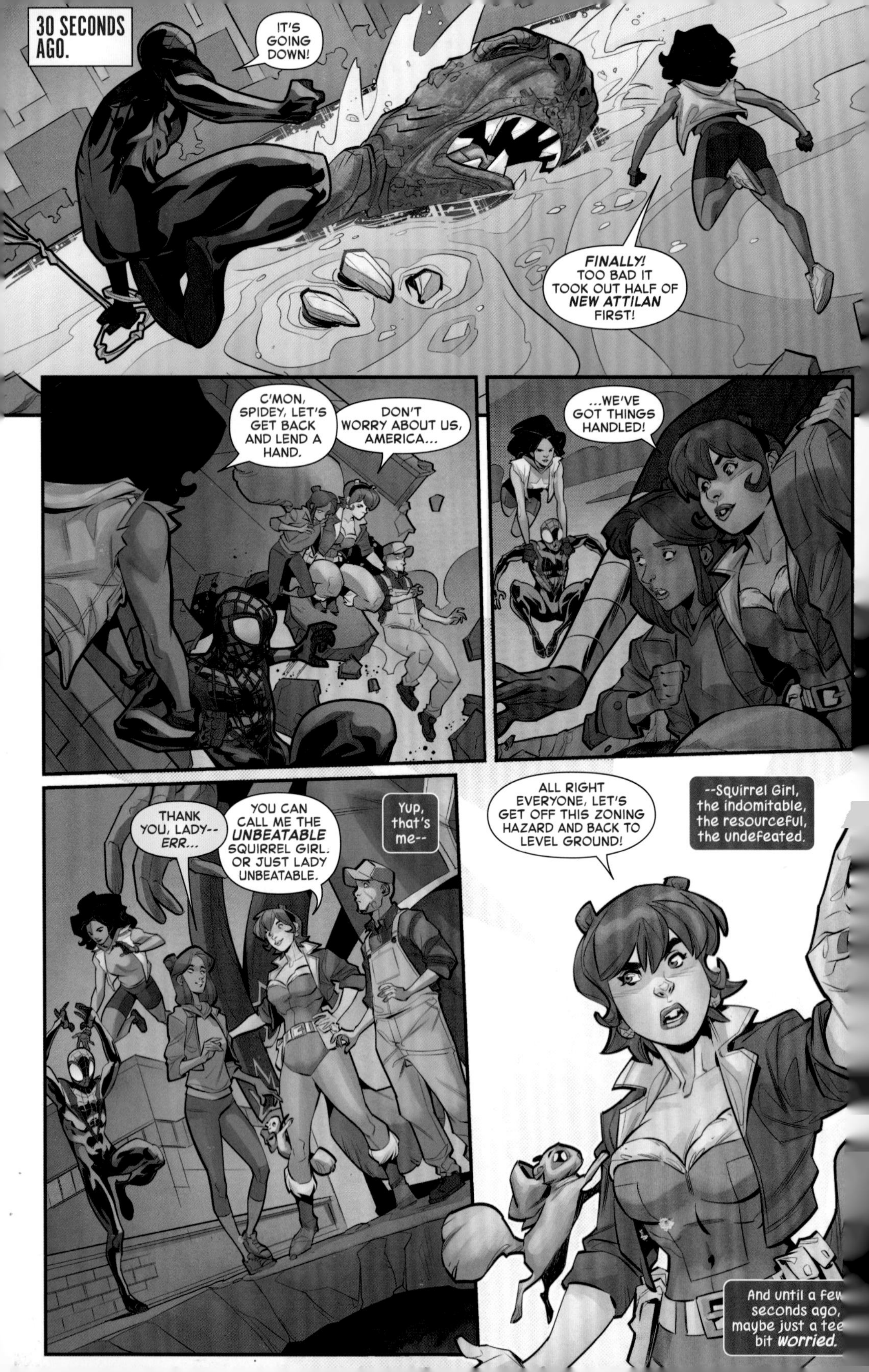
30 SECONDS AGO.
IT'S GOING DOWN!
FINALLY! TOO BAD IT TOOK OUT HALF OF NEW ATTILAN FIRST!
C'MON, SPIDEY, LET'S GET BACK AND LEND A HAND.
DON'T WORRY ABOUT US, AMERICA...
...WE'VE GOT THINGS HANDLED!
THANK YOU, LADY-- ERR...
YOU CAN CALL ME THE UNBEATABLE SQUIRREL GIRL. OR JUST LADY UNBEATABLE.
Yup, that's me--
ALL RIGHT EVERYONE, LET'S GET OFF THIS ZONING HAZARD AND BACK TO LEVEL GROUND!
--Squirrel Girl, the indomitable, the resourceful, the undefeated.
And until a few seconds ago, maybe just a tee bit worried.

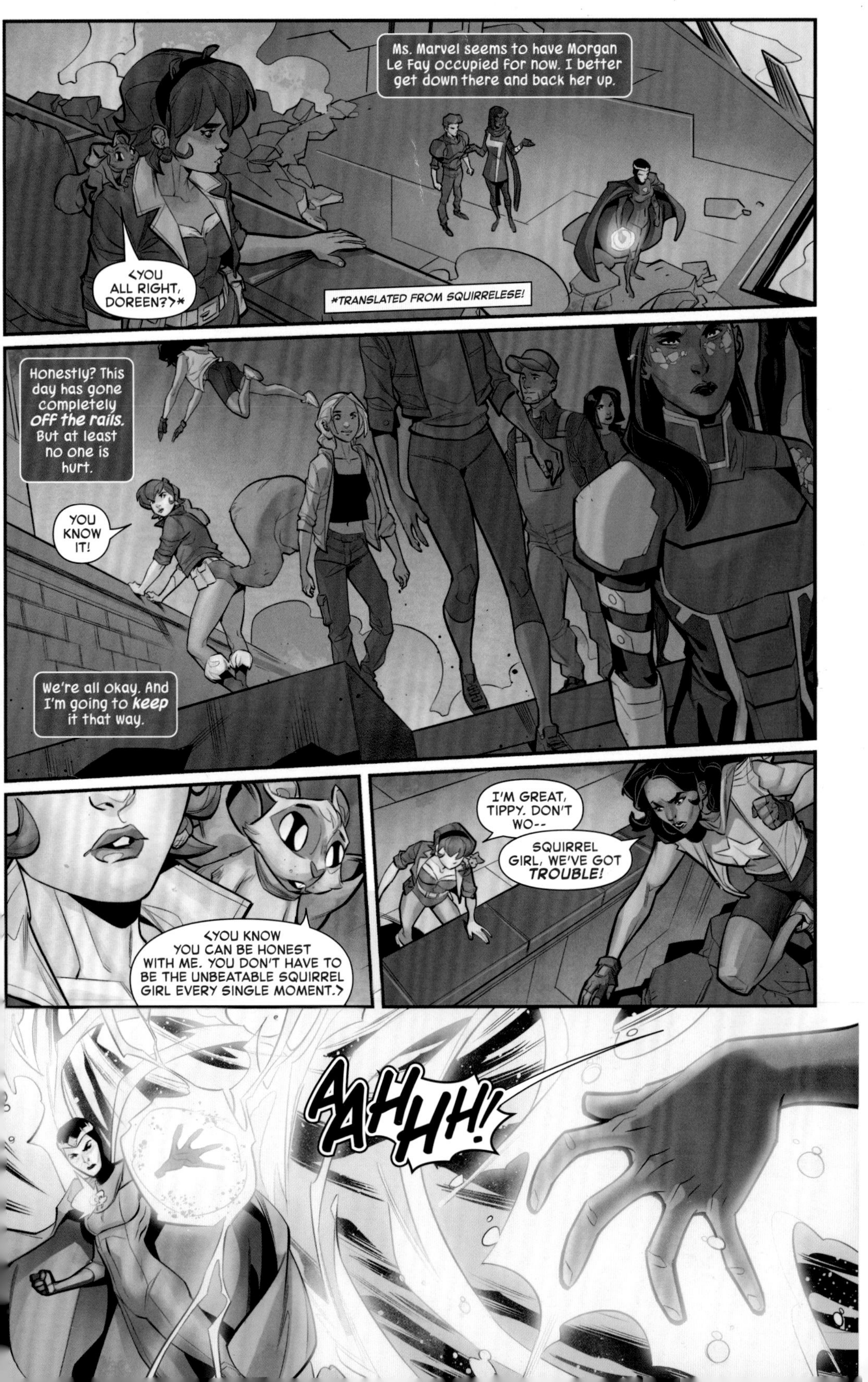
Ms. Marvel seems to have Morgan Le Fay occupied for now. I better get down there and back her up.
<YOU ALL RIGHT, DOREEN?>*
*TRANSLATED FROM SQUIRRELESE!
Honestly? This day has gone completely off the rails. But at least no one is hurt.
YOU KNOW IT!
We're all okay. And I'm going to keep it that way.
<YOU KNOW YOU CAN BE HONEST WITH ME. YOU DON'T HAVE TO BE THE UNBEATABLE SQUIRREL GIRL EVERY SINGLE MOMENT.>
I'M GREAT, TIPPY. DON'T WO--
SQUIRREL GIRL, WE'VE GOT TROUBLE!
AAHHH!

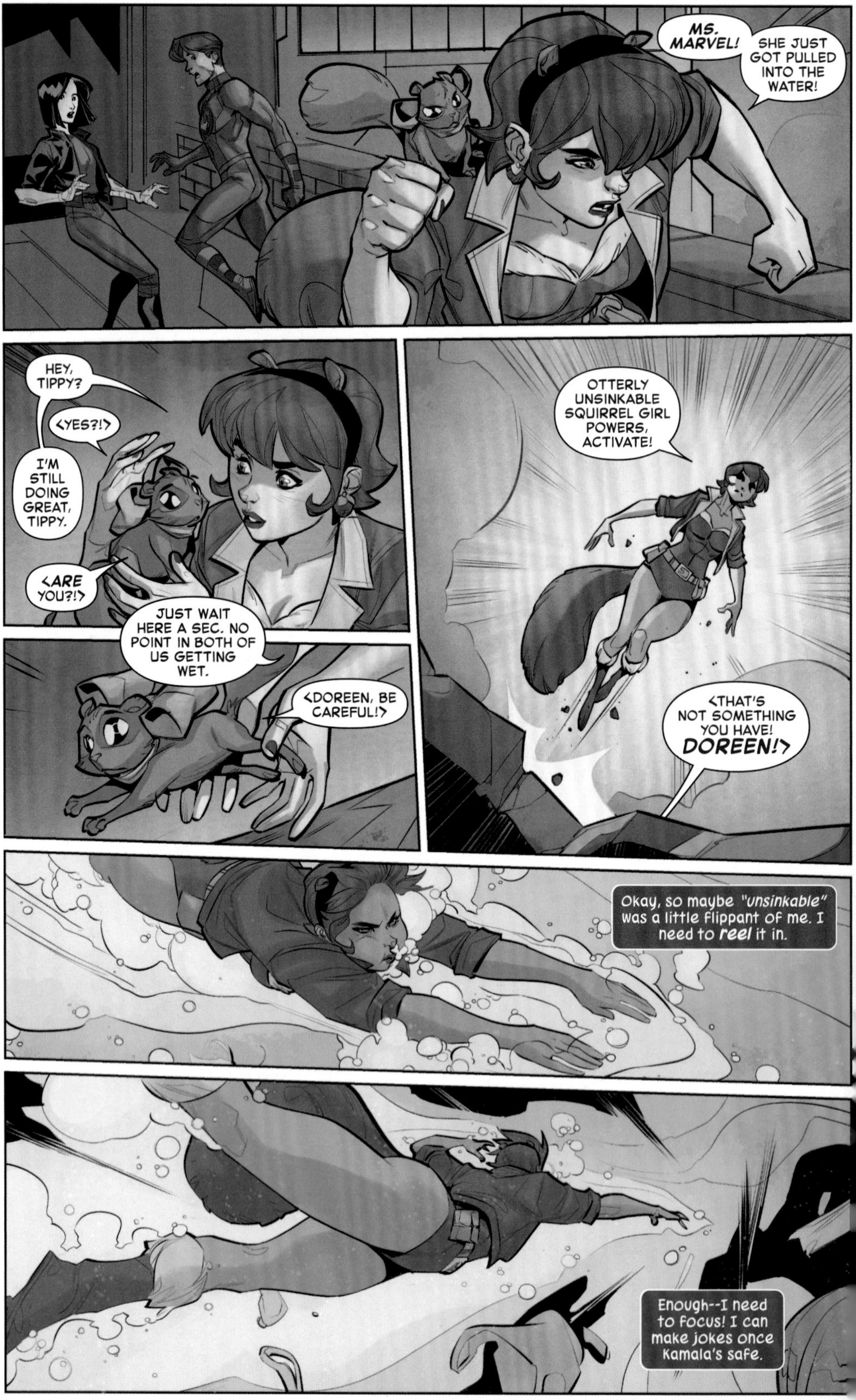

MS. MARVEL!
SHE JUST GOT PULLED INTO THE WATER!
HEY, TIPPY?
<YES?!>
I'M STILL DOING GREAT, TIPPY.
<ARE YOU?!>
JUST WAIT HERE A SEC. NO POINT IN BOTH OF US GETTING WET.
<DOREEN, BE CAREFUL!>
OTTERLY UNSINKABLE SQUIRREL GIRL POWERS, ACTIVATE!
<THAT'S NOT SOMETHING YOU HAVE! DOREEN!>
Okay, so maybe "unsinkable" was a little flippant of me. I need to reel it in.
Enough--I need to focus! I can make jokes once Kamala's safe.

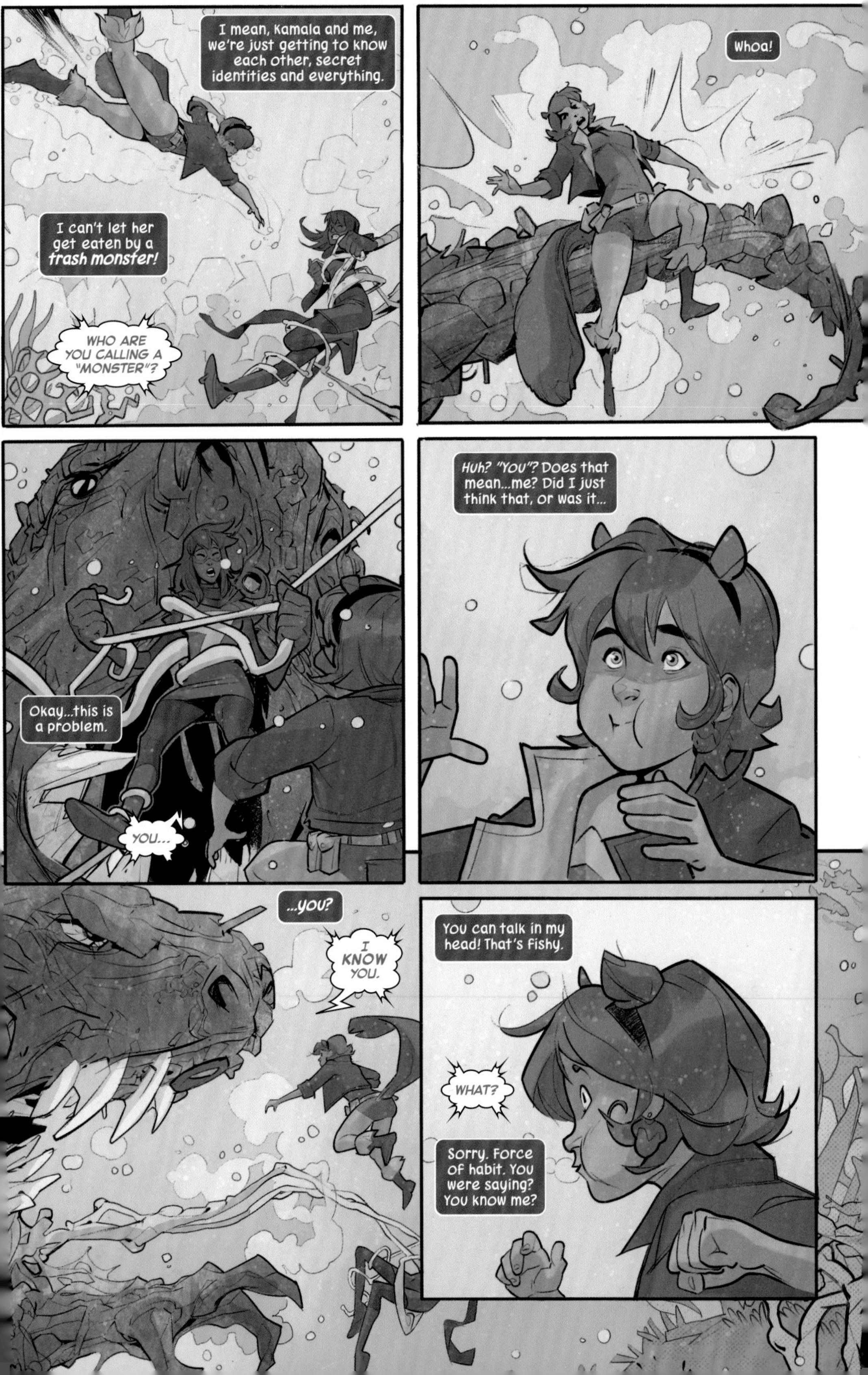

I mean, Kamala and me, we're just getting to know each other, secret identities and everything.
I can't let her get eaten by a trash monster!
WHO ARE YOU CALLING A "MONSTER"?
Whoa!
Okay...this is a problem.
YOU...
Huh? "YOU"? Does that mean...me? Did I just think that, or was it...
...YOU?
I KNOW YOU.
You can talk in my head! That's fishy.
WHAT?
Sorry. Force of habit. You were saying? You know me?

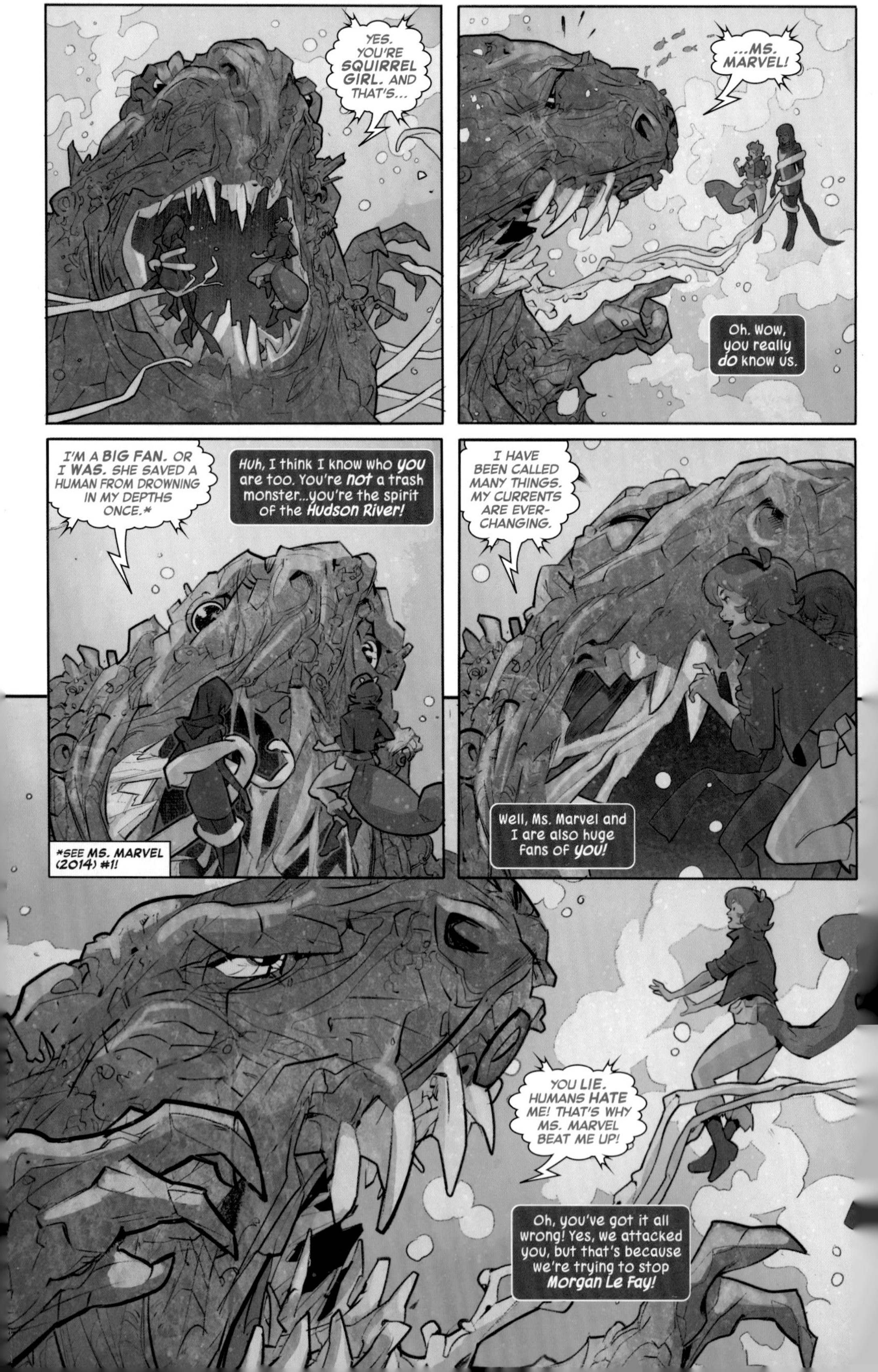
YES. YOU'RE SQUIRREL GIRL. AND THAT'S...
...MS. MARVEL!
Oh. Wow, you really do know us.
I'M A BIG FAN. OR I WAS. SHE SAVED A HUMAN FROM DROWNING IN MY DEPTHS ONCE.*
Huh, I think I know who you are too. You're not a trash monster...you're the spirit of the Hudson River!
*SEE MS. MARVEL (2014) #1!
I HAVE BEEN CALLED MANY THINGS. MY CURRENTS ARE EVER-CHANGING.
Well, Ms. Marvel and I are also huge fans of you!
YOU LIE. HUMANS HATE ME! THAT'S WHY MS. MARVEL BEAT ME UP!
Oh, you've got it all wrong! Yes, we attacked you, but that's because we're trying to stop Morgan Le Fay!

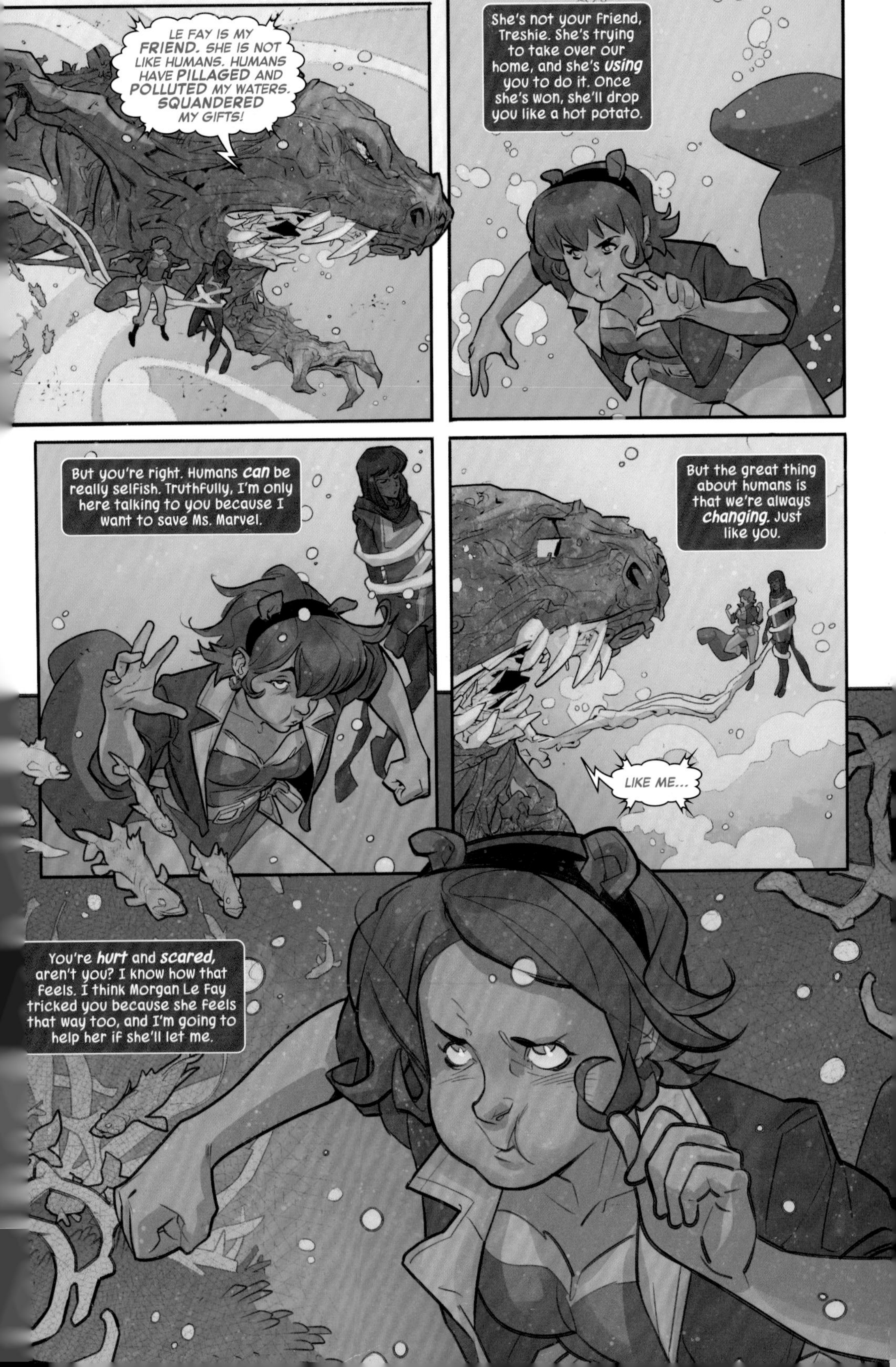
LE FAY IS MY FRIEND. SHE IS NOT LIKE HUMANS. HUMANS HAVE PILLAGED AND POLLUTED MY WATERS. SQUANDERED MY GIFTS!
She's not your friend, Treshie. She's trying to take over our home, and she's using you to do it. Once she's won, she'll drop you like a hot potato.
But you're right. Humans can be really selfish. Truthfully, I'm only here talking to you because I want to save Ms. Marvel.
But the great thing about humans is that we're always changing. Just like you.
LIKE ME...
You're hurt and scared, aren't you? I know how that feels. I think Morgan Le Fay tricked you because she feels that way too, and I'm going to help her if she'll let me.

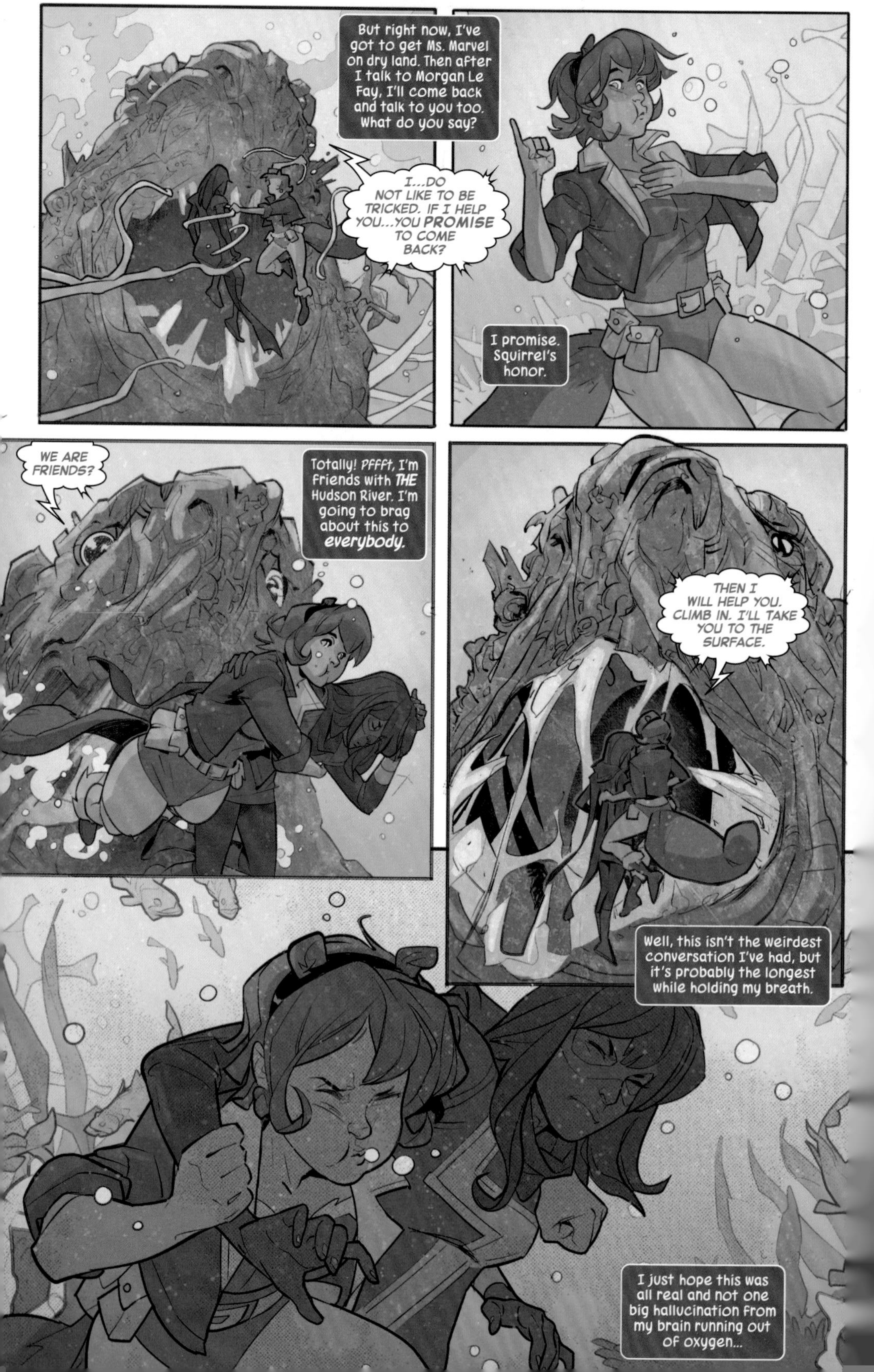
But right now, I've got to get Ms. Marvel on dry land. Then after I talk to Morgan Le Fay, I'll come back and talk to you too. What do you say?
I...DO NOT LIKE TO BE TRICKED. IF I HELP YOU...YOU PROMISE TO COME BACK?
I promise. Squirrel's honor.
WE ARE FRIENDS?
Totally! Pffft, I'm friends with THE Hudson River. I'm going to brag about this to everybody.
THEN I WILL HELP YOU. CLIMB IN. I'LL TAKE YOU TO THE SURFACE.
Well, this isn't the weirdest conversation I've had, but it's probably the longest while holding my breath.
I just hope this was all real and not one big hallucination from my brain running out of oxygen...

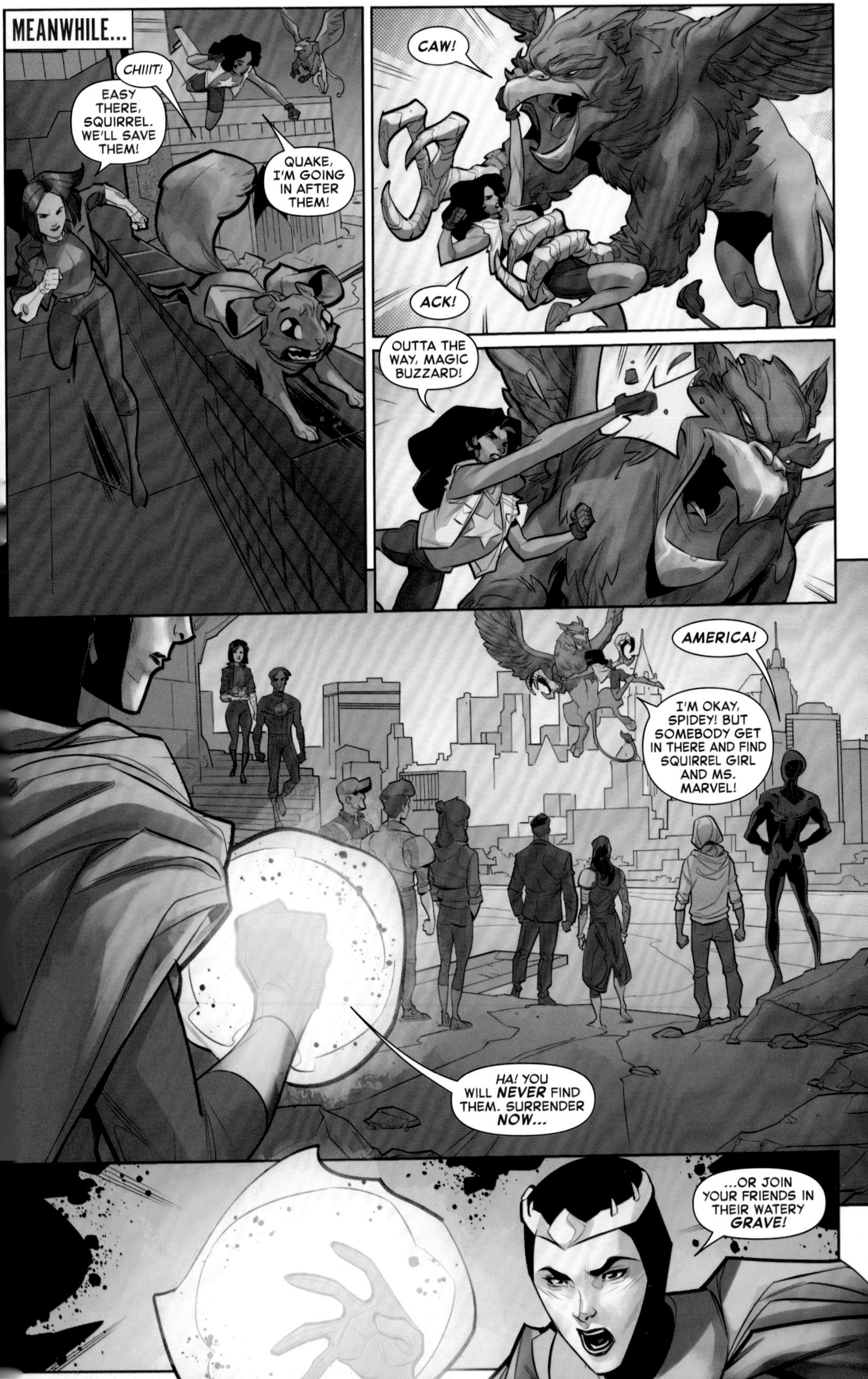
MEANWHILE...
CHIIIT!
EASY THERE, SQUIRREL. WE'LL SAVE THEM!
QUAKE, I'M GOING IN AFTER THEM!
CAW!
ACK!
OUTTA THE WAY, MAGIC BUZZARD!
AMERICA!
I'M OKAY, SPIDEY! BUT SOMEBODY GET IN THERE AND FIND SQUIRREL GIRL AND MS. MARVEL!
HA! YOU WILL NEVER FIND THEM. SURRENDER NOW...
...OR JOIN YOUR FRIENDS IN THEIR WATERY GRAVE!

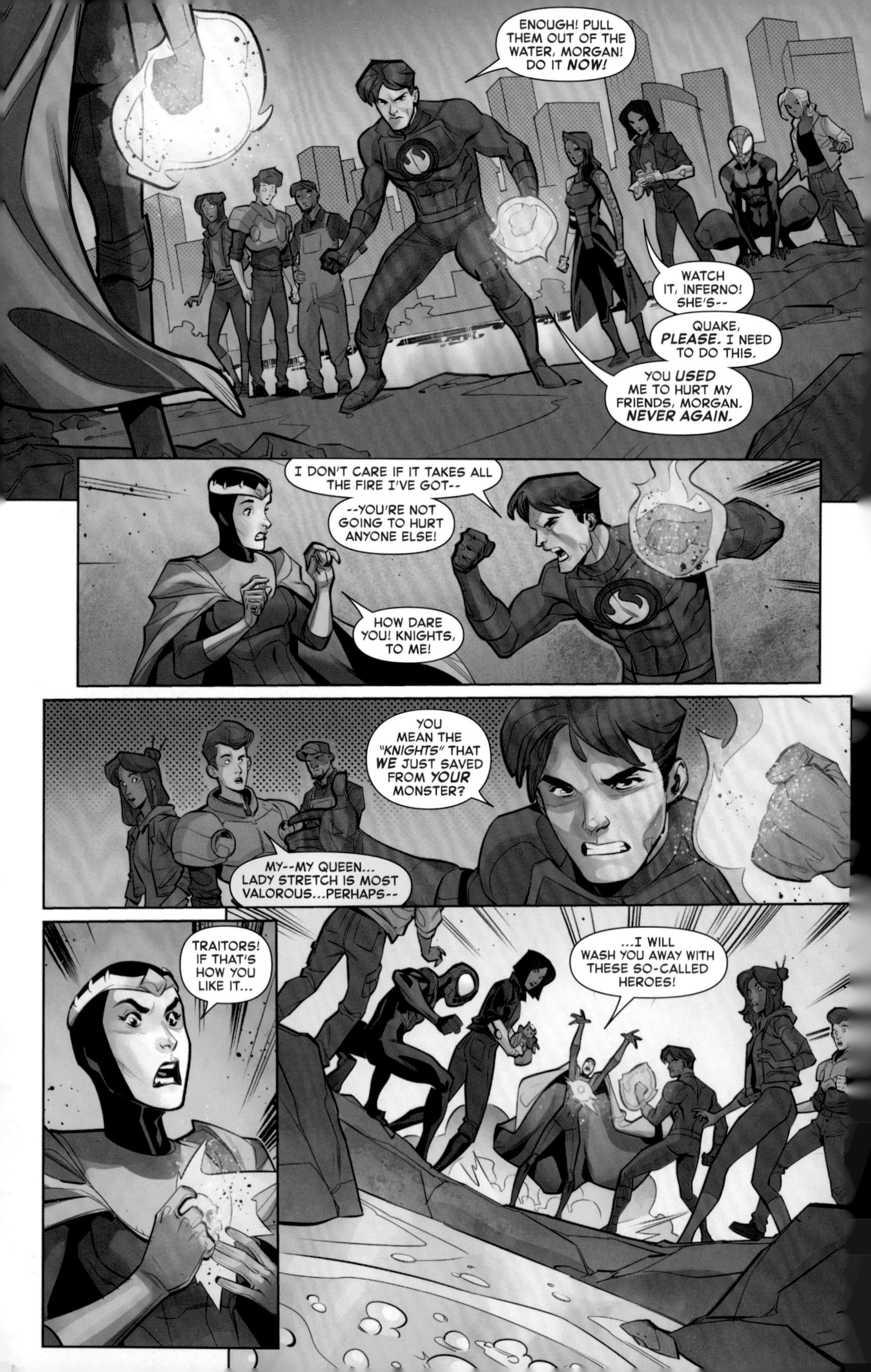
ENOUGH! PULL THEM OUT OF THE WATER, MORGAN! DO IT NOW!
WATCH IT, INFERNO! SHE'S--
QUAKE, PLEASE. I NEED TO DO THIS.
YOU USED ME TO HURT MY FRIENDS, MORGAN. NEVER AGAIN.
I DON'T CARE IF IT TAKES ALL THE FIRE I'VE GOT--
--YOU'RE NOT GOING TO HURT ANYONE ELSE!
HOW DARE YOU! KNIGHTS, TO ME!
YOU MEAN THE "KNIGHTS" THAT WE JUST SAVED FROM YOUR MONSTER?
MY--MY QUEEN... LADY STRETCH IS MOST VALOROUS...PERHAPS--
TRAITORS! IF THAT'S HOW YOU LIKE IT...
...I WILL WASH YOU AWAY WITH THESE SO-CALLED HEROES!

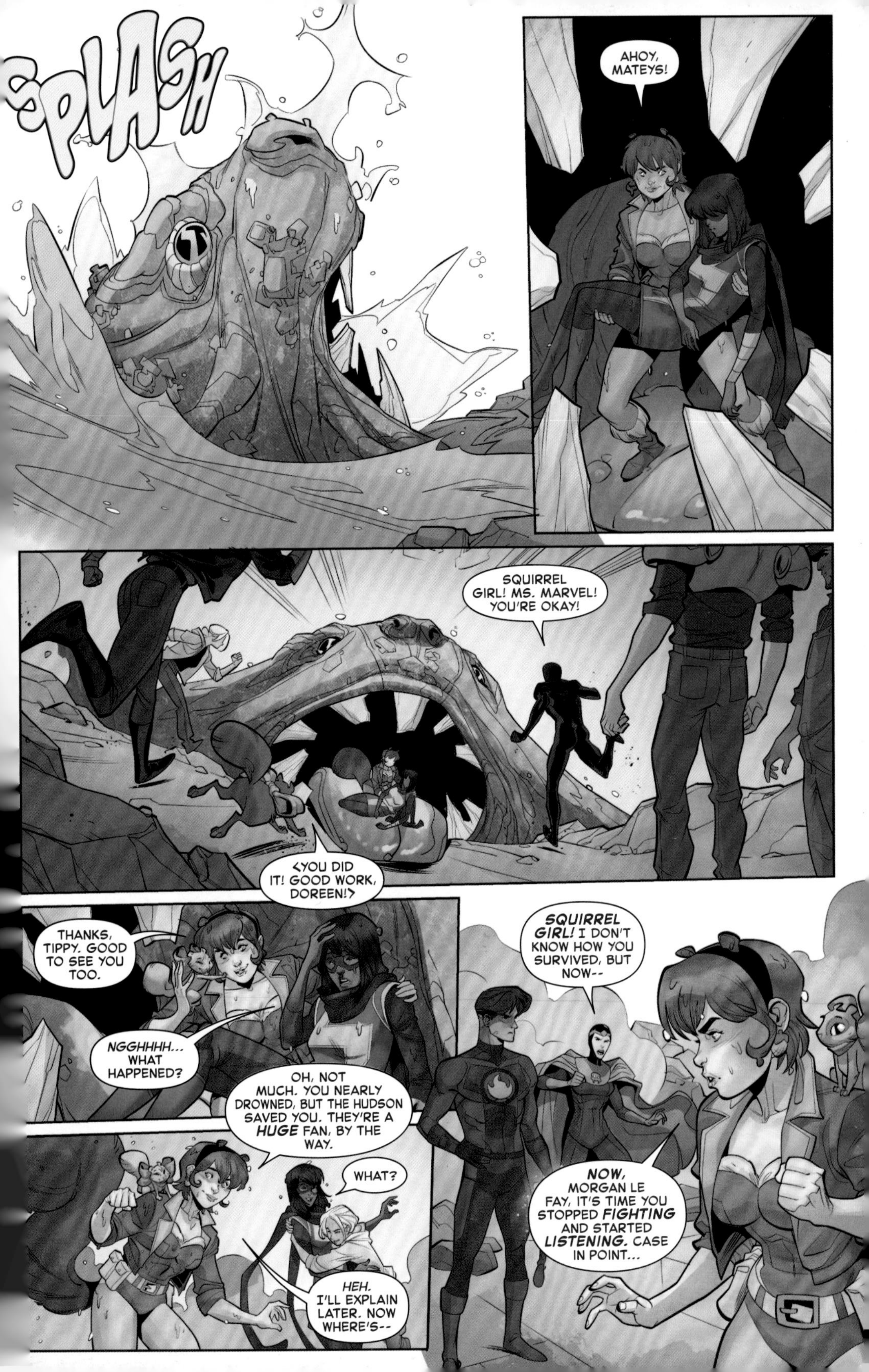
SPLASH
AHOY, MATEYS!
SQUIRREL GIRL! MS. MARVEL! YOU'RE OKAY!
<YOU DID IT! GOOD WORK, DOREEN!>
THANKS, TIPPY. GOOD TO SEE YOU TOO.
NGGHHHH... WHAT HAPPENED?
OH, NOT MUCH. YOU NEARLY DROWNED, BUT THE HUDSON SAVED YOU. THEY'RE A HUGE FAN, BY THE WAY.
WHAT?
HEH. I'LL EXPLAIN LATER. NOW WHERE'S--
SQUIRREL GIRL! I DON'T KNOW HOW YOU SURVIVED, BUT NOW--
NOW, MORGAN LE FAY, IT'S TIME YOU STOPPED FIGHTING AND STARTED LISTENING. CASE IN POINT...

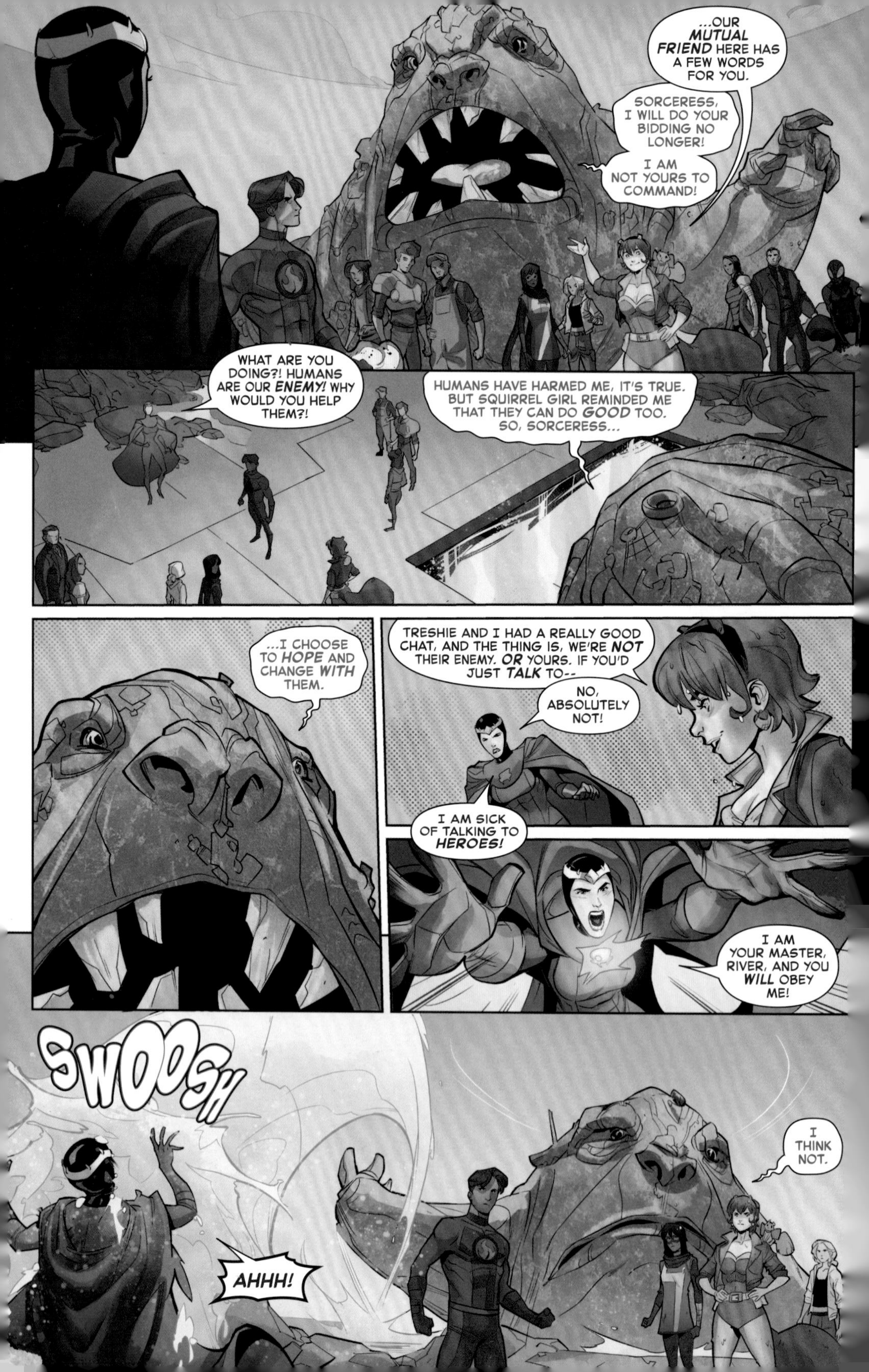
...OUR MUTUAL FRIEND HERE HAS A FEW WORDS FOR YOU.
SORCERESS, I WILL DO YOUR BIDDING NO LONGER!
I AM NOT YOURS TO COMMAND!
WHAT ARE YOU DOING?! HUMANS ARE OUR ENEMY! WHY WOULD YOU HELP THEM?!
HUMANS HAVE HARMED ME, IT'S TRUE. BUT SQUIRREL GIRL REMINDED ME THAT THEY CAN DO GOOD TOO. SO, SORCERESS...
...I CHOOSE TO HOPE AND CHANGE WITH THEM.
TRESHIE AND I HAD A REALLY GOOD CHAT, AND THE THING IS, WE'RE NOT THEIR ENEMY. OR YOURS. IF YOU'D JUST TALK TO--
NO, ABSOLUTELY NOT!
I AM SICK OF TALKING TO HEROES!
I AM YOUR MASTER, RIVER, AND YOU WILL OBEY ME!
SWOOSH
I THINK NOT.
AHHH!

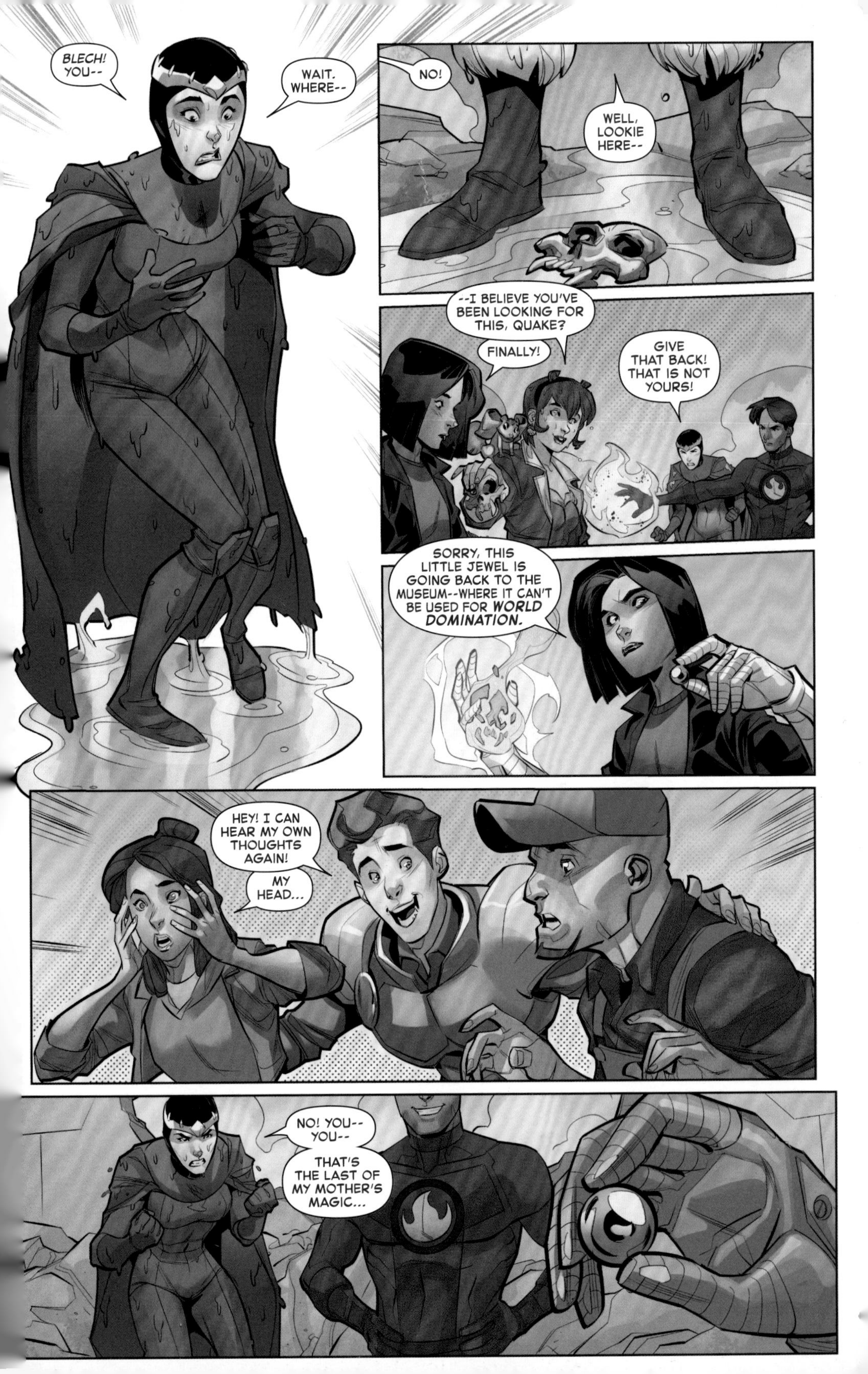
BLECH! YOU--
WAIT. WHERE--
NO!
WELL, LOOKIE HERE--
--I BELIEVE YOU'VE BEEN LOOKING FOR THIS, QUAKE?
FINALLY!
GIVE THAT BACK! THAT IS NOT YOURS!
SORRY, THIS LITTLE JEWEL IS GOING BACK TO THE MUSEUM--WHERE IT CAN'T BE USED FOR WORLD DOMINATION.
HEY! I CAN HEAR MY OWN THOUGHTS AGAIN!
MY HEAD...
NO! YOU-- YOU--
THAT'S THE LAST OF MY MOTHER'S MAGIC...

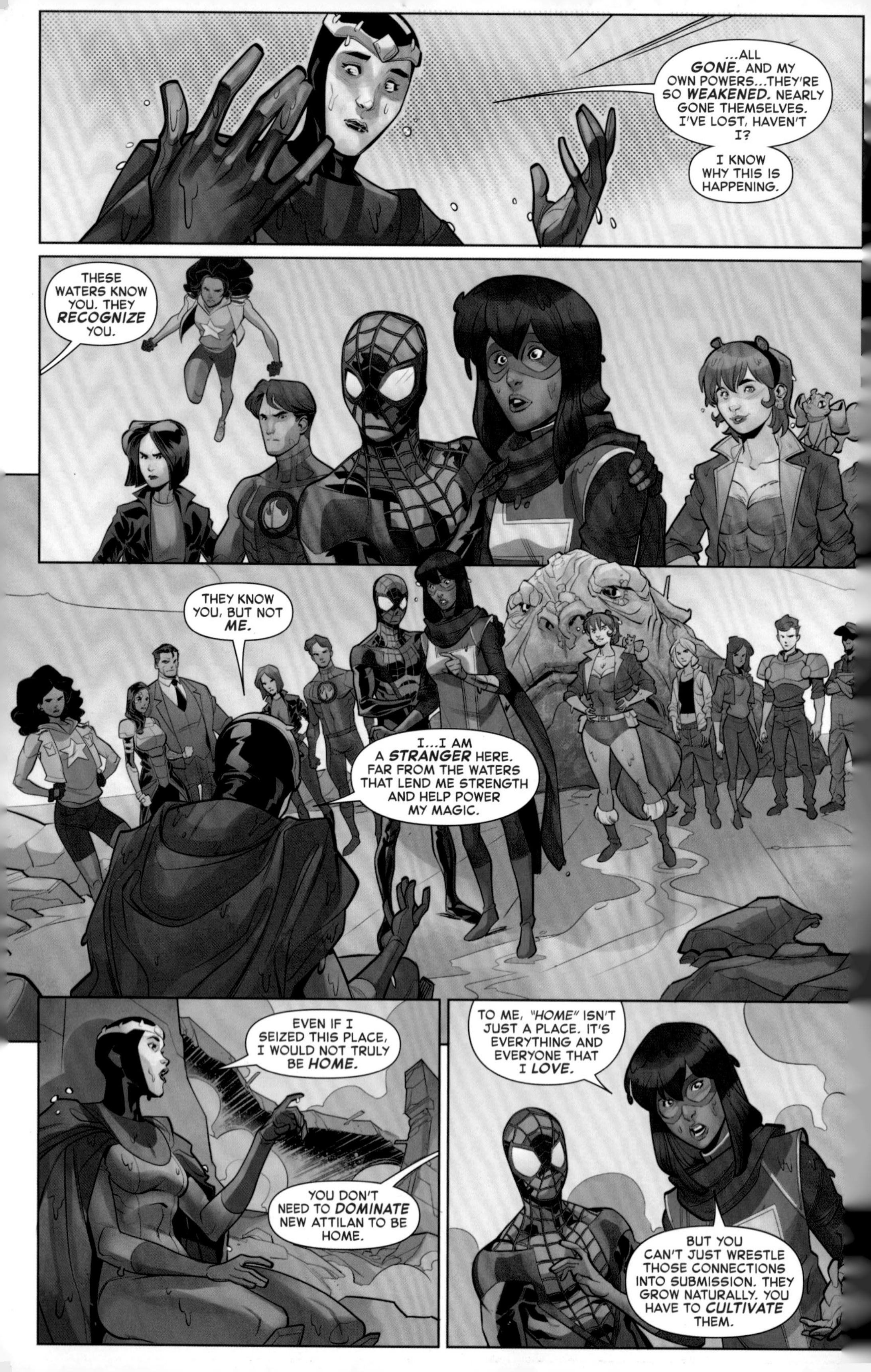
...ALL GONE. AND MY OWN POWERS...THEY'RE SO WEAKENED. NEARLY GONE THEMSELVES. I'VE LOST, HAVEN'T I?
I KNOW WHY THIS IS HAPPENING.
THESE WATERS KNOW YOU. THEY RECOGNIZE YOU.
THEY KNOW YOU, BUT NOT ME.
I...I AM A STRANGER HERE. FAR FROM THE WATERS THAT LEND ME STRENGTH AND HELP POWER MY MAGIC.
EVEN IF I SEIZED THIS PLACE, I WOULD NOT TRULY BE HOME.
YOU DON'T NEED TO DOMINATE NEW ATTILAN TO BE HOME.
TO ME, "HOME" ISN'T JUST A PLACE. IT'S EVERYTHING AND EVERYONE THAT I LOVE.
BUT YOU CAN'T JUST WRESTLE THOSE CONNECTIONS INTO SUBMISSION. THEY GROW NATURALLY. YOU HAVE TO CULTIVATE THEM.

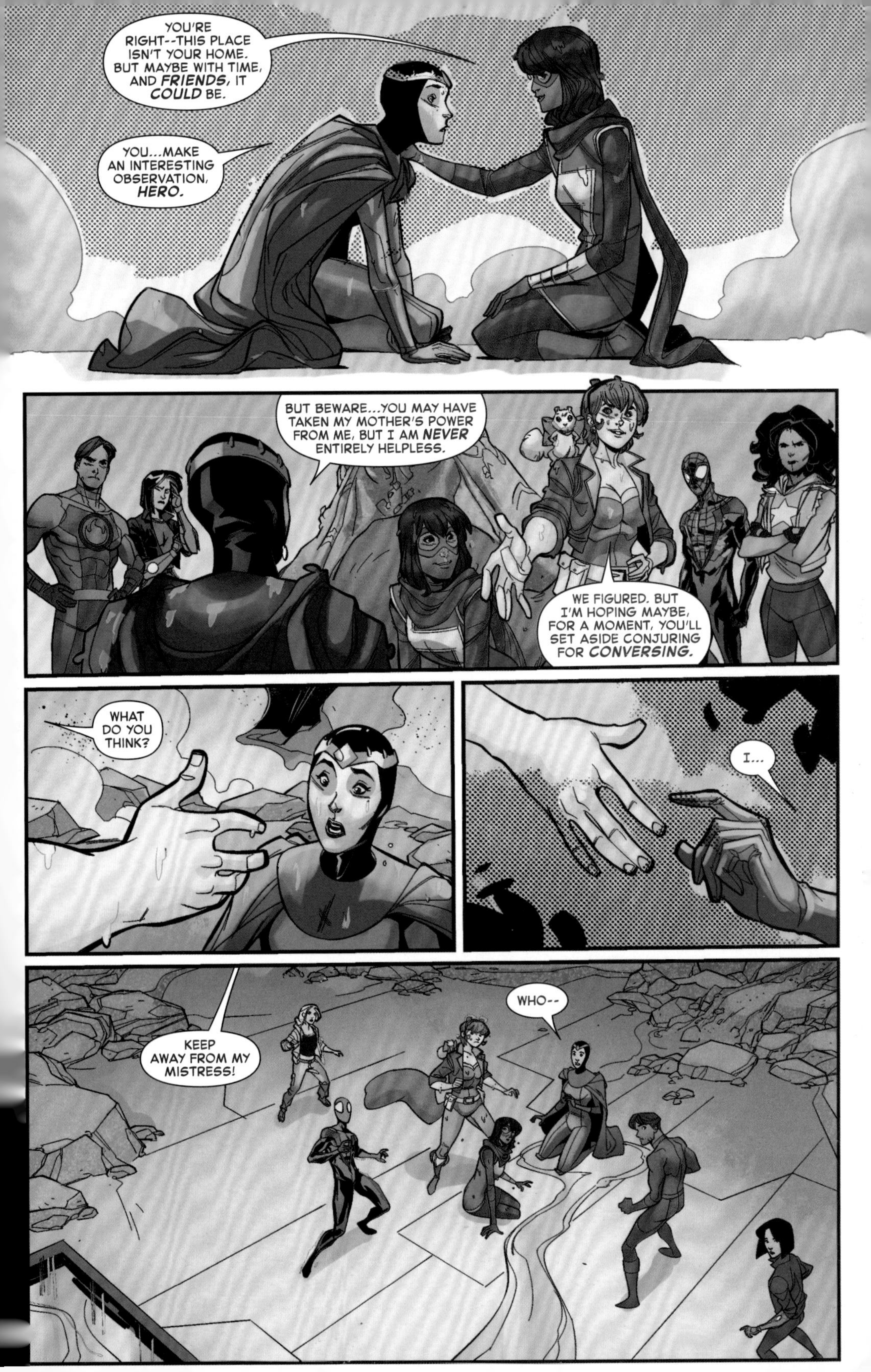
YOU'RE RIGHT--THIS PLACE ISN'T YOUR HOME. BUT MAYBE WITH TIME, AND FRIENDS, IT COULD BE.
YOU...MAKE AN INTERESTING OBSERVATION, HERO.
BUT BEWARE...YOU MAY HAVE TAKEN MY MOTHER'S POWER FROM ME, BUT I AM NEVER ENTIRELY HELPLESS.
WE FIGURED. BUT I'M HOPING MAYBE, FOR A MOMENT, YOU'LL SET ASIDE CONJURING FOR CONVERSING.
WHAT DO YOU THINK?
I...
KEEP AWAY FROM MY MISTRESS!
WHO--

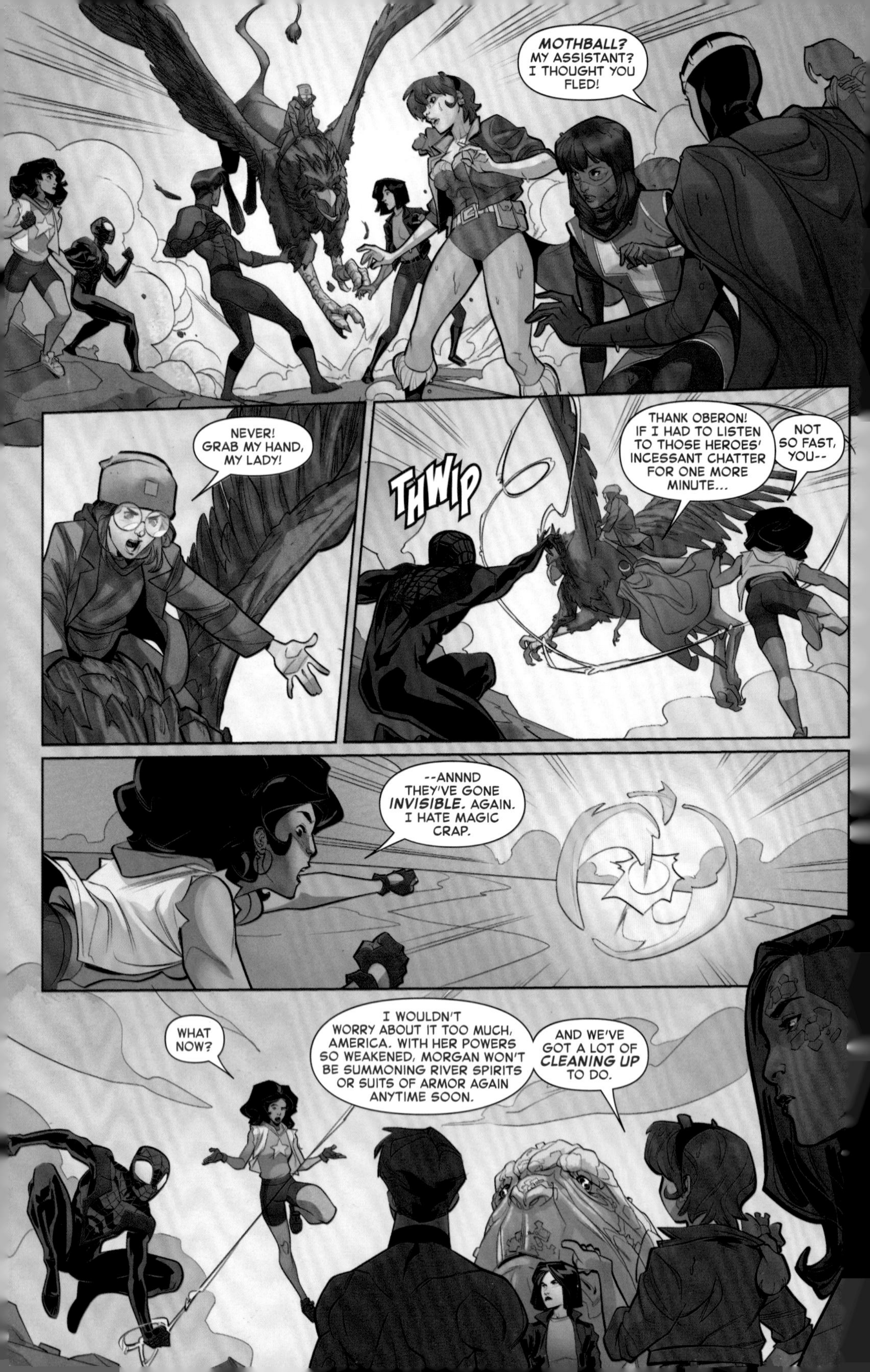

MOTHBALL? MY ASSISTANT? I THOUGHT YOU FLED!
NEVER! GRAB MY HAND, MY LADY!
THWIP
THANK OBERON! IF I HAD TO LISTEN TO THOSE HEROES' INCESSANT CHATTER FOR ONE MORE MINUTE...
NOT SO FAST, YOU--
--ANNND THEY'VE GONE INVISIBLE. AGAIN. I HATE MAGIC CRAP.
WHAT NOW?
I WOULDN'T WORRY ABOUT IT TOO MUCH, AMERICA. WITH HER POWERS SO WEAKENED, MORGAN WON'T BE SUMMONING RIVER SPIRITS OR SUITS OF ARMOR AGAIN ANYTIME SOON.
AND WE'VE GOT A LOT OF CLEANING UP TO DO.

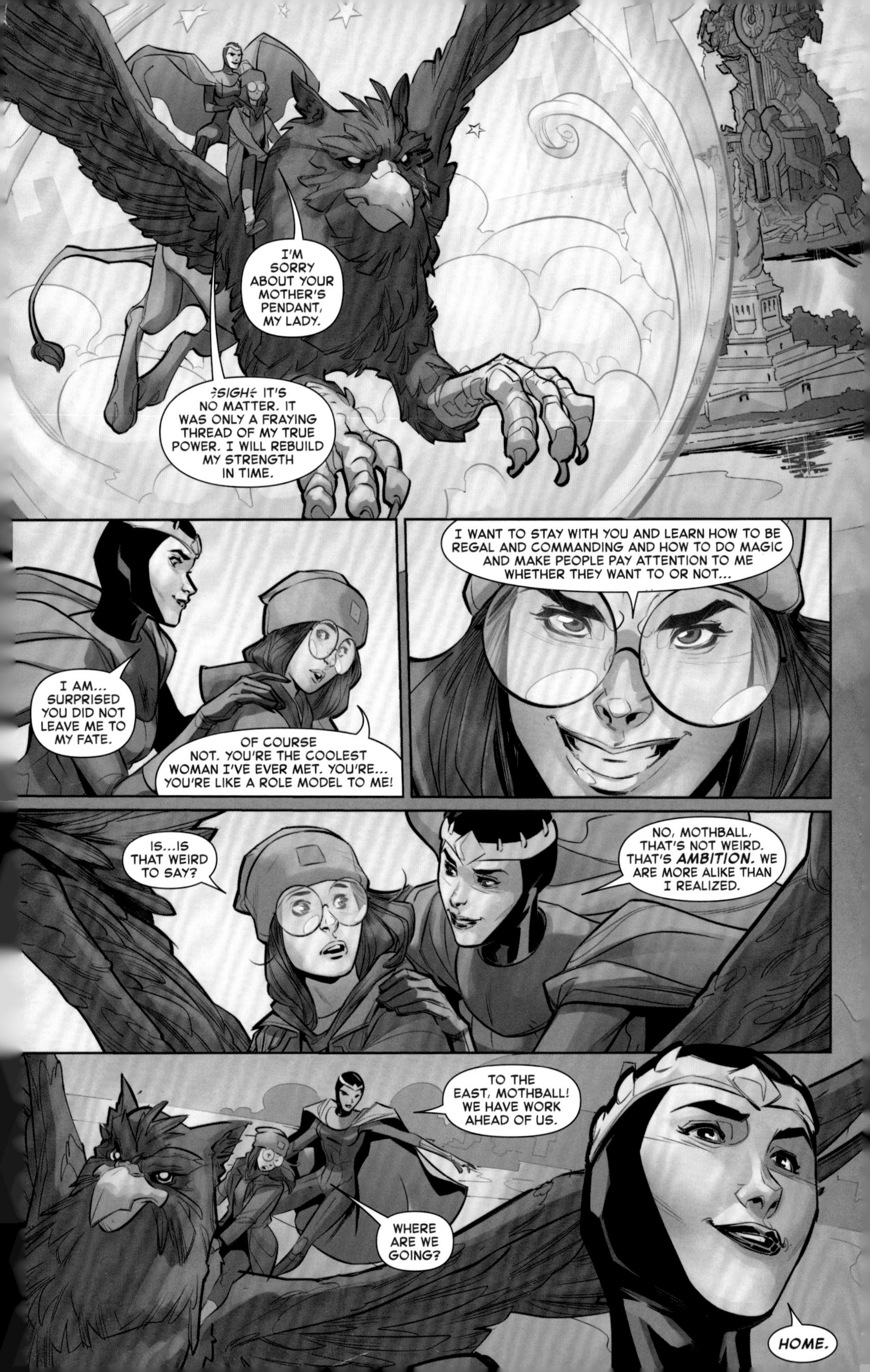
I'M SORRY ABOUT YOUR MOTHER'S PENDANT, MY LADY.
SIGH IT'S NO MATTER. IT WAS ONLY A FRAYING THREAD OF MY TRUE POWER. I WILL REBUILD MY STRENGTH IN TIME.
I AM... SURPRISED YOU DID NOT LEAVE ME TO MY FATE.
OF COURSE NOT. YOU'RE THE COOLEST WOMAN I'VE EVER MET. YOU'RE... YOU'RE LIKE A ROLE MODEL TO ME!
I WANT TO STAY WITH YOU AND LEARN HOW TO BE REGAL AND COMMANDING AND HOW TO DO MAGIC AND MAKE PEOPLE PAY ATTENTION TO ME WHETHER THEY WANT TO OR NOT...
IS...IS THAT WEIRD TO SAY?
NO, MOTHBALL, THAT'S NOT WEIRD. THAT'S AMBITION. WE ARE MORE ALIKE THAN I REALIZED.
TO THE EAST, MOTHBALL! WE HAVE WORK AHEAD OF US.
WHERE ARE WE GOING?
HOME.

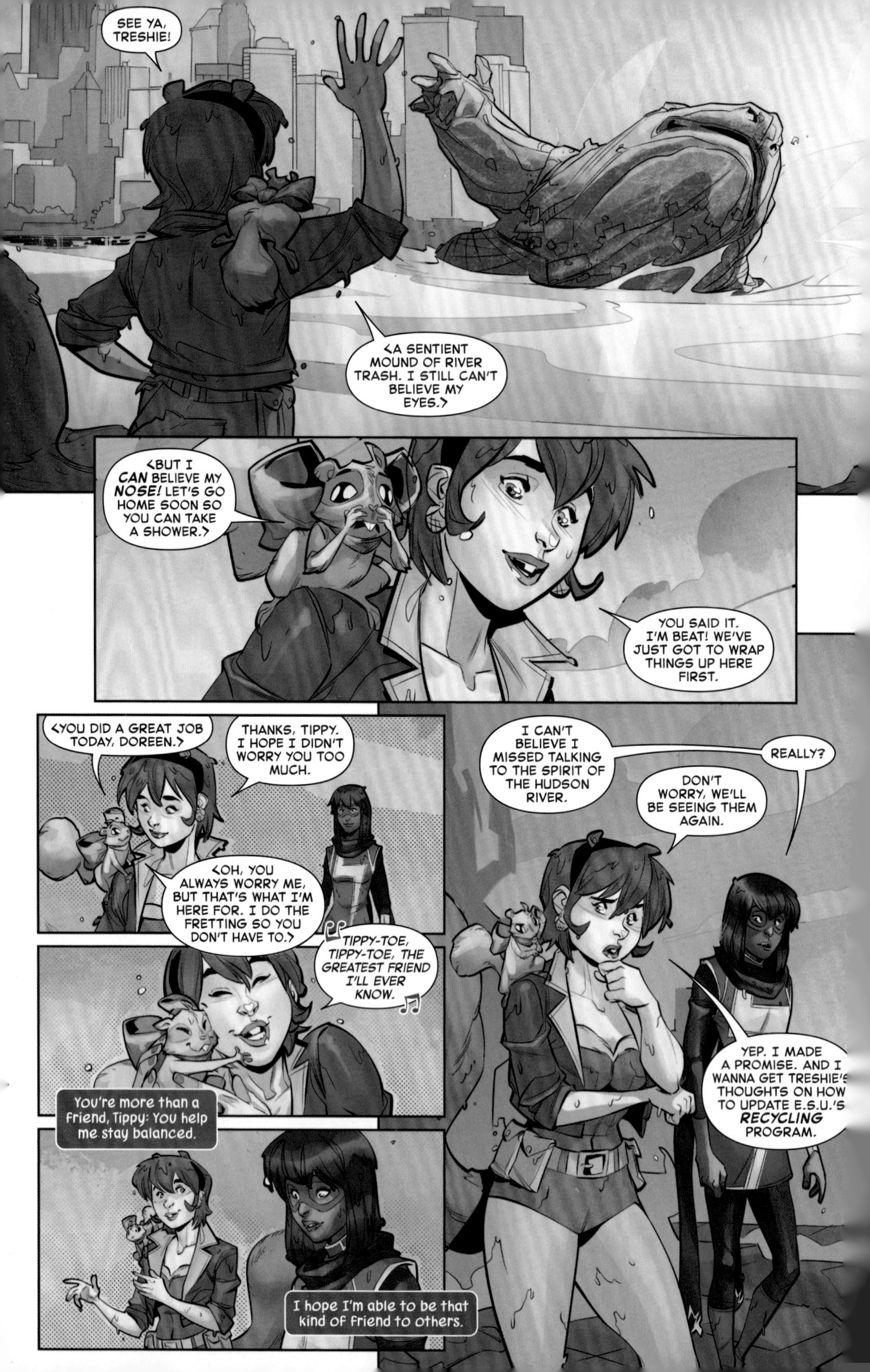
SEE YA, TRESHIE!
<A SENTIENT MOUND OF RIVER TRASH. I STILL CAN'T BELIEVE MY EYES.>
<BUT I CAN BELIEVE MY NOSE! LET'S GO HOME SOON SO YOU CAN TAKE A SHOWER.>
YOU SAID IT. I'M BEAT! WE'VE JUST GOT TO WRAP THINGS UP HERE FIRST.
<YOU DID A GREAT JOB TODAY, DOREEN.>
THANKS, TIPPY. I HOPE I DIDN'T WORRY YOU TOO MUCH.
<OH, YOU ALWAYS WORRY ME, BUT THAT'S WHAT I'M HERE FOR. I DO THE FRETTING SO YOU DON'T HAVE TO.>
TIPPY-TOE, TIPPY-TOE, THE GREATEST FRIEND I'LL EVER KNOW.
You're more than a friend, Tippy: You help me stay balanced.
I hope I'm able to be that kind of friend to others.
I CAN'T BELIEVE I MISSED TALKING TO THE SPIRIT OF THE HUDSON RIVER.
REALLY?
DON'T WORRY, WE'LL BE SEEING THEM AGAIN.
YEP. I MADE A PROMISE. AND I WANNA GET TRESHIE'S THOUGHTS ON HOW TO UPDATE E.S.U.'S RECYCLING PROGRAM.

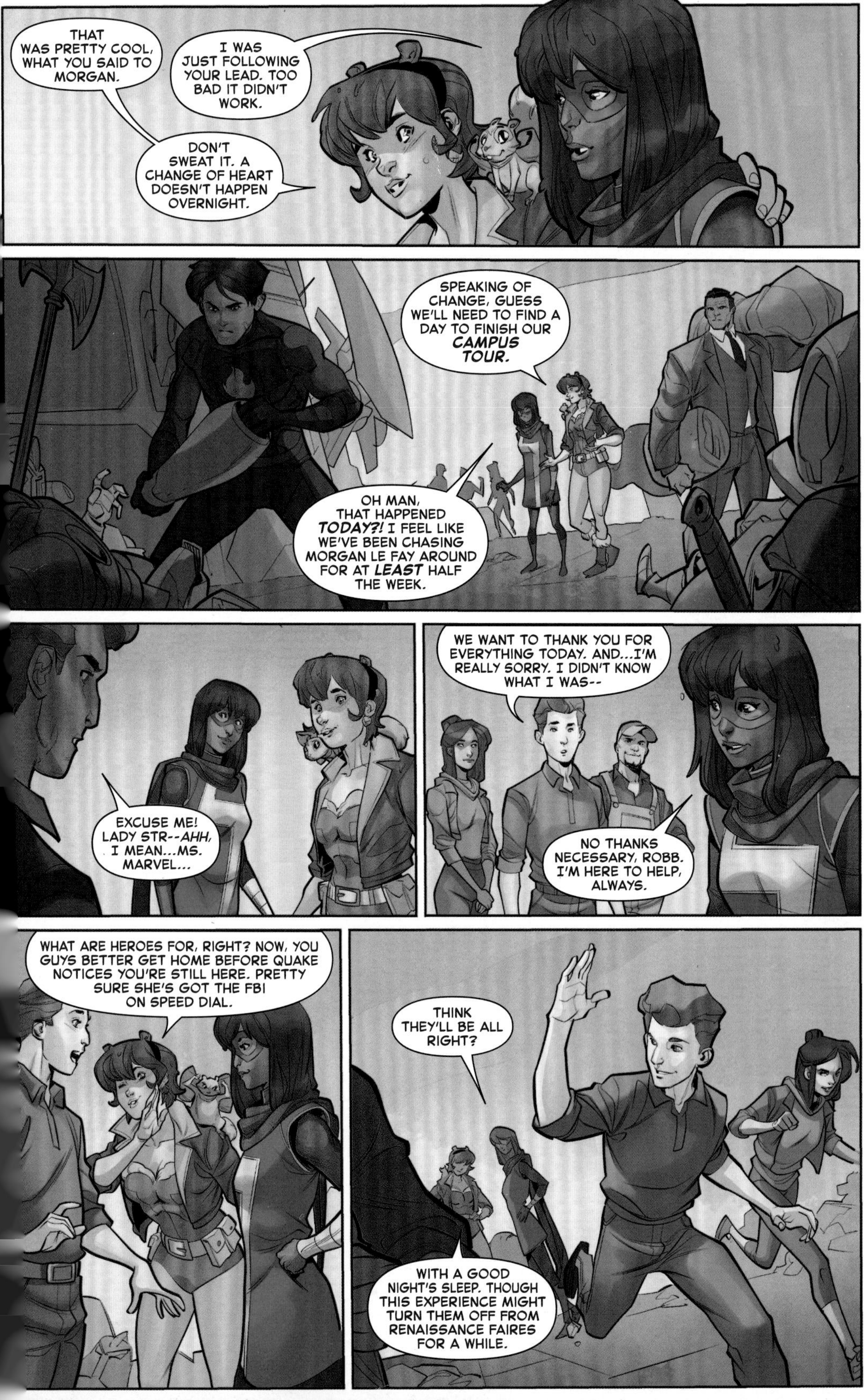
THAT WAS PRETTY COOL, WHAT YOU SAID TO MORGAN.
I WAS JUST FOLLOWING YOUR LEAD. TOO BAD IT DIDN'T WORK.
DON'T SWEAT IT. A CHANGE OF HEART DOESN'T HAPPEN OVERNIGHT.
SPEAKING OF CHANGE, GUESS WE'LL NEED TO FIND A DAY TO FINISH OUR CAMPUS TOUR.
OH MAN, THAT HAPPENED TODAY?! I FEEL LIKE WE'VE BEEN CHASING MORGAN LE FAY AROUND FOR AT LEAST HALF THE WEEK.
EXCUSE ME! LADY STR--AHH, I MEAN...MS. MARVEL...
WE WANT TO THANK YOU FOR EVERYTHING TODAY. AND...I'M REALLY SORRY. I DIDN'T KNOW WHAT I WAS--
NO THANKS NECESSARY, ROBB. I'M HERE TO HELP, ALWAYS.
WHAT ARE HEROES FOR, RIGHT? NOW, YOU GUYS BETTER GET HOME BEFORE QUAKE NOTICES YOU'RE STILL HERE. PRETTY SURE SHE'S GOT THE FBI ON SPEED DIAL.
THINK THEY'LL BE ALL RIGHT?
WITH A GOOD NIGHT'S SLEEP. THOUGH THIS EXPERIENCE MIGHT TURN THEM OFF FROM RENAISSANCE FAIRES FOR A WHILE.

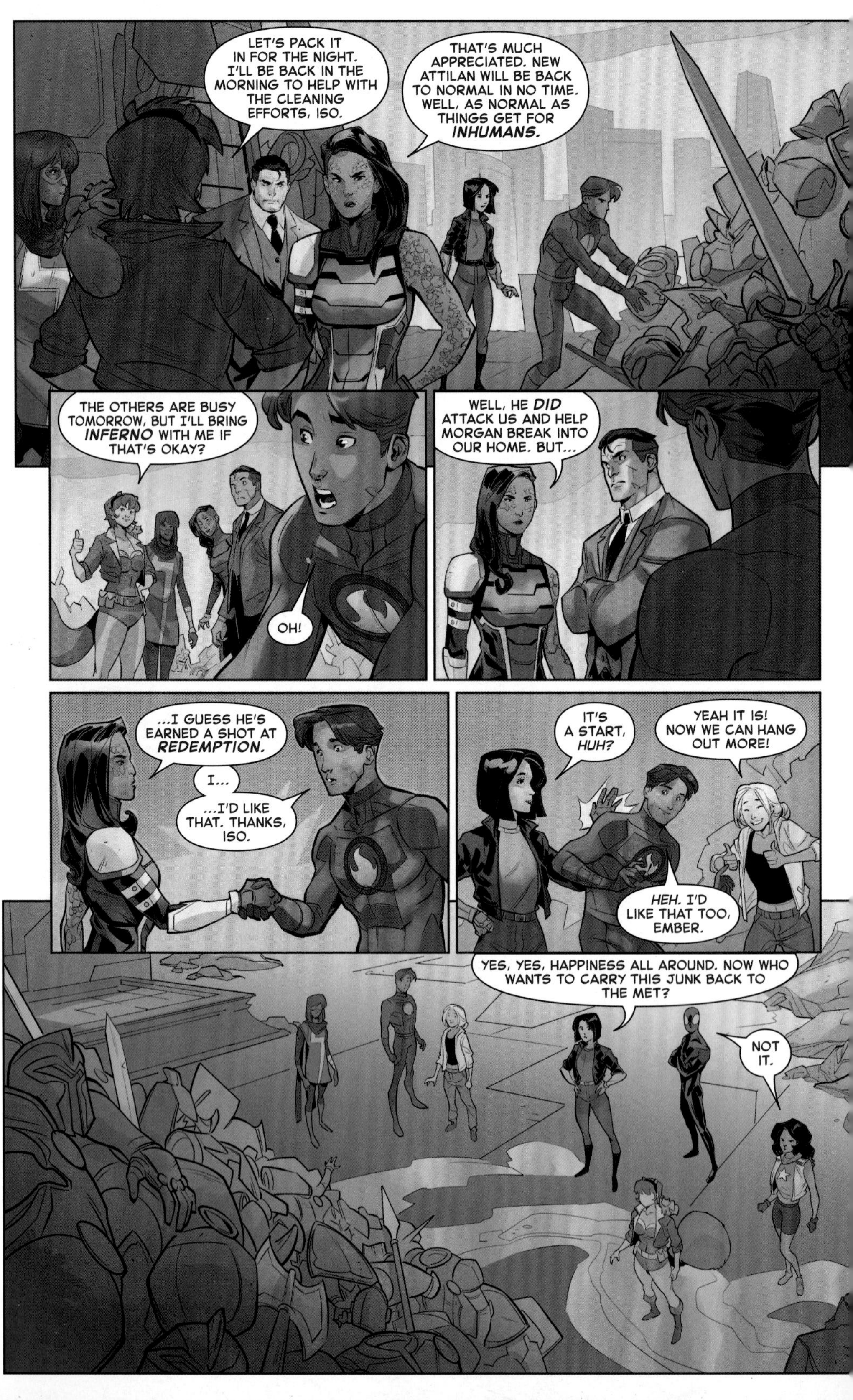
LET'S PACK IT IN FOR THE NIGHT. I'LL BE BACK IN THE MORNING TO HELP WITH THE CLEANING EFFORTS, ISO.
THAT'S MUCH APPRECIATED. NEW ATTILAN WILL BE BACK TO NORMAL IN NO TIME. WELL, AS NORMAL AS THINGS GET FOR INHUMANS.
THE OTHERS ARE BUSY TOMORROW, BUT I'LL BRING INFERNO WITH ME IF THAT'S OKAY?
OH!
WELL, HE DID ATTACK US AND HELP MORGAN BREAK INTO OUR HOME. BUT...
...I GUESS HE'S EARNED A SHOT AT REDEMPTION.
I...
...I'D LIKE THAT. THANKS, ISO.
IT'S A START, HUH?
YEAH IT IS! NOW WE CAN HANG OUT MORE!
HEH. I'D LIKE THAT TOO, EMBER.
YES, YES, HAPPINESS ALL AROUND. NOW WHO WANTS TO CARRY THIS JUNK BACK TO THE MET?
NOT IT.

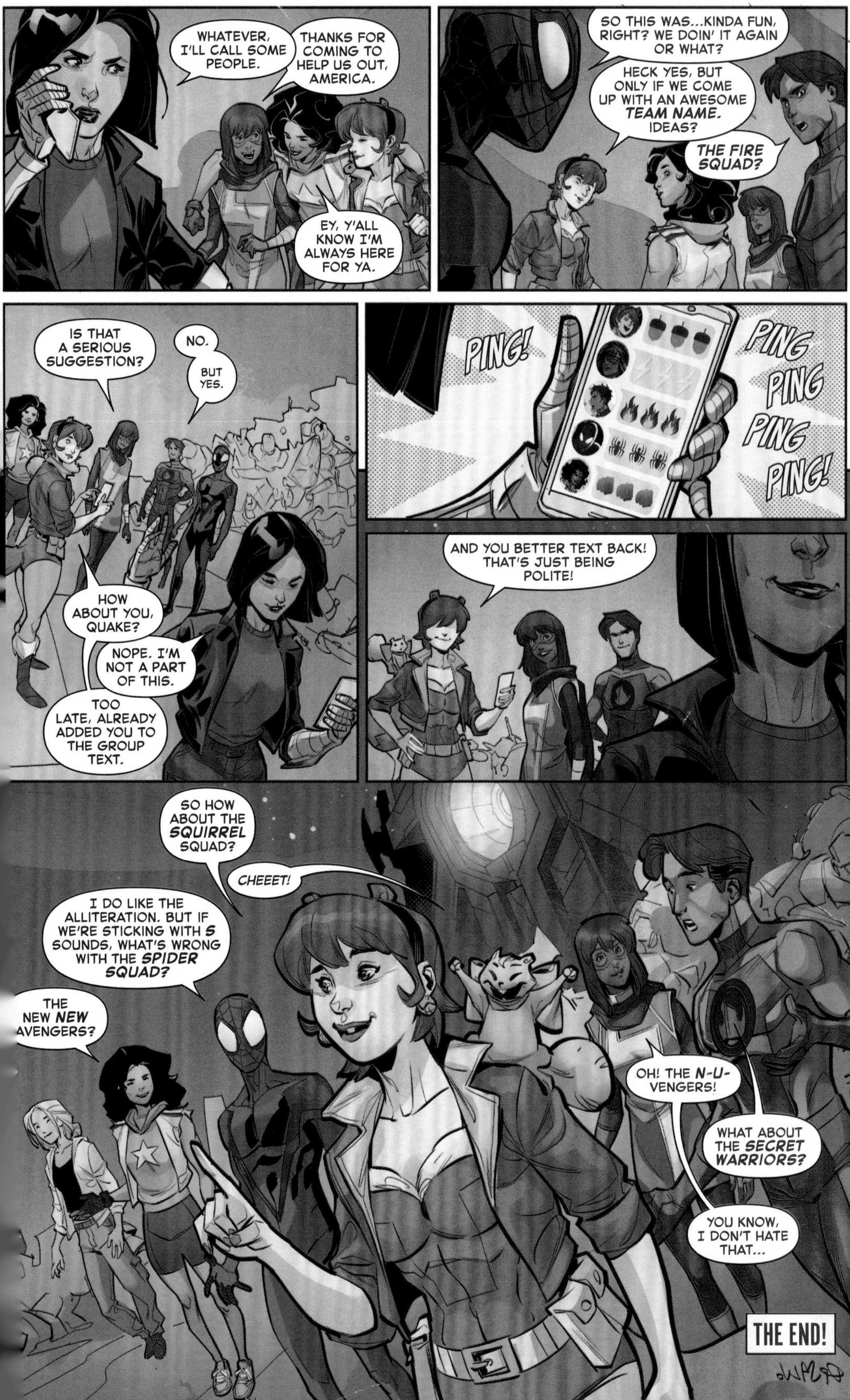
WHATEVER, I'LL CALL SOME PEOPLE.
THANKS FOR COMING TO HELP US OUT, AMERICA.
EY, Y'ALL KNOW I'M ALWAYS HERE FOR YA.
SO THIS WAS...KINDA FUN, RIGHT? WE DOIN' IT AGAIN OR WHAT?
HECK YES, BUT ONLY IF WE COME UP WITH AN AWESOME TEAM NAME. IDEAS?
THE FIRE SQUAD?
IS THAT A SERIOUS SUGGESTION?
NO.
BUT YES.
HOW ABOUT YOU, QUAKE?
NOPE. I'M NOT A PART OF THIS.
TOO LATE, ALREADY ADDED YOU TO THE GROUP TEXT.
PING!
PING PING PING PING!
AND YOU BETTER TEXT BACK! THAT'S JUST BEING POLITE!
SO HOW ABOUT THE SQUIRREL SQUAD?
CHEEET!
I DO LIKE THE ALLITERATION. BUT IF WE'RE STICKING WITH S SOUNDS, WHAT'S WRONG WITH THE SPIDER SQUAD?
THE NEW NEW AVENGERS?
OH! THE N-U-VENGERS!
WHAT ABOUT THE SECRET WARRIORS?
YOU KNOW, I DON'T HATE THAT...
THE END!

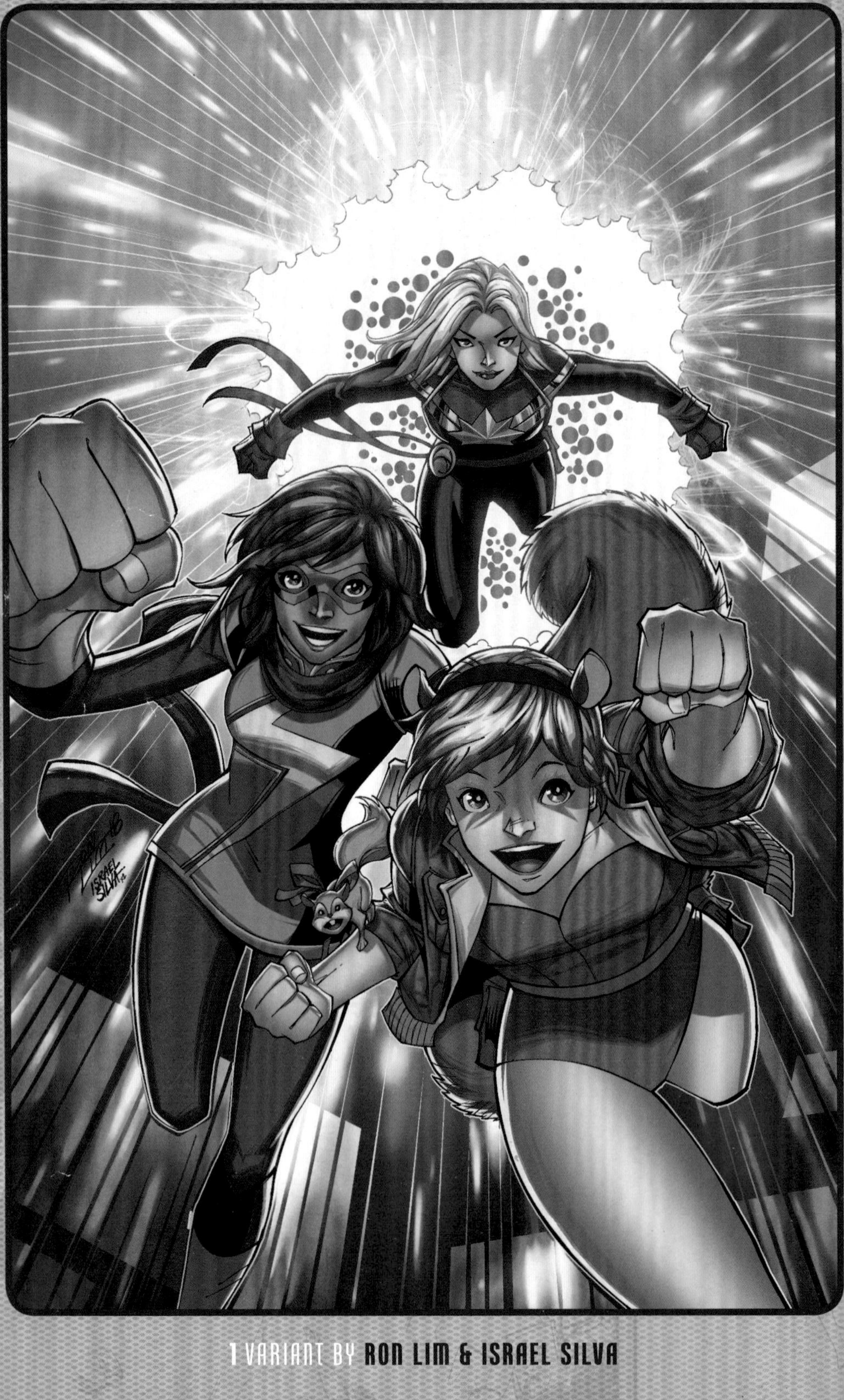

1 VARIANT BY RON LIM & ISRAEL SILVA

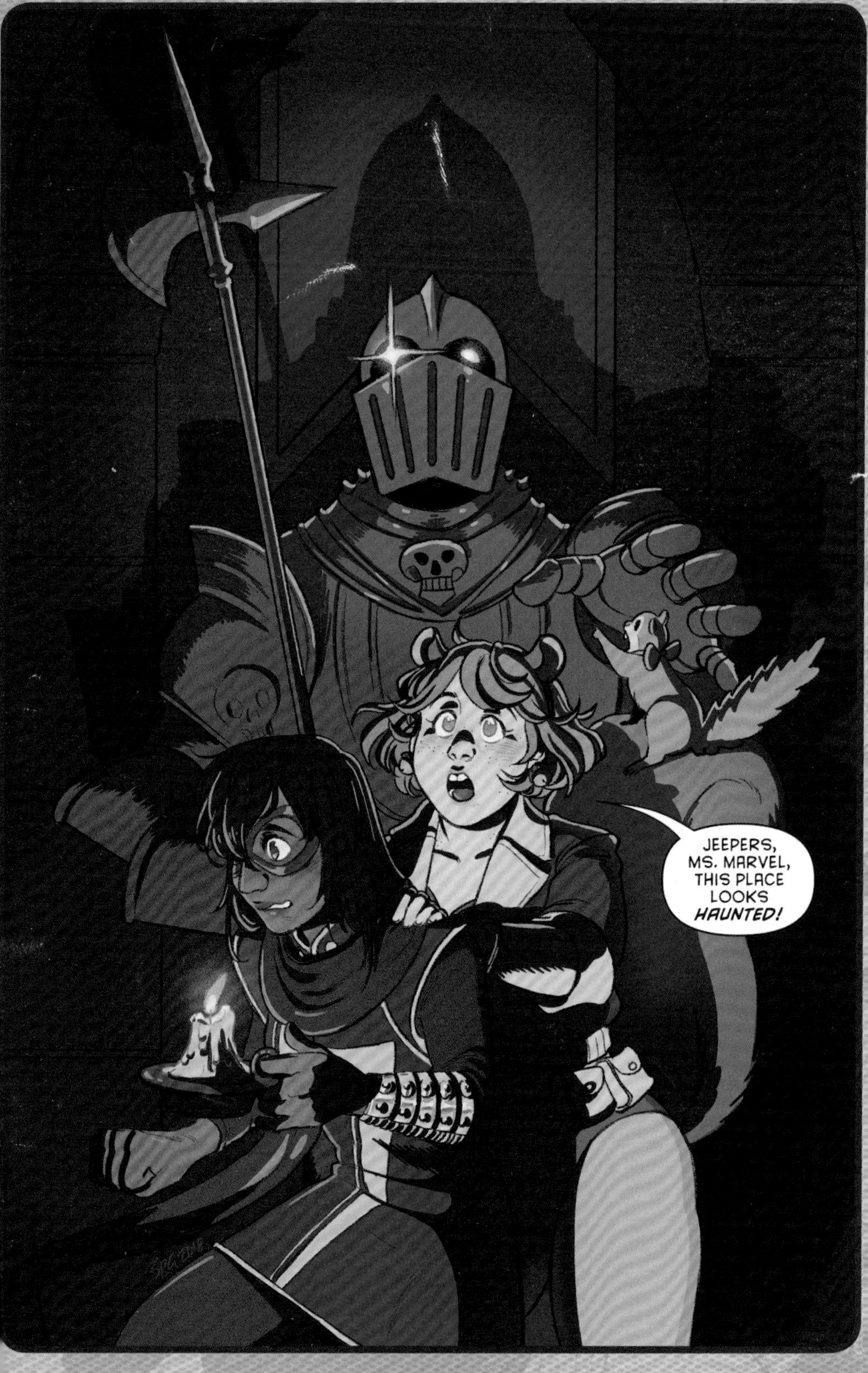
JEEPERS, MS. MARVEL, THIS PLACE LOOKS *HAUNTED!*

2 VARIANT BY **SAVANNA GANUCHEAU**

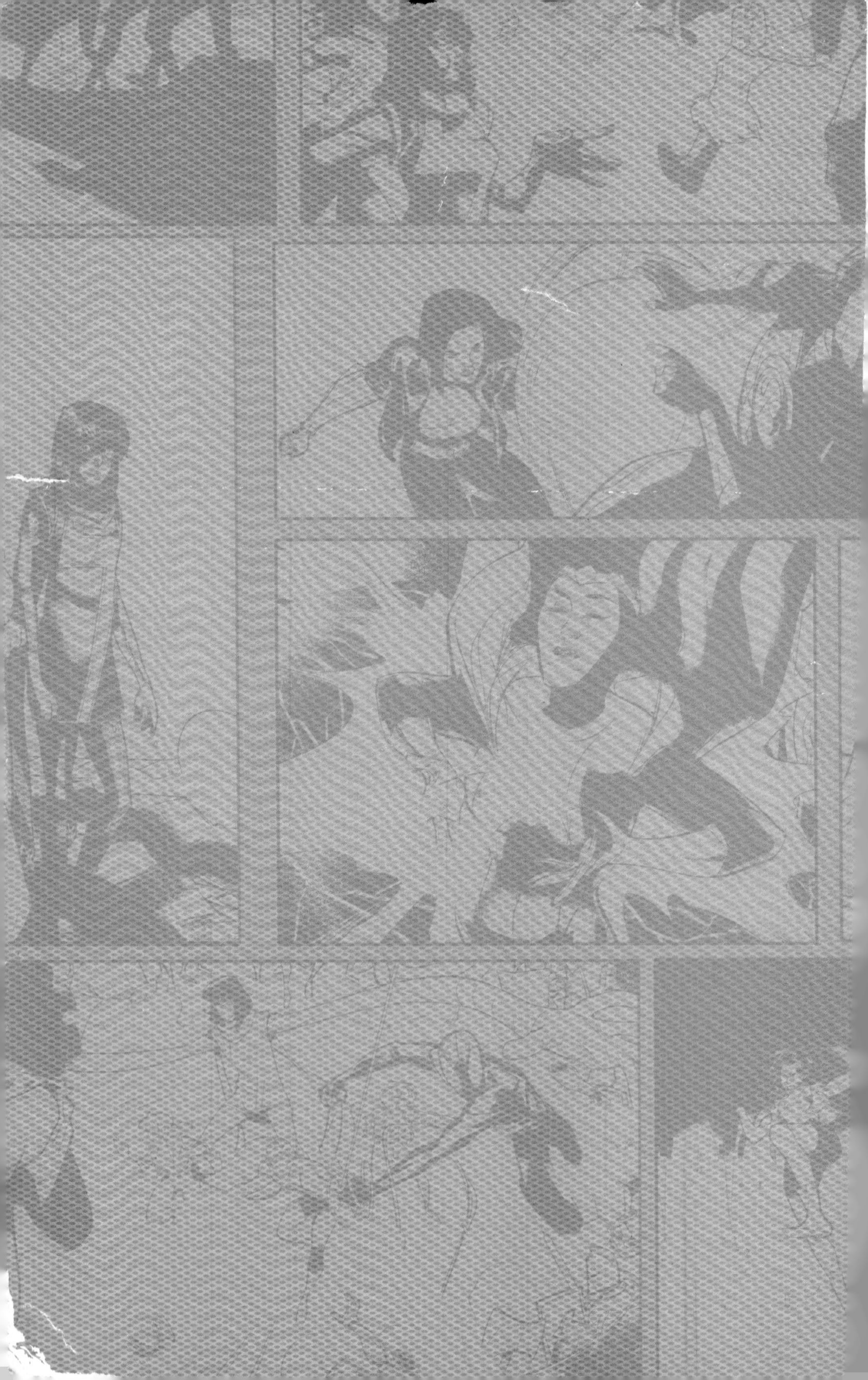